SANGUINE
AND
STYGIAN

SARA SELLERS

Copyright © 2021 by Sara Sellers
Published by Blackhearth Books

Paperback ISBN: 978-1-7372194-0-8

Cover Design by Ravven
www.ravven.com

Map Art by Z
www.twitter.com/xy01011010

www.sarasellers.com

Praise for *Sanguine and Stygian*

"It's hard to even put how much I love this book into words. It's intense, steamy, and had such a great dark fantasy vibe."

-Amazon Reviewer

"Hands down one of the best fantasy romances out there."

-CJ Connor

"This book grips you from the beginning and doesn't let go. From the opening scene to the last sentence, you are wanting more. You just have to find out what happens next, and suddenly it's 2AM and you have to get up for work in 4 hours! Action, intrigue, magic, and romance!"

-Amazon Reviewer

"From the first page, you dive into this amazing fantasy realm full of magic & mercenaries. Fast paced with great characters and steamy romance scenes, you won't be able to put this book down."

-Bridget K. Shapiro

"Good luck sleeping! You won't want to put this one down. Action packed and full of heat and intrigue, you'll love the merry band of bawdy characters from start to finish... this book will whet your appetite for much more."

-Amazon Reviewer

To everyone still chasing the dream.

ALSO BY SARA SELLERS

The Sanguine and Stygian Series:

The Stygian Crown

Standalone Books:

The Storm King

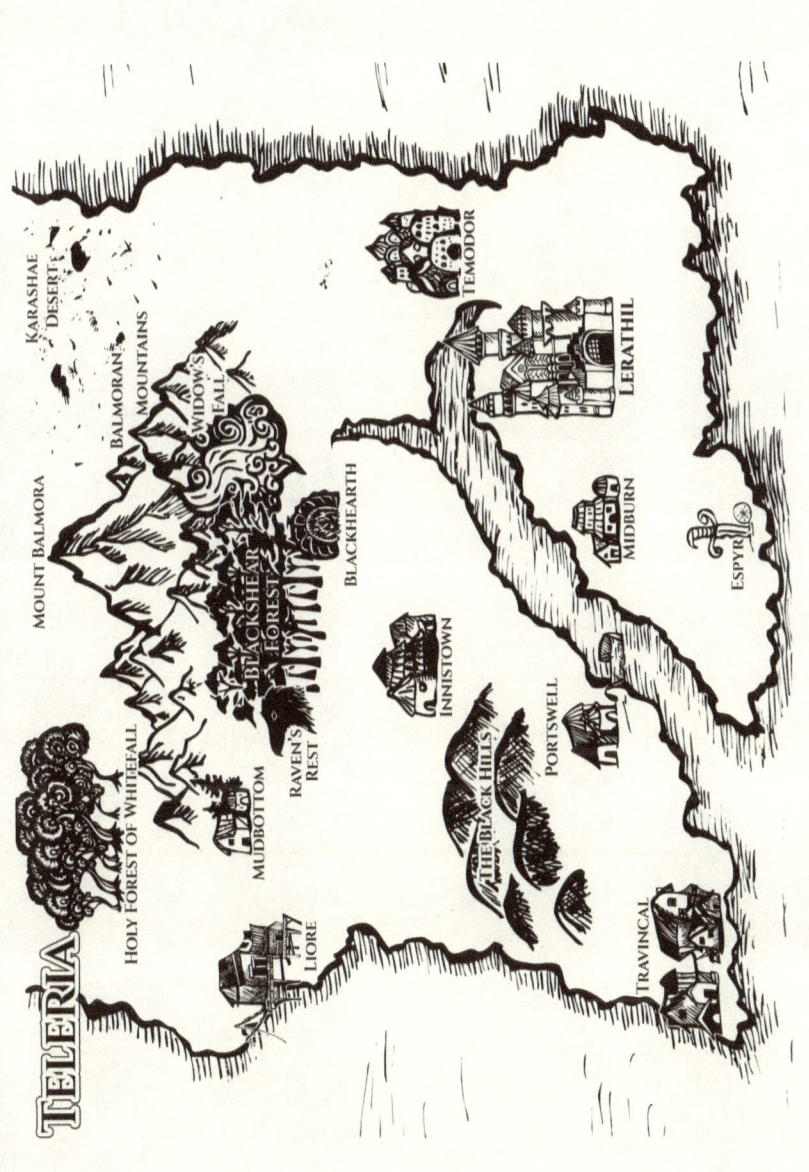

TELERIA

KARASHAE DESERT

BALMORAN MOUNTAINS

WIDOW'S FALL

TEMODOR

MOUNT BALMORA

LERATHIL

BLACKHEARTH

HOLY FOREST OF WHITEFALL

BLACKHEART FOREST

MIDBURN

ESPYR

RAVEN'S REST

MUDBOTTOM

INNISTOWN

LIORE

THE BLACK HILLS

PORTSWELL

TRAVINCAL

CHAPTER ONE

The molten heat of the forge buffeted Kara's face as she reached into it with her tongs. She gripped the glowing horseshoe and pulled it out, transferring it to her anvil. The fires of the forge growled low behind her as Kara yanked her hammer from her apron pocket and began flattening the shoe into shape. She choked the wood in her fist. A fat drop of rain fell from the sky and struck the glowing metal, sizzling out of existence. Kara glanced up and scowled. The horizon was pregnant with dark grey clouds.

Da and her brother Wesley had left at dawn to go hunting. Now she was stuck with the appointment to shoe her former lover's horse, something Da usually did so she could avoid Sean after he'd broken things off between them.

'We're just different people,' he'd said, by which he meant she was cursed and he wasn't, that he got to have a normal life and she didn't. He was fine to fuck her when no one knew about it, but once the villagers started gossiping, he'd dropped her like a hot coal.

Kara would've canceled the job altogether, but her

family sorely needed the coin. She swung the hammer again as the sky spat harder, striking the soft metal too hard and bending it out of shape. "Fucking hell."

A distant knocking from the other side of the house caught her attention. *Of course he'd show up early.* She still needed to move their horse out of the stable to make room for Sean's so she wouldn't have to work in the rain. She shoved her hammer into her apron and headed into the house through the back door. Using the window by the front door as a mirror, she tried in vain to pat down the fly-away hairs escaping her ponytail and brush the sweat-streaked coal dust off her arms.

The person on the porch shifted into view, and Kara stilled as she took in the man's scraggly brown hair and rain-slick cloak. It wasn't Sean. She didn't recognize the tall, hulking man standing outside, and Mudbottom was a small village where she knew all the faces. They got passers-through, but not often. Kara hesitated. She was reluctant to invite a stranger in when she was home alone, but Sean would be here soon. And for all their differences, she believed he'd still defend her if she were in danger. As Kara snuck a hand into her pocket to slide out her hammer, the stranger turned and caught her with his gaze.

Wind gusted outside, blowing open the man's cloak to reveal the red armor underneath. Kara rose her hand to her mouth and spun out of sight of the window. *Shit.* The Sanguine Riders had come early. The predatory merce-nary clan that extorted them for protection pay each month wasn't due for another two weeks. All the village actually needed protection from were the red dogs them-selves, but they had little recourse. What were they doing here?

Kara struggled to gather her thoughts as the mercenary pounded on the door again, her heart hammering in her chest. They didn't have the money to pay him yet.

"I know you're in there, girl," he called from outside. "I'd just like my horse shoed."

She doubted that. The Sanguines had never come to them for work before—their clan was big enough to have its own farrier. Even if it was true, she'd be a fool to let him in when she was home alone.

She couldn't stay here—it wasn't safe. What if he decided to break in or returned later with more of his fellows? Even if Sean showed up soon, he wouldn't stand a chance against the Sanguine. They were trained killers. Kara knew the region Wesley usually hunted in. If she could make it to the stable for Yuki and escape into the woods, she could track him and Da.

Kara straightened her back and took a deep breath. "Just a minute. I need to tidy up." The mercenary's heavy, booted footfalls as he paced across the porch raised the hairs on the back of her neck, but she tried to stuff down her fear. Kara pulled her leather apron off, pried up the loose floorboard where they stored their money, and took out the jar of coppers hidden there. It was barely half full, but if the mercenary stole it, they'd be ruined. She silently gathered the rest of her things, including her hunting knife, cloak, and waterskin. She spotted the wooden carving of the mother goddess Da had finished last night resting on the kitchen table and stuffed it in her bag, hoping it brought her some luck. It might be a while before it was safe to return to town.

Kara eased open the back door as quietly as she could, wincing when the hinges squeaked. She crept across the yard towards the stable, hunting knife gripped tight in her right fist. She wouldn't waste time saddling their mare, Yuki—she could ride bareback. The rain was falling thick and heavy now, and it sluiced down her face, soaking into her shirt and obscuring her vision.

The sweet, coppery stench of blood curled up her nose. Kara rounded the corner of Yuki's stall and stifled a scream. Yuki was stretched out on the ground with a wide, crimson slit cut into her throat. Scarlet stains spread across her dappled grey chest and the earth beneath her. Blood still leaked from the wound, and Yuki's eyes rolled in fear and pain.

Kara fell to her knees and reached for the mare, trying in vain to stop the flow of blood. Tears welled in her eyes, followed by a hot wave of rage. The Sanguine had killed Yuki, the sweet mare she'd ridden since she was a toddler. Kara bowed her head and stroked Yuki's neck, then grit her teeth and forced herself to stand. The mercenary was still here. She had to keep moving.

Hands wrapped around Kara's back, trapping her arms. Rain-soaked fabric and the stench of stale sweat pressed around her. She exploded, thrashing against his hold and screaming, but she couldn't shake him. He was strong, his grip on her arms tight enough to bruise. Kara flipped her small hunting knife up into her sleeve, hiding the blade. She'd only have one chance to use it.

The mercenary spun her around to face him and shook her, rattling her teeth.

"Don't fight me, lass. I may not be able to kill ya, but they didn't say nothin' about bruises."

Heat unfurled beneath her skin, swirling in her gut. She would not go easy.

"They didn't tell me you were pretty. Rare, for a pigsty like this. Shame about the horse, but I couldn't have you trying to escape. Boss would have my balls."

"What do you want? We don't have your money," Kara said, her voice brittle.

The merc laughed, revealing several teeth black with rot. "Ain't worried about a few coppers with a prize like you in the mix. Speaking of—" He yanked up her left sleeve, exposing the curse mark Kara was born with on her wrist. He ran his thumb across it, and Kara shuddered. The mark itched fiercely, and a fresh wave of fury washed through her. She thanked the mother when he didn't check the hand her knife was clutched in.

"Just making sure. You're the real deal, alright. Now, are you gonna behave?"

Kara nodded, lowering her eyes. She didn't know why the Sanguines were interested in Namirah's mark, but she wasn't planning to find out. A cord of fear ran through her when she realized she might have to kill this man to escape him. If she was responsible for his death, it would trigger Namirah's curse, and then she'd be compelled to take a life every month for the rest of hers to avoid falling prey to bloodlust. And after everything she'd been through—the hiding, the shame, enduring adolescence in this backwards mountain town because Da thought it would keep her safe —it would all be for nothing. Worse, the villagers would finally be justified in their hatred and fear of her.

The merc dragged her towards his horse, a tall bay courser with scars on its flank. He grabbed her wrists with one hand and reached for the rope slung over the horse's withers with the other. Kara's heart sped up. She couldn't let him bind her arms—it was now or never.

Kara threw her weight away from the merc, managing to rip her wrists free but stumbling to the ground in the process. He spun towards her. She couldn't run. She had to fight. Kara flicked her knife out of her sleeve and sprung off the ground towards him. She buried the tip of the knife into his eye, pulling her stab so she didn't go too deep and hit brain. Maybe it wouldn't kill him.

The merc screamed and swung at her, catching her across her brow with his bare fist. Her head blossomed in pain, and Kara faltered, momentarily dazed. Spots of light clouded her vision. She stumbled towards his horse, scrabbling into the saddle as he lunged for her. Blood poured down his face. His fingers dug into her ankle as she kicked the horse into a gallop, tearing her skin. They raced towards the woods together, and Kara glanced behind her at the merc. He was gripping his wounded face in both hands and stumbling towards their house.

Adrenaline pumped through her veins as she rode along the inner edge of the woods, close to the village outskirts. There was a commotion coming from the center of town. She led the horse towards it, pulling the bay to a stop to watch from the shadows of the trees.

The main Sanguine riding party had the townsfolk of Mudbottom lined up in front of the town well. They had a near-empty wagon with them, ready to carry the valuables of the households without the coin to pay them. A lumpy blanket was spread out on the wagon bed.

The Sanguines were at least fifteen strong, all armed to the teeth and mounted, their metal armor the color of old blood. The leader wore an antlered helm gilded in silver. He brandished something in his hand, swinging it in front of the civilians like a pendulum.

It took Kara a second to realize he held a decapitated head by the hair in his gauntleted fist. The mercenary swung the head around as he shouted to the townsfolk, "We met this one and his son on the road here. Thought you lot might need some incentive to continue paying for our valuable services."

His words hung in the air, and the world ground to a halt as they echoed over and over in her mind. *Met this one and his son on the road.* It couldn't be. That lifeless face...

Kara's stomach clenched. The man's pronged helm swam in her vision, and she slid, loose-limbed, off the horse. She retched violently in the grass.

It was Da, unmistakably so, even under all the dirt and dried blood. Glassy, lifeless eyes stared out at the crowd, and his grey beard ran red. Kara's chest heaved. She couldn't breathe. She wanted to scream, wanted to gouge out the eyes of the man who held him like he meant nothing.

Her eyes darted back up to the raiding party. *Wesley*. Where was Wesley? The mercenary had mentioned his son…Kara slowly looked towards the wagon, towards the dark, lumpy blanket. Dark hair and a familiar stripe of fur stuck out from beneath the blanket's edge. The white rabbit fur Kara had stitched to the collar of Wesley's winter coat. How he'd beamed when he'd trapped it. Her stomach seized. *No no no no*. She blinked, rubbed her eyes, willed the scene to vanish, to change. Willed herself to wake up from this nightmare. She retched again, then pulled her knees into her chest and sobbed. The only family she'd ever known, the people who'd taken her in when she had no one, were dead. Bile burned in her throat. Kara wanted to shut down. Wanted to lie on the ground and close her eyes and wait for the winter snows to bury her.

The merc's horse nuzzled at her hair, drawing her back. "We're looking for this man's daughter," the antlered Sanguine continued. "Anyone with information about her whereabouts will be rewarded."

She needed to leave, but she was frozen in pain. *Lie to yourself, Kara*. She could weave a fantasy in her mind to keep herself going, to keep herself from shutting down. Maybe it wasn't Wesley. Maybe it was some other boy who'd died today with a fur collar the color of a rare winter hare. *Lie to yourself until you're strong enough to bathe in their blood,* the dark part of her mind whispered, the part she was always trying to silence. The cursed part that regretted not screwing her dagger into that mercenary's skull as deep as it could go.

She scanned the crowd for Sean, some small relief breaking through the blackness when she spotted him standing with his mother. At least he hadn't met the same fate on the way to her house.

Kara struggled to her feet and dragged herself back into the saddle. She squeezed the horse's sides, cuing him to move deeper into the woods. When she came to the stream she and Wesley hunted near, she paused to collect herself and let the horse drink. She forced her eyes to slide over the evidence of the traps Wesley had laid mere days ago, struggling to swallow past the raw rock lodged in her throat. She had to focus, keep moving. The Sanguines would be searching the woods soon if they weren't already.

Wesley had been due to leave tomorrow for Liore, the last city in this year's Reaping Trials. He'd finally secured their Da's blessing to chase the reaper this year. Each fall, mercenary clans from across Teleria went on a tour of different cities, recruiting new members through a series of combat trials. The Sanguine Riders were the worst of the lot, feeding off their own countrymen during peacetime, but the other clans had better reputations. Wesley had wanted to join up with the Stygian Brotherhood, the Sanguines' biggest rivals, on a two-year contract and send part of his wages back to help with the tithe each month. Maybe even get them out of Mudbottom for good. Da had fought the idea tooth and nail until this year, when their waning larder and lagging business had given him no other choice.

The trials were due to begin tomorrow. Liore wasn't far; Kara could make it by nightfall if she rode hard. She didn't know how to fight, but she knew the farrier trade thanks to Da, and the clans had plenty of horses. Maybe it would be enough to convince them to sign her. They would arm her and pay her, and maybe the Stygians would even help her seek justice.

Kara put on her cloak, drawing it tight around her to fight the nip in the air. Her clothes were soaked through, and her head ached fiercely where the merc had hit her. She'd wager she'd have a wicked bruise on her browbone. She led the merc's horse southwest, towards Liore. Once Kara was well past the village borders, she slowed the bay's pace and looked back. Fire bloomed in the distance, smoke rising like a demon into the daylight. The rain had stopped. Kara led her horse deeper into the woods.

CHAPTER TWO

K ara arrived in Liore as the streets were emptying out and the sun set, the temperature sinking with it. Her breeches and boots were splattered with mud, and her threadbare cloak wasn't doing much in the way of keeping her warm. The Sanguine Rider's horse was spent, and she'd found nothing but booze and a ratty blanket in his saddlebags. She hadn't shed any more tears over Da or Wesley. Instead, she felt numb. Tears wouldn't serve her where she was headed.

Liore was a coastal town about five times the size of Mudbottom, but it was still modest compared to a real city. Houses and shops circled outwards from the town's center, where the main hive of activity was. The townsfolk decorated the city square during festivals, and various traveling acts set up stage here throughout the year. Da had brought her here once to see the Vespertines perform training exercises when she was just a girl. For weeks she'd harbored fantasies about being chosen to join the group of women responsible for the Queen of Teleria's safety, until Wesley had reminded her that they'd never choose a marked child for training.

Now a multitude of banners hung about the square, each representing a different mercenary clan. Flags of gold, crimson, and black snapped back and forth in the wind. They were the most numerous, but there was a smattering of olive green and royal purple as well.

Kara needed a place to stay for the night if she didn't want to catch ill. The Cat and Crow tavern glowed softly in the black night, and the sounds of its rambunctious patrons drifted outside. A banner of black silk hung next to the tavern's sign. Stygian colors. Kara headed for the tavern's stable and gave the stable boy the mercenary's flask in exchange for a good rubdown and some feed for the horse, then headed inside.

When she entered the tavern, a few heads glanced her way. Her hair and clothes were unkempt and dirty from her flight through the woods. Most of the tables were full. The smell of roasting meat and fresh-baked bread made her mouth water. She scanned the crowd with wary eyes, looking for the tell-tale red of the Sanguines, though she doubted they'd step foot in the tavern the Stygians were staying at. A loud poker game was going on in the back corner, and barmaids rushed back and forth from the kitchen to their tables. An enchanted harp with no harpist played itself by the fire.

Kara ordered ale and beef stew from a barmaid with straw-colored braids and found a seat set snug against the wall. It was pricier than she'd expected, but they may have raised their prices while the Reaping was in town. It was going to be difficult to make her coin stretch if her stay lasted more than a few days, and the locals weren't likely to be keen on hiring a marked woman.

A man at the poker table slammed his fists down and

shoved away from the table, yelling curses at his opponent. He raised his fists threateningly at the winner, but his companion laid a hand on his shoulder and whispered something in his ear before ushering him away from the game. Something he'd said had scared the loser off.

The winner stood up and bowed graciously to those remaining at the table before scooping his winnings into a leather coin pouch. He held a bracelet from the pile to the light, then turned to the girl on his arm and fastened it about her wrist. The girl blushed and rose to kiss him on the cheek, then dragged him back towards the stairs.

Kara snorted. Such games men and women played. Admittedly, she had limited experience with men. Twenty-three years old, and she'd only been with Sean. Their's had been no great love affair, but it'd still stung when he ended things a few months ago. She'd always been lonely in Mudbottom, even with Wesley's companionship. Since she was little, all the village children had been warned by their mothers to stay away from 'that cursed girl,' the farrier's daughter with Namirah's mark. Her mood sobered when she realized those same villagers may not have survived the Sanguine raid earlier today.

The barmaid appeared with her food and ale. Kara dunked her bread in the stew and started scarfing it down, though it tasted like ashes in her mouth. "Do you have any rooms available for tonight?" she mumbled around a mouthful.

"Full up with these mercs. Reaping, you know. Fools sign on for glory and riches and end up with they guts cut open. No thanks, I say. Doin' just fine for meself here in Liore." The barmaid paused, eyeing her. "Clean up a bit first, and I'm sure ye could find someone willing to share their room."

Kara sighed. "Do you know of anywhere else in town with space?"

"Doubtful, this time o' night with the trials startin' tomorrow. If you're real desperate there's the stable hayloft, but it'll be bloody cold."

Kara took a sip of the ale. It was swill, but she'd be needing some liquid courage. She wished she had something stronger. "Where are these mercenaries who might be willing to share?"

The barmaid pointed to a dark alcove behind the stairs. "They're taking applicants in that room back there. Stygian clan, real menacin' lot. Good luck." She winked, then spun around and headed for another table.

Kara finished her meal in silence. Her stomach no longer clenched with hunger, but she was unsettled and on edge. This was likely to be her only shot with the Stygians, and she needed their help. The area of her mind that she'd walled off and shoved all her grief into was starting to crack. She needed something to channel that pain into before it drowned her.

Kara wiped the dirt off her face with her sodden cloak, then drained the rest of the mug. She steeled her resolve and walked with purpose across the inn.

Dark curtains embossed with the sigil of the Stygian clan, a dagger with a snake wrapped around its hilt, obscured the entrance to the room. Kara froze outside of it. Her heart began to race, and cold beads of sweat formed on her temple. She could hear them talking through the curtain.

"Don't know why the guild had us recruit in Liore. Fucking mountain milksops."

"We've worn thin the hospitality of the southern cities."

"We don't have time for frightened rabbits, boy," barked the first voice.

Someone inside the room chuckled, and Kara realized they could see her feet through a gap at the bottom of the curtains.

She drew apart the heavy fabric and stepped inside, raising her head high in feigned confidence. "I'm not a boy."

"Clearly," said the copper-haired gambler who'd won the poker game earlier, smiling cheekily.

He sat between two other men at a wooden table with paper and quills scattered across it. On his right was a burly, bearded man with a weathered face—the one who'd barked at her, she guessed. At his left was a golden-skinned man with a clean-shaven head and a golden hoop through his right nostril.

"Hello," Kara said. It came out more softly than she'd intended.

The gambler spread his arms wide and said, "Hello, and welcome to the recruitment offices of the Stygian Brotherhood. Mercenaries extraordinaire—the original masters of shadow and death!"

Someone grunted in amusement, and Kara swiveled her head towards the sound. There was a fourth man in the room, leaning against the wall in the corner behind her. She couldn't make out his features in the weak lantern light. He stood in shadow, the only visible part of him a pair of big black boots.

"I'm Jonathan, Jon for short," continued the gambler. He held out his hand in greeting, and Kara stepped forward to shake it, making sure her grip was firm.

"Kara," she said, smiling at him. She liked Jon's theatrics.

"Athar," grunted the bearded man. He nodded curtly at her but didn't offer his hand.

"They call me Rahj," the man with the nose ring said. His voice was smooth as drizzled honey. He held out his left hand instead of his right, forcing her to swap the arm she offered him.

He grasped her palm and raised the back of her hand to his lips as if he were going to kiss it. He paused a hair's breadth from her skin and looked at her strangely, then began pushing her sleeve up. *Fuck*. How had he known?

"Let me go," she said, trying to pull away from him. His grip was like iron. She inhaled deeply, preparing for the worst as he exposed her mark. The mark didn't look like much, for all the fear and revulsion it inspired in people. It resembled the raised flesh of a scar, in the shape of two pronged crescents curving towards one another.

Rahj traced the curves of Namirah's mark with a light touch as Jon and Athar looked on. Her mark tingled, and Kara's face heated with shame. The man in the corner shifted his weight.

"Interesting," Rahj said as he released her.

Kara glared at the floor, cursing herself for being so careless.

"Cheer up," Jon said. "Us mercenaries are all cursed in one way or another, if not quite so literally as you. Now, what can we do for you?"

Kara let her denial fantasy unfurl a little further. She knew the chances were slim to none, but she had to ask. "Have you met anyone named Wesley McKenna? He's my brother. Our town was hit by Sanguine Riders. I thought he might come here. He's tall and thin. Brown hair, green eyes."

"Do you two bear a resemblance?" Jon asked.

"No, not really. I was adopted." Kara had dark brown

hair and hazel eyes, but Wesley had a strong brow and a hawk nose, whereas Kara's features were more delicate.

"What town?" Athar asked.

"Mudbottom. In the Balmoran Mountains."

"Small place. Surprised the Sanguines would hit there."

"They've been tithing us for years, but this time it was different. They were interested in my mark, tried to take me captive—I barely got away."

"They give you that shiner?" Jon asked, his voice gone cold.

Kara nodded. Jon padded his fingers on the desk as Athar thumbed through a stack of papers in front of him.

"No Wesleys here, sorry," Athar said.

Kara tried to mask the disappointment on her face. "Have you spotted anyone by that description in town?"

"Hard to tell, really—"

"City so full with the Reaping—"

"All kinds of boys here—"

There were mumbles of apology and a shaking of their heads all around. The man in the corner said nothing. Kara closed her eyes and took a deep breath so she could speak without her voice quivering. "In that case, I want to sign up for the Reaping Trials."

The room went silent for a second as they absorbed what she said, then Rahj smiled. Jon's face had fallen. Athar was rubbing his bare temples as if he anticipated a headache.

Jon's demeanor changed, his comic facade falling away. "The Stygians don't recruit just anyone. Our standards are very high. You're welcome to attend the trials of your own volition, but you won't be guaranteed a bid from us."

Kara stilled at his abrupt dismissal. They hadn't even asked her about her skills. Was she that obvious?

"Next," Jon called out into the hall. No one entered.

Kara braced her hands on the desk and leaned over it, getting into Jon's face. She looked a lot braver than she felt, but she wasn't going to give up that easily. "I'm not interested in the other clans. I need to join this one."

Jon wasn't fazed at all by her aggressive posture. "Why? This isn't an easy life. Few women ride with us. You would be isolated among the other recruits."

"I won't lie to you—I'm no great warrior. But I'm a fine farrier and groom, and I'm a damned fast learner. I need training, and I need gold. Please. Joining your clan is the best chance I have of avenging my family." Kara's voice cracked, and Jon's eyes softened. It was hard to speak about the events at Mudbottom, as if by saying it she'd make it more real. "The Sanguines took everything from me. Everyone knows of the enmity between your clans. And my curse might be awakening soon," she finished in a whisper. Kara didn't know how long it would take to trigger the curse if the mercenary she'd stabbed died. So far she felt normal, all things considered, but only time would tell.

The members of the recruitment panel looked to the man in the corner.

"They might be looking for her still," Jon said.

"Turn around, girl. Let me look at you," said the mysterious fourth member. His voice resonated through her.

Kara turned to face him, and in a last ditch effort, dropped to her knees. "Just give me a chance at the trials tomorrow. That's all I'm asking."

"Stop begging and stand up," he growled, moving into the light.

Kara raised her face and met the eyes of a savage man. He stepped forward again, his boots stopping just shy of crushing her fingers. When she rose to her feet, she was surprised by how much taller he was than her still—her head only came up to his chest. She scanned his body, avoiding looking into his eyes. Broad shoulders and powerful muscles filled out his black leather uniform, and a wicked looking dagger hung from his waist. The heat of his breath grazed her skin. She took a step back, and he immediately filled the space between them again. Kara looked up and tried to hold his gaze. Dark brown eyes with copper flecks in them burned into her, a sharp contrast to the soft black hair fluttering against his jaw. He looked like a devil painted with softness at the edges to appear urbane.

"First lesson. The Stygian clan does not beg."

Kara nodded, gulping. Did that mean she was in?

"Despite the history of bad blood between our clans, we're not here to enable your revenge fantasies. We don't war with the Sanguines unless we're being paid to do so. You will not receive any pity from my mercenaries. You are just another recruit, and we promise you nothing more than any other."

"I don't want your pity or your preference," Kara said.

He began circling her, assessing her with his gaze like she was a rabbit caught in a trap.

"You're untrained, you're entitled, and you're weak. None of this endears me to you. And I've a fine farrier already. Your curse, however, intrigues me. I will consider training you if you're willing to capitalize on its power once you awaken. You're of little value to me otherwise. What say you?"

"I…yes. Anything. What do I need to do?" She wasn't sure what he meant by the power of her curse—was he asking her to kill for him? She'd do it if it meant an opportunity to avenge her family.

He gave her a wolfish grin that held no warmth. "Give me your hand."

"Is this really necessary?" Jon asked.

"I don't want to hear it, Jon. This is what she wants." His tone had a hint of malice in it. He clasped Kara's left wrist in his warm, calloused palm and unsheathed his dagger.

"What—" she started.

He drew the dagger sharply through the twin crescents of Namirah's mark, splitting open her flesh. It didn't feel like a normal cut. It felt like she'd been kissed by fire.

He wet a finger with her blood and traced a circle that connected the twin halves of the mark. Kara tried to scream, but the sound stuck in her throat. Large, tan hands held her forearm still in a vise grip. His fingers were red with her blood.

"Don't fight it," he said calmly.

Kara looked on in horror as she bled out. Athar, Rahj, and Jon made no move to help her. In fact, they looked unsurprised.

Then the burning started. Phantom flames licked up her arm. Her veins burned beneath her skin, lighting up with a demonic red glow. Blood dripped from her wrist and sizzled on the floor. Her mind screamed. She couldn't speak. She shuddered and tilted her head back. The feeling was horrible yet ecstatic. It washed over her like a wave of fire, and power began flooding her body. The man stared down at her with unmistakable arousal.

And then it was gone. It faded as quickly as it came, and Kara felt incredibly tired. Her mind was fuzzy, her limbs useless and numb. She began to slump down, and the savage man caught her before she fell to the floor. He hauled her up into his arms like she weighed nothing.

"What are you doing?" her words were sluggish and half-formed.

He gazed down into her face. His animal eyes were too close, too knowing. She couldn't pass out in his arms.

"We'll see you at the trials tomorrow," he said.

"Who are you?" she asked, fighting to keep her eyes open.

"My name is Logan. *Commander* Logan."

Her world went black.

CHAPTER THREE

Kara woke to the sun shining in her face in a strange room at the Cat and Crow tavern. She looked around, not immediately recognizing her surroundings. Her head spun when she sat up in bed. Then memories of the day before crept into her consciousness. The Sanguine raid, riding to Liore, meeting the Stygian clan. *Da and Wesley*, her mind whispered. She shut that thought out, locking it in the back of her mind, and wrung her face between her hands.

Logan. The commander of the Stygian Brotherhood had sliced her wrist open and carried her to bed. She was off to a great start.

Kara pulled her wrist out from beneath the covers and inspected it. There was a thin, faded line where he'd cut her, as if the wound were weeks old. It didn't hurt at all. What the hell had he done to her? Cast some kind of spell? She quivered just remembering the sensation of the phantom flames licking over her. It had been intensely painful and pleasurable at the same time.

Someone knocked on her door, and Kara's eyes darted around the room. Whose room was she even in? *His?* She was dressed in her underwear, and her other garments were folded neatly on the dresser. Had he undressed her, too? The bastard. Kara tugged on her dirty clothes from yesterday, forcing her eyes to slide over the smattering of bloodstains on her cuff sleeves, and answered the door. It was Rahj and Jon.

"Morning, love. You look terrible," Jon said.

Rahj held out a thick vellum scroll to her. "Your contract."

She glared at Jon, then Rahj. "Before the trials? I thought the recruits performed, then the different clans bid on them?"

"Special circumstances. Are you interested in joining a different clan?" Rahj asked. He reminded her of a snake, all slithering tongue and golden scales.

"That depends. Is yours in the habit of stripping their female recruits after they've passed out?"

Their faces tightened. Rahj rolled his eyes.

"We asked one of the barmaids to change you," Jon said. "You were wet as a drowned rat and out cold."

"Oh. Well, thank you."

"Are you signing or not?" Rahj asked. "I have far more important things to be doing than paperwork."

She took the parchment and pen he offered. "In blood?"

"That won't be necessa—"

"If you like," Jon said.

Kara scanned the terms of the two year contract. It included details on the clan providing food, lodging, and a monthly wage, in addition to the pay from any Mercenary Guild contracts she earned money from.

"When do I get paid?"

"In a month, and every month after that," Rahj said.

"Any kind of signing bonus?"

Jon snorted. Rahj smiled, but it didn't reach his eyes. "No."

Kara scrawled her name, telling herself not to think of it as signing the next two years of her life away. Without Wesley and Da, the life she'd had was over anyway.

Rahj took the scroll and glanced it over. "Kara McKenna. Welcome to the Stygian Brotherhood, provided you don't die during your trial. Jon will take you to be outfitted." He turned and left.

Kara sighed. "Is he always like this?"

"Hmm. Most of the time, yes," Jon said.

THE CITY SQUARE had transformed into a bustling tournament grounds overnight. A large, fenced-in arena surrounded by wooden bleachers took center stage. They'd hauled in sand to cover and soften the cobblestones that made up the arena floor. Spectators filled the stands, some of them waving makeshift colored flags in support of a particular clan. It looked like all of Liore had come out to watch the trials.

She and Jon passed by a mother and her son bidding a tearful farewell to one another. He didn't look a day over thirteen.

"How old do you have to be to enlist?" she asked Jon.

"Old enough to kill a man. I joined when I was fifteen."

"It seems...wasteful."

"Not everyone goes straight into combat. Some clans have positions in support and reconnaissance available.

Many of these families wouldn't be able to survive without the earnings their children send them."

Jon led her to the Stygian tent. An assortment of men and women were pulling on leather hauberks and picking out weapons off metal-laden racks. Logan was nowhere to be seen. She wanted to ask him what he'd done to her yesterday.

Jon whistled to get their attention. "Everyone, this is Kara. Should your sorry asses ultimately be welcomed into our glorious establishment, you will have her esteemed company."

Most of them nodded at her in greeting.

A tall boy with glasses and a mop of curly blond hair approached her. He looked to be a few years younger than her. He was lanky, hadn't grown into his height yet. "I'm Thomas," he said, offering his hand. "Are you from Liore?"

Kara took his hand and shook it. "I'm from out of town."

Trumpets sounded, announcing the beginning of the trials. The crowd roared as someone entered the arena, and Kara's stomach dropped.

"Good luck out there, Kara from out of town." He winked at her and exited the tent.

Jon threw a leather hauberk at her, and she caught it with fumbling hands.

"I hope your reflexes are better than that in the ring."

Kara shrugged it on and fastened the straps as tight as they'd go. "It's too big."

"It's the smallest we've got. It'll have to do. We'll have you sized properly once we go home."

Home. She didn't even know where home was for these men. She wasn't ready to think of it as hers.

Jon passed her a flanged mace, and it was so heavy she nearly dropped it on her feet.

He plucked it back out of her hand. "Not that, then. Have you ever handled a sword?"

Kara shook her head. She was decent with a bow and arrow, thanks to Wesley's tutelage, but she'd only ever hunted game before. And archery seemed like a risky choice for the trials.

He sighed. "Aethyta is going to love you." Jon went back to the weapon racks, this time passing her a pair of crescent blades. "These are dangerous. You're going to have to get in close to be effective. Stay light on your feet."

She gripped the unfamiliar weapons tight in her palms. The blades curved back past her wrists into wicked points. She was going to have to slice into someone with these? An image of Yuki's scarlet throat flashed in her mind, and she took a deep breath. "I thought these were just combat trials. Is this a fight to the death?"

"This is a fight until you've hurt the other guy enough to determine you've won. So no death allowed. Not officially, anyways. Accidents happen, especially with the Sanguine recruits, so watch yourself out there. Come on, let's go."

They exited the tent and found a space by the arena railing where they could watch the duels. A man in a green and brown tabard and a tall woman in a yellow-gold one circled each other inside the arena, lunging and feinting in a deadly dance. If the recruits had pledged with a particular clan, they wore that clan's colors.

The duelist in green kneeled in surrender after being disarmed, which meant the bidding could begin. An officiator from the Mercenary Guild presided over the bidding from a tall platform overlooking the arena. The platform held a long table where the leaders of the various mercenary clans sat. Logan leaned back in his chair, looking bored as a man in brown leather with green accents talked to him.

"Accepting bids for our victor," the officiator announced.

At the high table, the man talking to Logan raised his hand, followed by a man with a silken yellow sash across his armor.

"We've got five gold pieces from Dreadnettle, raised to ten by the Golden Banner. Any other takers?"

Logan bid nothing.

"Golden Banner it is," said the officiator. "Recruit, please report to your clan's tent to receive your contract."

The loser was bid on for five gold pieces by the Dread-nettle commander. Kara imagined there was a good deal of clan politicking going on behind the scenes. "What happens if a recruit doesn't want to go with the highest bidder? What if they're pledged with someone else?"

"Then that's their prerogative. Bids are essentially a recruitment tax implemented to appease the guild and the hosting cities. Bunch of moneygrubbers. Though a higher bid is indicative of higher interest, and thus the possibility of better contract terms, be it in wages or position. Negotiating with different clans can even be done after your trial. It's all very diplomatic."

"Yet you had me sign a contract already." Kara found it odd that they'd been in such a rush to get her to sign, when yesterday they'd been reluctant.

"Hey, that was Rahj. Well, Rahj under Logan's orders, to be fair. But you came to us. Logan would never offer you a bid under normal circumstances. No offense.

Kara shrugged and looked back at the arena. She knew she wasn't the ideal recruit. Escaping the Sanguine in Mudbottom had been an adrenaline-fueled fluke. She wouldn't stand a chance against her family's killers in a real fight.

The last pair of fighters exited the arena, looking worn out. Thomas and a burly man wearing a purple tabard were the next pair called to enter the ring. They squared off in the sand. Thomas wielded a long, double-edged glaive as his weapon. He hadn't looked very intimidating when she met him, but that changed as he spun his glaive around in loud, whooping circles.

"Who is the purple clan?"

"Vispilio. They mainly operate around the southern coast. Dirty pirates, the lot of them. Led by a pirate queen."

There was a woman leading one of the clans? Kara glanced back at the commanders' table. A woman with jet black hair sat with her legs propped on the table. She wore a cocked leather hat adorned with a long purple feather.

The Vispilian pledge drew a curved scimitar out of his scabbard. He whispered over its hilt, and the blade burst into flame. Streaks of light lingered in the air when he slashed with it.

Kara sucked in her breath.

"Don't worry about him," Jon said. "He's all showmanship, no mettle. Wouldn't last a week in a real war. And I've seen Thomas with a glaive."

Jon had the right of it. The flaming sword was flashy, but Kara could see the panic in its wielder's eyes every time he had to lunge in beneath the glaive's deadly arcs. They parried off a few times before Thomas executed an impressive leaping sweep, drawing his glaive to a quivering stop just under his opponent's jugular. Kara looked at the close-quarters weapons Jon had given her with dismay.

He noticed her reaction and nudged her in the shoulder. "Don't be like that. If I'd given you a glaive, you'd trip over it coming out the gate."

He was probably right, but it didn't stop the knot of worry that filled her belly. She was anxious about having to fight, but she didn't think there was any getting out of this if she wanted to keep her contract with the clan.

Logan won the bid on Thomas for fifty gold pieces after a brief bidding war with the commander of the Sanguine Riders. It was an impressive amount. Kara wanted to get a better look at the Sanguine commander, but he was at the opposite end of the table from them, his body obscured by the Golden Banner leader.

"What's the name of the Sanguine leader?"

"That is the last thing you should be focusing on right now."

The next match was starting. A rotund boy with a skinny sword and a dented shield entered the arena. His face was red, and he was already breathing hard. He wasn't wearing any clan colors. His opponent was a hulking man from clan Sanguine who was covered in tattoos. He whirled a morning star flail over his head like it weighed nothing, his chest muscles rippling. The crowd screamed for blood.

Thomas joined Kara and Jon at the sidelines, his face flush with excitement.

"What is he even doing here?" Kara asked, gesturing at the boy in the arena.

Thomas glanced at the battle and shrugged. "Even mercenaries need meatshields."

All three of them winced as the boy barely raised his shield in time to block the flail's spiked ball from crunching into his skull. The Sanguine brute ripped the shield from the boy's hands and reared back for an overhead strike. The boy turned tail and ran, screaming, "I surrender! I surrender!" all the way to the fence. The crowd laughed and booed. Kara swallowed her spit. No one bid on the boy.

"Next up," the officiator called, "Kara McKenna, representing the Stygian Brotherhood, versus Rodrick Eckhart with the Golden Banner."

Kara's stomach twisted. Thomas gave her a hearty pat on the back.

"Don't panic," Jon said. "You can do this. Logan made sure you could do this."

"What?" she asked, perplexed.

"Here, take this," Thomas said, pulling the silky black tabard he was wearing over his head and handing it to her.

Kara tugged it on, wondering how many pledges had bled into the silk on days like this. She swam in the garment, but it would serve.

"You don't have to win," Jon said. "Just don't die."

Kara entered the arena on feet made of lead. Her hands were already sweating, making her grip on the blades slippery. No one entered opposite her.

"Rodrick Eckhart for the Golden Banner. Rodrick." Silence met the officiator's call. The Golden Banner commander shifted uncomfortably in his seat, and people in the stands muttered. She looked to Logan for guidance, but he was whispering fiercely with the Golden Banner commander. When she glanced back at Jon, he gave her a thumb's up.

Kara's hauberk squeaked as she turned, looking for anyone headed towards the arena. She thought she saw a silver-pronged helm moving through the crowds of people by the stands, but when she jerked her head back, it had vanished.

"In that case," mumbled the officiator, "we'll move on

to the next recruit. Kara McKenna for the Stygian Brotherhood versus Sebastian Vardis, unaffiliated."

Logan cursed from the officiator's stand. The wind whistled, picking up speed, and small eddies of sand shifted around the arena floor. The gust brought with it the scent of dead fish from the docks. Her stomach flopped over.

Sebastian entered through the far gate, casually dragging his rapier in the sand behind him. He looked strong and solidly built, probably in his early thirties. Oily black hair fell to his shoulders, and a puckered scar ran down his right cheek. She sincerely doubted she was going to win this fight, but she'd try to hold her own. He gave her a feral grin. "Little Stygian spider. A black widow, perhaps," he murmured to himself as he strolled towards her. His voice had an unctuous quality to it.

He struck at Kara with a lightning fast swing of his blade as soon as he was in range. She jerked her blades up in defense. Their weapons scraped together with a metallic whine. They disengaged, and Sebastian struck again. She didn't move fast enough to dodge him, and his sword made a shallow slice into the meat of her left shoulder. She sucked in a breath at the sting of the cut, but the pain was manageable.

As the fight went on, Sebastian never stopped grinning at her. It made her uneasy. Her attempts to penetrate his guard were parried with ease, and the cut on her shoulder burned. Sebastian jumped from foot to foot and darted in to slice at the skin her hauberk left exposed. After a few minutes of this and several shallow cuts to her arms and legs, Kara realized he was toying with her. He could have ended to fight as soon as it'd begun. The gash on her shoulder wept blood, staining her shirt. Sebastian licked his lips at the sight of it. Kara began to pant from the effort of blocking his attacks as her arms grew heavy. She needed to end this soon—one way or another.

Sebastian stilled for a moment, and Kara whirled and sliced into his thigh. He snarled and kicked her right knee out from under her, then swung his blade at her neck. Kara fell to the ground in a desperate attempt to avoid the blade. Her knee smarted, blossoming in pain. She scuttled backwards in the sand as Sebastian walked towards her. The game was up.

She let go of her weapons and held up her hands. "I surrender."

He kept coming.

"I surrender!"

He dropped the point of his rapier into the sand and bent over to offer her a hand up, still wearing that same smile. She caught the scent of lavender oil on his skin.

Time slowed to a standstill as she clasped her sweaty hand in his. She saw him raise the blade again, saw it sinking slowly towards her gut. The noise of the audience faded. She couldn't move fast enough. Behind Sebastian, she saw Logan vault over the commanders' table and leap off the platform. He landed and broke into a run, eating up the distance between them. He would never make it in time. The officiator dropped his list of recruits and stared, mouth agape.

A vibrating hum filled the air. The sword rapidly heading for Kara's gut was pulled out of Sebastian's grip. It soared across the arena towards the stands, and everyone clustered by the railing ducked. All except for one woman who stood tall, her arm outstretched to catch the sword by its hilt. The revelers surrounding her shifted, backing away. Someone yelled, "Witch!"

Logan collided with Sebastian, knocking him to the

ground. His eyes glowed a hellish red as he wrapped his hands around Sebastian's throat.

Kara collapsed against the sand and tried to catch her breath. Her first day as a mercenary had barely begun, and she'd almost died. She laughed, overwhelmed. Maybe she was in shock.

One of the Mercenary Guild's guards pounded up to them and tried in vain to pull Logan off Sebastian. Logan shook him off like a fly. Sebastian's face was beginning to change colors. His eyes bulged, and he clawed at Logan's hands around his throat.

Then the woman who'd caught the sword arrived. Her forest green cloak was clasped at the neck by a brooch of golden antlers. Underneath she wore a simple riding habit, her tan skirt split down the middle to allow riding astride.

"Vakarian. How...typical."

Logan finally released Sebastian, who rolled away, sputtering for breath. His throat and face were a livid blotch of red. The guild guard knelt beside him and put him into handcuffs before escorting him out of the arena.

"Serena," Logan said to the woman, standing up and brushing the sand off his pants. Then he looked to Kara. "Are you okay?"

"Yeah, I think so." Her knee was bruised and the cut on her shoulder stung fiercely, but she was alive.

Logan offered her his hand and hauled her to her feet. Kara wobbled, still overwhelmed, and he steadied her with a heavy hand on her back. Then he ripped the bottom half of her torn sleeve off and inspected her shoulder. Kara was going to need to supplement her wardrobe soon.

"You need to have this tended to."

"I see you still have issues with control," Serena said. Her eyes had narrowed on Kara's mark, exposed by her ripped sleeve.

"Likewise."

Serena laughed. "Would you rather I have let her die?"

Logan narrowed his eyes at her. "You're not usually so charitable with your powers. I'm thinking there's a catch."

"I want her. For the Vespertines." She looked at Kara. "Kara, was it? How's saving your life for a bid?"

"Uhh—" Kara started. Was she serious? She must be joking.

"She's mine, Seeker," Logan growled.

"I think that's for her to decide."

"Actually—" Kara began again.

Logan pulled her contract out of his pocket, snapping it open in front of Serena. "It's been decided."

Kara looked back and forth between them. They obviously had a history together.

"You signed her before the trials even started? My, my, Commander. You're getting desperate." Serena took the contract and looked it over, then started laughing. "You're kidding me, right? And what happens when her curse awakens?"

"I'll train her," Logan said.

Serena's eyebrows furrowed. "God's teeth, you're serious about this. You're the last person who should be training her." She passed the contract back to Logan and looked at the two of them. "I almost wish I could see it. Two of you destructive, willful, keening bastards stuck together on that rock you call a fortress in the Blackshear. You'll ruin her."

Logan's lip curled in anger.

Serena patted him on the chest dismissively, then took Kara's hand in hers, "Come find me when you come to your senses, dear." Then she dropped her hand and made her way out of the arena.

"Who was that?" Kara asked.

"The Seeker for the Vespertines. Handles all of their recruitment. She's also a very powerful mage."

"Commander Vakarian," the officiator announced, "as always, pre-emptive signing of contracts is ill-advised behavior. However, given the nature of today's events and the fact that the Vespertines hold no sway in these proceedings, we'll let it stand. Now *please* clear the arena."

CHAPTER FOUR

K ara watched the rest of the trials, looking for anyone in Sanguine colors that had been at Mudbottom, but she didn't see anyone she recognized. The Sanguine recruits were distinctly brutal, usually winning their matches with ease. Logan was more selective with his bidding than the other commanders, but he bid high for anyone he was particularly interested in.

Along with her and Thomas, two other recruits signed on in Liore. One was a burly, one-eyed man named George who smoked like a chimney. He was a retired fisherman. The other recruit was Jasper Kendrick, the fifth son of some local noble who wanted him out from under his feet. He had wispy white-blond hair and a willowy frame that moved with grace. He'd been classically trained by a swordmaster at his father's estate, and his victory at the trials had been impressive.

After the trials ended, they stayed another night at the Cat and Crow, finalizing contracts and readying supplies for their departure for the Stygian fortress. Logan had the bay courser she'd ridden from Mudbottom sold when he heard how she came by it, saying he'd find her a new mount. Kara didn't argue with him about it. It would put any Sanguines looking for her on the wrong path.

The clan gathered outside the inn the morning they were set to leave. There were no supply wagons. Instead, Jon passed out saddlebags—each packed with a sleeping roll, rations, and a full canteen. The town square was crowded with couples and families saying their farewells.

Logan called Kara over to the stable. There were dark shadows under his eyes, and he'd let his stubble grow in. "I have something to show you."

He led her inside to a stall that held a majestic black mare. She was tall and muscular, with a coat sleek and dark as raven wings. "Her name's Drum," he said, patting the mare on the neck.

Kara held her palm out for Drum to sniff and was rewarded with a wet tongue lapping. She smiled and rubbed the mare's silky muzzle. "Where'd you get her?"

"The commander of the Golden Banner owed me a favor. She's yours."

Kara swung her head towards him. "You must be joking."

"I don't often."

"But—she looks to be worth half a year's wages, Logan. I can't afford that. There's no way I could repay you—"

"Enough. You don't owe me anything. I sold the horse you were using, so unless you're planning to sit in someone's lap for the journey to Raven's Rest…" His eyes darkened, and he quirked an eyebrow at her.

Kara swallowed hard and quickly buried the image that rose in her mind of being sandwiched between his powerful thighs in a saddle. "Not exactly."

"She'll be invaluable for your training exercises. Saddle

her up; we're riding out soon." Logan gave the mare a final pat and left.

Kara looked Drum in the eye. "What have we gotten ourselves into?" The mare nickered softly in response.

Kara let herself into the stall and ran her hands over the mare's feathered legs, testing for lameness and gauging the horse's temperament. Drum stood quietly, swishing her tail while Kara checked her hooves. Her father had been a consummate horseman, and Kara had had a horse between her legs before she'd learned to walk thanks to him. Buying a horse off someone could be a tricky business, but the mare was perfectly healthy, with a beautiful conformation and coloring. Either the Stygian clan had very deep pockets, or their commander had called in a hell of a favor.

THE JOURNEY to Raven's Rest would take them two days at a clip, according to Jon. It was deep in Blackshear Forest, far from any major hubs of civilization. They rode out before noon, passing through Liore's eastern gate as the townsfolk dismantled the dueling arena behind them. Kara rode in the middle of their procession, next to Jon and the new recruits. Logan took the lead, while Athar and Rahj brought up the rear. Drum was proving to be a dream mount, her gaits smooth and balanced. Kara let her have her head and relaxed into the saddle once they were out of the city.

Teleria was succumbing to autumn's embrace, the trees ablaze with deep reds and hues of yellow and orange. Fallen leaves crunched beneath the horses' hooves with each step. Kara considered Serena's dubious offer to join the Vespertines. Perhaps she'd just wanted to get a rise out of Logan. Kara didn't think the trend towards prejudice against Namirah's Chosen had shifted so much that Telerian royalty would accept a cursed bodyguard. She was on a different path now, anyways.

"Copper for your thoughts?" Jon asked. He was dressed in the Stygian uniform today—all tight-fitting black leather, shiny buckles, and a chest harness that held several knives. It didn't look particularly comfortable.

"Tell me about Raven's Rest."

"Not much to tell, really. It's an old fortress that was abandoned after the Curse Wars. Parts of it are crumbling about our heads, but we make do."

"I heard you had an oubliette," Thomas said.

Jon nodded. "True. Floods when it rains, nasty business. Had to fish a recruit out of there once. You lot will be acquainted soon enough. With the fortress, that is. Not the oubliette. Unless—"

"Thomas," Jasper interrupted, "You're from Liore. What's your family's name?"

"I doubt you'd know it."

"Humor me."

"Carrington."

"Carrington. I thought you looked familiar. What does your mother do? We used to have a maid by that name. Pretty thing. Up and vanished one day. Father thought she'd stolen something and ran off, but we never could identify what was missing."

Thomas glared at Jasper. "It's a common name."

"If you say so."

Thomas's grip tightened on his reins. "Why are you joining a clan, anyways? Your family has plenty of money."

"Got to make a name for myself somehow. And my four older brothers have taken all the usual career routes.

It's important that a man distinguish himself. Especially a Kendrick."

"There are five of you? Mother have mercy," George said.

Jon snorted.

"Before the trials, father and I were debating which clan I should join. Sanguine or Stygian, obviously, but which one? Then he told me it didn't really matter. I might as well choose my favorite color, because they used to be one and the same. And black is so slimming."

"*What?*" Kara said.

Jasper nodded. "During the Curse Wars, the Sanguines got quite big. There was a power struggle amongst their highest-ranking members, and the Stygians split off and formed their own clan."

Kara swiveled towards Jon. "Is that true?" What exactly had she gotten herself into? Had she joined a clan no better than the one responsible for her family's death?

Jon shrugged. "The split was over twenty years ago, soon before the Curse Wars ended. We're our own clan now, but we've a bloody past."

Kara turned to George and Thomas, still reeling from the news. "Did you two know this?"

Thomas looked sheepish. "Didn't you learn clan history when you were in school?"

Kara shook her head. Tuition for school in Mudbottom had been expensive, and Kara had convinced Da to home-school her once the other kids had started calling her 'Kara the Cursed' and moving away from wherever she sat. While she'd learned her sums and letters, the forest had been her true teacher. She and Wesley would speed through their lessons so they could go outside and explore the woods and hunt game. Da had done his best, but he'd been busy trying to keep his business afloat and food on the table.

"I was surprised to see you receive a bid after such a dismal display of skill," Jasper said, "But I hear you bear the mark of Namirah."

Kara stilled. Drum came to a stop, and Kara nudged her back into a walk. "Who told you that?" She'd figured she wouldn't be able to keep it a secret from her fellow recruits for long, but she hadn't expected it to come up so soon.

"Athar's rather loud when he's drinking."

Kara pinched her lips together. "I do bear the mark."

"My father says Namirah's Chosen are nothing but rutting, murdering degenerates. However, I reserve the right to change my mind."

Kara clenched her teeth and ignored him lest she said something she'd regret.

"Whoa," Thomas said. "You're marked? I hear you get demonic powers and shit once you awaken. Remind me not to piss you off. Are you taking notes, Jasper?" He winked at her.

Kara struggled to suppress a frown. It was easy to forget that awakening might be creeping up on her even now. Would this be her last month of freedom? It was refreshing to be around open-minded people for once— Jasper aside—but she hoped the Sanguine merc would live. She had enough to worry about as it was without being overcome by magic-fueled bloodlust on the regular. Only revenge would be worth that price.

"I don't think I'd mind it so much—all that power, you know?" Thomas said.

She shook her head at Thomas. He had no idea; he was all youth and bluster. "It's called a curse for a reason. People fear it."

"Yeah, I know. That's the idea."

"A foolish wish," said Jasper. "Namirah's Chosen are baser beings who aren't fully in control of their instincts."

"Watch your mouth, lordling," George said, blowing smoke from his pipe into Jasper's face. Kara had never known a man to smoke a pipe and ride a horse at the same time, but George seemed proficient at it.

"What'd you call me, fisherman?" Jasper said.

"So George," Kara said, trying to change the subject away from her, "why'd you quit fishing to sign on with the Stygians?"

"The sea's a fickle bitch. She took my eye n' my coin. Figured mercenary work would be steadier. At least ya know what to expect." He chewed on his words like he had a wad of spit in his mouth.

"Tell me, do they pay you less because of your handicap?" Jasper said.

George swiveled his eye towards Jasper and drew deep on his pipe. "They'll save a chunk on two years' wages when I kill you before we even reach the fortress."

"Who said I was talking to you? Having one of Namirah's Chosen among us could be a liability."

Kara's face went hot.

"Liability? Come on, Jaz. I'm sure *you* had a fancy tutor coming up. Namirah's Chosen were notorious for decimating royal forces during the Curse Wars. In the end they only lost because they were overwhelmed by sheer numbers," Thomas said.

"Do not call me 'Jaz.' And I simply question her ability to control herself if she awakens."

"Keep questioning, and maybe she'll be obliged to give you a demonstration," George said.

Kara rolled her eyes. She kicked Drum forward and rode to the front of the procession, drawing even with

Logan. He cut an imposing figure atop the tall black stallion he rode. The dark cut of his jaw and bunching of muscles beneath his shirt drew her eye, distracting her from her purpose.

"Have you come to stare?"

Kara blinked and shook her head. "I need to talk to you."

He sliced his dark eyes towards her. "Do you always announce your intentions before you begin, Ms. McKenna? We'll have to teach you subterfuge."

Kara felt a blush begin to stain her cheeks. Quarrelsome man. "What did you do to me when you sliced open my arm the other night?"

"A little blood magic. There's power in your blood because of your curse. You'd been through a lot; it was meant to replenish your energy and invigorate you."

"Does the fact that it…that it happened the way it did —" *That it felt like I was being kissed by fire and caressed by velvet lips.* "—mean my curse has been triggered?"

"No, not necessarily. The power's in you regardless, it just needs someone that can manipulate it."

"Someone like you. Are you a mage, then?"

"Something like that."

So the man she'd entrusted her future to was a menacing warrior who could do blood magic. Fantastic. "I'm not sure you did enough invigorating."

"It wasn't a fair fight. Vardis is experienced, but unaffiliated with any particular clan. That's the only reason he was allowed in the ring to begin with. He's the kind of mercenary that does the dirty work of other mercenaries."

"You think someone sent him to kill me?"

"Maybe, or to ensure your performance was poor, leaving you open for the Sanguines."

Kara quieted. Would they go to such lengths? "So you

think I could have won against someone else?"

"Probably not," he said, the corners of his mouth tilting up.

Kara sighed. She had a lot of work to do if she wanted a chance at vengeance.

"What did you end up paying for my bid?"

"A transactional fee of twenty-five gold pieces."

It was a hefty sum to pay on top of her wages. Logan's hulking black stallion nipped at Drum's shoulder and pawed at the earth. The horse was at least seventeen hands tall, with a back wide as a barrel. Drum laid back her ears.

"Hmm," she said, guiding Drum away from his horse. "Thomas got more."

"Thomas didn't fall on his ass five minutes into his fight."

He had a point. The stallion pranced up to Drum again, fighting Logan's rein. If her mare was in heat this was going to be a hell of a trip. "He's feisty. What's his name?"

"Char."

"I think I'll call him brute."

"Apt."

She and Logan fell into silence. His dark hair was swept back into a queue today, and the sun highlighted the stubble dusting his jaw. His eyes constantly scanned their surroundings, always on alert. Jasper and George were still arguing behind them.

"How do you know Serena?"

His lips quirked. "You ask a lot of questions."

Logan said nothing further, so Kara decided she would take the hint. The East Road stretched on endlessly ahead of them. It was called such because it spanned Teleria, all the way from Liore on the west coast to Temodor on the east. Kara wondered if people traveling westward called it the West Road, instead. Their procession rode past fields of desiccated farmland long turned to shrub as the sun beat down on them, making the nip in the air tolerable. When the jagged border of the Blackshear came into view, Logan finally spoke.

"I know Serena from the time I spent at the royal palace in Lerathil. We were a couple for a bit."

Kara's eyebrows crawled up her face. That would explain the tension between them. "What happened?"

He sighed and glanced at her, bidding her to be quiet with his eyes. "People like us don't do well in long-term relationships."

A charged silence hovered in the air between them. Kara let the gentle creak of saddle leather and the shuffling of hooves lull her into a relaxed state. She yawned.

Jon rode his chestnut gelding into the space between her and Logan's horses, the jingle of buckles on his saddlebags announcing his arrival. Char laid back his ears. "Sorry about Jasper," Jon said to Kara, "there's a bastard in every lot."

"It's fine. I'm used to it." It was a comfortable lie. It wasn't like she could insist they drop him in favor of the woman who'd nearly died the first time she stepped into the ring.

"You'll stay in the broken tower room when we arrive at Raven's Rest. We don't have many female recruits, so they're allowed private living quarters," Logan said.

"That dilapidated hovel? It's a wonder we never get visitors," Jon said.

"She can hardly room in the barracks with the rest of the men. The tower is serviceable."

"'*Serviceable*,' he says." Jon cupped a hand around his mouth and mock-whispered to her, "It's got *broken* in the name for a reason."

"I could hack it in the barracks."

"No," Logan said. "You'd be a distraction."

"For once, I agree with him," Jon said, shrugging. "The new recruits live in close quarters. You wouldn't have much privacy."

Kara hadn't given much forethought to what her living situation would be like once they arrived. She was far more worried about the training. From what she'd seen at the trials, all of the recruits were skilled with at least one kind of weapon.

"Living in the tower may be an exercise in awareness and agility, but it's private and spacious. You won't do better," Logan said.

"If you insist." She wasn't looking forward to being alone with her thoughts.

"Take what leniencies you're offered," Logan said. "They'll be few and far between. Your fellow recruits are likely to test you even more than usual."

"I'm no stranger to adversity, Commander."

"Maybe so, but the people of Mudbottom weren't wielding swords."

THEY MADE camp that night in a small clearing just within the border of Blackshear Forest. The pines stretched high, casting their motley group in shadows. A small fire blazed in the center of their camp, crackling and spitting embers occasionally. Jon was roasting a fat hare he'd shot on a spit, and its tantalizing scent crawled up Kara's nose and lingered there. Her legs were sore from spending all day in the saddle, and she was enjoying the opportunity to sit down.

"Gotta take a piss," Thomas said, heading into the woods.

Athar called out after him, "Best watch yourself. Black-shear's not verra hospitable at night. Full o' arachnae and wolves, snakes as long as a man is tall."

George looked out at the shadows slinking in on the clearing. "Don't like the forest at night. Especially when the moon's new. I'd climb a tree and bed down in chainmail if I could."

"I'd rather be here than out on the water," Athar said, shuddering. "Fucking jellyfish. And sharks. Can't forget sharks. Unnatural creatures."

"To each their own," George said.

"When's that rabbit going to be ready?" Jasper groaned. "I'm starving."

Jon gave him a cold grin. "Who said I was sharing? There's food in your pack."

"Kara, come here," Logan called. He was a few yards away from the campfire ring, sitting on the gnarled stump of an oak tree, his form obscured by shadow. The horses grazed nearby, chuffing softly to one another.

Logan motioned for her to sit, but there was virtually no room left on the stump. Did he expect her to sit on his lap? Kara stood still and glared at him until he grinned and scooted over.

"Better?"

She sat down, but her legs and arms still brushed up against his. The warmth of his large body pressing against her smaller form unnerved her. Blood rushed to her face, and she was thankful for the darkness.

"I wanted to change your bandage."

Kara shrugged off her cloak and angled her right shoulder towards him. She was still wearing the cream-colored blouse she'd put on the morning of the raid. It was stained with blood and torn now.

"These are the only clothes you brought?"

She nodded. "I had to leave in a hurry."

"We'll have you outfitted once we get to Raven's Rest." He unwrapped the old bandage carefully, his calloused hands hot against her skin. "This is going to sting," he warned before rinsing the cut with water from his canteen. He leaned closer and blew on it gently.

Her skin broke out in goosebumps. His scent enveloped her as he bent close—leather and sweat and horseflesh. Logan's gaze rose to meet hers. Kara's sudden puff of breath fogged in the night air, and his eyes flashed yellow.

What was that? Kara blinked, and his eyes were back to their usual dark brown. His hands fell away from her, and she immediately missed their warmth.

"I'm sorry about your family. I know what it's like to lose a parent at the hands of the Sanguines. Do you have anyone else? What about your birth parents?"

Kara shook her head. She had no idea who her real parents were. Da had been a ranking officer in the royal army during the Curse Wars, and he'd found her during one of his patrols. A baby hidden in the back of a wagon in an empty, razed village. The wagon had been packed with the belongings of a couple preparing to flee. Da hadn't expected her to make it through the night, but when she'd woken him in his tent the next morning with her screams, he decided to bring her home to his wife and young son. Wesley's mother passed away two years later of the consuming sickness, though the residents of Mudbottom blamed her death on the shame and misery of sheltering a cursed child.

Kara swallowed the sudden lump in her throat, fighting the urge to cry. "If Wesley had left a day earlier…" Images from the raid began flashing through her head, threatening to breach the wall she'd built in her mind, brick by bloody brick. One of the bricks crumbled.

Logan cradled her face in his gigantic hands and wiped away her tears with his thumbs. "Some people will tell you revenge won't satisfy you. I'm not one of those people."

"But you said—"

"That I wouldn't enable you? I can't risk a war with the Sanguines for the sake of my people, but I've no love lost for them. Two years will go by quickly, Kara. You'll have your chance. Your brother wanted to be a mercenary?"

She nodded. "With your clan."

"Maybe you're taking his place." Logan slid his hands off her face, pulled a tiny tin jar of salve from his pocket, and applied it to her cut. The cooling relief it brought was instantaneous, and it hardly stung once he finished.

"Thank you, Logan. For everything." She was surprised by his gentleness and sincerity. This didn't seem like the same man she'd met that first night at the Cat and Crow tavern.

"Listen, Kara. We may be familiar on the road, but you really ought to address me formally."

"Right. Commander." She smiled.

"It's healing well," he said, wrapping her arm with a fresh cloth. "The scar will be small." He drew back and tucked a stray strand of her behind her ear, scanning her face for something.

Then his expression changed, his sharp eyes darting towards the woods. He was over the stump, knees crouched low and knife drawn in one smooth motion. The speed at which he moved was alarming.

Something crashed through the brush on the edge of the clearing seconds later. "Guys," Thomas huffed out as he came into the light, bending over at the middle to catch his breath, "I think I saw a cougar."

CHAPTER FIVE

They arrived at Raven's Rest the following day at sunset. It was nestled deep within Blackshear Forest, and Kara would be hard-pressed to find her way back here unassisted, even with her tracking skills. The horses picked their way through trails invisible to the naked eye, avoiding massive fallen trees and deep gullies in the earth. When they finally emerged from the treeline, Kara took in the view.

Set against the backdrop of the falling sun, Raven's Rest was almost beautiful. A crenelated stone wall surrounded the keep, and a portcullis with two sets of barred iron drop-gates formed the entrance. Four turreted towers framed the inner courtyard, one of which Kara assumed contained her new quarters. There were signs of disrepair, even from here. The outer wall crumbled in on itself at certain places, and it was covered with a thick layer of moss and climbing vines. Scouts patrolling the battlements spotted them and sounded their arrival with a hunting horn.

The portcullis doors creaked upward, and the group

rode inside. Anticipation unfurled in Kara's belly. The central keep rose like a stone monolith before them. The architecture was simple, utilitarian. The keep's only unique feature was a large stained glass window on the second floor that depicted the Stygian sigil in a kaleidoscope of colors. The artistry in the intricate design was impressive; it must have cost a fortune to have made. Colored glass was an expensive rarity, and it usually needed to be imported from coastal cities like Espyr.

A few Stygian mercenaries stood clustered around the courtyard to greet them. Logan dismounted, and a jovial-looking man with a head of thick brown hair ran through with grey took Char's reins. He looked the new recruits over and whistled.

"She's a beaut, Commander. Is she mine? Please say it's so."

"The horse or the girl?" asked Jon.

"Either one'd be fine by me." He winked at Kara. The man was at least forty.

"This is Rohan," Logan sighed. "He's our—"

"Horselord," Rohan supplied.

"—stablemaster," Logan finished.

"Old goat," Athar said.

"That's rich coming from you, dwarf," Rohan said.

Athar harrumphed. "My family's dwarf blood was diluted centuries ago."

"Once a dwarf, always a dwarf."

"Cut it out, you oafs. We have a visitor," said a squat man with a potbelly and bulging arms. His pate was smooth as a baby's bottom, yet his chin sprouted a bushy grey beard that grew to his chest.

"She's not a visitor, Ridley. Are the weapons I ordered ready yet?" Logan said.

Ridley's eyes widened. "Ahh—not yet."

"See to it that they're finished."

"Yes, Commander."

Kara's eyebrows rose. They must be producing a lot of weaponry to warrant their own blacksmith. And the amount of respect Logan commanded from men who looked twice his age was impressive. The men slowly dispersed, the new recruits following Jon to the stable. Kara dismounted and made to follow when Rohan stopped her.

"Let me," he said, taking the reins from her. "I'd like to get acquainted."

Kara looked skeptically at Logan's brute of a stallion. "You don't have your hands full with Char?"

"You mean Baby Bear here?" He scratched Char under his forelock, and the horse lipped at Rohan's shirt. "Never. He's a sweetheart—loves peppermints."

Kara shrugged and passed him the reins. Rohan led the two horses away, whistling a tune. The horses looked quite the pair with their twin black coats.

"*Baby Bear,*" Logan muttered under his breath. "Follow me. I'll show you to your room."

"Quite the crew you've got here," she said as they walked towards the northwest tower.

"You met the civilized lot. They're not all so pleasant, as you'll figure out in training."

"But they respect you."

He looked at her, assessing. "That surprises you?"

"You just seem young, to be leading one of the big clans. How did you come into power?"

Logan pried the tower door open, and the wood groaned. The winding stone staircase they faced was thick with a layer of moss that'd built up on the stones. He strode up the steps on long, muscular legs. Kara followed, watching her feet to keep from slipping. There was no railing to grab onto, and cobwebs clung to the rusted sconces on the wall.

"My father was the last leader of the clan," Logan said from up ahead.

"So you inherited it?"

"No," he snapped. "I earned it with sweat and blood."

"Is your father still here?"

"No more questions."

Kara relented, though she wondered how young Logan had been when he'd taken over. Was the clan all he'd ever known?

Midway up the tower, sunlight beamed in through a breach in the stonework that'd never been repaired.

"Well, that explains the greenery. Water must come in when it rains," Kara said.

"A trebuchet busted through here, back when this was an outpost for the royal army. It can get a bit drafty."

"I hope you aren't expecting any more sieges."

"They'd be dead before they ever got that close."

They reached the top of the stairs, which opened onto an arched wooden door. Logan pulled a black metal key out of his pocket, put it into the lock, and twisted. The door creaked open, and he stood aside to let her pass.

The room within was spacious but barren. The only pieces of furniture remaining from its last occupant were a four-poster bed and a worn dresser. A dusty mirror with a splintered crack down its middle adorned the wall.

"You'll be responsible for the cleaning," Logan said. "We don't have any servants or maids. The well's in the courtyard."

Kara groaned internally at the thought of dragging bucket after bucket of water up those stairs. And the trouble she'd have to go through to bathe…maybe she'd just live in filth for a while.

A door across the room opened onto the fortress ramparts, and a window adorned with simple wooden shutters looked down on the courtyard below. A ray of sunlight shot through it, capturing a thousand tiny motes of dust in its path. The bed bore a single pillow and a patchwork quilt embroidered with flowers. It was rather feminine for a mercenary fortress. Who had this room belonged to before? The furnishings looked too simple for someone like Serena.

Logan gestured towards the other door. "Men patrol the ramparts at all hours, but they won't disturb you. The mess is located in the keep, along with the barracks and the officer's rooms. Dinner's at six. You're expected in the training yard tomorrow at first light." He set the key down on the dresser and turned to go. "Any questions, recruit?"

"No, Commander." She was ready.

()

DAWN CAME EARLY, and the twenty-some recruits gathered in the training yard were bleary-eyed. Kara was surprised when an older woman in tan breeches and a navy jerkin belted at the waist entered the yard. She wore her long grey hair in a braid that fell to the middle of her back.

"Students," she said. "My name is Aethyta. *Mistress* Aethyta to you lot. For the next ninety days, I will be your god. You will do what I tell you, when I tell you, and how I tell you. If you should fail to exhibit the necessary skills by the end of this period, your contract with the Stygian clan will be terminated." Her words clipped out sharply as she walked down the line.

"Who is she?" Kara whispered to Thomas. She'd been expecting Logan or one of the other men from the Reaping Trials.

Thomas shrugged.

"The head trainer," said a girl that appeared on Kara's right. She was tall and muscular, with tousled red hair and green eyes bright with excitement. "Faedra," she said by way of introduction.

"Kara." Kara was relieved to discover another woman in the pool of recruits.

"Aethyta. Ahem—*Mistress* Aethyta lives in Blackhearth, but she's been training Stygian recruits since before Logan became commander."

"How do you know that?"

"My older brother, Feron, has been here for three years. Thought I'd keep with the family tradition."

"I see we already have people who would rather chat than pay attention," Aethyta said, approaching them. She gave them both a once-over.

"Feron's kid sister and a farrier's apprentice. What was the Commander thinking?"

Kara swallowed. So she knew her history already—did she know about her mark, too? She tried to suppress the sinking feeling in her gut. She knew she wasn't in combat shape, but the woman was discounting her before training even began.

Aethyta gave them a flinty, grey-eyed stare, then moved on along the line. Faedra released the breath she'd been holding.

"For five days a week, I expect each of you to be at this training yard at dawn, weapon in hand and bodies ready. I do *not* tolerate tardiness." She clapped her hands together. "Now. Weapons, everyone. We begin with staves. We'll move on to swordplay once everyone has mastered the basics."

The recruits took up training staves from a wooden bin at the arena's edge and paired off with each other. Aethyta took them through the optimum positions for their hands and feet, then ran drills where they parried and struck at each other with the polished wood.

Kara partnered up with Faedra. She was more skilled than Kara—certainly stronger, and Kara struggled to score any strikes on her body. She saw Aethyta heading towards them from the corner of her eye.

"Your form is pitiful," Aethyta barked. "Goddess knows why you were contracted."

"Because she's marked," Thomas muttered next to them.

Kara glared at him. She lost track of Faedra's stave, and it caught her on the collarbone. She kept swinging, rapping Kara on the wrist and then her knee. Kara winced, nearly dropping her staff on the last hit. Her knee was still bruised from her skirmish with Sebastian.

"Sorry," Faedra said, a sheepish look on her face.

"It's fine." Kara shook out her wrist.

"Don't go easy on her," Aethyta said, then walked away with her arms clasped behind her back.

Kara sighed and blew a loose strand of hair out of her face in frustration.

"It will get easier," Faedra said. "According to Feron, Aethyta can be a real hardass, but these training exercises are child's play compared to what we'll eventually be doing."

"You're incredibly reassuring, Faedra." Kara put her frustration into the force of her next swing, and she was pleased to see Faedra's grip wobble on contact.

Aethyta completed her circuit of the other duelists and clapped again. "Swap partners!"

Faedra left, and Kara found herself face to face with an enormous man she hadn't met yet. He had a torso like a tree trunk, a nasty scar marring his upper lip, and long brown hair. His padded jerkin was damp with sweat stains, the look in his eyes uncertain. He bowed his head to her then started swinging.

Kara danced left and right, frantically meeting him swing for swing. She was winded, her grip on the wood slick with sweat. She missed a beat, and his swing caught her hard on her bruised clavicle. White hot pain flashed through her, and Kara staggered to her knees. She bit her tongue and blinked rapidly to keep her tears at bay. She spotted Aethyta at the other side of the arena through blurry eyes and thanked the goddess that she wasn't paying attention.

Her opponent held out a huge tan paw to help her, and Kara's gut clenched as Sebastian's twisted smile flashed through her head.

"Name's Bear," he grumbled in a rough voice. "I don't like fighting women—makes me uncomfortable. I've got a daughter of my own at home." He looked down at his feet.

Kara clasped his palm and leveraged herself up, giving him a weak smile. "Don't worry about it. I need the practice."

THE TRAINING SESSION continued for hours. When the sparring drills were done, Aethyta had them run the inner perimeter of the fortress and perform body-weight exercises until all of the recruits were red in the face and panting. Kara was going to have nightmares rife with the sound of Aethyta's gnarled hands clapping together.

Their second trip around the fortress, Kara noticed some rope rigging on the wall adjacent to the broken tower. It looked like it'd been used as a weighted pulley system to transport cargo to the top of the battlements.

She'd have to investigate it later and see if it could be used to haul water.

The recruits who had some training and were in shape were faring well enough, but the drills were kicking the shit out of Kara. By day's end she was covered in dirt and dried sweat, and her limbs felt like jelly. She hardly remembered what it felt like to be clean anymore, and she desperately needed a change of clothes.

The sun began to fall lower in the sky, and Aethyta clapped her hands twice. The recruits looked at her expectantly from glazed eyes. "You lot are done for today. We reconvene tomorrow. Don't be late."

Kara trudged after the other recruits heading to the great hall, where they lined up to be served food by a wiry man named Olly.

"I don't trust a thin cook," Thomas whispered beside her in line.

Jasper was a few recruits in front of them, sporting a split lip and mussed hair.

"What happened to our lordling?" Kara asked.

Thomas grinned. "That might have been me. A little payback for the East Road."

"He could be a powerful enemy."

He shrugged. "I'm not going to spend the next two years letting him piss on me because his father's a rich bastard. Better to make that clear now."

They took their plates and sat down at one of the long tables spanning the hall. Faedra and George sat down opposite them once they'd been served.

"Where's your brother?" Kara asked Faedra between bites of bread.

She nodded towards several tables at the head of the room, positioned by the hearth. A cluster of people in black leather sat around them, laughing and tossing back mugs of ale. "That's where the initiated members sit."

"They separate us?" Kara asked.

"It's more like a rite of passage. Besides, training doesn't last that long."

Kara scanned the group for Logan, but he wasn't there.

Athar pounded the table with his fist and bellowed, "They always drag ass in here like a sack of half-drowned kittens on the first day." Ale spittle flew out of his mouth and into his beard as he spoke, and he was met by a round of laughter.

"I know what you're thinking—three more months of Aethyta sounds like hell," Faedra said. "But she's not the only trainer. Feron said that members of the inner circle give lessons sometimes."

"Inner circle?" Kara asked.

"The highest ranking members of the clan. The Commander and Jon—he's second-in-command. Athar, the quartermaster. And Rahj—he's the spymaster. You should have met them at your host city," Faedra said.

Kara nodded, trying to imagine what a training session with Logan would be like. Then something occurred to her. "Why did Aethyta say we only had ninety days to prove ourselves? Aren't we already contracted?"

Thomas sighed and pushed up his glasses. "Did you even read your contract?"

"Yeah," she said, forking a piece of chicken into her mouth.

"Then you saw the three month termination clause. Either party can choose to part ways if they're unsatisfied after three months."

"You get your wages and the boot if you don't pass muster," George said.

Kara shook her head. "My contract didn't have that."

"*Huh*. That's interesting," Thomas said, frowning slightly.

Faedra grinned. "Guess you're trapped."

The boys finished eating and joined another group of male recruits headed towards the public baths. Kara stared after them wistfully. Part of her wanted to strip down and join them. She doubted they'd mind, but the prospect of facing Jasper naked turned her stomach.

"I'd go with them, but I don't want them to be picturing my tits in their head every time we spar, you know? At least not yet." Faedra said, winking.

"I don't know. Might give you an edge in sparring."

Faedra giggled and drowned her glass.

"What dilapidated tower do they have you in?"

"The northeast one, near the keep. 'Fraid you drew the short straw there."

Faedra finished eating and went to interrogate her brother about what training exercises to expect so she could start practicing. Kara scarfed down the rest of her meal without tasting it and returned to the tower, fetching a bucket of water from the well to wash with on the way.

She lugged the water up the slippery steps and kicked her door in, then paused. There was a neat pile of folded clothes on her dresser. She set down the bucket and went to examine them. Black breeches, undergarments, an assortment of shirts, and a pair of leather gloves. No one had taken her measurements, but everything looked like it would fit well enough. She felt a hard lump in one of the pant pockets and pulled it out. It was a tiny tin jar of salve.

CHAPTER SIX

Kara's muscles screamed in agony when she rose from bed the next morning. The bell clanging in the courtyard made her head pound. Her whole body was stiff, and her bruises ached. She sneezed, and the convulsion sent pain wracking through her. Kara sighed. She'd have to use her spare time over the weekend to rid the tower of its dust and grime.

She dressed and exited via the ramparts' door. No one was currently patrolling this section of the fortress wall. The rising sun cast a pink wash over the distant Balmoran Mountains. Kara turned to face it and began a series of stretches to loosen her muscles. The rope pulley she'd spotted during training yesterday was mere feet from her door, affixed to the wall. The rope was threaded through two rusted metal wheels, and a large sandbag resting on a wooden platform at the foot of the wall served as a counterweight. She wondered if it could support her weight. It looked dangerous. But she ought to be embracing danger, right? She finished stretching and fetched her gloves from her room.

There was some excess length in the rope. Kara took hold of it and climbed into an embrasure in the wall. She took a deep breath, steeling herself, and jumped. The rope whistled through squeaky wheels as she plummeted towards the earth, wind rushing through her hair. The sandbag catapulted up past her. It occurred to Kara as thirty feet of stone wall hurtled past that perhaps she should have double-checked the length of the rope before hurtling to her death. She clenched her eyes shut in anticipation.

The rope snapped taut, and Kara blinked her eyes open slowly. She hovered a mere foot off the ground. She let her breath escape and scuttled down until her feet touched wood. She looked around for something sturdy enough to hitch the rope to and spotted a spiked metal ring at the edge of the platform. She hauled the rope towards it and tied it off, anchoring the sandbag at the top of the pulley. To travel back up the wall, she'd simply need to untie the rope and tug on it to release the sandbag's catch, then ride its downward momentum back up the wall. She backed away and smiled at her handiwork.

Kara arrived at the practice yard early, her heart still racing with adrenaline. Today Aethyta was having pairs of them duel one at a time while the other recruits watched and critiqued their performance. In short, Kara's worst nightmare.

"Any volunteers to begin?" Aethyta asked.

Thomas stepped forward and grabbed one of the practice staves, followed quickly by Jasper.

"Jaz!" Thomas said, grinning. "How's your lip?"

"Carrington," Jasper said as he circled him, eyes focused. Thomas twirled his staff one-handed in a fancy arc before bringing it center. Aethyta clapped, and they were off, swinging at one another in a flurry of wood.

They thwacked staves together a few times before Thomas darted in with a quick thrust to Jasper's gut. Jasper skidded back in the dirt, dodging him.

"You know," Jasper said, voice low, "you do bear a striking resemblance to that Carrington maid. The one my father thought was a thief. But I heard she skipped town because her husband couldn't handle his drink."

Thomas advanced on Jasper, his swings increasing in speed.

Jasper clucked against his teeth. "Did he hit her, too? Is that why she abandoned you? You think you're so special, swinging around that pigsticker of yours." He dodged Thomas's quick slash at his shin. "But I know you're just another fishfucker from the docks."

Thomas reared back for an overhead strike, and Jasper slipped under his guard. He slammed the butt of his staff into Thomas's face. The sound of crunching glass was audible from the sidelines. Thomas stumbled back, blood trickling down his temple.

"Fuck!" he muttered, tearing off his mangled glasses and inspecting the damage. Jasper performed a sweeping bow for the other recruits.

Aethyta clapped twice. "Alright, boys. Enough. Someone escort him to the infirmary."

Kara hopped over the fence and went to Thomas, grabbing his arm and leading him out of the arena. "Are you okay? Can you see?"

Thomas winced as he touched a hand to his busted brow. "Poorly. So stupid! I can't believe I let him get to me like that." He turned back to look at the arena. "Give me my glaive, and I'll—"

Kara tugged him forward. "He's on our side, Thomas. You can't kill him."

"Doubt I'd be the first one to murder a fellow recruit."

"Do you think he did it on purpose?"

Thomas nodded. "Payback for that scratch I gave him yesterday."

They climbed the stairs to the keep, and Kara paused. "Where's the infirmary?"

Thomas pointed her towards a hallway branching off of the great hall. "How's the tower treating you?"

She shrugged. "It's dirty, but private."

"You ought to try the baths under the keep. Simply divine."

They turned left after passing by a weapons room and came to a closed door banded with black iron. Kara rapped on the door.

"Actually, Kara, I may have taken a wrong turn—"

Thomas cut off as the door opened. Logan stepped into the doorframe, filling it with his presence.

"Commander!" Thomas said, snapping up straight.

Logan's eyes went from Kara to her hand on Thomas's arm before flicking to his bloodied face.

"What do you want?" he growled.

"We were looking for the infirmary," she said.

Logan's gaze swept over Kara. His copper-flecked eyes pierced through her. "You're unharmed?"

"She's fine, sir."

"I wasn't asking you, recruit. And if she's fine, why is she here? With *you*?"

"M-my—my glasses broke," Thomas stuttered. "Bad vision. You know how it is."

"Actually, I don't." Logan made to close the door, eyes intent on Kara. "If that's everything?"

She and Thomas both nodded, and the door slammed shut.

Kara stared at the banded iron, befuddled by the tone of the exchange. What was he so pissy about?

"Shit," Thomas said. "I can't believe we interrupted him in his office. Come on, we're in the wrong wing."

"You're afraid of him," Kara noted as they walked to the other side of the keep.

"Of Commander Vakarian? Mother Night, who wouldn't be? The man's a legend. Do you know how many kills he's rumored to have? Before the guild cracked down on contract killings, he was infamous as an assassin. There are even rumors that he's taken out members of royalty."

Kara raised her eyebrows and resisted the urge to glance behind them and check if he stalked their shadows. "I didn't know he was so notorious."

"The Stygian Scourge? The Shadow that Lives? Lerathil's Bane? All of those, him."

"A lot of names for one man."

"That's just the beginning. It's all speculation, of course. He's never been caught or tried, but people know. Can feel it just by lookin' at him. Can't you sense it?"

Kara didn't think Thomas would appreciate the sensations the commander inspired in her. "He can be rather menacing, but he's been kind to me," she said.

"Don't let him fool you. There's a beast under all that black leather." Thomas glanced at Kara. "Maybe he wants something from you."

She sighed. "You don't even know him, Thomas."

"And you do? I've been at the trials for the last three years, trying to get a bid from him. And trust me, the last man whose *head* he severed did not think he was very 'kind.'"

When they found their way to the infirmary, the door was open. A thin, grey-haired man sat at his work desk, grinding herbs. Small vials of murky liquids and glass jars brimming with dried herbs surrounded him. The room was outfitted with two cots.

He looked up from his work when he heard them approach. "Ah, the first misfits of the season. Come in, come in." He turned his creaking wooden chair to face them. "You must be Kara. And your friend?"

"Thomas," Thomas supplied.

The man peered at Thomas through narrowed eyes. "Sit, before you bleed on my floor." He reached into a drawer behind him, rummaging through for a magnifying glass and a bundle of gauze. "Name's Bartholomew, but most people call me Bart."

Bart blotted away some of the blood on Thomas's brow, then peered through his magnifying lens at the wound. "You've a fine sliver of glass wedged beneath the skin there. I'll need my tweezers. And you'll need stitches. Five, by my guess—it will hurt."

"I'm no stranger to pain," Thomas said, a lop-sided grin on his face. "Will it scar?"

"Probably. The ladies will love it. Kara, dear," Bart said without turning to face her, "lovely to meet you, but you mustn't dally, or Aethyta will have our hides. A bug's been up that woman's ass for the last forty years. Think it's a holdover from her royal army days. Anyways, I expect you'll be back here before long."

"That doesn't bode well, Bart," Kara said. Bart snorted and drew a large, hooked needle out of his desk.

KARA LEFT the infirmary and returned to the practice yard, where she was promptly walloped in her duel by a dark-skinned man named Aaron. The critiques of her fellow recruits were harsh, and she left practice feeling weary and downtrodden. She hated this feeling of ineffectiveness. The Sanguines were continuing unchecked, and she was stuck here, flailing wooden sticks around until she improved. The Stygian Brotherhood was a fine organization, but she wasn't sure where she fit within it yet.

Dinner proved to be a solemn affair. Thomas was still missing, and everyone was too tired and sore to do much more than shovel food into their mouths. Kara was conscripted into helping Olly clean the tables afterward. Once they were finished, she plodded back towards the tower, her body aching. She just wanted to crawl into bed, close her eyes, and sink into oblivion for the night.

She exited the keep and spotted Logan in one of the training arenas. He was going through a sword drill, executing a pattern of strikes and spins like the weapon was a natural extension of his body. The swift precision of his movements and the power of his swings were hypnotizing. She stopped and stared. The muscles of his broad back flexed under his shirt as he moved, the blade of his sword glinting in the twilight.

He spun towards her, the tip of the sword halting midair as it pointed towards her chest. "Like what you see?" His voice was gravelly.

Kara swallowed. She stared at her feet and forced them to move towards the tower.

"Kara, wait," he called, loping up to her.

She turned, and he was right behind her. Sweat dripped from the ends of his hair, and his chest steadily rose and fell with each breath.

"I wanted to apologize for this morning. I was out of line."

Commander Vakarian *apologizing*? A stiff giggle escaped her lips. "You seemed rather on edge."

"I'm always on edge, Kara."

Her mouth had gone dry. "You don't dine with everyone else in the great hall?"

He smiled. Such a man should not be allowed such a beautiful smile. It was far too disarming. "I usually take meals in my quarters and use the opportunity to run drills when the yard is clear. Otherwise I find my presence can be…distracting."

She shivered in the night air as the wind picked up speed, and Logan's nostrils flared, his eyes glowing amber.

"You could use a dip in the baths. I was heading there myself. You can come, if you'd like."

Kara's eyes popped open. Had he just *sniffed* her? "*With you?*"

"The pools will be empty by now. They're spacious."

She raised an eyebrow at Logan. Her body thrummed with insistence that she say yes, but Thomas's warnings about him snaked through her mind. Though he'd *also* said that the baths were divine, and her skin was covered in several layers of dried sweat thanks to Aethyta.

"Continue to use that pitiful bucket then if you prefer," Logan said as he strode off towards the keep. Kara glanced to the well in the courtyard, then ran to catch up to him.

She followed him through the keep to a stone staircase behind the kitchen that descended into darkness. Halfway down the steps, the light from the keep succumbed to shadow.

"I can't see where I'm going."

A large, warm hand brushed across her midriff before finding her hand. "Hold on to me. One of the torches must have gone out."

Kara followed him with careful steps, gripping his hand tightly. "How can you see down here?" The temperature increased, and a flickering light became visible as they descended. They rounded a corner, and Kara stilled. They were at the entrance to a large, warm cavern. Slick black stone walls surrounded three natural pools curling softly with steam. Torches lit the area and cast dancing shadows against the dark rock.

"Whoa. I've been missing out." She noticed she was still holding his hand and quickly let go.

Logan chuckled. "The springs were discovered after a siege, when part of the keep's original foundation crumbled. They incorporated them when rebuilding."

"Is the cavern stable?"

Logan nodded. "We have a mage who reinforces the rock with a spell every year, just in case."

Kara's eyes roved the cavern. The sheer rock walls provided no niches or alcoves that she could hide in to get undressed. Logan was already unbuckling his scabbard and a chest harness full of knives.

"You first."

Logan grinned, peeling off his dark leather jerkin and a black shirt that fit him like a second skin. Her breath caught in her throat. His tan body rippled with muscle as his arms stretched overhead. The torch flames cast seductive shadows over the ridges of his abdomen. He started to unbuckle his pants, and she squeezed her eyes closed, fighting the desire to look. She didn't know if it was wise to add any more flame to this particular fire. His clothes rustled as they fell to the ground.

"Are you getting in?" he asked.

He sounded closer. Was he closer? She peeked an eyelid open in time to see a pair of muscular buttocks slip beneath the water as he waded in. The groan he made as he sunk down until his shoulders were submerged sent a trill straight to her core. She wanted to strip down and press her skin against his. Kara shook her head, an icy shiver trailing down her spine despite the relative heat of the cavern. What had gotten into her? She wasn't usually so distractible. Not that she'd known any men like *this*, but getting involved with the Stygian commander was the last thing she needed to do. Logan surfaced and shook out his hair, splashing her with the droplets.

"Don't look," she said.

His laugh was hot and breathy. He closed his eyes, and Kara's gaze dropped to his soft-looking lips bordered by dark stubble. Lips made for sin. *Mother Night.* Kara stripped out of her practice clothes in record time, crossed her arms over her hard nipples, and padded towards the water. She opted for the pool next to his—joining him was too tempting.

She slipped in up to her shoulders, relishing the immediate heat of the water. It infused her sore muscles with a silky warmth. She waded in deeper until her feet barely touched bottom. Logan's eyes were still closed, but a smirk crossed his lips.

"You can open them," she said.

His lids rose slowly, eyes glowing in the dark of the cavern. "I don't bite, you know."

The splash of firelight melded with the shadows shrouding his face and torso, making him look like some shadow creature summoned from the depths to tempt and devour her. "I highly doubt that."

His gaze sharpened on her, and he dived beneath the pool's surface. Kara stifled a shriek as Logan resurfaced in a burst of water inches from her—in *her* pool.

He slid forward through the water and stroked the mottled bruise on her collarbone with light fingers. "You said you were unharmed."

He was too close. And they were both completely naked. Her heart pattered in her chest, and she took all of him in with wide eyes. His black hair fell in silky strands dark as ink, begging to be touched. Kara found herself tracking the rivulets of water streaming lazily down his chest.

"Kara," he snapped.

She blinked. "What?"

"You said you weren't hurt. This morning—with that boy."

"Oh." Kara shrugged. "It's nothing."

"Who was it? *Him?*" he said in a low, dangerous growl.

The hairs on the back of her neck rose. "*His name* is Thomas. And no. It happened during one of Aethyta's drills."

Logan drew his hand away from her skin, but his intense gaze held her frozen in place. "You must improve then."

"Erm, yeah. Working on it. Thank you, by the way. For the salve."

"A trifle."

"Even so."

"Use it on your bruises. It will speed the healing process."

Kara couldn't keep staring into his eyes—they were too hypnotic. She glanced down. He hadn't removed his leather bracers before entering the pools. "The water will ruin those, you know."

His brow furrowed, then he put a wet finger to her lips, pointing at the keep above them with his other hand. The press of his finger against her mouth was the most distracting sensation. She had an insane urge to draw his finger between her lips to taste it.

There was a clatter of footsteps on stone, and Logan's eyes darted towards the stairwell.

"Take a deep breath," he said.

"What? Why?"

"Someone's coming."

Kara inhaled, and Logan put his hands on her shoulders and urged her beneath the water. She resisted the impulse to immediately resurface. Blurry shapes moved around the edge of the pool. He was talking to someone, but she couldn't make out their words. Long seconds passed, and Kara's lungs strained. She urgently tapped his thigh, and the corded muscle tensed beneath her fingers. The conversation above continued.

Seconds later, her chest began to burn. She sank her nails into Logan's thigh, and he didn't even flinch. The man was made of stone. Speckles of black floated at the edge of her vision. What the hell was taking so long? Kara slid her hands up between Logan's thighs and gripped the weight of his balls in her palm, her threat clear.

Logan's whole body stiffened, and he barked something out. Kara felt the heavy bob of his erect cock against her arm, and her cheeks burned beneath the water. The figures finally vanished from sight.

Kara surged to the surface and gulped in deep breaths of air. Her breasts were exposed above the water line.

Logan's eyes ate her up hungrily. "You should go," he growled.

"Mother Night, Logan. What the fuck?" She was officially unnerved.

"I wasn't sure who it was. If one of your fellow recruits found us down here, they might get the wrong idea."

He had a point, but the heady attraction between them and nearly running out of breath had unsettled her. What would have happened if they hadn't been interrupted? Kara banished the image of their bodies twined around one another, water dripping down the muscled planes of his back as he devoured her mouth. She climbed out of the pool as Logan looked on. Anger made her brave, scorching away any shred of self-consciousness. She yanked on her clothes even though she was still dripping with water. Kara could feel the lingering heat of his gaze on her all the way back to the tower.

CHAPTER SEVEN

The beginning of the weekend marked their first free day since training began. Kara was in the stable grooming Drum after an indulgent morning sleeping in. She slipped the mare a sugar cube she'd taken from the mess. Rohan's legs dangled from the hayloft as he played an otherworldly tune on his pan flute.

He caught her looking at him and shrugged. "The horses like it."

Drum nickered in assent, and Kara smiled. Rohan was spry and handsome for his age, and he worked magic with the horses—even had the likes of Char eating out of his palm.

"Visitors!" he announced, hopping down from the loft as Thomas and Faedra entered the stable. They waved to Rohan as they approached Kara.

"We're all heading down to Blackhearth tonight for drinks," Faedra said, hanging over the door to Drum's stall. "Care to join us?"

"I'm getting my glasses replaced while we're there," Thomas said, a knobby patch of raised skin and black stitches marring his youthful face. "Bart told me there's a lenscrafter in town. Absurdly lucky in a village that size, really. You ought to come."

Kara continued to brush Drum and considered the offer. She'd planned on going for a ride, but the journey to Blackhearth would serve as adequate exercise for the mare. Plus it would be a welcome distraction from her troubles. "Alright. I'll go."

Thomas whooped, and the pair went to saddle their horses.

THEY REACHED BLACKHEARTH BEFORE SUNSET. The tiny hamlet was nestled in a valley about an hour's ride east of Raven's Rest. The town shouldn't exist at all, it was so stunningly remote, but Kara supposed the mercenary traffic kept it afloat. Small houses and storefronts built out of wattle and daub with thatched roofs lined the main street. Dirty children gathered by the roadside, gasping and pointing as the Stygian procession made their way into town. A blond girl with threadbare skirts and a painted face, no older than sixteen, came out of one of the houses. She lingered in front of it, making eye contact with the men as they passed. Jon flicked a golden coin to her. She snatched it out of the air and folded it tight in her fist. Kara was surprised Jon had decided to come with them, since the group was mostly made up of new recruits.

"That was generous of you."

Jon shrugged. "Her family's fallen on hard times recently. I've known men who spent every copper they had and ten they didn't. And men who clutched and hoarded till they died unexpectedly, having spent nary a cent. Better to spread it around while I'm still breathing."

They hitched their horses in front of the Blackhearth

Inn and paid the stable boy to stall them for the evening before going inside. An enormous fireplace carved out of black stone spanned the entire back wall of the inn. George made a beeline for the bar.

"Forty years old, and I'm not allowed a drink in that shitstack of a fortress for another three months," he grumbled to the bartender. "It just ain't right." The barkeep just smiled and filled him a tankard full of ale.

Kara found a seat at a table with Jon. "I'm surprised by the kind reception you get here," she said. "Whenever the Sanguine Riders came to Mudbottom, people would hide in fear. Do they pay for this peace?"

Jon snorted. "No. Victus is a brute, and the men he employs are even worse. We don't tithe the people of Blackhearth for our protection. They provide us with valuable services, and we support their economy. It's a beneficial arrangement."

"Victus. That's the Sanguine leader?" Kara filed the information away for later.

"Yup. Speaking of, I need to give my little speech." Jon jumped up in his chair and whistled, and all the heads in the room swiveled towards him. "Listen up. You lot start any fights with the townsfolk, you hurt any of the girls— you're out. No pay, no exceptions. The Commander will not tolerate it. You are not to undermine the respect we've established here. Am I clear?"

They all mumbled in assent.

"Good. Now, enjoy yourselves while you can! Aethyta will make you pay for it later."

That garnered a round of laughs and groans, and Jon hopped back down.

"Why *did* you hire Aethyta?" Kara asked, leaning back in her chair. "She's a nightmare."

Jon grinned. "For precisely that reason. Hell, she was

training back when I signed on. The woman survived the Curse Wars under King Urian's banner, then left when Urian's grandson Calim ascended the throne. Reckon she wouldn't know what to do with herself if dirt and steel weren't involved."

"Why'd she leave the army?" Kara wondered if she'd known Da.

Jon shrugged. "Better pay? After the war ended, the clans were the strongest fighting forces in Teleria. Urian died, and Calim couldn't afford to pay the troops competitive rates with the treasury depleted from the war. The royal army never really recovered."

"Sounds rough."

"Aye. I think she prefers this, though. She gets to share her knowledge with others and still kick men's asses every day. Yours too, of course," Jon said, winking.

Thomas plopped down at their table. "Why aren't you two drinking yet? Two more!" he yelled to Faedra at the bar.

Three drinks later, a fiddler had taken up a lively tune, and Jon was dancing a reel with one of the barmaids. Thomas poured them two more shots of Balmoran whiskey. Kara's belly burned with the warmth of it, and her head felt a little fuzzy. She didn't usually drink this much.

"Jasper was right, you know," Thomas said, downing his glass. "About my parents. My da was a jackass when he was sober, but he turned into a right devil when he drank. My vision started to fail after he threw me against the corner of our kitchen table as a kid. He blamed me for the cost of the lenses I needed to see, of course."

"Did you and Jasper know each other, back in Liore?" Kara asked.

Thomas snorted. "The lordling and the fisherman's

whelp? Hardly. Mum worked for his family, but she left my da as soon as I was old enough to fend for myself. Made for a juicy bit of gossip. Jasper probably heard it from one of his servants."

"He's a righteous prick," Kara said. She laid her hand over Thomas's and squeezed. "I'm sorry about your mum, though. And your da. I know what it's like to lose family."

Thomas nodded and stared into the bottom of his empty glass. "I miss her," he mumbled. "Haven't seen her in five years. It's why I trained so hard. To get out of that house, that town. Maybe find her again."

The table fell into silence, and Kara finished off her drink and poured them another round.

Faedra plunked down in her chair when she returned from her pee break. "Y'all are a sorry sight," she said, stretching her arms out behind them. "I know just where to take you later to cheer you up."

"Do tell," Kara said.

"The Velvet Chamber. Colette will help you rediscover happiness between a pair of legs."

Thomas's throat constricted before he finally managed to swallow. "They have a brothel in this town?" he coughed. "Mother have mercy."

"Of course they do. Fortress full of horny mercenaries right down the road? They'd be fools not to. You're welcome too, Kara. Feron said they've got lads, if you've a preference." Faedra waggled her eyebrows.

A pair of meaty, sea-chapped hands squeezed Thomas and Faedra's shoulders, and Kara looked up into George's weathered face. "Time enough for that later, you degenerates. We're starting a game of poker in the back. You in?"

"Anything but this drudgery," Faedra said, dragging Thomas to his feet.

"Kara?" George asked.

She smiled and shook her head. "I'm dreadful," she feigned. Da had taught her a mean hand of cards using the skills he'd picked up during his army days, but she couldn't risk what little coin she had right now on a game.

They left, and Kara migrated to one of the large leather sitting chairs in front of the fireplace. The crackling hearth had been drawing her eye all night, and the warmth emanating from it felt good in her bones. The unnatural bright blue flame blazed high over several gnarled white logs stacked on the grate.

Kara glanced around. The inn was crowded now, and the air buzzed with the muffled undertones of conversations and laughter. She could feel the drinks she'd downed with Thomas creeping up on her as she gazed into the oddly colored flames.

"Entrancing," Jon's voice whispered in her ear. His breath tickled her neck, and she swiveled towards him as he sat down on the oversized arm of her chair. "They're enchanted logs, you know. Fire keeps blazing all year long, even during the summer months."

A piece of wood flaked off one of the logs as he spoke, glowing molten in the ash beneath the grate before fading into darkness.

"And when the logs burn up?" Kara asked.

"*If* they do. Never stuck around long enough to find out myself. Rumor is the current barkeep's father cut down an undying oak in the holy forest of Whitefall and hauled it back here before dropping dead of the plague. To burn the goddess wood…" Jon whistled.

"It's sacrilegious?"

"Incredibly. Whole family line's probably cursed if it's true. Then again, it could just be some spell on the wood."

Kara looked over at the barkeep as he rapidly filled mugs for clamoring patrons. He had dark circles under his eyes and a sheen of sweat on his brow, but he didn't seem any more cursed than the rest of them.

The fiddler started up another fast song and people began to rise from their seats and pair off for dancing. Jon was staring at her. His dark eyes seemed larger than normal. Enticing. The air brimmed with vibrant colors and the warmth of too many people under one roof. A reckless, hazy energy suffused Kara.

"Dance with me?" She'd never been asked to dance at Mudbottom's harvest festivals. There was always too much fear from the villagers, too much reservation on her part. Year after year she'd sat in the audience and watched as kids her age paired off one by one, until she was left alone among the elders. Even Wesley abandoned his frequent post by her side to dance during the harvest festivals. As she'd aged, she stopped going altogether. It was too depressing.

Jon's eyebrows rose, but he turned in the chair and offered her his hand. "Of course."

Kara took his hand, and they stood together. "I don't know any of the steps," she confessed as he led her to the dance floor.

"Just follow my lead."

Jon grasped her waist with one hand and spun them into the formation of people already dancing. His steps were quick and smooth, and she let herself be tugged along instead of thinking about her feet. Lights spun around her, and women's skirts twirled in wide blooms of colored fabric in the periphery of her vision.

Jon's shoulders were warm and comforting beneath her hands—something solid and reassuring in the storm of motion. His muscles bunched beneath his shirt as he lifted her in time with the music.

"Do you fight like you dance?" she asked, breathless from the relentless spinning.

His lips split in a smile. "You mean do I fight to win? I'm a Stygian, aren't I?"

Kara snorted. She wasn't sure if he was flirting with her or if he was like this with everyone. "I'm getting dizzy."

Jon's response was drowned out by a roar of commotion from the poker room and the sawing of fiddle strings.

"What?" she yelled.

Another couple swung dangerously close to them, and Kara stumbled over Jon's feet. He winced and pulled her tighter against him. "I said that we may have plied you with too many drinks." His freshly-shaved cheek felt like velvet against her ear.

"Please. I feel wonderful. So light." It was the first time she'd felt relatively trouble free since the raid on Mudbottom.

Jon's eyes crinkled at the corners. "The wondrous effects of alcohol."

They spun past a window, and Kara caught a glimpse of a tall figure dressed in black looming in the darkness outside. There was a flash of glowing red, then nothing.

Jon had seen it too. His face fell. "I have to go," he said, halting mid-step and pulling away from her. "I'll be back. Stay here."

Jon pushed his way through the bustling crowd and disappeared. Kara sighed and made her way to the bar. Her skin was flushed, and her shirt was stuck to the center of her back with sweat.

"Water," she told the barkeep.

A bespectacled older man in suspenders climbed onto the stool next to hers, frowning at her attire. "You with those mercenaries?"

Kara nodded warily.

"Stygian boy came by my shop earlier, put a rush order on for some glasses. Come time to pay, he's nowhere to be found. You know anything about that?"

"Oh, uhm—" Kara craned her neck around, trying to spot Thomas in the packed inn, but the recruits had vanished.

"Wouldn't be trying to cheat me, would he? Ought to charge the little bastard double," the man grumbled.

"Easy, Abner," the barkeep said as he passed Kara her water. "They'll all be at Colette's by now, missy."

Abner spat on the floor. "Got time and coin for whorin' but none for me, eh?"

"Hey, watch it!" the barkeep said. "I ought to make you lick that up."

Kara rubbed her forehead. "Look—Abner, was it? How much does he owe you for the glasses?"

"50 gold pieces." He smirked, revealing browned teeth under his pale lips.

Kara swore. It was too much for her to pay in Thomas's stead. They hadn't even received their first month's wages yet.

"I'll go find him for you, alright? Meet us by the hearth in an hour." She stood up from her stool with a groan. "Point me towards the brothel?" she asked the barkeep.

BLACKHEARTH'S BROTHEL was located in a large, two-story building on the edge of town. A torch-lit porch extended out from the front of the house, and the ornate roofing hung low overhead as Kara climbed the entrance steps. She slid through a pair of burgundy velvet curtains into the central lounge. It was dimly lit, the walls covered in tapestries the shade of bruised plums. Women and men in various stages of undress and inebriation hung like silk-clad ornaments about the room. Several of the women sipped from wine goblets and tugged on thin cigarettes, while others dangled off furniture and the laps of men.

A woman in a green brocade gown with auburn curls piled high upon her head approached Kara through the haze of smoke in the air. "Welcome to the Velvet Chamber. I'm Madam Colette, the proprietress. May I interest you in anything? Vhaidra here would be delighted to serve you." She gestured to a bronze-skinned woman with kohl-rimmed eyes who lounged on a nearby chaise. Vhaidra looked up at the mention of her name, then swept her hair off her chest and arched her back to reveal a thin golden chain that looped around her neck and hung down between twin nipple piercings.

Kara gulped. "Not exactly. I'm looking for someone—one of the Stygian men."

"Ah, I see." Her eyes twinkled mischievously. "I'm afraid they're all occupied upstairs at the moment."

"I'll wait, if that's alright."

Madam Colette's rings clinked against one another as she steepled her fingers in thought. "Hmm. I suppose. Try not to start any fights in my drawing room, though. The blood takes forever to get out."

Kara took a seat on an unoccupied sofa across the room from Vhaidra. The sound of pounding headboards and breathy moans drifted down the stairs, and Kara drew in tight on herself and tried not to squirm. She wasn't opposed to brothels, but it was her first visit to one, and she felt out of place. A serving girl clad in a sheer shift asked her if she wanted any wine.

Kara shook her head. Her senses were compromised enough already.

A well-dressed man with tousled hair and a loose cravat

stumbled in through the entranceway, a silver flask clutched in his hand. He reeked of liquor. His eyes fell on Kara, and he leered.

"A little covered up, aren't ya?"

Kara blanched, her stomach shifting uncomfortably. He thought she worked here? He must be knackered—she was still wearing her practice clothes. "I think you're confused."

"Where's the goods?" the man slurred, lurching forward and palming Kara's chest with his sweaty hands. "Give me a peek."

Kara froze at first, appalled. Then she shoved his hands away and stood up from the sofa. The urge to retaliate swelled within her, but Jon had asked them not to get into it with the townsfolk.

Vhaidra rose from her chaise behind the man, long curves unfolding beneath her. A jewel dangled from the pert indentation at her navel. She approached the man and tapped him with one bored fingernail. "That one is not selling anything, Willoughby. She is a customer." Her voice was husky, her accent lilting and foreign.

Willoughby swatted Vhaidra away with his flask, scowling. "Please. All you bitches have a price. What's hers? Maybe I'll have the two of you at once."

"A delicacy that would be wasted on you. You smell like the type who pisses the bed as soon as you're brought up," Vhaidra said.

His face went livid. "You little desert slut. I'll have you whipped for your insolence." He swung at Vhaidra with the metal flask in his fist, but his swing was slow, and Vhaidra managed to duck out of the way.

Anger surged through Kara, and her mark itched fiercely. *Fuck the rules.* She could handle insults, but she wasn't going to stand by while this guy beat on women.

Willoughby rose the flask again, and Kara dove for him. She tackled him around the waist, and they both fell to the floor. Vhaidra shrieked and kicked at him with her bare feet. Kara snatched the knife from her belt and held the tip of it to the soft hollow at his throat.

"Do you know who I am?" he gurgled against the sharp point.

"You're rude," Kara said. "I ought to bleed you like a pig."

Willoughby's eyes swam in his ruddy face. Heavy footsteps pounded down the stairs. Madam Colette rushed over, her jeweled hands fluttering. The other Chamber girls looked on with bloodlust in their gaze. Kara got the impression this guy was a regular nuisance. Maybe she ought to do them all a favor. It would be so easy. Just a slip of her knife, the slightest application of pressure. He squirmed between the grip of her thighs. A bead of scarlet peeked out from beneath the blade. Kara licked her lips. Her curse might be triggered already anyways. It was inevitable, one way or another.

"Enough!" a familiar voice roared behind her. *Logan.* Strong hands hooked under her arms, pulling her away from her prey. Willoughby scrambled back, fear lighting his eyes as he stared at her arm. He crossed his hands in front of him in the ward sign against evil. Kara glanced down. Her mark was glowing a dim orange color and tingling faintly.

Logan cursed and jerked her head up to face him. "Look at me. What the hell are you doing here?"

"*Me?* What are you—" Kara paused. Logan was naked from the waist up, and he wasn't wearing any boots. His face was unshaven, his hair loose and falling around his shoulders. A pale, freckled girl with a face as flushed as her fiery curls stood by the stairwell, wrapped in only a sheet.

Understanding dawned. Kara had no claim to him—no reason to be jealous, but her stomach plummeted all the same.

More footsteps clattered outside, and Madam Colette made a high-pitched wailing noise as Jon careened in off the porch. He untangled himself from the curtains, and his mouth rounded in a small 'O' of surprise as he took in the scene. Then he regained his composure and smiled. "Kara McKenna. Didn't you hear my speech?"

"You were supposed to be watching her!" Logan snapped.

"I was!"

Kara pulled away from Logan and stood up. That's why Jon had been paying so much attention to her tonight? Danced with her, even. Bitterness burned through her blood. "Why would you have him watch me?"

"So you didn't do something stupid, like assault the local judge."

Kara looked at the sniveling heap of drunken man in the corner. He was responsible for upholding the law? She spat at his feet.

"My rug!" Colette moaned.

Willoughby's eyes bulged in his face. "She's one of yours? This Namirahn whore?" He gave a bark of harsh laughter. "You have gone too far this time, Commander. You drag the Stygian name through shit when you consort with their kind."

"*Silence*, Willoughby," Logan roared.

Vhaidra stood in the corner picking at her nails. "Your girl defended me, Logan. This drunk's just angry she was not for sale. Wanted a grope."

Logan's eyes shuttered, and he inhaled deeply. "Very well. Kara, I'll deal with this. Please leave."

"You can't just let her go!" Willoughby yelled, spittle flecking his lips. "She attacked me!"

"She is *my* recruit, and I will punish her according to *our* rules."

"You're lawless heathens! When the people find out you're harboring a cursed whore, they will riot!"

Logan's eyes narrowed on him. "If you try and incite a witch-hunt, I will bury you and your good name. Your wife doesn't know about your regular visits to the Chambers, does she?"

Willoughby paled but remained silent.

"Punish *Kara*?" Jon asked, stroking a hand through his hair. "Logan, come on—"

"I will deal with you later, *Second*. Out—now! Both of you."

KARA MARCHED down the brothel steps, fuming. She wished she'd never come tonight, wished she'd stayed back at Raven's Rest with Rohan and Drum and ignored Faedra and Thomas's stupid invitation. There was no telling what sick task the Commander would dream up as punishment for her assaulting the judge. What if he let Aethyta determine it? Kara shuddered.

Jon jogged to catch up to her and swung an arm around her shoulders. "You know, next time you want to hit up the Chambers, you ought to sample the wares instead of starting a brawl. I think you gave Colette palpitations."

"I'm not in the mood, Jon."

"I'd recommend Arden. Vhaidra's too feisty—you two would clash."

Kara jabbed him in the gut, and he let out an *oomph*. "Which one is Arden?"

"Red hair, freckles. A true flame, if you know what I mean."

Kara blew air through her nose. "The Commander's leftovers? I'll pass. Is that all you lot do for entertainment?"

"What else should we do for distraction? Start scrapping with the townsfolk?"

"He deserved it."

Jon shook his head. "I shouldn't have left you alone."

"Are you my keeper now?"

"No. Well, maybe a little. Namirah's Chosen are known for their volatility. Logan told me to keep an eye out."

"So that's what you were doing when you danced with me? Keeping an eye out?"

"That's not—Kara—"

They reached the inn, and Kara veered off towards the stable.

"Hey," he said, tugging on her hand. "Where are you going?"

She pulled away from him. "I'm leaving."

"Come on, Kara. You can't ride back alone. They'll be done at the Chambers soon."

"I'm not sitting around waiting for them. The lenscrafter's expecting Thomas at the inn, by the way. He was very displeased earlier. Better handle that if you want Thomas to be able to see for shit this week. I'm through trying to help."

Jon sighed and ran a hand through his hair. "Fucking recruits. When did I become the bloody nanny?"

"I'll be alright, Jon. I just need some space."

"Fine. Logan's going to have my head regardless. Be careful, okay? Stick to the main path. The Blackshear's dangerous at night."

Kara nodded and entered the stable. She scowled when

she spotted Char in the stall next to Drum's. The stallion's head hung over the wall between them, and he made soft moon eyes at the mare.

"Horny brutes," Kara muttered, stroking Char's silken muzzle. His nose twitched as he sniffed her person for food.

She had half a mind to steal Logan's mount and leave him stranded, but managing two horses in the dark would only slow her down. And while the idea entertained her now, further incurring the Commander's wrath wouldn't be wise.

Kara saddled up Drum and headed out on the road back to Raven's Rest. The path had been much easier to follow by daylight. Now the trees loomed in close, scratching jagged shadows across the night sky, and shy shafts of moonlight broke through the canopy overhead. The shadows pressed in close, and Kara felt like the tree limbs were reaching out to grab her.

An owl hooted and burst from the treetops, sending Kara's heart racing. Her nerves were frayed around the edges. Even Drum, usually unflappable, seemed more skittish. Maybe she should have waited for Jon and the others. But she didn't want to *need* them, especially when Jon was only around because the Commander had ordered him to keep an eye on her.

The wind picked up, and something dark and ameboous skittered across the path in front of them. Drum reared, and Kara clutched the mare's mane until she fell back to the earth. What the hell had that been? A susurrus whisper swept through the trees, and a chill of foreboding crept up Kara's spine.

Squelch. Pop. Squelch. A wet sucking sound emanated from the forest floor, and Kara looked down with dawning horror. Black amorphous blobs the size of plums clustered around Drum's hooves—writhing spots of night encased in a gelatinous skin. The forest path teemed with the creatures, all scooting towards her with surprising speed. Drum pinned her ears flat and neighed in pain. They were oozing their way up the mare's forelegs, leaving smudges of fresh blood behind them.

"Shit!" Kara swung down out of the saddle, squishing one of the creatures beneath her boot when she landed. It popped, leaving behind a pool of black blood that sizzled in the air and smelled like decay.

Drum's eyes rolled wildly, the whites flashing as she jerked her knees high in an effort to dislodge the creatures. Kara stroked the mare's neck, trying to soothe her. "Shhh. Easy, girl. It's okay, I've got you. I'm here." If she bolted, Kara would have a hard time finding her in the forest at night.

The dark blobs began to cluster around Kara's feet, and she stomped on them until their stink filled the air. More of them wriggled in to replace the dead ones. There was no end to the creatures. Where were they all coming from? Kara looked up as hoofbeats sounded in the distance. "Jon?" she cried out. Maybe he had followed her. Maybe it was something worse, lured by the scent of blood.

A stallion black as night trotted up through the moonlight, steering clear of the wave of amoebic creatures.

"Guess again," Logan said.

The Commander. *Great.*

Logan took in the dark blobs verging closer on her and Drum. "God's teeth, I've never seen so many at once before. You must have trampled through one of their nests."

"What the hell are they?"

"They're called obara. Humans weren't the only ones

affected by Namirah's curse. They're unnatural shadow creatures created by dark magic runoff." Logan dismounted and dug through his saddlebags, pulling out a striking flint. "We need fire. It will scare them off."

Kara glanced from him to Drum. The obara were up to Drum's knees now, and the mare's flanks heaved in pained quivers.

"Fuck it," she said, "There's no time for that!" Kara waded into the cluster of obara and began pulling them off of Drum's legs and flinging them to the ground. There were so many of them. The reek they released when they splattered apart on the ground burned Kara's nostrils.

Logan cursed and strode after her, snatching her around the waist and pulling her away from the horse.

"You little fool." His voice trembled with fury. "Right now they're only leeching her blood. If one of them bursts on either of you, their toxin will eat the flesh off your bones in a matter of seconds. Now *don't fucking move.*"

Logan shoved her away and ripped off his shirt, wrapped it around a stick in a makeshift torch, and ignited it. The obara hissed as the fire blazed to life, and swarms of them began to peel off Drum's legs and wriggle away as Logan edged them with the flames. Her legs were spotted with bloody patches, but the wounds were clotting quickly.

Kara felt a sharp pain on the back of her neck as something burrowed its teeth into her. She made to swat at it, then froze abruptly. "Logan," she whispered, voice shaky. "Help me."

Logan looked back, eyes flaring when he spotted her neck. He slowly circled her with the torch. Kara whimpered.

"Look at me." His voice was calm, commanding. "You're okay. I'm going to burn it. It's going to hurt, but you can't move. Do you understand?"

Kara grit her teeth. "Yes."

He raised the torch to the back of her neck. The flames licked at her skin, the heat blistering. Kara clenched her fists against the pain. She could smell singed hair, but at least she'd worn it up in a ponytail. There was a soft *plop* as the creature dislodged itself from her skin and fell to the earth, where Logan quickly crushed it under his heel.

Kara shivered violently and released a ragged breath. "Holy shit. I think I'm going to puke." Logan checked the rest of her person for any stray obara, then fanned the torch out over the trail to chase off the stragglers.

Drum walked over and nosed Kara, and she buried her face in the mare's neck. "I didn't know there were creatures like that in these woods."

"Which is why you shouldn't be out here alone at night to begin with. I'm going to kill Jon."

"It's not his fault."

Logan raised an eyebrow. "That's twice in one evening I've had to bail you out, recruit. It's unprecedented."

"I didn't need saving at the Chambers."

"Only from yourself."

That quieted Kara, and she sighed. "Thank you. For Drum and me."

"If you really want to thank me, stop being so reckless. At this rate it'll be a miracle if you earn out your bid price before you end up dead."

Logan mounted Char and held a hand out to her. "Come on. We'll give your mare a break."

Kara eyed his bare chest skeptically. "I can walk."

"And get back by daybreak? Stop wasting my time."

Kara let him pull her into the saddle in front of him. His legs, flush against hers, were like iron.

They rode back in silence, his bare chest brushing against her as he moved his body in subtle cues for Char.

He was so warm and solid behind her—she had to fight the urge to relax against his chest and close her eyes.

"You can sleep if you want," he whispered, so quiet she questioned if he'd really said it. She shot up, stiffening her back, and Logan chuckled.

When they got back to Raven's Rest, Kara immediately slid out of the saddle and began to lead Drum to the stable. She wanted Rohan to check on the mare before she went to sleep.

"Kara," Logan called after her.

Kara paused but didn't look back.

"Don't endanger yourself so carelessly for the sake of pride ever again. I won't always be there to rescue you."

CHAPTER EIGHT

A week later they began training with swords. Kara's arms were toned from her farrier work, but she didn't have the stamina for swordplay. Even the lighter training swords felt heavy after swinging them about for hours. The training was grueling and relentless, and her bones still ached from the impact of steel on steel long after practice was over. The other recruits were progressing nicely, but many of them had prior experience with sword-work. Bear noticed her struggling and showed her where the free weights were kept in the keep so she could work on building her strength, but it was slow going.

When she had time, she visited Drum in the stable, bringing her half-eaten apples from the mess. Some days she longed to mount up, ride out the fortress gate, and never look back. Then she would remember Da and Wesley and her obligation to them. It was difficult to hold onto her anger when her body and mind were so distracted by exhaustion, but a spark of rage still burned low in her gut when she thought back on the events at Mudbottom.

Occasionally Aethyta abandoned the training yard for

the forest so the recruits could practice tracking and hunting. Kara felt more confident in her skills on these outings. Wesley had been teaching her to hunt and read trails since she was ten so she could go hunting with him and help stock the cellar for the long winters in Mudbottom. She could shoot down a deer or rabbit at thirty paces, but Aethyta wasn't impressed.

One morning when Kara came down, Logan was waiting in the training yard, casually leaning against the fence railing. Aethyta and the other recruits were nowhere to be seen. Logan looked hale and tan in the morning light —more composed than he'd seemed in Blackhearth last week.

"What's going on? Where is everybody?"

Logan stepped away from the fence. "About time you showed up. The other recruits are in the woods with Aethyta, tracking wild boar."

"Why did they leave without me?" Kara had been looking forward to the boar hunt. It was something other than flighty herbivores to sink her arrows into.

"Aethyta tells me you're falling behind the other recruits. And since I decided to contract you, it's my responsibility to rectify that. You'll be training with me through the weekend."

"You have time for that?"

"Of course not. Don't flatter yourself. But I like to think I don't make bad investments, which is what you're proving to be. And even though your contract didn't have a termination clause, I want you to perform well at the final evaluations."

"Why wasn't that in my contract, by the way?"

Logan frowned and glanced away from her. "Several parties are becoming more interested in marked individuals. The Sanguines and Serena, for example. I suppose I wanted to protect you from yourself. In Liore you were desperate—ready to charge headlong into a Sanguine camp with your farrier's hammer and blazing eyes. And they wouldn't do you the mercy of killing you, Kara."

Kara let that flop around in her head for a minute. It was an oddly compassionate move from the Stygian commander, if manipulative. He was right. She still wouldn't put it past herself to do something reckless if she spotted one of the Sanguines from the raid.

"So what have your weak areas been in training?"

Kara laughed. "Everything? I've been struggling a lot with swords. I'm not as strong as the others."

"You'll frequently be overpowered in contests of brute strength. You need to cultivate speed, awareness, reflexes. Now grab a sword."

Kara tugged at the collar of her shirt. It was suddenly very hot outside. "You want me to spar with you?"

"How else am I going to teach you?"

"Alright," Kara sighed. Her stomach twisted in on itself.

They each grabbed a practice sword and squared off, circling one another. Logan crouched low to the ground, his knees supple as he shifted his weight from foot to foot.

"Come on."

Kara swung. He dodged the strike and dashed behind her, drawing his sword even with her hamstring.

"You just lost mobility five seconds into the fight. You're a dead woman walking."

She struck again. He dodged effortlessly, this time whacking her on the ass with the flat of his sword. Kara jumped and rubbed her stinging flesh.

"You're signaling your attacks and leaving your defenses open in the process. Never reveal anything to your opponent until it's too late for them to react. Keep them guessing."

Kara schooled her features and focused her mind. She needed to find the rhythm of the fight rather than forcing it. Logan parried her next swing.

"Better, but you're still too slow. Speed must be on your side if you're to have a chance of winning. Don't think about the weight of the sword in your hand. It's just an extension of your arm. You are weightless."

Kara darted forward through the dirt, and they locked swords at the hilt. Logan forced her blade down with the weight of his own and tore the hilt out of her hand.

He stepped forward over the fallen blade. "Maybe the longsword isn't your weapon. A staple, certainly, but we're mercenaries, not knights. Any sharp edge will do. And it's good to practice with a variety of weapons." He drew two daggers from his belt and handed them to her hilt first. "Try these."

Kara frowned. "A close quarters weapon? Have you forgotten the crescent blades?'"

"Unfortunately not. But you'll have to overcome that fear. Close range is risky but rewarding. Stay light on your feet. Move like a snake through tall grass, striking and departing before they even know what hit them. Now attack me."

"But these blades aren't dulled." The smooth handles felt good in her palm. The daggers were well-balanced, and they curved into wicked points that promised violence.

Logan raised an eyebrow. "I'm aware, Kara. You're not going to hurt me."

"If only." He smiled at that, then she came at him, slashing the air in front of her wildly. He grabbed her wrists and twisted the blades away.

"Control, Kara. Patience. Don't strike without explicit

purpose. Envision the cut you want to make before you make it, then follow through." He released her wrists. "Again."

Kara circled him warily. She imagined she was stalking prey in the forest, waiting for the right moment to strike. She crouched low to the ground. Logan's eyes burned into her. His hands were in a defensive posture, ready for her attack.

This time she vaulted forward, and he was forced to grapple with her to keep the blades from his face.

"Much better," he said, releasing her. "Again."

They fell into an easy rhythm of skirmish after skirmish, where Kara attacked and Logan disabled her with relative ease. Sweat soon soaked them both. After landing on her ass for the fifth time, he helped her up and asked, "What did the Sanguine Riders who raided your village look like?"

It was the first time he'd mentioned it since they left Liore. Kara shrugged. "Aside from the one I stabbed in the eye, I didn't get a close look. Their leader wore an antlered helm cast in silver. Do you know of him?"

Logan nodded, pensive. "Cervus. We were aware of him extorting the mountain villages, but it's out of our territory. I'd hoped someone would interfere by now."

"We petitioned the guild and King Calim, but nobody ever came. Just some half-assed response about their forces being needed elsewhere."

"Without proof of the Sanguines murdering civilians, the guild won't do much. Even with it, Victus might have to pay a fine and hand over some of his men, but it wouldn't matter in the long run. The Sanguines have deep pockets and men to spare. As far as the king goes, the crown is weaker since the Curse Wars. The royal army used to be able to challenge the Sanguines. Now, I'm not so sure."

"I'd appreciate any information you have about Cervus."

Logan tilted his head to the side and considered her. "And if you kill him? What then?"

"Then he can't hurt anyone else."

"You'll never run out of bad men to kill, Kara."

"Why haven't you done anything about it? You could challenge them."

"Victus has a lot of resources at his disposal. Support in unexpected places. When I start a war with him, I want to know it's going to end my way. I can have my contacts look into Cervus, but you can't take any action while you wear the black. An act of aggression from you is an act of aggression from my clan."

"I understand." But Kara she wasn't sure she'd be able to keep that promise. She wasn't equipped to take Cervus on now, but if the opportunity ever presented itself, she wouldn't be asking Logan's permission.

THE OTHER RECRUITS filtered back in from the woods at dusk, hauling their prize. A group of them gathered around the training yard to watch her and Logan spar. It made Kara self-conscious. She preferred to get her ass kicked in private.

Logan lunged at her to capture her in a waist hug, and she vaulted over his back.

"Go Kara!" Thomas cheered from the sidelines.

Kara blushed. Her blood was high, her shirt damp with sweat.

Logan flicked his eyes to their onlookers with disdain. It was the first sign of distraction he'd shown all day. Kara decided to bait him. She was never going to get the advantage on him if he remained focused.

"Jealous, Commander?" She raked her gaze over him and spun one of the daggers between her fingers. "Want me all to yourself?"

"Stop it, Kara."

"I'm surprised. Don't the girls at the Chambers keep you happy?"

He began striding towards her. "I'm warning you."

"Still have issues with control, I see," Kara said, parroting Serena's words.

Logan's eyes flashed amber. Kara threw a dagger at his torso, knowing he would snatch it out of the air or dodge it. It missed. He charged.

Before she could take two steps, he'd grabbed her by the shoulders and lifted her in the air. She writhed, trying to escape his grasp, but her arms stayed sandwiched in at her sides. His pupils shifted colors, and he leaned in and ran his nose along her throat. "I can smell your fear, Kara. You're playing with fire."

A delicious shiver ran down her spine as his stubbled cheek rasped against her skin. It was like she'd snapped her fingers, and the docile kitten who'd been toying with her all day had finally unleashed his claws. Kara leaned in towards him and whispered in his ear, "Then can you smell my lust?"

Logan shuddered and dropped her, and she stumbled forward when she landed. The crowd had gone silent. Jon cleared his throat and clapped his hands. "Alright everyone, enough gawping. Show's over—get out of here. Olly will poison us all if we're late to dinner."

That garnered a few laughs, and the tension broke as the crowd began to disperse.

"Be here in the morning," Logan said to Kara and left the arena.

Jon jogged forward as she stood up and dusted herself off. He frowned at the streaky layers of dirt covering her clothing.

"You two been at it all day?"

"Yeah. Don't know what got into him," she lied.

"Moody bastard. I heard about your little adventure with the obara. I feel terrible for letting you go alone—the Commander was *not* pleased with me."

"You couldn't have known," Kara said. "And I was being stubborn."

"Well, I'm glad you're still here, and with all of your flesh still at that. Come on, let's get you some food. You have a long weekend ahead of you." He laughed. "Hell, you might even prefer Aethyta by the end of it."

( )

THE NEXT MORNING DAWNED EARLY, and Kara woke up sore and grumpy. She plaited her hair into a tight braid to keep it out of her face and donned a fresh shirt, then regarded herself in the shattered mirror. Her breeches were a tight, dark leather that laced up the front. She'd gained muscle since coming to Raven's Rest, and her silhouette curved attractively in her clothes. The planes of her cheeks were more prominent, and hours in the sun had graced her with a golden tan.

She left the tower room and rode down the wall on the rope pulley, enjoying the rush of the wind in her hair. Instead of catching air as the rope went taut, she fell into hard, muscled arms. Her captor grunted as her weight slammed into him. Kara looked down into Logan's fiery eyes as they darted across her face.

She released the rope and wrapped her arms around his neck. Her skin lit up in awareness of his closeness. Her breasts were sandwiched against the hard breadth of his chest, and he was breathing heavily, like he'd run to catch her. He smelled like the sun. His gaze was starting to turn hypnotic, and she had to shake herself out of it. "What the hell, Logan? I was fine. Put me down."

The arms wrapped tight around her squeezed harder. "Do you have a death wish? Those ropes are older than sin. What if they frayed? That wall's thirty feet high. Your legs would snap like twigs."

Kara shrugged her shoulders. He was right—perhaps she should have been more careful—but she was in a surly mood. She was still feeling embarrassed by how he'd overpowered her in the ring yesterday in front of the other recruits, even though she'd been egging him on. "I haven't had any problems. It's efficient."

"Bloody night. I'll have them replaced, okay? Until then, you can take the godsdamned stairs like the rest of us."

"Are you planning to carry me to the ring?"

Logan dropped her on her ass into the dirt and strode off, and Kara supposed she deserved it. She followed him to the empty practice yard, where a tall wooden column marked with curved notches stood in the middle of the ring.

"What's this?" Kara asked.

"Your exercise for today. Strike all of notches on the column with your sword without missing any."

Kara raised an eyebrow at him. "Seems…simple."

He smiled at her. "Seems that way."

Kara began to swing at the column, executing clever slides and arcs to connect her attacks together. When she finished, she looked around for Logan. He was lounging under a nearby tree, oiling a leather bridle with a rag.

"I'm done," she called out.

"Continue," he said without looking up.

Kara sighed and started hacking at the wooden column until she'd completed another two circuits. When she looked at Logan, he hadn't moved. He wasn't even paying attention. She began again.

The sun was rising swiftly now, and she began to sweat in earnest. The cling of her clothes against her skin was oppressive. A fly circled her, buzzing incessantly. She swatted at it, and it dodged her. Sweat started to drip down Kara's face into her eyes, and she wiped it away with her sleeve.

"This is getting tedious, Logan."

"Again, recruit."

She repeated the exercise until she lost count, abandoning all finesse to conserve energy. Her arms grew tired, and the point of her sword began to tip drunkenly through the air.

The wood shuddered beneath her blows. One of the notches was particularly deep, and Kara hacked at it, abandoning the exercise altogether. It began to splinter. She gripped the hilt in two hands and swung with all her might. The top half of the column teetered, then fell to the ground.

"Destroying training equipment?" Logan asked as he approached.

Kara dropped the sword and stared up at the sky, trying to compose herself.

"It's practice, Kara. Giving up already?"

"So I'm to toil in the sun while the others receive real training?"

"You misunderstand the purpose of the exercise. It's

meant to test your patience, resolve, and ability to conserve energy. Not your skill with a blade."

"Am I training to be a monk, then?" Kara asked, throwing up her hands.

Logan fought back a smile. "A marked monk, eh? I'd pay to see that. But those skills will save your life more times than a blade ever will. Trust me."

"So I've failed your test."

"Astoundingly."

Kara sat down in the dirt, head bowed. The sun pounded at her. "It feels like you're punishing me for yesterday."

Logan shrugged. "You're reckless. Don't start fights you know you can't win. It might save your life one day."

She looked up at him. "From who? You?"

"If I were going to kill you, you'd already be dead. Now pick up the sword."

"Can we work on something else? It's so humid out here."

"What would you suggest, *recruit*?"

She considered his question. One on one training time with the Commander was valuable. But while his combat skills were impressive, Aethyta or the other mercs could teach her those techniques.

"Teach me how to use blood magic."

Logan laughed at her. "You're an even bigger fool than I thought. Absolutely not."

Kara grit her teeth. "Why not?"

"First of all, I can't. You can't use it until your curse awakens. And unless you've been feeling strange murderous urges recently, you're probably in the clear. I'm afraid whoever you injured is either still alive or suffering a very slow death."

"Does the urge to murder you count?"

Logan smirked. "Afraid that's universal."

"If I did awaken—would you teach me then?" Kara would wager that Logan knew some very useful blood spells.

"If you wish. Though I imagine for the first few months you'll be too distracted by adjusting to the changes to maintain the focus required of learning magic."

"Like the bloodlust?"

Logan's lips twisted. "Among others. Did anyone ever teach you about the curse? What to expect?"

Kara shook her head. "Da was always tight-lipped on the subject. I know being responsible for someone's death, even indirectly, will awaken it, but most of that I learned from the villager's insults. He thought moving us to the middle of nowhere would keep me safer from awakening."

"The curse always finds a way."

Rahj came galloping into the courtyard on a flashy palomino. He signaled to Logan, and Logan nodded at him.

"Mother Night. Alright, we're done for today. We'll... revisit this conversation later. I'll see you in the morning. *And use the stairs.*"

( )

THE NEXT MORNING, Logan awaited her in the courtyard with Char and Drum already saddled. Kara frowned at the storm clouds rolling in overhead. It would rain soon.

"Where are we going?" she asked.

"You'll see."

Logan led them deep into Blackshear Forest, which seemed much less menacing by daylight. The trees rustled pleasantly as a light breeze blew down their path. They rode until they reached a small clearing encircled by trees and covered in a thick blanket of fallen leaves.

"This will do," Logan said, dismounting, and Kara followed suit.

He pulled a length of black silk from his pocket and gestured for her to come closer.

She eyed the silk skeptically. "What's that for?"

"An exercise in sensation. Close your eyes."

A tingle ran up Kara's spine as he draped the soft cloth over her eyes and tied it off behind her head. He gave her braid an experimental tug, and Kara's cheeks flushed with heat. This was certainly different.

When she opened her eyes, the world was black—no light peeked in through the fabric. The sounds of the forest intensified around her. Leaves crunched beneath Logan's boots. A branch snapped in the woods, and the trees sighed softly. The darkness was strangely peaceful, her senses more alive than she'd expected them to be.

"What now?" Kara asked.

"Now you fight me."

She laughed. "You have got to be joking."

"I'm not." He took her hands in his and placed them on his broad chest, and she resisted the urge to trail them down his muscled abdomen. "I'm right here. Attack me."

Kara punched at his chest and met thin air. She had no idea where he'd dodged to—the crunching of leaves was indeterminate chaos to her ears. A whisper of leather to the right, and she swerved and swung again. She teetered forward when her fist made no impact, losing her balance. She must look a fool right now.

"You're not listening," Logan said from behind her.

"You're not making any noise. The leaves are just confusing me."

"Block that out. Focus on me. No living thing is ever

completely silent. Listen for the beat of my heart—the blood rushing through my veins. The whisper of my breaths."

Kara stilled, quieting her mind. She found that she could vaguely sense his location, the parameters of his body, if she strained her mind and ears. This time when she lunged, she felt strands of hair against her fingers.

"Better."

They continued the exercise, and Kara managed to get a few hits in as her muscles warmed up. Logan was still incredibly fast, his feet skidding through the leaves as she jabbed and kicked at him. She considered any contact made a victory.

"Good," Logan said as she caught him in the thigh. "You're progressing, but no opponent is going to stand back and let you wail on them. I'm going to be offensive now."

Kara bit her lip and nodded.

She didn't even sense his first punch. It caught her in the ribs, not hard enough to hurt but still knocking the breath out of her. He gave her a second to recover, then his next hits were lighter, more forgiving.

"Focus," he said.

Her muscles tensed in preparation. Instinct told her he was preparing to swing, but she wasn't sure where it was coming from. Kara stopped straining so hard and let her instincts guide her. She dodged quickly to the right and grinned when she felt a whiff of air to her left. She managed to block the next attack with her arm.

Kara began to sweat as they danced around the clearing, lunging and feinting. The air grew heavy with humidity, and the wind picked up speed. Logan grabbed her by the hips and jerked her towards him. Heat pulsed off his body, and she could feel the shadow of his presence as he loomed over her. She tilted her head up towards him and made to release her blindfold, but he caught her hands and lowered them. Kara stepped closer, until a breath of air separated them. He smelled like sweat and leather. She wanted to kiss him.

The sky cracked open, and the first trickles of rainfall slithered through the canopy overhead.

Logan leaned down towards her. "You should run," he growled into her ear.

"Why?"

"So I can catch you." His breath was hot, his voice full of silken promises. Trepidation snaked its way up her spine. She bolted.

Kara crashed through the trees. She let her senses free, extending them like fingers into the environment around her. She had a strange, preternatural awareness of her surroundings, allowing her to run without tripping or slamming into any trees. Logan tore through the forest after her, giving chase. She was being hunted.

Lightning flashed white through the blindfold, giving her a skeletal outline of the forest ahead. The rain began to fall in torrents, sluicing down her face as she ran. A new sound filtered in through the trees—the dull roar of swiftly moving water. It called to her, beckoning her forward. She turned in its direction.

"Kara," Logan yelled from behind her, "Be careful. The rain will distort—"

The hairs on the back of her neck raised. He was too close. The path in her mind's eye blurred and grew hazy, but she rushed blindly forward, picking up her pace. She bounded off roots and leapt over fallen logs, kicking up clods of earth as branches whipped past her face. Power thrummed through her as thunder rumbled in the sky overhead. The pull of the water pounded in her ears. It was calling her name, whispering her promises of power. A voice like an echo underwater filled her ears. *Come, daughter of my blood.*

The voice pulled her out of the trance. Something was wrong. She was being tugged in two directions, intuition telling her to stop but some other force pulling her forward. She skidded to a stop, panting.

Logan barreled into her from behind, and they both toppled to the ground. The length of his body pressed into her backside, all hard muscle and hot flesh. His breath was warm against her neck. They were both soaked through from the rain.

"You caught me, Commander."

He tugged on the silk blindfold and it fell away from her eyes. Kara craned her neck up and gasped. They were steps away from a cliff-face that dropped off into a sharp ravine. Across the ravine, a waterfall poured off the side of a mountain, crashing down below and sending clouds of wet mist into the air.

"A waterfall? Here?" Kara squirmed beneath him until he rose up on his arms, allowing her to roll over and face him. That's when she saw that he wore a twin blindfold, still tied behind his head.

"The whole time?" Her voice shook with amazement.

Logan nodded. Kara slowly pulled the fabric down over his nose and lips, leaving it to hang from his neck. She laid a hand on his cheek.

He stared down at her with blazing eyes. His lips parted, and he bowed low, so close that his stubble scraped her cheek. Rainwater dripped from his face down between her lips.

Kara's heart raced in her chest. Was he going to kiss her? She lifted her head, raising her lips towards his. Just before they met, he pulled back.

Logan gave a great shudder, then cursed and rolled off her. Kara sank back to the earth. Why was he so determined to resist the connection between them?

"I didn't realize we'd come so close to the ravine," he said, leaping up and pacing near her feet. He ran a hand across his face and bent over to shake the water out of his hair. He ripped the blindfold off his neck and stuffed it deep into his pocket.

The roar of the falls still called to Kara faintly, not as strong as before. It was hauntingly beautiful, but she made herself block it out. "Why is its pull so strong?"

Logan's eyes slid to her. "You feel it?"

Kara nodded. She could still feel it in her chest, luring her forward like a siren's song.

"Usually it takes months of living near it to affect someone, otherwise I would have never brought you in this direction." He grasped her hand and tugged her farther away from the precipice.

"What are you talking about?"

"That's Widow's Fall. Namirah hid in the network of caves behind the falls when she was being hunted by King Urian's men. Eventually they found her, though, and she made her final stand there. She'd absorbed so much power at that point that her magic was quite volatile, and the magic runoff from the battle tainted the water of the falls. Now it has the power to ensorcel others. People from the nearby mountain villages are prone to wandering off, lured to the falls after hearing a woman calling for help. Then Namirah's grief becomes their own, overcoming them until they fling themselves to the rocks below."

"That's terrible." Kara took a few steps farther away from the cliff's edge. "But why did Urian hunt Namirah down? Weren't they a couple? I'm not that familiar with the story."

Logan's eyes narrowed on her. "That farrier kept many secrets from you, Kara. But why? Who was he hiding you from?"

Kara bristled at the implication. "I don't know. Maybe he didn't want me to feel like any more of a freak than the townsfolk already did. Perhaps he planned to tell me more but never got the chance. He was a good man. He took care of me when my own family left me to die." *Or were killed. Just like everyone else.* Kara's mood deflated.

"Perhaps," Logan nodded. "Come on, let's get out of here before I have to fish you out of the ravine."

CHAPTER NINE

Kara's sparring improved immensely over the next week thanks to Logan's training. Her fellow recruits weren't nearly as quick as Logan, and their defenses were sloppy. The more she dueled with someone, the more she grew accustomed to their strengths and weaknesses. Faedra, for instance, was weak at defending her left side. Jasper was quick, but he had a habit of overextending. Bear was freakishly strong, but he moved slowly and his attacks were easy to anticipate.

Aethyta begrudgingly complimented Kara on her improvement, telling her that maybe she wasn't so worthless after all. Kara intensified her training outside of the scheduled sessions. She'd begun to rise early and run along the parapets, steadily increasing her stamina and speed. She wanted to work her way up to going into the forest alone and running blind again. The rush of it had been exhilarating.

One evening after practice, Jon sought her out in the great hall.

"Jon!" she said, surprised. He usually ate by the hearth with the other initiated members.

"Afraid I can't stay to chat, love. Logan wants to see you in his office."

Kara paled. "Why?" Was this about her punishment for attacking Willoughby? There'd been no mention of it since their return from Blackhearth. She'd almost forgotten that there might be repercussions.

Jon flicked his eyes to the side. "Haven't the slightest."

Kara glared at him. "There's something you're not telling me."

Jon stole her roll from her plate and shoved it in his mouth. "Really must go. You shouldn't keep him waiting," he mumbled around the bread.

KARA STEELED herself before Logan's ironclad office door and knocked firmly.

"Come in, Kara."

She pushed on the massive door and slid inside, taking a seat in the chair across from him. A bottle curved like a snake eating its own tail sat on his desk next to two glasses. The inky black liquor inside it was already half gone.

Logan was fiddling with a spherical paperweight made of black marble. He set it spinning on the table and filled two glasses with the liquor, passing one to her as the sphere slowed to a stop. "Shadow spirits from Verdeen. Strong stuff." Logan's eyes were glassy, his speech slow and relaxed. Apparently he'd had a headstart.

Kara took the glass and frowned at the swirling black syrup. "I don't think—"

"You'll want it by the end of this conversation. Trust me."

She grimaced as she swung back the glass and downed

it. The oily liquid swam down her throat, leaving a burning trail in its wake. Kara coughed and pounded her chest.

"Mother Night. That was strong."

He smiled. "We've an important issue to discuss."

"Is this about Willoughby?"

Logan looked confused. "What about him?"

"You said I would be punished."

"Forget it," he said with a flick of his hand. "That man's a git. I'd have let you kill him if it wouldn't hurt our image in Blackhearth. That and your wee curse."

"Then why were you so angry, back at the Chambers?"

"I didn't expect to see you there. I wasn't…prepared."

Kara nodded, even though it was a half-answer. "Then what is this about?"

"It's about you being one of Namirah's Chosen and not knowing everything that entails, apparently. I didn't realize your education was so deficient."

Her heart began to thump louder in her chest.

Logan refilled her glass and slid it back across the desk. "If you do awaken, you need to know all your options. It's less dangerous for all of us that way." Logan took a large gulp from his glass, sighing and stretching his neck as it slid down his throat. "Might as well start from the beginning, since your history is incomplete. Nearly seventy years ago, King Urian fell in love with a very powerful mage named Namirah. Their passion was legendary, their love for each other absolute. Years passed. He made her his consort, but he never married her. She wasn't royal, and some parts of the realm still harbor a deep distrust of mages. His advisors counseled him against marrying her, fearing that people would revolt if he named her queen. Urian grew older, and his need of an heir grew with him. As far as we know, Urian and Namirah never had any children, but they would have been illegitimate regardless. So, on the advice of his counselors, Urian married Genevieve, the Princess of Demma, and made her his queen.

"So that's what caused their falling out?" Kara was on the edge of her seat. She'd heard bits and pieces of this story, usually hand-in-hand with people railing against Namirah and romanticizing the Curse Wars, but never the whole thing. Da had always avoided talking about it.

"In part. It gets worse. Urian was greedy and perhaps still in love with Namirah. He kept her around as his mistress even as his new wife rounded with child. Namirah grew jealous. She flaunted Urian's favor in front of Queen Genevieve and all the courtiers, seeding dissent between the royal couple. When Princess Laura was born, Genevieve demanded Namirah be removed from the palace. She claimed she feared for her baby daughter's life. Urian conceded, and Namirah was heartbroken. She thought the king's heart had truly belonged to her, even if she could never be his queen. She vowed to make Urian regret his actions."

"Nothing like a woman scorned, eh?"

Logan nodded with a grimace. "An understatement. Namirah performed a dark blood spell that bound her soul with a demon from the shadow realm, the realm between worlds, giving her immense power. She was strong before, but the demon bond gave her powers that totally eclipsed that. Before leaving the palace, she broke into the royal nursery. She channeled all of her heartbreak, rage, and jealousy into a curse on Princess Laura. But she wasn't accustomed to the huge reserves of power she now had access to, and the magic overflowed its intended vessel. In addition to infecting other children nearby, researchers at the mage college think it affected the crops, water, and air in the area surrounding the palace. That's how it spread so far initially."

"And that's how creatures like the obara came to be?"

Logan nodded. "There are others, too. Creatures warped by living off land suffused with dark magic. There are new, dangerous species that we don't entirely understand yet."

And she'd walked into a nest of them, completely unaware of the danger. Kara shivered and rubbed her neck. "So what happened to Princess Laura? I know she was the first to awaken."

"She was a normal child, all but for the strange marks on her wrist. Eighteen years passed in peace, and Namirah stayed away from the royal palace. The curse went so long without manifesting that the king and queen were lulled into a false sense of security. Then, on the day of her eighteenth birthday, Princess Laura and her friend went riding in the royal forest. Laura adjusted her friend's saddle cinch for her before they made their way back to the palace, but it was too loose, and the girl fell and broke her neck."

"But she wasn't trying to kill her."

"No, but she was responsible for her death, and that's all it took for the curse to trigger. Even marked children whose mothers die in childbirth are doomed from the moment they draw their first breath. Eighteen years of peace, then they awaken."

Kara blanched. "It's that sensitive?" It explained why Da had kept her so sheltered and insisted on living in a village as small as Mudbottom. Less chances for the curse to trigger through happenstance.

Logan nodded grimly. "The curse has cruel logic. How old are you again?"

"Twenty-four in a few months."

"You've been lucky. It's rare for the curse to go so long without baring its fangs."

"So what happened to the princess after that?"

"A month after the riding accident, Princess Laura killed her handmaiden in a fit of anger. The murder was swept under the rug, but every month after that, another palace inhabitant died—usually one of the attendants to the royal family. Eventually the princess was locked away from human contact. After a moon's turn, she began to cry out from her room in pain, raving about flames licking at her skin and fire burning her from the inside. No medicine or healers could help her, and the palace doctors declared her mad. She started to waste away, writhing and screaming in her sleep as she succumbed to the curse. Then she began to change, began to become something *other*. Without satiation, the dark magic took over. A priestess of the Night Mother attending her took mercy on her. She left a knife in the princess's cell so she could ease her own suffering. Around the realm similar cases started appearing as children born under Namirah's curse began to awaken. Mayhem and murder reigned—no one knew how to control the curse without more killing. In a last-ditch effort to contain the chaos, King Urian combined his forces with that of the mercenary clans to hunt down and kill all of Namirah's Chosen. And thus the Curse Wars began. Back then they believed the curse was hereditary, so Urian wanted all of the chosen and their families eradicated. It was genocide."

"I'm surprised they were able to resist as much as they did."

"They weren't without resources. An affinity for blood magic, heightened senses, augmented strength and speed, and a facility for murder will take you a long way. And not everyone sided with Urian. Some supported the Namirahns outright. Others were convinced to turn—among them were skilled generals and entire clans. It wasn't enough, though, and eventually their main army fell. In the years after, several rebellions cropped up, but they were swiftly put down on Urian's command."

Kara felt sick to her stomach. There were people who still believed in Urian's insane crusade. "So many deaths… for nothing. It didn't stop anything. Do you know how many of us are left?"

Logan shrugged. "It's not a status most people readily advertise. Some of the chosen didn't want to fight, so they went into hiding when the Curse Wars started. And while less prolific, Namirah's outpouring of magic lingers in the earth to this day, marking unfortunate newborns with her curse."

"What happened to Namirah?" Kara asked, sipping on the shadow liquor.

"After the death of his daughter and the awakening of so many of the chosen, Urian had her hunted down like a dog. He brought in magic hunters from Verdeen to sniff her out, and they chased her across the country until they cornered her at last—at Widow's Fall. She felled hundreds of soldiers before they finally captured her and burned her at the stake. Story goes that she cried out to Urian with her last breaths, begging him to save her."

"I had no idea the origin of the curse was so tragic."

Logan nodded. "So much blood shed, so many lives ruined because of two people's selfishness."

Kara finished off her second glass of the shadow liquor, and Logan eyed the empty glass.

"Don't you have training tomorrow?"

"That's tomorrow's problem, this is today's."

He snorted. "Some scholars view the curse as the twisted embodiment of Urian and Namirah's relationship —all corrupted passion and burning anger. She wanted Princess Laura to suffer the same fate they had. Others think the curse is a weaker version of Namirah's soul bond with a demon, the demon demanding to be sated in exchange for its power."

"Where are you going with this?" The liquor burned warm in Kara's gut, emboldening her.

Logan looked world weary. "Can't believe I'm about to do this." He filled her glass again, then downed the rest of the bottle, tipping it back to get every last drop. Kara was surprised he hadn't passed out yet.

Then he propped his arm on the table and began unbuckling his left bracer. The leather fell open to expose the twin crescents of Namirah's mark curving around his pale wrist. The tanline from his bracers was stark—he must never take them off. His mark was identical to hers, except his was lit from within by a dim, fiery glow.

Kara sucked in her breath. Her brain was slow to comprehend the enormity of what she was seeing. She slowly lifted her gaze to meet Logan's. "You...you're cursed," Kara stuttered.

"Yes." His eyes were haunted.

"Who else knows?"

"My inner circle."

"How did you survive?" Most marked males weren't allowed to survive past infancy, let alone awaken. They were notorious for their lack of control. In the past too many of them had given over to their bloodlust completely, becoming serial murderers that killed even when they weren't sating the curse. People eventually started killing them in their cribs.

"Through great sacrifice from my father."

Kara polished off her third glass in one swig, and it made her eyes water. "You have any more?" she croaked.

He smirked. "Not if you want to remember this conversation in the morning. Namirah cursed us with souls that are part demon, part man. And thus, once the curse awakens inside you, you're prey to a demon's proclivities. Anger, rage, passion, lust. All vying against each other, demanding to be quenched month after month when you start keening."

"Keening?"

"That's what we call it, the monthly toll. Fortunately, we've discovered an option other than killing to stave off the bloodlust since Namirah's time."

Hope fluttered within Kara's chest. "What is it?"

Logan's voice went gravelly. "Giving in to lust."

Kara's cheeks heated. "And if I do neither?"

"That's not an option. You'll lose yourself, Kara. Princess Laura's fate was no exaggeration. I revealed my mark to you because I want to help guide you. When I awakened, I had no idea what to expect—how strong the compulsion would be. I wouldn't wish that on anyone."

Kara leaned back in her chair. "Well, getting myself off once a month doesn't sound so bad. I do it already—" Her cheeks flamed as she realized what she'd said. The shadow spirits had certainly loosened her tongue.

Logan's gaze on her was hungry, heated. His eyes flicked to a brilliant yellow color, then back to normal as he took a deep breath. She averted her eyes from that molten gaze.

"Unfortunately, Kara, the curse demands that you take your pleasure with a partner. That fits the storyline, after all."

"Fuck." Kara's mind rebelled at the idea, that she'd be compelled to kill or be with someone, *anyone*, in order to not lose herself. She enjoyed sex, but she didn't want to be controlled by it.

"It's less heavy on the soul than random killing. Trust me on this one. Perhaps you could arrange something with one of the men or women from the Chambers. Your partner need not be of the opposite sex…"

Kara took a deep breath before she spoke. "What about us?" No one had ever looked at her the way Logan did, and her thoughts had often drifted to what it'd be like to be with him.

Logan's gaze fell to his empty glass. "What do you mean?"

"We're both cursed. Why not keen together? Two birds, two orgasms. Or something." Heat crept up her neck.

His amber gaze crawled up her skin. "You haven't even awoken yet, Kara."

"And?" She crossed her arms and held his gaze.

A muscle in Logan's jaw flickered. "It's a bad idea."

"Why? I've seen the way you look at me."

"I will admit that there's an…attraction, between us. One I've been struggling to resist."

Kara's eyebrows raised. So he *did* feel it too. "Are you afraid of what the others would think?"

"That would complicate things, but no. I don't let what people might think of me dictate my decisions."

"Well then?"

"I prefer to keep things simple. Uncomplicated. What if one of us began to develop deeper feelings for the other? A job could separate us for more than a month, and then what? You get jealous. *I* get jealous. Emotions start to cloud our thinking. On the battlefield we begin to worry about each other's safety more than the objective. That's the kind of thing that gets people killed. And if we had a falling out? You're still under contract with the clan for two years. Like I said, it's a bad idea."

"You've thought about this a lot." Which meant he'd

been considering it as an option. Satisfaction curled inside her.

Logan nodded.

"It's just sex. It doesn't have to be more than that." Even as Kara said it, she wasn't wholly convinced it was the truth.

"I'm not so sure, Kara McKenna." Logan's voice was a low growl.

Heat flooded Kara's core. This man thoroughly unnerved her. "So I'm left to my own devices." Her pride stung a little at being shot down, but his reasoning was sound. Which meant that if her curse awoke, Kara was going to have to choose someone else—or find someone that needed killing—when the man she wanted was right in front of her.

She stood up from her chair too quickly, and the room spun around her.

"I'll help you where I can."

Kara needed to leave. She didn't want to be in this room any longer, with the weight of all he'd told her pressing in and his rejection staring her in the face. She stumbled to the door, her legs unsteady from the alcohol. She left without looking back.

When she got to the tower, the ominous darkness of the stairs unsettled her. She was tempted to curl up at the bottom of the stairwell and sleep there, but she began to climb. Kara slipped on a step and fell forward, banging her knee and catching herself with her hands. There was something wet and slimy under her palms. She jerked away, teetering dangerously on the stairs until she clutched the grooves in the stone wall with both hands. She kept her balance by leaning against the wall the rest of the way up. When she reached her room, she fell into bed still fully clothed and passed out.

()

When the morning bell rang for a second time, Kara was still abed, mouth fuzzy and dry and her head pounding with pain. She'd drooled on her pillow in her sleep, and half of it was sticking to her face. Someone was rapping on her door urgently. She groaned.

Jon swung open the door and sauntered over. "What got into you?"

"Bottle of black stuff," she mumbled groggily.

"Expected as much. Shadow spirits, noxious stuff. Came to see if you were still alive." Jon pried her left eyelid open and gave her a stern look. "Aethyta will have your ass if you don't make it to the training yard soon."

"Never missed before."

"Perhaps not, but getting drunk as a skunk with training in the morning is a poor excuse for absenteeism."

"How'd you get in here, anyway?"

"I have a key."

"What?" she squawked, sitting up in bed.

"Too easy," Jon laughed, the rich timber of his voice filling the room. "You left it unlocked last night. Seems your little heart to heart with Logan really put you on your ass. I wouldn't recommend drinking with him. He's got nightmarish tolerance."

"Probably because he's a bloody demon!"

Jon's face tightened, his expression closed off. "He's told you, then. I suppose there was no helping it."

Kara swung her feet over the edge of the bed and tried to stand, clutching her head as the motion rang in her ears.

"You look like shit," Jon frowned. "If you'd rather I take you to Barty—"

"I'm fine. I'm on thin ice with Aethyta already. Let's go."

Kara didn't bother changing out of yesterday's practice clothes. She moved gingerly down the stairs, each step sending a lance of pain through her skull.

The training yard was bright and bustling with recruits. Jon veered off towards the keep, and Kara squinted at the arena, the sun blinding her. Several horses were hitched to the railing, and the practice swords were out. How bad could this be?

Aethyta turned as she approached. "Ah, Ms. McKenna. How considerate of you to grace us with your presence. We're practicing mounted combat techniques. In light of your tardiness, I'm sure you won't mind volunteering for the first lesson?"

As if she actually had a choice. Kara trudged into the ring, her stomach roiling with nausea.

Jasper volunteered next, and Kara cursed him into the depths of the sea.

"Excellent," Aethyta said. "Jasper, mount up. Kara, arm yourself. The horseman's objective is to swiftly cut down their opponent without losing their seat or injuring their mount. Our groundsman's goal is to dismount the rider, allowing them to fight on even footing. In a real battle, mount casualties are an unfortunate reality, but for the purpose of today's lesson, please refrain from injuring the horses. Let's begin."

Kara sighed and scratched the tip of her sword through the dirt. Of all the days for her to show up to practice hungover. This was going to suck.

Jasper chose a mean-looking russet gelding who was already foaming at the bit. He raised his sword in one hand, reins in the other, and kicked the horse into a canter. He bore down on her immediately. She stood in his path until the last second, then ducked low and rolled out of the way as he swung at her. The knee she'd smacked on the steps last night smarted painfully. Jasper wheeled the gelding in a circle and came at her again. This time when she dodged, she smacked the horse's rump with the flat of her sword, just enough to startle him. He bucked, jostling Jasper, but the lordling kept his seat.

Jasper recovered his balance and heeled the horse into a hard gallop, coming straight for her. He was going too fast. Kara's vision blurred, and she ran, hopping over the top of the fence just as the gelding slid up against it, stopping hard.

"Please remain in the arena," Aethyta said, voice cold.

Did the woman prefer she be trampled to death? Kara shot her a look that could curdle blood and climbed back inside. She crouched low under the pretense of catching her breath and grasped a handful of arena sand. Jasper smirked, thinking her beaten.

Kara stood directly in his path, waiting until the flashing hooves were almost upon her to throw the sand in Jasper's eyes and slide to the side. She grabbed a rein and tugged hard, pulling the horse around. Jasper was rubbing his eyes and swinging his sword blindly. She tore his foot out of the stirrup and yanked down on his leg, and he began to slide off the side of the horse.

Jasper tumbled to the ground then scrambled up, eyes narrowed in fury. "That was dirty."

They circled each other. The tip of his sword wobbled. He was getting tired, but Kara's head was pounding relentlessly. She needed to make this quick. She struck, and their swords clashed together, ringing off one another. Kara waited for an opening in his aggressive attack style, then hooked the hilt of her sword around his and popped it out of his hand.

Her sword was shaking in her grasp. She was pushing

her limits, overtaxing her body. "Enough," she cried to Aethyta.

"I'll let you know when you're done. Now drop your sword and continue."

Kara's nostrils flared. Aethyta was determined to see her fail. Kara reluctantly released the hilt, letting her only weapon go. Jasper drew his fists up. He dove for her, and she caught him in the eye with a punch as he brought her down to the ground. This wasn't good. She was in an unfavorable position, and Jasper was stronger than her when it came to pure physicality.

They tussled in the dirt, and Kara did her best to fend off his attacks. Then one of his punches caught her in the gut, and her stomach heaved. She rolled over in the sand and puked. The result was a black tarry mess that smelled like death.

Jasper held off finally, not sure whether to continue.

"I yield," Kara mumbled around a swollen tongue. She wasn't sure whether any words had actually come out. Her head swam, her vision starting to go dark as she tried to stand up. Was she going to puke again? There was a commotion by the arena railing as someone barked orders.

The next sensation she knew was warm, strong arms lifting her off the ground.

"Logan?" she murmured.

"Guess again."

Jon. He carried her to the infirmary, where he laid her down on one of the cots. Bart bustled over and peered down at her, tsking to himself. "I told you," he said matter-of-factly.

"I'm fine," Kara grumbled.

"No, you're not," Jon said, his tone angry. "And you're not to leave this room before sundown, after which you will eat and go directly to bed."

"Bossy Jon. This is new."

"Feel better," he said, sweeping a hand across her brow. He strode out the door and slammed it behind him. The noise sent another painful jolt through Kara's skull.

"Ow."

Bart was busy brewing her a cup of tea. "You're dehydrated. You need to rest, let your body recover. Stop putting it under so much stress."

"I need to keep up with the others. Today was all Logan's fault."

"I wouldn't doubt it. But you need to stay healthy."

"Aethyta will be the death of me."

Bart chuckled. "You're not the first one to say that. She has a marked daughter, you know. Maybe you remind her of her."

"Must be in a bad way."

Bart passed her the tea. It was piping hot, and it tasted of old leaves and lavender. Her eyelids began to feel heavy after a few sips.

"Hey—I have things to do."

He pulled a blanket over her and went back to tinkering at his work desk, and soon Kara sunk into sleep.

CHAPTER TEN

The next two months passed quickly at Raven's Rest. Kara focused on training and tried not to dwell on the story about Princess Laura's fate. The Sanguine she'd stabbed must be alive, but she still felt the curse creeping inexorably towards her, like a malignant shadow. She began to worry during training that she would accidentally injure someone, and that injury would lead to their death via a thousand different possibilities.

Occasionally Jon or Rahj would join the recruits and teach a session on a particular fighting technique, but by and large it was Aethyta training them. Kara and Logan mostly avoided each other. She was exhausted all the time from practice, and he didn't spend much time with the recruits. Sometimes he'd workout or run drills in the yard while they trained, and trying to sneak peeks at his shirtless body, pumped with blood and pouring with sweat, earned her more than a few bruises.

Her peers had begun to buzz with speculation about what their final evaluations would involve. Their performance would determine whether they passed their trial period and were formally inducted into the clan. Kara wasn't worried initially. She felt like she was beginning to come into her own, thanks to her extra time spent training, but everyone else's stress was beginning to get to her. She wanted to perform her best at the evaluations regardless of the anomaly in her contract.

One morning when the recruits gathered in the yard, Logan, Aethyta, and the members of the inner circle were already there. Kara's stomach dropped. Today must be the day.

"Nervous?" she asked Thomas.

"As hell."

Logan waited until everyone arrived to begin. "A clutch of arachnae have been sighted near Blackhearth. I've decided to make eradicating them your evaluation exercise. They're deadly creatures. Don't abandon caution once we reach their nest."

Kara swallowed.

"*Arachnae,*" George muttered. "Call them what they are, man. Giant fucking spiders. Makes my skin crawl."

"Is he serious?" Thomas whispered.

"We're getting off easy," Faedra said. "Feron told me that one year the recruits fought against a rival clan in a minor border skirmish. Another year they hunted down a rabid ogre."

"Alright," Aethyta yelled, clapping her hands together. "You'll be divided into teams for the evaluations. Your team captains are Jasper and Kara."

Kara stilled. *Her?* Why would they pick her? She didn't know how to lead anyone. Several recruits began to grumble at the announcement, and cold sweat broke out on her brow.

Aethyta continued, "The team that brings me the most arachnae heads will win a gold purse, to be split among yourselves. Everyone's performance in training and during the exercise today will be evaluated equally, regardless of if you're on the losing team or not. Team leaders, make me proud. A lot of responsibility is on your shoulders. Do your best not to get anyone killed. In the event of any injuries, Bart will be at the Blackhearth Inn."

Kara's stomach dropped. What were they thinking? Did they *want* to awaken her curse? She ran a hand over her sweaty brow.

Aethyta had them flip a coin to see who would choose the first team member. Kara won. She looked over the pool of recruits, considering her options. She knew next to nothing about hunting giant spiders, but she knew she wanted her friends beside her. "Thomas," she said, and he came over to stand beside her.

Jasper's first pick was Everett, one of his cronies who was wicked with a blade.

Kara chose Faedra next. When Jasper took Bear, she bit back a curse. George looked at her hopefully, but she hesitated to pick him. He'd already confessed to his fear of spiders, and his swordsmanship was only average. Then again, she didn't know the other recruits that well. She'd work better with people she was familiar with.

"George."

Thomas groaned beside her.

AFTER THEY FILLED out their teams, Logan led them through the woods towards Blackhearth. He rode tall and proud in front of the procession, his black leather uniform blending seamlessly into Char's midnight coat. He had an enormous black bow she'd never seen before strapped across his back. It looked like it was made of bone. When they reached the town, they left their horses at the stable there. Kara was sad to let Drum go—she felt safer with horseflesh between her legs.

"The horses would just bolt anyways," Thomas said as they began their hike up the craggy terrain surrounding the arachnae lair. "Arachnae are natural predators of equines. They'll drop down from trees onto the horse's back, sink their fangs into their flesh, and cling to them until their venom brings the horse down. Then they feast."

"Thanks for that imagery," Kara said.

"Maybe they'll like you. They're also a byproduct of Namirah's curse, after all."

"I don't plan on letting them live long enough to find out."

Logan called them to a halt once they reached a dense thicket of trees sticky with old webbing. The grey strands were thick as ropes, and some of them spanned ten feet across. A skinny kid named Tanner, whom Kara had picked near the end of the team draft, marveled at their size. His face was still hairless as a babe's—he couldn't be older than sixteen or seventeen.

"Teams, fan out," Logan said. "We'll be shooting flaming arrows into the nest to antagonize them and draw them out. Be prepared. These aren't normal animals— they're warped by dark magic. Don't underestimate them."

"I would have preferred the element of surprise," Kara told Thomas. "Are they trying to make this *more* difficult?"

"Eh," Thomas said. "I wasn't exactly keen on traipsing into the caves they nest in."

She motioned for her teammates to follow her down a side path dense with brush. They all slipped their weapons out of their sheaths and held them at the ready as they cut a path ahead. An arrow whistled through the sky, and a cloud of smoke bloomed in the distance. They pushed forward through the woods. The webs grew larger and more frequent the deeper in they got.

"This stuff is fresh," Faedra said, pointing at a glistening white liquid that dripped from the strands of web to the forest floor.

"Everyone on the lookout," Kara said. "Aaron, keep an eye above us. They might drop down."

A member of Jasper's team screamed in the distance, and everyone stiffened.

Tanner had his back to the trees, sword brandished in front of him like he expected the beasts to appear out of thin air. A sharp chittering noise came from the treetops, and a strand of web shot down behind him.

"Tanner! Watch out!" Faedra yelled.

He was too slow. A black chitinous mass the size of a pony descended down the web and wrapped its furred, spindly legs around him. Each of its eight legs were capped by glistening black claws. Tanner screamed and thrashed in its grasp, and the arachnae bit into his leg. Kara scrambled forward, grabbing Tanner with one arm while she kept her sword trained on the creature. Eight glittering eyeballs stared back at her, blinking rapidly. It released Tanner and dropped down to the ground, where it skittered left and right, looking for an opening to attack. She lunged forward and plunged her sword into its face. Hot blood burst out, smoking as it splattered on her sword. The creature screeched and lunged towards her even as the blade slid through its body. It collapsed mere steps from her. Kara braced her boot on its hard outer shell and tugged the blade out.

Tanner lay curled up on the ground, clutching his leg. Aaron kneeled beside him and cut off his pants leg. Sickly green striations emanated from an inch-long fang lodged deep in the meat of his calf. Tanner was shivering, his face pale and scrunched.

"He doesn't have a lot of time," Aaron said. He put the leather-wrapped hilt of his dagger between Tanner's teeth. "Bite down. We have to get the fang out before the poison spreads."

Tanner clenched down, and Aaron pulled out the arachnae's fang with a gloved hand. Tanner thrashed, his eyes wild with pain. Faedra handed Aaron a strip of cloth so he could wrap the wound and staunch the bloodflow.

More clacking, chittering noises came from behind them. Shadows shifted in the treetops. Kara backed away from the trees as more arachnae began to descend on their webs. They were surrounded.

"Kara!" Faedra yelled. "What do we do?"

Fuck fuck fuck. Why was she asking her? She scrambled for a solution. "Circle Tanner! We have to protect him until we can get him to Bart."

She was surprised when they listened, clustering around his prone form and forming a wall of sharp points for the approaching monsters.

"Hold steady," Kara said. "Let none through."

Beady eyes blinked at them from the shadows, and several massive forms moved forward in unison.

"There shouldn't be this many!" someone shouted. "Where's the other team?"

Thomas swung his glaive in warning as one of the arachnae edged closer in. The extra reach it provided was deadly. When the spider darted in closer, Thomas sliced its head off in one clean stroke. The beheaded body continued twitching for a moment before it fell.

Three arachnae approached Kara's side of the circle, converging on her as they gnashed multiple rows of toxic teeth. She was shoulder to shoulder with her neighbors, blade at the ready. The middle spider approached, and she jabbed at its eyes. The spider ducked, and her sword lodged under the hard, armored carapace atop its back. The monster pulled back before she could dislodge her sword, and she was forced to let it go.

"Fuck." The other two arachnae chittered rapidly and blinked with interest at her. How intelligent were these creatures? They both leapt for her at once. Faedra intercepted one of them, delaying it, but the other toppled her back against the grass. She struggled beneath its monstrous body, trying to grip something vulnerable. She could hear Tanner moaning. The arachnae stabbed at her face with its clawed leg, and she barely jerked to the side in time. Its spiky leg fur brushed against her cheek. Rancid breath that smelled like rotting meat came from its maw. Kara pulled her dagger from her belt, yanked it up, and dragged it through the arachnae's flesh, slicing its vulnerable belly open. Hot entrails spilled out onto her. Kara gagged at the smell and struggled to roll the beast off of her. Thomas helped drag it off and grimaced at the mess of entrails covering her torso.

"I hope none of that's yours," Thomas said.

"Gutted him like a fish," George said, nodding approvingly. Kara stood up, and viscera sloughed off of her into a wet, bloody pile at her feet. One of the men made a retching sound.

"That's all of them?" Kara asked, looking around. Her heart was beating so hard she could hear it in her ears. It was over as quickly as it began. Black carcasses littered the forest floor; grey webs glistened with bright blood. There were at least ten of them, enough to be an entire arachnae brood.

Tanner gave a shallow, rattling breath. His skin was damp with sweat.

"We need to get him out of here," Aaron said. "His pulse is weakening."

One of the recruits looked up from where he was hacking at a dead arachnae's armored neckline with his sword. "We need the heads. Aethyta wants heads."

Kara looked from Tanner to the corpses. It would take precious minutes, and they still had to trek back to Blackhearth. "We don't have time for that. Getting him to Bart is our first priority, and I don't want to split up the team. There could be more of them out there."

A few of the recruits grumbled, and one of them snatched up the head severed by Thomas's glaive as Thomas and Aaron helped ease Tanner's body onto George's back. Kara squeezed Tanner's hand tight in her own. "Hold on. We'll be there soon." He would *not* die on her.

"Hate working outside my infirmary," Bart muttered as he entered the room they'd set Tanner up in at the inn. "Deplorable conditions. Blackhearth Inn? Might as well have the patient in the stable amongst the horse dung and flies." Bart swatted Kara away when he saw her at Tanner's bedside. "Out of my way, girl." He paused to stare at her clothes, slick with blood and bits of questionable grey matter. "You're filthy and contaminating my work space. You want him to live, don't you? Out!"

Kara watched from the doorway as Bart unwrapped Tanner's leg and prodded the striated flesh with his fingers.

"Bloody arachnae hunts. You'll be lucky not to lose your leg. Let's hope the venom hasn't set in."

Bart began to pull out his instruments from his bag, and Kara went back downstairs.

Thomas was arguing with Aethyta by the hearth, while Jasper leaned back in a chair, looking smug and satisfied. His teammates were already celebrating with rounds of alcohol.

"Ten?" Aethyta scoffed. "You take me for a fool, boy."

"I'm telling you! We weren't even near the smoke— they came out of nowhere. Ambushed Tanner before we realized we were surrounded."

"You bring me *one* head and a gravely injured team-mate, then have the audacity to lie to me? Your chances at passing your trial period are rapidly dwindling."

"Aethyta," Logan said, silencing her, "I believe there was a second nest that the villagers were unaware of. We'll need to sweep the area for it and burn it out in case they've already laid eggs."

Aethyta bristled at the interruption but didn't dare argue. "Very well, Commander. But rules are rules. Jasper's team brought me six heads. They're the winners."

The barkeep curled his nose at Kara as she climbed into a bar stool. "Mother Night, girl. You look like you bathed in one of 'em."

"Beer," she said.

He slid her a cold, frothy mug, and she took a big sip.

"Make that two, on me," Logan said as he sat down beside her. "You did well."

"We lost."

"Next time you might draw your daggers before a giant spider is on top of you."

Kara stilled and slowly turned towards Logan, blood

pounding in her ears. "You were there watching, and you didn't help?" she said through clenched teeth.

"My job is to evaluate, not to intercede. Athar was with me. Rahj and Jon evaluated the other group. You saved your teammate. That counts for a lot."

"He could die! And trigger *my* curse. What the hell were you thinking?" Kara struggled to keep her voice down.

"He's not going to die, Kara."

"He might lose his leg!"

"He knew what he was signing up for."

"You're a bastard, you know that? He's just a kid."

"At that age Jon and I were already hunting men, not the local village monsters. I was confident you had it under control."

Kara stared into her mug. He was sorely mistaken. "Despite all of that, you still won't vouch for us to Aethyta?"

"The gold, the competition—it's meaningless. A token to encourage everyone. You'll make five times that on a real contract."

"That's not the point! You put me in charge, and he almost died. You think I want that on my conscience?" She wanted to hurl the heavy mug at his skull. Rage boiled inside her, threatening to overflow.

Logan laid a hand on her marked arm. "Easy. I know you're angry, but I'm aware of the speed at which arachnae venom operates. I had my bow. Do you think I would have let him die or lose his leg?"

"I don't know. Yes! Maybe. You do whatever serves your purposes. Including awakening my curse."

Logan sucked in a breath, and anger flashed across his face. "I'd never inflict that on another, Kara. Especially you. And letting a young boy be crippled serves me how? You're smarter than that. What's really bothering you?"

She felt tears threatening to spill over, so she bowed her head. "I wasn't ready. I was—I *am*—scared." She'd almost failed Tanner, just like she'd failed Wesley and Da.

"I made you captain because you're capable, Kara. You're a mercenary now. A member of the Stygian Brotherhood. Human casualties are a byproduct of our lifestyle. Why do you think we do these exercises?"

Kara was surprised to hear that he'd nominated her as captain. She'd thought it'd been Aethyta trying to set her up to fail. "How do you handle it?"

Logan sighed and ran a finger through the water condensing on the outside of his glass. "You have to remind yourself that you did everything within your power to save them. That their sacrifice meant something in the end. If you let it haunt you, eat away at you, then you're as good as dead. We have to worry about the living."

"Do you have anything stronger?" Kara asked the barkeep.

( )

TANNER AND A HANDFUL of other recruits didn't make it past their trial periods. They were given the remainder of their wages and dismissed. They packed their things while everyone else prepared for the induction ceremony. Tanner sought Kara out before he left. He thanked her for saving him and told her to visit him at his home in Lindenvale if she ever passed through.

That night the recruits were summoned to the great hall for the induction ceremony. Kara sought out Thomas and Faedra in the cluster of people milling about excitedly. No one knew quite what the ceremony entailed, but the gossip ranged from naked rites to animal sacrifice to bare-handed brawls to the death. Kara thought the ideas were a bit far-fetched until the senior mercenaries entered the hall. They were clad in black cloaks that swept the floor, their faces hidden deep within their hoods. The room fell into a hush, and the senior members guided them down the stone stairwell that led to the baths. Kara tried to pick out Jon or Logan, but the cloaks concealed too much.

The leader of the procession stopped at the landing before the final descent to the baths and turned towards the sheer rock wall. He murmured something unintelligible and traced a pattern onto the rock. When he took his hand away, the pattern lit up with a violet glow. A rune. Who in the clan knew rune magic?

The walls began to rumble around them, and the rune faded as the sheer stone slid to the side, forming a doorway.

"God's teeth," Faedra whispered. "Feron never told me about this."

"Silence," one of the hooded members said, "or we'll make an offering of your flesh."

The cloaked mercenaries led them through the newly opened passage, and they slowly filtered into an awning cavern as dark as pitch. Once everyone was inside, the stone rumbled shut behind them, trapping them. Kara couldn't see anything, and she didn't like the idea of being trapped down here beneath the earth. Four pot-bellied braziers nearly six feet in diameter blazed to life, filling the cavern with an eerie glow. A thick fog hovered above the cavern floor, clouding around their ankles.

The cloaked mercenaries who'd escorted them stood in a semi-circle behind a tall, imposing figure in the center of the room. He wore a cloak that moved like a sheet of moonless night, sucking up all the light around it. He stood in front of a crude stone slab stained with old blood, some kind of ancient altar. Behind him an obsidian obelisk jutted up towards the cavern's ceiling. Kara looked closer and saw that it was covered in names and dates that'd been carved into the stone. A monument to the fallen members of the Stygian Brotherhood, likely dating back to the clan's origins.

The cloak fell in a whisper of silk, revealing black hair and a muscled back painted with a crude rendition of the Stygian sigil. Kara knew that back; she'd stared at it often enough. Logan turned around to face the recruits and stepped forward. He was naked but for his leather bracers and a black loincloth loosely tied around his waist. Kara's eyes drifted over him. Every inch of his bare flesh was covered in swaths of red blood and black ash. His eyes burned like coals beneath the dark, livid streaks, and his hair framed the hard planes of his cheeks. Logan padded silently towards the altar on bare feet, corded muscles flexing in the low light. Kara bit her lip, hard.

Who had painted him? There were trailing streaks from fingers and hands across his chest, and intricate whorls wrapped around his legs. He looked like some dark pagan lord pulled straight from her dreams.

Logan's voice boomed throughout the cavern, and everyone startled from the hazy dream state they'd been in. "Welcome, recruits. Brothers and sisters. Tonight you'll take part in a sacred ritual of our clan. I'll call upon each of you to make an offering upon the altar. An offering that symbolizes your commitment to the Brotherhood—one you're expected to honor until such time as your contract expires or your spirit departs this plane. Once your offering is accepted, your initiation will be complete."

An offering? Fuck. Why hadn't they been warned? Kara rummaged through her pockets and pulled out a piece of hay and a sugar cube for Drum, then quickly shoved them back. Her blades weren't unique—they were the same weapons Athar had requisitioned for all the new recruits. What was special to her that she could offer? She'd abandoned most of her belongings when she'd fled Mudbottom. She thought of Da's carving of the goddess sitting on the dresser in her room. But it was just a sentimental bauble—useless to the clan, and she didn't have it with her, anyways.

"Bear, approach the altar," Logan said.

Kara thanked the goddess she wasn't first. She had no idea what to offer.

Bear approached the altar stone and knelt, looking perplexed. He glanced from Logan to the hooded members with a question in his eyes. At least she wasn't the only unprepared one.

"Make your offering, recruit," Logan said

Creeping seconds passed. Finally Bear reached for his belt, untied a small furred object on a leather loop, and placed it on the altar. It was a gnarled old rabbit's foot.

"I offer my luck," Bear said.

Kara didn't know Bear to be particularly lucky, but the object seemed to mean something to him. He looked at it with a sad fondness.

Logan nodded. "Your offering is accepted, recruit. Welcome to the Brotherhood."

"Am I going to be able to get that back?"

"It belongs to the clan now." One of the senior members passed Logan a folded black cloak identical to the ones they were wearing. Logan draped it over Bear's shoulders, lifted the hood over his head, and hooked the cloak's clasps around his neck. Bear bowed low to Logan and went to stand amongst the senior members.

The ceremony proceeded like so, with no discernible

order to the names being called. When Jasper was summoned, he unsheathed a thin rapier with a pearl-encrusted hilt and laid it on the altar. "I offer my blade."

Kara found it suspicious that he should be carrying around such a valuable sword on the eve of induction, when none of them had known what to expect. Perhaps he'd bribed someone for information.

"More like 'my wealth,'" Thomas whispered.

"Both useful," Kara admitted.

Aaron was next. He knelt and wiped tears from his face before presenting Logan with a highly stylized dirk. The blade was inscribed with a message. "I offer my purpose," he said.

As the stone altar grew crowded with trinkets, coins, and blades, Logan periodically cleared it off, passing the offerings to the senior members. People grew impatient and began to shuffle restlessly. A recruit named Ned was noisily rummaging through his coin purse during George's offering. Kara kept raising up on her tiptoes to try and see what he'd given.

"Ned!" Logan shouted. The purse clattered to the stone floor, coins spilling everywhere. "How generous," Logan said, smiling. "We'll take all of it." Ned paled and muttered angrily, but offered the entirety of the bulging purse when he was called.

The line of remaining recruits began to dwindle, and Kara grew anxious. She'd had no new ideas for her offering. She supposed it couldn't go any worse than it had for Thomas, who'd offered his glasses and 'his vision' before reconsidering and taking the glasses *back*. He'd then offered 'his regrets' and laid down a small paring knife used to fillet fish. "I offer my expertise," he finally said.

Logan was glowering, but he gave Thomas his cloak and moved on to Faedra.

Faedra pulled a knife from the band of her pants and laid it down. It was the same stylized dirk that Aaron had offered earlier. "I offer my cunning," she said, which garnered a round of chuckles. Kara was impressed; she hadn't even noticed her moving about the crowd.

"Kara, approach the altar," Logan said.

Kara froze, then forced her legs to move forward. She should have been thinking of a plan instead of watching the other offerings. Her mind was a giant gaping hole of nothing. She sank to the floor and looked up into Logan's intense gaze.

"What do you offer the Stygian Brotherhood?" Logan asked.

Her mind raced, supplying nothing. An eternity passed as everyone stared at her, waiting. A memory of the night she met Logan flashed through her mind.

Kara picked up the stylized dirk still resting on the altar. The inscription on the blade read, '*To my lover. My heart.*' She slid the blade through the crescent shapes of Namirah's mark, hoping she didn't pass out in front of everyone this time.

Pain flared hot as the wound burned, and a strange, heady sensation swept over her. She swayed on the spot. "I offer my blood," she said, the words thick on her tongue.

Logan's eyes burned bright. He dragged a finger through the pool of blood collecting on the stone altar and drew it across his chest, painting another whorl. There was something incredibly intimate about it—as if they were sharing the same flesh. Her knees quivered against the stone floor. "Your offering is accepted, Kara."

One second she was staring up at his molten eyes, the next she was flat on her back against the stone altar. She could hear the tinkling clatter of bones. Logan approached from the darkness and leaned over her. He crawled on top of her, still painted like a pagan god. His hands were every-where, his body sliding against hers, smearing blood and ash across her naked flesh. Kara was hot—burning from the inside out. She wanted him to sheathe himself inside her. She wanted to be devoured. She moaned his name.

He bit her on the neck and said, "Welcome to the Brotherhood."

Kara blinked, and she was back in the stone cavern on her knees in front of the altar. Her mark was pulsing with a hot glow.

Logan was staring at her intently.

"What happened?" she asked, panting.

"I said welcome to the Brotherhood, Kara McKenna."

( )

AFTER THE CEREMONY WAS FINISHED, a feast awaited them in the great hall. Kegs of mead and barrels of wine were tapped for everyone's enjoyment. Olly had outdone himself with the food. A giant smoked boar from a recent hunt formed the centerpiece. There were stuffed pheasants and savory meat pies and tureens of mushroom and leek soup with bacon crumbled on top. He'd even prepared sweet honey almond tarts for dessert. Everyone mingled together at the dinner tables—there was no more separa-tion by ranks. Even Logan joined them for the meal.

"They didn't cull the herd as much as I expected," Thomas said. "Thought there'd be less of us after the eval-uations."

"The clan needs bodies," Feron said. He was the spit-ting image of his sister Faedra, plus some muscle and a rugged red beard. "Most of the work is done at the Reaping Trials. The evaluations are just a precautionary measure."

"Louts and oafs, that's what we bought at the trials," Athar grumbled, stabbing his fork into a hunk of boar. "Bleeders, blind men, and thieves. In my day the offering used to mean something."

"Did you guys...see anything? When you made your offering?" Kara asked.

They shook their heads no. "How much blood did you lose?" Thomas asked, raising his eyebrows.

Jon squeezed into a seat beside Kara, his goblet full of wine. "Some of the old timers say that if the altar stone likes your blood offering, it'll show you the future."

"Well? You see anything?" Faedra asked.

Athar snorted. "Maybe if they were high on scag. Pure drivel."

"Uhm...no." *Impossible*, Kara told herself as blood rushed to her cheeks. It'd been some trick of ritual and fog playing havoc with her mind, that was all. Maybe the air was thin down there. Yet she couldn't shake the feeling of Logan's eyes on her from his position at the head of the table. She met his gaze, then looked away.

"What did you guys offer when you were inducted?" she asked, trying to change the topic.

"My destiny," Jon said. "My parents are successful merchants. As their only child, I was poised to inherit the business, but I didn't want my future handed to me. I craved adventure, spontaneity."

"So your pockets were empty," Athar said, and they all laughed

"What about you, Athar?" Thomas asked.

"That's between me and old man Vakarian. Ain't no one else round here old enough to remember, 'cept maybe Rohan, and I like it that way."

"Wait. You mean Logan's father? Is he still alive?" Logan had brushed her off when she'd asked him before.

"The *Commander's* father, missy. And no. He led the clan when it split off from the Sanguines, but that got him killed, just like he knew it would. He was a great man—a king among men. The Mother took him too soon."

Jon nodded, his eyes downcast.

"And don't go askin' me how he died, either. That ain't my story to tell."

CHAPTER ELEVEN

The routine at Raven's Rest didn't change much following the induction ceremony. Kara and the other former recruits still trained most days of the week with the senior members of the clan to stay in shape and develop their skills. They also gained new duties, like patrolling the keep's walls and scouting the borders of Stygian territory on horseback.

The new inductees received their third month's wages and a bonus for passing their trial periods. Kara had never had so much money at once before. She'd had little occasion to spend any of it. The sum would have kept her, Da, and Wesley comfortably fed and clothed all winter long.

Kara's group of friends joined Jon and Feron in their morning training sessions. She quickly learned why Jon was second-in-command. He was deadly with a blade, and his clownish behavior evaporated in the ring, where he transformed into an intimidating force. Kara had as much chance of besting him in a fight as she did Logan. When she wasn't on duty or training with them, Kara intensified her blindfolded training, often going on long runs throughout the Blackshear without sight to guide her.

One afternoon Kara was perched on a stool in the stable, trying to take off her mud-splattered riding boots, when Jon came in. Kara and a team of Stygians had been trekking through a cold, rain-soaked bog all morning, helping a local farmer herd his escaped cattle back into their enclosure. The farmer's daughter had gone missing along with the cows, but they'd been unable to pick up her trail after hours of searching the mucky terrain.

"Team this morning have any luck?" Jon asked, leaning against a stall door. His copper hair was in need of a trim. It dangled around his eyes, and Kara found herself fighting the urge to brush it out of his face.

"No. I'm worried. At final count he was still missing three head, and the paddock fencing had clearly been vandalized. They didn't escape on their own."

"She'll turn up. They always do, sooner or later. Let's hope she just ran off with the miller's son."

"Hopefully."

"A little bird told me it was your birthday today."

Kara groaned. "You and the rest of the fortress. I never took Thomas for a gossip." At breakfast she'd been plied with trinkets and gifts, including a tortoiseshell comb from Ned, who'd advised her to put it to good use. Everett had asked if she'd killed anybody lately and offered her a roll in the hay once her keening began, an encounter that had almost ended in bloodshed.

"Not keen on receiving gifts?"

"I don't need anything," Kara said as she pried at her boot.

Jon moved towards her and motioned for her to give him her leg. She lifted her foot and put it in his hands, mud and all.

"What happened to the soles of your boots?"

"Obara."

Jon shook his head. "Don't think it's time for new ones?" He gripped her heel and gave the boot a swift tug. The stool beneath her wobbled precariously as her foot slipped free.

Kara smiled and lifted her other foot to him. "They're fine."

Jon rolled his eyes. "So you need nothing. What do you *want*, then?"

Impossibilities. "Let's see. An emerald ball gown. A team of six black horses and a carriage to match. A coat of diamonds. What do you think?"

Jon tossed her dirty boots back to her. "I think you want none of those things. Besides, red's more your color."

Kara stood and stretched, flexing her stockinged toes in the hay littering the stable floor. "You could tell me when we're going to start taking contracts. Patrol duty and night watch are getting boring." While the monthly pay was generous, contracts offered by private parties and organized by the Mercenary Guild were what made the clans their real money.

"Ever eager to run into danger. Logan should have something new for us soon, now that you tadpoles have grown legs. Stick with us, and you'll never be poor again."

( )

WHEN KARA RETURNED to the tower for a fresh change of clothes, a thin box fashioned of rich cedar planks awaited her on the foot of her bed. She paused upon seeing it, immediately suspicious. Who had managed to get into her room? She lifted the box gingerly, testing its weight. Then she lowered her ear to it, listening for the sound of snakes or bugs that might be wriggling about inside. She wouldn't put it past Jasper to prank her on her birthday, but the box was silent. Satisfied that it wasn't a trap, she lifted the lid.

Kara's jaw went slack. The box held twin jeweled daggers set within a velvet embrasure. The metalworking was phenomenal, and Kara could see her reflection clearly in the polished metal blades. The silver cross-guards were engraved with intricate, interlocking knotwork, and the grips were wrapped in black leather. A fat ruby the color of blood sat within each pommel. There were also two finely-tooled leather scabbards featuring the same knotwork that looked like they'd been custom fitted to these blades.

She searched the cedar case for a note, even taking out the velvet lining to look beneath it. Nothing. She scoured the room, but there were no clues as to who had left it. It unnerved her, this priceless gift with no acknowledgment of who'd sent it. It was impractical. What fledgling mercenary needed weapons like these? Weapons better kept on the mantle or in a display case. Who were they from? Logan had trained her with daggers, had been the first to suggest she start using them. Could they really be from him?

She picked up the daggers with trepidation. They were light and well-balanced, and they fit perfectly in the palms of her hands. They begged for blood when she held them. Kara removed her old scabbards and hooked the new ones to her belt, then slid the daggers home and headed towards the keep.

Kara entered the great hall and went up the main staircase, past the barracks on the second floor. She didn't know the exact location of Logan's quarters, but they had to be somewhere hereabouts. On the third floor she discovered a long hallway with several doors branching off it that looked like residential quarters. It was well-lit, and several paintings of horses hung on the walls. Did Rohan paint in his spare time?

Kara moved down the hallway, looking for a sign of which room could be Logan's. She came to the door at the end of the hall and stilled when voices came from within. It sounded like Rahj and Logan.

"One of my scouts in the Black Hills got a report to me."

Kara almost pulled away from the door and left, but the mention of the Black Hills made her pause. That was Sanguine territory. She pressed her right ear against the door, keeping an eye on the stairs for anyone that might come up. She tried not to think about what they'd do to her if they found her eavesdropping.

"Are more girls missing?" Logan said.

What girls?

"Yes. Several."

"I expected as much. Kara was lucky. What do you think he's after?"

"What is he always after? More power."

"He's building an army of cursed warriors. But who does he plan on fighting with them?"

Kara's heart sped up as their words clicked into place. The Sanguines must be gathering girls with Namirah's mark. It explained the interest of the merc back in Mudbottom and his insistence on keeping her alive.

"He hasn't made any moves. He's biding his time still."

"We need to do something," Logan said.

"We don't know where he's keeping them yet. It'd be a suicide mission."

"Put more people on it. Track everyone you know is involved. This doesn't sit well with me."

"If we interfere, it will end bloody. You know this."

"Even I have my limits. He's hunting my own. But we wait for the right time."

"Very well."

Footsteps headed towards the door, and Kara's heart jumped into her throat. She plastered herself against the wall beside the door hinges, praying that Rahj went towards the stairs.

The door swung open, and she clamped her mouth shut and didn't dare breathe or move a muscle. Rahj turned towards the stairs. The door swung shut a second later with a heavy thud. Once Rahj cleared her sight, Kara resisted the urge to bolt down the hallway. She forced herself to wait a few minutes more, in case Logan came out, too. Once she felt like it was safe, she crept back down the stairs and headed for the mess.

Kara mulled over the information she'd learned at dinner. She'd feared the true reason the Sanguines had come early to Mudbottom was for her, not the tithe, but this as good as confirmed it. Which meant she was the reason Da and Wesley were dead. The realization sobered her. She was surprised their deaths hadn't triggered her fucking curse. But how had the Sanguine mercenary known about her mark? Had one of the villagers sold her out? She wouldn't put it past them. And if the cursed warriors the Sanguines were gathering weren't all joining willingly, what was happening to them?

Kara waited until the mess hall cleared out and most of the mercenaries had gone down to the baths to return to Logan's room with the daggers. As she reached the third floor, she heard heavy footsteps on the stairwell behind her. Kara hurried to Logan's door and tested the latch. Unlocked. The door swung outward on oiled hinges, and Kara ducked inside. She was in a luxuriously appointed antechamber, complete with a sprawling mahogany desk and an armoire. An enchanted fae lantern floated by the desk, casting the papers covering it in a soft blue light. The orange glow of a fireplace came from the room beyond, but there were no sounds of movement coming from within.

Kara poked her head into the open bedchamber and immediately regretted it. Logan was standing naked before the fire, one hand braced on the mantelpiece, a towel slung casually over his shoulder. A towel which may have previously occupied his waist, but certainly no longer did. His bare feet were cushioned by a bearskin rug stretched in front of a towering four-poster bed. Kara's eyes dropped to the sculpted planes of his muscular butt and legs.

He didn't look up from the flames when he spoke. "You really ought to knock, Kara. Or was that your laughable attempt at being covert?"

Logan turned to face her, and Kara struggled to keep her eyes on the upper half of his body. "Why are you always naked?"

"You're in *my* chambers."

"Well, it's distracting."

"It's your birthday today, isn't it?" He said it low and soft, like a threat. Or a vow.

"Yes. Can you…" She gestured at his crotch, sneaking another glance. He was hard. And *big*. The longer she stared at him, the more erect he became. Saliva flooded her mouth.

"Any interesting gifts?"

Kara swallowed and jerked her gaze away. "Some lewd offers."

Logan lifted one dangerous eyebrow as he drew the towel off his shoulder and slowly knotted it around his waist. "*Offers?*"

"Not important. I came here to thank you for your gift, actually. I found it when I returned to the tower."

Logan looked confused for a moment. "Oh, the new ropes? They were installed yesterday. It is an efficient method of travel, I must admit. If incredibly dangerous."

Kara paused, taken aback. He'd had the ropes for the pulley outside her room replaced? She hadn't even noticed.

"I meant the daggers."

"Show me."

Kara slid one out of its sheath and handed it over to him. Logan examined the blade, running an experimental thumb over the edge until blood welled.

"Someone's certainly trying to impress you. It's fine steel, quality craftsmanship. And rubies the size of robin's eggs. The jewels seem impractical, though. Makes you a target for thieves more than anything. Pretty, I suppose."

Kara's face fell. Logan passed the dagger back to her.

"They're not from you?"

"Why would I give you such gaudy rubbish? No, they're not from me. Perhaps you have an admirer."

"Fucking hell," Kara said, shoving the dagger back into its scabbard. "I've had enough of admirers." She tried to shrug off the wave of disappointment that had washed over her when he'd said they weren't from him.

Logan shrugged. "You could always pawn them at the markets. Fetch a tidy sum."

"Seems a bit rude."

"Do what you will, then. I'll not involve myself in your love troubles." Logan picked up a poker from the hearth and prodded the fire. "You ought to know that I'll be announcing a mission tomorrow. Rahj has received reports that the Sanguine Riders are extorting tithes from the people of Innistown, a small settlement within our southern border."

Kara's ears pricked up at that. She was eager to get her hands on Sanguine flesh, especially after what she'd overheard earlier. "What are you going to do?"

"Victus is testing us. I can't let the exploitation continue without appearing weak, but I'd prefer to resolve the matter diplomatically if possible."

"When do we leave?"

"You're not coming, Kara."

"Oh," she said, her voice dropping. "Who all is going then?"

"Most of your fellow recruits. That's why I wanted to tell you personally, before it's announced."

Kara's chest constricted. He was going to force her to sit out? "I'm just as good as them, though. And I'm familiar with the Sanguine tithes. My family—"

"Is exactly why I'm not bringing you. I know you haven't abandoned your rage where the Sanguines are concerned, and this needs to be handled with tact. I don't need you distracting me or jeopardizing the current peace."

Kara clenched her fists. Logan kept his back to her, staring into the fire. Hiding.

"Please, Logan."

"I'm sorry, Kara."

Kara left without saying a word.

CHAPTER TWELVE

A day later, Kara rose at dawn and watched from the battlements as the Innistown mission rode out. She was furious. All of this training, and her first opportunity to get close to the Sanguines was a total bust. She considered tailing the group, but they'd likely spot her tracking them and send her back. She was tempted to leave altogether, to trek out on her own in search of information on Cervus and the other members of the raiding party. She was getting nowhere here. But she had limited funds and no idea where to start. Would the Stygians hunt her down if she broke her contract? She didn't think she could hide from them forever.

The fortress fell into silence as the sounds of the riding party faded into the distance. Kara dropped into her usual series of morning stretches to warm up her muscles. The fog was dense this morning, forming a thick carpet over the forest floor. She needed to go for a run and get her frustrations out. The gloom and stillness permeating Raven's Rest following the group's departure was only aggravating her further.

Kara rode the weighted pulley down the wall after testing the strength of the new ropes and landed with a soft thump in the courtyard below. She donned Logan's silken black blindfold as she left the fortress via the postern gate and headed for the forest.

The Blackshear was unusually quiet this morning. No songbirds accompanied the cawing of crows and soft flitting of the tree beetles. Kara began with a light jog, feeling her way through the well-worn paths at the forest's edges. The deeper she went, the thicker the undergrowth became. Footpaths tread by men in boots faded into faint deer trails.

Kara focused on her breathing, inhaling and exhaling deep and slow. As she picked up speed, the cold air bit at her face, and branches and leaves whipped her skin. She tore through a sticky spiderweb and shuddered but kept going. When she heard the roar of Widow's Fall in the distance, it curled around her like a warm embrace. She forced herself to veer away from it, heading northwest instead. The smell of mildew and dead leaves invaded her nostrils. Kara leapt over a wide root in her path, but her feet met air instead of earth, and she was falling.

She came crashing down against something hard that snapped beneath her. Pain blossomed across her back. Kara tore off her blindfold and swore. She was at the bottom of a deep pit riddled with wooden spikes. A white goat was impaled on the spikes in front of her. It had died recently. The blood that had coagulated around its wounds was still fresh, and the corvids and carrion beetles had yet to pick it over. Some kind of animal trap, then. Who had made it? To her knowledge, the Stygians didn't have traps like this in the forest. They tended to track their prey. Kara pulled the stake she'd broken during her fall out from beneath her. Her back was sore and scraped where she'd landed against the spear, but she was able to move around with only dull pain. She was lucky she hadn't been impaled.

Kara looked up, gauging the distance to the top of the pit. Ten feet of earth separated her from the forest floor. She tugged one of the spears out of the ground and impaled it in the dirt wall of the pit, then stepped onto it. It began to bend and sink in the wet dirt. It'd been raining off and on all week, and the ground was soaked. Kara hopped down and cursed. She tried with another spear, stepping onto it and jumping as high as she could. She sunk her fingers into the damp earth, scrabbling for purchase. She was still far from the pit's edge. Earth began to crumble between her fingers and fall into her eyes. She lost her hold and slid back towards the bottom.

Kara tried several more times to scrabble up the wall, but there were no roots or rocks to hold onto, and each time she lost her grip and began to fall. "Fucking fuck!" she screamed, kicking one of the spears. As if today could get any worse. Kara didn't know how long the mission in Innistown would take. Rohan and Ridley were still at the fortress, but it would be hours before they noticed she was missing, and she wasn't near any of the patrol paths. Someone might come to check the trap, sooner or later, but that begged the question of who had built it in the first place. The only people who hunted the Blackshear were the mountain tribesmen, but they rarely came so far south of the mountain. How deep into the forest had she gone? Kara cursed Logan to a thousand hells for not just taking her with him.

She pried one of the stakes out of the ground to use as a weapon, in case the scent of the goat's blood drew predators. She usually brought a pair of daggers with her on her runs, but she'd forgotten them in her rush to leave this morning. She was angry at herself for her own incompetence. If she'd been paying more attention—

A fat droplet of rain plunked down in the center of Kara's head. More droplets swiftly followed. Kara looked up to the sky. Dark clouds loomed over the forest, casting her in shadow. "Of course." She pulled the hood of her cloak up and dragged the goat's corpse off the spikes, draping it across her body for warmth as she nestled against the wall of the pit. All there was left to do was wait.

KARA AWOKE to the sound of squishing leaves and rough voices, and relief surged through her. Maybe she wouldn't die in this hole after all.

A man with thick, gnarled hair and a thin face smeared with soot leaned over the edge of the pit. His eyes widened in surprise when he saw Kara, then they narrowed on the dead goat.

"Girly in hole," he yelled. "Girly has goat."

"Please help me," Kara called up to him. She squinted up against the sun stabbing at her eyes.

The man shook his head vigorously. "Murk build trap," he said, pointing to himself. "Murk's goat. Girly steal goat."

"No!" Kara said, shoving the dead goat away from her. Mud and blood had soaked through her breeches overnight and dried, leaving them a crusty brown color. "You can have the goat. I just want to get out."

Two more men joined Murk at the edge of the pit and peered down at her. Kara palmed the wooden spear and hid it behind her, eyeing them.

"My, my, boys. It's our lucky day, we got a two-for-one," said a man in a patchy cloak with a hood that hid his eyes.

The third man had a copper ring in his eyebrow and a greasy blond ponytail. He clapped Murk on the back. "Did well, Murk. Is she comelier than the last one? I can't see under all that mud. Come on, pull her up."

Murk didn't look pleased by the idea. He shook his head again. "Girly scrawny, no meat. Goat first. I want hooves. And eyeballs."

"Whatever you say, Murk," the greasy one said.

Murk beamed, then slithered a rope down to the bottom of the pit. "Give me goat!" he yelled.

Kara tied the rope around the goat's hooves, trepidation curling in her gut. What were these men doing so close to Raven's Rest? They lifted the goat out of the pit, and Murk disappeared from the edge. A grotesque sawing noise came from above.

The blond man made to toss down the rope again, and the cloaked one stopped him with a hand against his chest. He was looking over the bottom of the pit.

"Wait, Segen. One of the spears is unaccounted for. Drop your weapon, girl, or we'll leave you here to rot."

This one was keen, Kara noted, which meant he was dangerous. She reluctantly rolled the wooden spear to the center of the pit and clambered to her feet. She still had a small throwing knife tucked within her boot, provided they didn't find it.

"Go ahead," the cloaked man said.

Segen lowered the rope into the pit, and they hauled her up. Kara scrambled over the ledge and sunk her fingers into the forest mulch. The men surrounded her. They were armed with bows and flinthead spears. Murk had blood on his lips, and the goat was missing one of its horns. Her only route of escape was behind her, back into the pit.

"People are expecting me," she said, trying to keep her

tone calm and measured as she began to stand. "Thank you for—"

The cloaked man shoved her flat against the ground, straddled her waist, and jerked her hands behind her back. Panic flared. Kara struggled beneath him, and he twisted her wrists painfully. He was heavy—he'd be hard to flip, and she doubted she'd get far against three of them.

Segen crouched down in front of Kara, inspecting her with a leering grin. He ran a hand through her hair, and she tried to jerk away. His nails were crusted with dirt and blood. "Pretty, this one. She's even got all her teeth. How refreshing."

The man on top of her tied a length of rope around her wrists, yanking it tight, then hauled Kara up and spun her around.

The hood had fallen off his head, and Kara's blood ran cold when she saw his face. A gnarled, hollow socket full of scar tissue stared at her where his left eye used to be. It was the Sanguine she'd stabbed in Mudbottom. He was thinner now, with long, matted hair, but she recognized his face from her dreams.

Recognition dawned in his eyes. *"You,"* he spit. "You cost me everything, you little bitch."

Kara tried to pull away, and he gripped her by the neck, squeezing tight.

"One-Eye," Murk whined. "We got a goat."

"Shut up, Murk. We can't let her go. She's a Stygian. She escapes, she'll tattle, and we'll all be dead in our beds come morn."

"You know her?" Segen asked.

"Saw her at the trials," One-Eye said. "Before Victus kicked me out. She owes me something very dear." His grip on her neck tightened, and Kara's vision started to go dark at the edges. She tried to silence the horror gripping her mind. She had to remain calm if she wanted to get out of this alive. Fear would cripple her.

"Think she learned how to suck cock over in Castle Birdshit?" Segen asked.

One-Eye chuckled. "I intend to find out." He released her throat, and Kara gasped for air. He jerked her against him and took his time rubbing his hands up her legs and abdomen, feeling for weapons.

"Murk!" Kara yelled, turning to look him in the eyes. "Please help me!" Murk glanced up from gnawing on the tattered meat at the end of the goat's horn, seemingly torn.

Kara's head snapped back as One-Eye's fist hit her square in the jaw. She tasted blood, and her jaw ached when she stretched it out.

"Shut up, Stygian whore, or I'll cut out your tongue and fry it for my supper. Or perhaps your eyes," One-Eye said.

Segen and One-Eye hauled her up by the shoulders and began dragging her northwest, deeper within the shadow of the mountain.

HOURS LATER, well past the range of the Stygian patrols, they reached a camp set up against the base of a mountain. Dusk loomed on the horizon. Human skulls pierced by tall wooden stakes formed a ring around their sleeping tents. The tents were covered with a strange, stretchy leather that looked unnaturally pale in the firelight.

One-Eye drug Kara over to a tiny, rusting cage and pulled out his dagger. He dragged the sharp tip across the top of her right cheekbone, splitting the skin. Blood dripped down her face. Kara grit her teeth against the pain. She dared not move, lest the dagger slip.

"You owe me an eye, girl. I've a mind to carve it out."

"Come on!" Segen said. "At least let us have our fun first. I don't wanna be reminded of you when I'm fucking her."

"Soon," One-Eye whispered, then he shoved Kara into the cage and locked the latch behind her. Kara fell forward on her face. She used her legs to twist herself around and get a better view of her surroundings. The stench was nauseating. Situated next to her cage was a putrid cow carcass, wriggling with flies and maggots after being stripped of most of its meat. On the far side of the tents, two other cows grazed on sparse grass within a crude enclosure. Kara had found the cattle thieves.

One-Eye and Segen set to skinning the goat and spitting its body over the fire. They threw the hooves at Murk, nailing him in the head and side as he fumbled to dodge them. Murk gathered up the hooves and began hammering at them with a rock, breaking them into small slivers. A roach skittered through the bars of Kara's cage. She suppressed a shudder and crushed it beneath the heel of her boot.

Once night fell, two more men returned to the camp. One was older, wiry, and he wore a mask made of tiny bones wired together. The other was the youngest of the group. He wore a red suede vest embroidered with flowering vines. The old man bowed before the skulls and crossed his face with a ward sign before entering the camp. The beady eyes behind the mask immediately focused on Kara.

"What's this?" he said. "We don't need another offering this month. What have you done?"

"Relax, Harren. She came to us. Found her in one of Murk's traps, just waiting for us to come and rescue her," Segen said.

"She's a black 'un," One-Eye said, picking at his teeth with a sharpened bone.

"You brought a Stygian *here?* To my camp? Have you gone mad, boy? Do you know what they'll do to us?" Harren started to pace before the fire and scratch at his forearms.

"We're not letting her go, Harren," One-Eye said.

"They ain't found us yet, have they?" Segen said.

"And now you've taken one of their own. A woman, no less. They'll come looking for her, come sniffing around our mountain."

"Calm down, old man," One-Eye said.

"Out of my sight, both of you!" Harren yelled. "Patch, take watch tonight. No one touches the girl." Harren began stroking his mask and muttering to himself. "Perhaps it's a sign. Must consult the sorceress."

Murk brought Kara a bowl of grey gruel and attempted to feed her through the cage. Kara took a cautious bite, then spit it out when she bit down on sharp, brittle shards of hoof. Murk looked at her with sad eyes and scampered away, taking the gruel with him.

Kara kept herself awake, waiting until Patch was dozing at his post and the other men were asleep to retrieve her knife. A strange calm had come over her. She had to keep her head if she was going to get out of this alive. She lifted her feet overhead and twisted and shook, trying to shake the blade loose from the hidden sheath in her boot. Finally it slipped out, falling in the dirt beside her. *You're going to be okay*, Kara told herself. *You can do this*. She sidled over to the knife and stretched out her fingers, feeling for the hilt. She grasped it, flipped it up, and started sawing through the ropes binding her hands.

Her stomach growled and hummed with hunger. She was going on two days without food. The sentry began to snore, and the fire gradually died. Midst the glowing embers was a long, charred bone—not the right size for a goat or a cow. A human femur, Kara realized with dread. Were the skulls studding the perimeter fresh? She had to make her escape attempt soon, before she grew any weaker.

Once she was through the ropes, Kara crawled over to the cage door and attempted to pick the lock with the tip of her knife. The rusted metal whined, and Patch jerked his head up, blinking his way back to alertness. Kara froze, fear wrapping its fist around her heart. It pounded in her chest like a drum. She silently crept back to the rear of the cage and slid her wrists through the loose loops of rope, keeping her knife gripped tight in her palm.

She tried to rest to regain some energy, but she slept fitfully, waking up in jerks throughout the night. This high in the mountains, sometimes the blistering wind sounded like screams. Maybe they were Namirah's, still echoing across the range years later. Trapped.

THE NEXT MORNING Kara's arms were sore from being twisted behind her back all night, and her back and jaw ached fiercely. Her mark itched as well, but she couldn't move to scratch it without arousing suspicion.

Murk was playing a game with himself using some tiny white rocks over by the cow enclosure. Segen relit the fire and put a hunk of dripping meat on to roast. The smell of it made Kara salivate.

"She looks hungry," Segen said, walking over to the cage.

"Murk gave her some gruel," One-Eye said, laughing.

"Then maybe she's hungry for something else, eh, girl?

Or didn't the black ones keep you busy? Where's the key, Harren? I've waited long enough."

Harren ducked out of his tent, waving his arms. "Stop, you rutting bastard. You defiled my last offering, surely ruining the viability of the ritual. Namirah will shower favors upon us if we do it properly this time, I'm sure of it. If you just show restraint until the full moon—"

Kara swung her head towards Harren. He was worshiping Namirah? Had he missed the news that she was forty years dead?

"No mate. Bad mate," Murk chattered to himself, tossing the white stones and scooping them up again.

"She lived with the Stygians, you git. She's been defiled a thousand times over by now," Segen said.

Kara watched silently as One-Eye picked up the hatchet beside the wood pile and came up behind Harren. With one forceful swing, he buried the hatchet in the back of Harren's skull. Harren fell, twitching, his mouth still agape. *One down.*

Segen stepped back from the widening pool of blood. "The fuck, One-Eye? What'd you do that for?" Patch glanced up, then resumed rotating the spit over the fire.

One-Eye shrugged, bending down to fish the cage key out of Harren's trouser pocket. "Old badger's been grating on my nerves since we left the village. Didn't come out here so I could be preached to in the wilderness. He was no prophet, just some scagged up old loon with a peculiar appetite that thought a dead woman was talkin' to him." He smacked the cage key down in Segen's hand. "Besides, now you can fuck her without him yipping in your ear. Go on, then. We all want a turn. Maybe Murk will even have a go, eh?"

They all laughed. Kara shook against her bonds, rage boiling up inside her. Fear evaporated like smoke. She tried to quell the anger, to tamp it down and get control of it. Her wrist burned beneath the ropes.

Murk covered his head with his arms and rocked back and forth. Segen opened the lock and ducked inside the cage. He dragged Kara out, yanking her up by the hair and inhaling her scent. His grisly beard scraped against her face.

"Do you know how long it's been since I've lain with a woman who didn't stink of barbarity? I'm going to savor this."

One-Eye yanked the hatchet out of Harren's skull and wiped the blood and brains off on his pants.

Segen's hands began to roam over Kara's chest, ripping at her blouse.

"Don't you worry. I'm a real gentleman compared to these two. Won't bloody ye up or nothin'. Hell, I'll even use spit—"

Kara twisted out of the loose rope bonds and slammed her knife into Segen's throat. Blood gurgled out of his mouth, his eyes wide with surprise. Kara screwed the blade in deeper, taking pleasure in the crunch of cartilage as she mangled his windpipe. She yanked the blade out and whirled on One-Eye.

"You bitch!" he yelled, lifting the hatchet and racing towards her. He was so slow, a glacier compared to Kara. Power pulsed through her veins, a relentless drumbeat calling for blood. She dodged his swing and stabbed him in the gut. Once. Twice. Three times. She wanted him to die slow. She ripped the hatchet out of his fingers and whirled around.

Murk screamed. Blood was everywhere. Patch scrambled up from the fire and grabbed his bow. He sent an arrow straight at her, and she slid to the right. A blaze of pain shot through her left shoulder. Patch reached for his quiver, and Kara hurled the hatchet at him. It somersaulted through the air, landing with a sickening squelch in the meat of his thigh. He staggered to the ground, clutching his leg.

Kara snatched up one of their spears and ran towards him, keeping a careful eye on his bow arm. "Please. I didn't do anything," he begged, eyes wide with fear.

"Exactly." Kara used her momentum to shove the spear up under his sternum, impaling him on the shaft. His breath rattled in a dying gasp.

Kara walked back over to One-Eye. He was still alive, his breaths labored as blood leaked out of his abdomen.

Kara knelt beside him. "That was for my father. And this—" Kara dug a finger into one of the holes she'd made in his stomach. "—this is for my brother."

One-Eye screamed and clutched at her forearm, digging in with his nails. She didn't feel the pain.

"Where is Victus keeping the marked women he's captured?" she demanded.

"You'll hang…just like all the others."

"Tell me!"

One-Eye laughed, and it made a wet sound. His face was going pale. "Blooded yourself for a traitor brother that's still alive."

"My brother's dead, asshole."

His voice was a raspy stutter. "Not dead. *Red.*"

Kara grabbed him by the collar and hauled him up. He had to be lying—she'd seen Wesley's coat, the body, but if there was even a chance… "Where is he? What happened to him?"

"Already. Told ya." His grip on her arm went lax, his eyes losing focus.

Kara dropped him, still seething. Was he just fucking with her, trying to get into her head? Could Wesley really be alive still? She hated the seed of hope that sprung in her chest.

A whimpering came from the other side of camp. Murk cowered by the tents, mewling. Kara walked over to him, letting rage drape over her like a familiar cloak.

"Only goat, girly. Only goat," he kept repeating. He held up one of the white stones in his hand, offering it to her. It was a human tooth. She looked over at the pale, freckled skin stretched to form the tent flaps and the skulls studding the camp's perimeter. The farmer's daughter had met a worse fate than she ever could have imagined.

Kara's blood sang with rage. She drew Murk's head towards her in a gentle embrace, stroked his tangled hair, and laid her knife against his throat. One-Eye's blood stained his neck. Adrenaline pumped through her veins. She imagined cutting into his skin, imagined his hot blood trickling over her fingers and his body going limp in her arms. She shuddered and unclenched her fingers one by one, until the knife fell to the earth. Murk turned to look at her with wide eyes, then scrambled into the woods.

They were all dead—she was soaked in their blood— and still it wasn't enough. Bloodlust hammered against her skull, insistent. Kara pulled the hatchet out of Patch's leg and started to hack.

CHAPTER THIRTEEN

Night had long fallen when the shadow of Raven's Rest came into view through the trees. Kara stumbled onward. The barbed arrowhead embedded deep within the muscle of her shoulder had started to ache three miles back, and now it burned viciously with every step. The sentry on duty spotted her as soon as she cleared the trees and blew his warning horn. Rohan met her by the postern gate. The grounds were quiet.

"Kara? Is that you? We've been looking everywhere—"

"Is Logan here?" she asked.

"Nae, they've yet to return."

"Good." Kara stepped forward into the pool of weak torchlight, and Rohan blanched. Blood dripped from the burlap sack she carried onto her boots.

"Shivans, you're covered in blood…Who did this? Are they still alive?" he growled. She'd never heard Rohan sound so menacing.

Kara lifted the sack and dropped it on the ground "No."

"What's in the bag, lass?"

"A souvenir." Her tongue was thick with thirst, her lips chapped and cracking. She swayed on her feet.

Rohan rushed forward and caught her in his arms before she fell over. "Come on, let's get you to Bart."

When they staggered into the infirmary, Bart looked up and swore. He slipped the book he'd been reading into his desk drawer and lit a fire beneath his alembic.

"Put her on the cot."

Rohan laid her down and smoothed a hand over her brow. "She's feverish."

"Rouse Olly and have him heat up some broth. Something simple—no chunks. She'll need to eat when I'm done."

Rohan appeared reluctant to leave. "Is she going to be okay? I don't know what happened, but it looks ugly…"

Bart's gaze darted between Rohan and Kara. "There are some wounds I can't heal. Now go, I need to be alone with her."

Rohan left, and Bart came at Kara with a large pair of scissors. He cut away her bloodied, muddy clothes, then bundled them up and tossed them in his wood furnace.

"Hey," Kara said, sitting up.

"Sit back and stop fretting, or you'll burrow that arrowhead even deeper. Those rags are nothing but blood and bad memories now." Bart shuffled over to his desk and began taking down various herb jars from his shelves. His voice turned grave. "Kara, you should know…I can brew you an elixir that prohibits fertility if…should you need it. I already have the ingredients."

"No need, Bart," Kara said, her throat hoarse.

Bart let out a deep sigh. "Good, good." He drew the alembic off the burner and poured its contents into a cup. "Here, drink this."

"What is it?"

"Something to knock you out. I need to operate without you squirming about like an eel."

Kara downed the cup quickly, eager for oblivion.

BART KEPT Kara on bedrest in the infirmary for another two days before giving her the all clear to leave, arming her with a jar of poultice and instructions for re-dressing her shoulder. He also gave her a leather necklace that was strung with a smooth black stone carved into the shape of a rune.

"What's this?" Kara asked.

"A contraceptive charm, should you need it in the future. I know your keening approaches, now that…well, after what happened. I picked it up in town. It's simpler than brewing a tea, but that's also an option. And if you'd prefer the charm on a different item, we can contact a mage who specializes in them."

"This is very thoughtful, Bart. Thank you." Kara took the necklace and looped it around her neck, then tucked it into her shirt. She was more relaxed about having triggered the curse than she'd anticipated. In a way, she was glad it was over—no longer looming over her like a threat. The men she'd killed had deserved it, and it'd been her only way out of a terrible situation. She was lucky to be alive.

One-Eye's dying words haunted her, though. She'd played them over and over in her head on the slow, excruciating journey back to Raven's Rest, committing them to memory. She wanted to believe that Wesley could be alive. Her mind clung to the idea like a raft in the ocean. But she felt like a fool to take the Sanguine at his word. What if it was his idea of a cruel joke, an attempt to get into her head? She needed to find another Sanguine that'd been at Mudbottom to get answers.

Kara went to the great hall for dinner and was in the middle of eating a hearty stew when the clamor of horses and voices in the courtyard signaled the clan's return from Innistown. The doors blew open, and Logan was the first one through them. He was dressed in full black leather, and dark shadows marred his cheeks where he hadn't shaved. His gaze swept the room, landing on her. His face tensed when he saw her. She could see him scanning each of her injuries, calculating the damage. She had dark, mottled bruises on her jaw and back. Scabs on her forearm. A new hole in her shoulder, plus twenty other tiny scrapes and bruises.

Logan sat down in front of her and began pulling off his gloves. The muscle in his jaw ticked. "Why are there four severed heads collecting flies atop my gates?"

Kara blew on her stew and took another sip. "What makes you think I had anything to do with it?"

"You're done up in Bart's swaddling, for one. And I'm familiar with your proclivity for disaster."

"I don't want to talk about it," Kara said, lowering her eyes.

Logan snapped his gloves against the table. "You don't decorate my walls with dead men and then *not talk about it*."

"Rohan put them up there, not me. It wasn't my idea."

"He was with you?"

"No. I was alone, running the Blackshear. Fell into their trap, and they——" her voice cracked. "They dragged me to their camp. They'd turned cannibal, Logan. Took the farmer's daughter and his cows. Likely others before her. It was horrible."

"You took on four of them?" Logan raised his eyebrows.

"Three. There was in-fighting." She waited for his admonishment. He'd warned her about going into the woods alone. He'd berate her for not being more careful, for endangering herself. Tell her she'd been foolish to get caught. Kara rolled her shoulder and winced at the sharp pain. Something flickered in Logan's eyes. He took her hand between his own, the intensity of his grip belying his relative calm.

"Are you okay, Kara? I don't just mean your injuries."

"I don't know," she answered honestly. "I'm still coming to."

"I'm here to talk when you're ready. I'll give the farmer the news."

"What?" *Was that it?*

"You did well. I'm glad you're safe. But you know what will be coming now."

"Yes."

"Let me know when you feel it."

"Why? You going to help me feed it?"

Logan's eyes flared, and he ran his tongue along his teeth behind his lips.

"I still don't think that would be wise. But I don't want you to suffer, Kara. We need to make arrangements. If you don't want to go to the Chambers or elsewhere, it may be possible for us to find you a prisoner—someone who's already destined for execution, if you'd rather take that route. I know of a noble girl who addresses her keening that way, since her parents would like to keep her pure for her future husband."

Kara glanced up at Logan. He didn't seem at all fazed by suggesting she kill someone in cold blood. She didn't think she was ready to start playing executioner, especially after her encounter with the mountain men. "I—I'll think about it. Maybe Vhaidra?" The courtesan's sloe-black eyes and lithe curves flashed in her mind, but Kara felt numb. "I don't know." She still wanted what she couldn't have.

He gave her hand a tight squeeze. "You'll have to choose eventually. Mind that shoulder. I'm going to need you soon."

CHAPTER FOURTEEN

Rumor of Kara's encounter with the mountain men spread quickly throughout Raven's Rest, and everyone began to look at her with newfound respect. There were sparks of fear in some eyes that hadn't been there before. Thomas and Faedra wanted a detailed account of how she'd killed them and escaped, but Kara refused to talk about it. She didn't want to relive those blood-crazed moments, to remember the light slowly fading from their eyes. It was the first time she'd killed someone, and she'd done it ruthlessly. In a manner that made her question herself. It unnerved her, how normal she felt. What was she becoming?

Her shoulder healed surprisingly quickly, and she was able to return to exercises after they celebrated the new year. Bart told her that fast healing was a benefit of the curse. She could feel it unfurling inside her, like some long-dormant beast rising from hibernation. And it was hungry.

During simple sparring drills her nerves were piqued and pulsing, her body calling for blood with each swing. Everyday moments around the fortress began to feel sexually charged. Kara became acutely aware of how many muscular men in various stages of undress she was surrounded by on a daily basis. A lingering look, an innocent touch on her bare arm, and her core would heat, sending her mind racing from thoughts of blood and death to more lascivious things.

Kara ran to stave off the unwelcome sensations and exhaust herself. She didn't don any more blindfolds and stayed far from the mountains, exploring the southern reaches of the Blackshear instead. Yet when she fell into bed every night, bone-tired, she was still plagued by dreams. Nightmares of what might have happened had she not escaped the mountain men woke her, her limbs heavy with sleep and her heart pounding in her throat.

The nightmares were interspersed with dreams of sweat and skin. Logan's burning eyes and the pulsing glow of his mark seared themselves into her mind. In her dreams he ran rough hands over her naked flesh, kissed the undersides of her breasts, and bit her on the neck as she strained against him. She woke twisted in the sheets and soaked in sweat despite the chill winter air, haunted by a wanting, a need that felt just out of reach. She begged the mother goddess to take her dreams, or at the very least change the subject of them. Logan had already rejected her twice. She wasn't going to beg him to reconsider. Worry about who she would find as an alternative hung heavy on her mind. She needed to come up with a solution soon.

Kara went out of her way to avoid Logan around the fortress, going so far as to take her meals to the tower room when he made the rare appearance in the great hall. She was afraid to look him in the eye, lest he read her thoughts in a glance.

After sparring drills one morning, Kara pulled Thomas

aside. He'd begun to fill out his lanky form with muscle, though the scar marring his eyebrow did little to counteract his boyish features.

"I need to talk to you in private."

"Alright," he said and sheathed his sword.

They walked to the far side of the yard, away from the groups of Stygians in various stages of warming up and running drills.

"I have a favor to ask you."

"What do you need, Kara?"

Kara took a deep breath, steeling herself. "Would you be willing to…to keen with me?" Thomas was one of her closest friends in the brotherhood, but things had always been strictly platonic between them. He was the easygoing sort, and she thought that they'd still be able to be friends after her keening.

Thomas froze, his cheeks going red. Then he took off his glasses, rubbed the lenses with his tunic, and put them back on. "Kara? That is you. Had to check."

"Please be serious, Thomas."

"What would keening with you even entail, exactly? You know what, I don't want to know. I'd be crazy to even consider it. I'm sorry, Kara, but I can't."

Kara frowned and bit her lip. "I thought you were open minded where the curse is concerned."

"I am. Don't get me wrong—you're fantastic, beautiful—any man would be lucky to have you. And I'm flattered that you asked," he stammered, "but I don't have a death wish."

"I wouldn't kill you, Thomas."

Thomas fiddled with the pommel of his sword and glanced around before speaking. "Not you. The Commander. I've seen the way he looks at you. Like a hawk eyeing its prey."

"He doesn't want me," Kara said. *Or maybe he does, but not badly enough.*

"Bullshit. You remember that day we interrupted him in his office? He wanted to bite my head off."

"He's made it clear he's not interested."

Thomas's head snapped towards her. "You asked him? You've got some balls on you, I'll give you that. Look, maybe he's trying to keep up appearances. Maybe it's a guardianship thing—he feels like he has to protect you, and keening with you would get in the way of that. But whatever it is, I don't want to get involved."

"Fine," Kara sighed. "Leave me. I need to think."

"You going to be okay?" He tried to nudge her chin up with his hand, and she tore her head away as her blood heated, unbidden. She stared at her feet, avoiding eye contact, afraid of what her eyes might reveal.

"Yes. Just go, Thomas."

( )

As THE DAYS passed and Kara's urges grew worse and her dreams more intense, she began to sleep less and drink more. She invested in several flagons of Ridley's special autumn brew, as he called it—a thick apple cider that got her tanked in three cups.

Jon was absent from their morning training sessions, as he was frequently called to meetings with the inner circle, and soon Kara stopped sparring with the others in the yard altogether. She was afraid of losing control and hurting someone. She gave her friends an excuse about pain in her healing shoulder and instead went to the forest, armed with flask and sword, to practice by herself until she grew clumsy from drink. When she stared into her cracked mirror at night, fighting sleep, her eyes had dark shadows beneath them. Her hair fell limp and lackluster, and the edges of her irises crawled with filaments of yellow and orange that hadn't been there before.

One unseasonably warm afternoon, Kara donned her coat and took a stroll to a small pond she'd discovered whilst exploring the southern reaches of the Blackshear. It was tucked away within a sunny little glade surrounded by evergreens, their branches heavy with snowfall. The forest was quiet, muted. The water wasn't frozen over yet, but it was sure to be frigid. It'd be a welcome change to her sweat-slicked nights.

Kara unbuckled her sword belt and undressed, and the frosty air bit at her bare skin. She waded into the shallows, and the cold rushed up her spine. It was invigorating. Water lilies encrusted with frost parted in her path, and tiny golden fish darted between her legs, tickling her skin. When her toes could no longer reach the bottom, she relaxed and let her body float to the surface of the water

The icy water lapped around her head, distorting her hearing each time her ears submerged. Some of the fervor in her blood cooled, and the water soothed the angry scar left by Patch's arrow. Kara cleared her mind and let the serenity of the moment sink into her. The gentle current pushed her to the center of the pond, where a beam of sunlight broke through the trees and washed over her face. It was the first time she'd felt at peace in weeks.

Something rustled in the bushes, and Kara slowed her breathing and gradually lifted her head. A deer or moose in the area, maybe. A man snickered. Kara sank beneath the water and began gliding towards her weapons, moving slowly so as not to disturb the surface above. When her feet touched the shore, she pushed up with force, exploding in a burst of water and reaching for her daggers.

Daggers that weren't there. Everything was gone—her

clothes, her boots, her weapons. There was a snap of branches and the thudding of hooves as the thieves fled. Kara glimpsed a shock of white-blond hair through the trees as she rushed forward. Something snapped inside her, and all the rage she'd tried to suppress over the past week came bubbling up with a vengeance.

She would wager that today's southern border patrol—the one Jasper had been assigned to this morning—had decided to play a trick on her. Apparently they were acquainted with her pond. And they'd left her here, in the middle of Blackshear Forest in winter, defenseless and naked. Kara strode forward, batting tree branches out of her way, her body flush with anger. And then she broke into a run.

Luckily most of the ground snow had melted this morning. Her feet were supple against the roots that crawled the forest floor. More than one prickly spur wedged itself into the soft flesh between her toes, but she kept going, numb to the pain. Anger fueled her. Namirah's mark pulsed with ragged insistence. She was so sick of Jasper and his conniving, belittling antics. He was a worm. He was nothing. *All* she'd wanted was a moment of peace, some time away from the dark urges that plagued her. He was going to pay. *Weakling man.* A little slip of the dagger was nothing.

Kara picked up her pace as she neared the fortress, and she sprinted from the edge of the trees to the open portcullis. Her chest heaved with the effort, but she wasn't winded yet. She'd been conditioning herself for this for months. The members of the patrol wouldn't expect her back so soon. They'd been on horses, after all. As Kara crossed the courtyard, Rohan came out of the stable. He dropped the pail of grain he was carrying and stared.

She rushed up the keep steps and pushed through the

great hall doors, striding inside with single-minded intent. Her bare shoulders, chest, and calves were scratched up from whipping through branches and brush. Blood pooled around a toe that she'd smashed against a rock hidden in the earth, but all she felt was rage

Stygians filled the great hall. Their guffaws and intakes of breath, their mutters of interest and appreciation were deafened by the blood rushing through her ears. She was stone. She was fire. Kara honed in on Jasper's table. He and Everett laughed about something with their friends over mugs of ale. Jasper turned to see what the commotion in the aisle was about. When he spotted Kara, he stood up from the table, looked her over, and licked his lips.

Kara didn't slow her stride. When she was within arm's reach of him, Jasper smirked at her and made a lewd gesture. She spotted the glint of a ruby pommel at his hip and lost it. With her marked arm she gripped him by the throat and lifted him up off his feet. She snaked her other hand towards his waist and tore her dagger out of his scabbard. In a flash the tip of the blade was under his chin, threatening to impale him. The laughter in Jasper's eyes faded, quickly shifting to fear.

"Put me down, you bitch," he gurgled around the tip of the knife.

"Say one more word, lordling, and I will kill you."

"You wouldn't dare."

Kara pricked Jasper's throat with the dagger, and blood welled around the sharp tip. It excited her.

"Last warning. I need someone to kill this month." Namirah's mark pulsed with a fiery intensity. Doors slammed in the distance. People stared on in mute horror and fascination. She was going to kill him.

"Kara!" Logan's voice boomed. "Put him down."

Her mind flickered in recognition at the voice. There

was some vague aspect of authority in it, something signifi-
cant she ought to remember, but her body wanted blood.
She tightened her grip on Jasper's throat, her nails biting
into his skin.

"Everyone out. Now!" Logan yelled, and then the cold
steel of his dirk was tickling the hollow of her throat. She
hadn't even sensed him move.

"Feels good, doesn't it?" he whispered in liquid tones.
"He probably deserves it."

Kara shuddered, fighting the urge to slice open Jasper's
throat. Logan licked the rim of her ear, and heat flooded
her loins. *Mother Night.* What was he doing to her?

Jasper's eyes began to bulge in his head. Logan scraped
his teeth down the back of Kara's neck and wrapped a
strong arm around her abdomen.

"Make your choice, Kara."

Kara dropped Jasper. He fell to the floor and wheezed,
then yanked her dagger's twin out of its scabbard. One
look at her and Logan's expressions, and he sent it skidding
across the floor towards them. Kara brought her bare foot
down on the dagger's hilt to stop its spinning. Jasper scrambled to his feet and fled the great hall. They were alone.

Logan lowered his dirk and tugged the dagger out of
her hand. Kara spun on him. His eyes widened when they
saw hers. "Fuck," he said just before she pressed her lips to
his. It wasn't a tame kiss. She devoured him, plunging her
tongue into his hot mouth. His beard stubble rasped
against her face. Logan growled in the back of his throat
and kissed her back. Kara's hands went to the fastenings of
his breeches, and he pulled back.

"Wait, Kara. Listen to me. You're keening. We
need to—"

Kara bit his lip and pulled his head back down to hers.
Logan's eyes flashed a deep glowing amber, and he

captured her mouth in his. She wanted him, needed him. Her body demanded it.

Logan gripped her bare ass and lifted her against him. "You taste like cider," he groaned. "Have you been drinking?"

Kara ignored him, wrapping her legs around his waist and ripping at the buckles on his leather jerkin. He wore a dark shirt underneath. She rose, pressing her breasts into his face, and he burrowed into them and inhaled her scent. His lips encircled one of her nipples and sucked, and she moaned, low and long.

Kara ground herself against him mindlessly. He felt so good; she burned for him. Logan sat her down on the edge of a dining table, and her ass met the hard, rough wood. He nipped at her nipples, then bit and kissed his way up her collarbone and neck.

She ran a questing hand up his inner thigh and tugged at the laces of his breeches once more. The hard bulge they confined pressed against her hand. He wanted her.

Logan caught her hand, stilling it. "Not like this," he said, breathing hard.

She gnashed her teeth and rolled her hips at him.

"Bloody hell, woman. Why are you even naked?"

He snatched her off the table and carried her to a storeroom off the kitchen. *Good enough.* She was so fevered, she'd have fucked him atop the tables strewn with everyone's half-finished meals.

Logan sat her down on a large crate and laid her back, trailing fingers over her flesh. "Close your eyes," he whispered.

Kara obeyed. His palms traced her body all the way down to her toes, then lifted. She awaited his next touch, but nothing came. Her eyes snapped open. Logan was gone.

Kara leapt up from the crate and tested the door. The wooden frame rattled, but the door refused to budge. The bastard had locked her in, left her wanting. She could sense him standing on the other side, just out of reach. Her brain flooded with rage. She screamed.

HOURS LATER, when her bloodlust had subsided some and she'd begun to feel the chill in the room and the after-effects of her dash through the forest, Jon came to let her out.

"You look like shit," he said, throwing a blanket at her. He set down the clothes she'd been wearing earlier, now carefully folded. Her jeweled daggers and their scabbards lay on top.

"Jasper was, uh, convinced to return these."

Kara ran her hands down her face in exasperation. "So that wasn't all just a bad dream?"

Jon shook his head, and she groaned.

"How am I supposed to look them in the face after this? Everyone saw me naked."

"You didn't seem to care much when you burst into the keep with your tits bouncing." Jon grinned. "Nothing compared to what Logan did when his first keening began, but still...alcohol and keening. Not a good combination. Loss of control is what you're trying to avoid, in case you've forgotten."

Kara narrowed her eyes on him. "How did you know?"

"Look at you. You're a mess. The boys said you've been missing practice, and Ridley fessed up about you relieving him of *three jugs* of his stock."

"I don't need a lecture right now, Jon."

"Very well. The Commander wanted me to relay that

he's made you an appointment tonight at the Chambers with Vhaidra."

"Thinks he can tuck me in a box," Kara muttered.

Jon didn't meet her eyes. "He encourages you to leave immediately, lest you start stabbing anyone who looks at you the wrong way. I can escort you, if you wish."

"I'll be fine," Kara bit out. "Give me my boots and piss off."

KARA LEFT her daggers in the tower before riding out, in case she ran into Arden or Willoughby. Even Colette had a way of pushing her buttons, and her nerves were still on edge.

Drum enjoyed the opportunity to stretch her legs during the journey to Blackhearth. The Chambers hadn't changed much since her last visit. Madam Colette tracked her with suspicious eyes when Kara came in, as if she expected her to destroy the furniture as soon as she turned her back. Vhaidra appeared from behind a velvet curtain and beckoned her to follow. She led Kara upstairs to a bedchamber lit with candles and incense. She poured Kara a glass of wine from a wicker demijohn and brought it to her. Vhaidra's burgundy silk dressing robe parted as she crossed the room, revealing the curved mounds of her ample breasts. Her perfume reminded Kara of an overripe fruit, all cloying and sticky.

"Your eyes are different from when I saw you last. It seems you and your Commander share an affliction. Perhaps the two of you can come together sometime."

"I don't think so," Kara said, tamping down the jealous rage Vhaidra's suggestion summoned in her.

"You know, at first I thought he was a mage, but now I'm not so sure," she said as she trailed a long fingernail across Kara's mark. The motion sent a shiver down Kara's spine. "Where I'm from, the curses are much worse."

"And where's that?"

"Perhaps one day I'll tell you." Vhaidra sat down on the edge of the bed and patted the space beside her. "Come."

Kara sat and took a large gulp of her wine. She'd burned off the effects of the cider hours ago, and she could use a little liquid courage.

"I was with a warrior like you once before. Unprofessionally," Vhaidra added. "She treated me better than any man ever has."

"I'm afraid I'm not very experienced," Kara admitted.

"A virgin?" Vhaidra asked in her sultry lilt, her long lashes sweeping her cheeks when she blinked.

"No," Kara coughed. "But I've never been with a woman before."

"Don't worry about that. Just follow my lead."

Vhaidra shifted on the bed, moving to straddle Kara from behind. Her robe fell open again as she began massaging Kara's neck with cool, manicured hands. "You're so tight. Relax."

Kara let her head hang loose as Vhaidra worked at loosening the taut muscles of her shoulders and neck. Her mind drifted, and she began to imagine Logan working her muscles with his rough palms and strong fingers. She pictured him making his way down her lower back, kneading the dimples above her ass, then moving lower still. Kara sunk her head back against Vhaidra's breasts with a soft sigh. This was all wrong. Vhaidra was lovely, but she didn't send heat flashing to Kara's core like Logan could with a single look.

Vhaidra kissed her—her plump lips and soft pink tongue prodding at Kara to open up. Kara responded weakly, going through the motions of the kiss. But Vhaidra tasted of smoke and strong wine, not the crisp, violent passion she craved.

Vhaidra pulled away and tugged the sides of her robe together. "Why are you here, Kara? This isn't what you want. I can tell when my patrons are thinking of another. Will they not have you?"

Kara shook her head. "Apparently not."

"Men are stubborn creatures. Sometimes they need to be shown what they want."

"I'd be a fool to go down that path anyway."

Vhaidra combed through Kara's hair with her fingers. "Matters of the heart make fools of us all, but you must give them that chance. Regret can be a bitter burden."

Kara's blood pulled at her, demanding. She eyed the soft curve of Vhaidra's neck, where her pulse beat just beneath the skin. "I'm running out of time."

Vhaidra's painted lips curved in a soft smile. "Then go to him."

Kara rose from the bed in sluggish motions and pulled out her coin purse. "Thank you for your time. How much is it? I'll pay the full price—as if we had gone through with everything."

"Put away your purse," Vhaidra said, waving her hand. "Your Commander already took care of that when he made your appointment."

Kara stiffened, her mind bristling at the revelation. What else had he taken care of during his visit, while she was locked away in the bloody pantry? Kara fought for calm, for serenity. She blew a huff of air out her nose.

"Is he still here?" *Please say no.*

"No. He told us to expect you and left. I've never seen him so unraveled, actually."

"Very well. Thank you. Goodbye, Vhaidra."

( )

KARA'S STOMACH began twisting painfully on the ride back
to Raven's Rest, and her forehead beaded with sweat
despite the chill air. It wasn't time for her period, and these
cramps were more severe than what she was used to. After
untacking and brushing down Drum, she headed straight
for the tower, fighting the clenching in her gut all the way
up the steps. She could suppress the curse's urges again,
give herself time to get over this illness and figure out how
to approach Logan once more.

Kara locked her door and dragged her dresser across it
in case she was tempted to leave or someone came looking
for her. She didn't need any distractions or interruptions
when she was this volatile. Then she sank into bed, her
knees shaking with tremors.

The next hour was one of the worst hours of her life. It
passed in a haze of pain and sweat. Her stomach pains had
gotten progressively worse, and her whole body burned
with fever. Kara felt like she was holding her face to a forge
and someone kept stoking the flames. She considered
seeking out Bart for something to knock her out, but the
thought of navigating the tower steps was nauseating.

Kara dimly registered the sound of quick, heavy footsteps on the tower stairs. Someone pounded on the door.

"Kara? Let me in."

Logan.

Kara rolled over in bed and groaned. She tried to quell
the shaking in her legs to no avail.

"I will kick this fucking door in if you don't come open
it. I heard you scream. Stop hiding."

"Leave," she yelled hoarsely. She didn't remember
screaming, but her mind was foggy and thick with pain.

"Stand aside." The wooden door quaked and splintered under the force of his kick. The dresser shook as the door thudded into it. Logan heaved, and the dresser inched forward as he pushed against it. He slid into the room once he'd created enough space. "Are you okay? What's going on?" Logan looked up at her and swore.

Kara's naked skin glistened with sweat. She'd torn off her clothes in an effort to escape the oppressive heat. Namirah's mark burned like a branding iron as she convulsed in pain. Logan knelt beside the bed and took ahold of her chin, turning her to face him.

Kara shuddered and looked up into his eyes. "What's happening to me?"

"You're keening. Your eyes are shifting over from amber hues into red. Not a good sign."

"Will it be this bad every time?"

"No. This is what happens when you wait too long to satisfy the curse, and it only gets worse from here. Your stages came on fast—I should have been paying closer attention, but I've been distracted. I'm sorry. What happened with Vhaidra?"

"I didn't want her. You should have just taken me in the great hall," Kara said before turning her head and coughing into the pillow.

"I'm not 'taking' anyone," Logan growled, his eyes flicking amber.

"Even though you desire me?"

"I'll see you through this, and next month I'll help you find a proper partner, however much it may pain me to do so."

Kara laughed, but it came out more like a feeble croak. Maybe she was imagining it, but the pain seemed dampened with Logan at her side. "I asked Thomas."

Logan's lip curled in distaste. "Thomas? That little prat? And he refused you?"

"I want you." She tossed her head back as a fresh wave of pain wracked her.

Logan smoothed a hand over her brow. His touch was like silk against her fevered skin. "Shh. You have me. I'm here." Logan lifted Kara's back off the bed, pulling her to him and cradling her in his arms. Kara sighed and burrowed her head into his chest, enjoying his scent enveloping her. He smelled *right*, like leather and sweat.

Logan lifted her head and kissed her while he stroked her back. His lips were soft and gentle. Then he cupped her breasts in his palms and massaged them, rolling her nipples between his fingertips. Kara's eyes shot open, awareness flooding her body as the pain in her belly pooled lower, transforming into an insistent, molten heat. She clenched her hands in the front of his shirt and tasted his lips with her tongue, begging him to let her in. She wanted him to ravage her with his mouth. Ravage her with his body.

Logan tore away from her and pulled off his shirt and boots.

"The bracers," Kara said.

"What?"

"Take them off. Don't hide from me."

Logan hesitated for a moment. "So be it," he said and unbuckled them. His marked wrist glowed in the dark room. He roved his eyes across the curves of her body and crawled atop the bed, stretching out over her like a great cat.

"You're not a virgin, are you?"

"No," she grit out.

Logan trailed his fingers down her stomach to her inner thigh, spreading a tingling sensation throughout Kara's body. Heat bloomed in her face as desire for him tugged at her.

"You blush like a virgin," he said, his eyes sparking.

Kara gripped his biceps and tugged him down on top of her, wanting to feel his skin against hers. She cursed him for not taking off his breeches—she wanted to feel all of him. Her hands dove down the hard planes of his stomach that rippled with muscle. Logan's breath hitched when she slid one inside the waist of his pants. He grabbed her questing hands and pinned them above her head.

"Uh-uh," he said, voice heated. He bit her nipples gently in admonishment. "We do this my way."

Kara locked her calf around his, pulling his hips down to meet hers. She arched her pelvis, wanting—needing —more.

Logan slid a finger through the wet slit between her thighs. "Mother Night, Kara. You're so wet." His fingers found her clit and stroked it once. Twice. "Is this what you want?"

Kara squirmed her hips beneath his hand. "Please." Logan caught her mouth with his, devouring her. He slid a long finger inside her and slowly pushed it in and out. Her skin was on fire; her mark smoldered. Logan slipped in a second finger, stretching her out. Kara moaned and spasmed around him, but it wasn't enough.

"I need you inside me, Logan." She could feel the hard ridge of his cock through the constraints of his pants. "I know you want me."

Logan moved down lower on the bed and spread her legs apart. "Of course I want you, Kara," he said before scraping his teeth over the sensitive skin of her inner thigh. Then he parted her lips and laved her core with his tongue. Kara writhed, hands fisting in the sheets as she went wild with desire. Sean had certainly never done *this*. She felt like she was coming apart at the edges. Logan's lips and tongue were on her clit, driving her wild. Her head fell

back in ecstasy. Pleasure suffused her down to the tips of
her toes.

Logan held her to the bed as she quaked beneath him,
undulating and bucking her hips as the pleasure became
too much. She let out a long moan, and Logan sheathed
two fingers inside her again as he licked, bending them in a
beckoning motion that sent her into a frenzy.

"Logan!" she screamed, clutching his head between
her legs and grinding herself against him. The pressure
built. The thrust of his fingers grew more relentless. The
muscles in her neck seized, and Kara cried out as an
orgasm washed over her. She collapsed against the bed,
filled with euphoria. Her thighs continued to tremble with
the aftershocks of pleasure.

The symptoms Kara had been experiencing before
Logan arrived had vanished. She felt wonderful, like power
was surging through her veins. The pleasure he'd given her
settled in her bones with a warm heat. She looked at her
wrist and was surprised to see her mark glowing a faint
orange color, like Logan's.

Logan rested his cheek on her stomach and took long,
deep breaths. Kara still wanted him despite her keening
being satisfied. She wanted to watch him thrash and moan
beneath her hands and mouth, to experience his pleasure.
Kara tugged his left hand away from its white-knuckled
grip on the sheets and interlaced their fingers. Their marks
met as their wrists closed together, and a zing of pleasure
shot straight to her core. Logan shuddered, and his eyes
snapped open. They were pure molten gold. She'd never
seen them look like this.

He tore his hand away from hers as if he'd been burnt,
then climbed out of the bed and began putting on his
boots.

"Stay with me. Please."

Logan shook his head, refusing to look her in the eye as he buckled on his bracers. "I can't. *We* can't."

Kara pulled up the sheets to cover herself. Why was he doing this?

He scrubbed a hand over his face. "We talked about this, Kara. Tonight changes nothing."

It'd changed *everything*. She could still feel the heat of his touch lingering on her skin. "I don't understand, Logan. You obviously want me—"

"It's not a question of want, Kara. My body, this fucking cursed vessel, will start to think it *needs* you. You know what I am. When I'm keening, I'm dangerous. Ask Jon to show you his back sometime. I don't want to hurt you. I fought too hard for the control I've gained to jeopardize it over some girl."

Kara stiffened as his words hit her. She was just *some girl* to him? After all this? She bit her lip to distract herself from the lump swiftly rising in her throat.

Logan picked up his crumpled shirt and strode for the door without looking back. He shoved her dresser out of his way and left, slamming the splintered door shut behind him.

Kara tucked her knees beneath her chin and sighed. So much for Vhaidra's advice.

Minutes later she heard a whinny from the stable, and Kara rushed out onto the parapets with her bedsheet wrapped around her. Logan led Char through the stable doors, then swung into the saddle and heeled him hard. They raced together towards the black forest.

CHAPTER FIFTEEN

Two days later, hail pinged off the roof of the keep as Kara rushed inside, cloak pulled over her head. Lightning flashed outside, and wind slammed the door shut behind her as soon as she let it go. The training yard had turned into a muddy mire in a matter of minutes once the deluge began.

Kara untied her wet cloak and hung it on a coat peg to dry. A group of Stygians were all clustered around the large table by the fire, drinking. Kara squeezed into a spot between Thomas and Jon, and Jon passed her a mug.

"You're looking better," Jon said. "What'll you have?"

"Ale's fine." Kara was surprised to see Rohan and Rahj amidst the group, as they usually kept to themselves. Athar was in the middle of one of his tirades, spewing spittle and breadcrumbs across the table as he spoke.

"We laugh at the Banner and the Vispilians for humping the trade routes, but during peace time they've got solid employ. Meanwhile we sit in this rock with our thumbs up our collective asses, getting fat."

"Speak for yourself, old man," Rohan said.

"We didn't make our name by shepherding caravans across sand and sea, Athar," Jon reminded him.

"You forget that I rode with the Banner in my youth," Rahj said. "When war breaks out, those trade route commissions are a bloody and infrequent affair."

"Is it true the Golden Banner ride on camels instead of horses?" Thomas asked.

Rahj smiled. "Miserable animals. That and the sand. Sand in places sand should never be. Why do you think I left?"

Thomas grimaced. Kara chuckled and took a sip of her ale.

"The clan's due in Travincal for the guild meeting in a few weeks. We'll sniff something out," Jon said.

"Hmph," Athar said. "Not with the other clans hoarding information like a gold crown clamped between a peasant boy's arsecheeks. Dreadnettle's man may be forthcoming, but not the others. Things were better back in my day, before the guild began their meddling, pitting us all against one another."

"Were you not a Sanguine defector during the split?" Rahj said, arching an eyebrow at Athar.

"That was *personal*. This is business. I dream of the days before the guild and the paperwork and so-called 'rules.' When the clans ruled the land and the earth ran red with blood."

"God's teeth, he's on one," Jon said. He smacked the top of the table with his hands. "Who's down for cards?" He threw an arm around Kara's shoulders. "I'm not letting you worm your way out of it this time, Kara."

"I'm really no good," she protested, thinking of her modest savings.

"Nonsense. Anyone who can fight can gamble. At its

core all the necessary skills are the same—awareness, intelligence, and a little bit of recklessness."

"What about luck?"

Jon winked at her. "We don't rely on luck. She lies."

"Fine, deal me in."

Rain hammered against the keep windows as they played. Kara was bunched in between Thomas and Jon's wide shoulders, and the heat coming off their bodies warmed her up quickly. When Jon offered her advice on the basics of the game, she struggled to keep from laughing. She'd spent many such evenings during Mudbottom's long, dull winters with Wesley and Da by the hearth, playing into the wee hours of the morning with fruits and nuts as stand-ins for coin. Wesley had always been a sore loser.

Kara took care to keep her cards hidden as the pot grew larger and larger, and she maintained a calm and unaffected expression as the men laid down their final hands. Athar was blustering and cocksure that he had the best spread. Kara smiled and laid her cards flat when she was the only one remaining.

Thomas groaned and shoved away from the table.

"Wench fleeced us!" Athar hollered, pounding the table with his mug, slinging foam. "Bloody untrustworthy women, always my downfall."

Jon smirked and swept the sizable pile of coins and valuables towards her. "Well, well, *Ace*. Who taught you to play like that?

"My da."

"You certainly strung me along. I shan't go so easy on you next time."

"Says the man who insisted I play." Kara smiled. "But

I am sorry I misled you. I only gamble occasionally—too much chance in the cards for my liking."

"You should play with us more often. I could use a little healthy competition."

The front door battered against the wall as a gust of wind blew into the keep, and everyone turned towards it. A looming black figure came in out of the storm, muddy and dripping water on the stone floor. He drew back his hood to reveal dark eyes and hair damp with rainwater. Logan had returned.

His eyes locked on Kara, sitting so close to Jon, then swept past her. Kara tried to ignore the heat that flared in her gut upon seeing him for the first time since her keening.

"I see the weather hasn't kept you from enjoying yourselves," Logan said, his tone dark. "Mind the drink; we head for Travincal tomorrow. I want all of you ready to ride at dawn." Logan stormed up the staircase towards his rooms, dripping water all the way.

"What's gotten into him?" Faedra asked.

"He's a moody bastard," Athar said.

Kara was eager for the trip to Travincal. The Sanguines would be there, which meant she might be able to find out more information about Wesley. It'd be dangerous, but she'd go mad not knowing. She'd caught herself entertaining outlandish scenarios where she discovered Wesley was happy and healthy and far from the clans, but it was delusional. If he'd survived, he was likely a Sanguine prisoner.

The group continued playing for several hours, but as the evening grew late, people began to drop out of the game and drift off to their beds. Soon it was just Kara and Jon left.

Jon made to stand up as the last player filtered out of

the hall. "Welp, that about does it for me. You've cleaned me out anyways."

"I have a favor to ask, Jon."

"Keening again already?" he said with bite in his voice.

Kara frowned. Jon was usually the farthest thing from mean-spirited. "No, I—Logan told me to ask you to show me your back. What did he mean by that?"

A shadow passed over Jon's eyes. He scrubbed his hand through his hair and sighed. "You should tell him I'm not his pet to be shown off when it pleases him."

"I know, Jon. I'm sorry. Don't do anything you're uncomfortable with. I'm just trying to understand where he's coming from."

"Good luck," he muttered. "I suppose I've never denied a woman asking me to strip before, and I shan't start now." Jon peeled his shirt up slowly, teasing her. Each inch of fabric revealed tight, pale skin studded with muscle. He was leaner than Logan, and he had a tattoo of a black sun inked into the indentation of his hip. Jon finished his strip tease and tossed her his shirt, then slowly turned his back to her.

Kara gasped when she saw the muscled planes of his back. A huge, puckered scar spanned his back diagonally, shoulder to hip. It was old and faded at the edges, but the cut had been deep. He was lucky to be alive. Kara crossed to him and touched his bare shoulder, and his skin rippled in surprise.

"Who did this to you?"

Jon spun around and yanked his shirt back out of her hands, quickly tugging it on.

"It was an accident."

"It was Logan, wasn't it? That's why he's so afraid of losing control—because it's happened before."

Jon sat down at the table and took a long sip of his ale,

then turned to face her. "Logan was eighteen when he awakened. His father's death triggered his curse. He didn't kill him, but you know what a fickle bitch the curse is. And he blamed himself regardless, of course. His mother was gone at that point, all he had was the clan. When his first keening came, he was determined to resist it, to ride it out. We told him it was impossible, but he refused to listen to any of us. Made us chain him up inside a locked cell in the dungeon and promise not to let him out."

Kara winced. She'd only resisted her keening for a few days, and she'd been in agony once her clock had run up. "He was torturing himself."

Jon nodded. "He was—*is* my best friend. I couldn't stand to see him like that. In so much pain, tearing at his own skin to try and escape flames that weren't there."

Kara brought her hand to her mouth and bit down on her knuckles. He'd been so young.

"After a week, the demon started to come out. And he was *persuasive*. I was eighteen, too, and stupid. He talked me into unlocking the chains binding him, said they felt like molten iron on his skin. As soon as his hands were free, he disabled me and pulled my sword out of its sheath. We'd always been on even ground in fights before—I thought I could handle him if he tried to fight me, but he was so strong, Kara. Totally overpowered me. I tried to run, and he cut me down."

Kara's heart twisted. The guilt Logan must have felt—she couldn't imagine. And he was still punishing himself for it. "How did you survive?"

"I shouldn't have. I think there was enough of him in there still to pull the swing before it severed my spine. By all rights I should be dead. Bart's a hell of a healer, but they had to bring in a mage to fix me up. It still pains me sometimes, but I'm lucky it didn't cripple me."

Kara chewed on her lip. "What happened to Logan afterward?"

"He stole the cell keys and escaped into the Blackshear with nothing but the clothes on his back. We searched for him, but it was like he'd vanished. He didn't come back for a year. When he did, he was different. Less carefree. Haunted. I love him, but I never forget what's inside him. And you shouldn't either. Be careful with him, Kara. I don't want to see you get hurt."

()

THE RAIN HAD LET UP ONLY MARGINALLY by morning, and Kara trudged to the courtyard after packing her things. She was pleased to be included in the trip to Travincal, but the weather conditions were miserable. The horses were already saddled and huddled together, heads hanging low to the earth. Jon tried to have Logan postpone their departure to no avail.

"I want to get there early, before the other clans have an opportunity to start stirring things up, making deals behind our backs. Victus will use any advantage he can get. I can spare a few bodies, if any of you want to stay."

No one took Logan up on his offer. The lure of potential contract money was too strong, and chances were the rain would ease off soon. Rohan, Ridley, and some of the other senior members stayed behind to guard the fortress.

The weather only worsened as their journey progressed. Kara's fur-lined winter cloak couldn't withstand the persistent downpour, and soon water had soaked through the fibers of her hood and dampened her hair. The wind cut through the cold, wet fabric like knives, and she struggled to keep from shivering in the saddle as they made their way through the Blackshear.

Theirs was a solemn procession; no one felt much like talking. When they finally stopped to pitch their tents for the night along the outskirts of the forest, most of their company looked like drowned rats.

The horses had picked their way through the slurry of melting snow and mud on the ground, and Drum's legs and underbelly were covered with it. Kara used a stiff bristle brush to clean her coat before joining the others gathered nearby. The group was trying in vain to start a fire, but the kindling was proving too damp to catch flame.

George cursed and rocked back on his heels, pocketing his flint. "Whole forest is soaked after two days' rain. We're all gonna get the blasted sniffles and lung crud at this rate."

"Stand aside," Rahj said. He looked remarkably dry compared to the rest of them, and everyone eyed him enviously. Rahj stretched out a bubble of air over the kindling with his hands, then thrust them forward and uttered a spell. The words came out in a sibilant whisper that filled Kara with unease. She thought she felt sand shift beneath her fingers, but when she glanced down, there was nothing there. The fire blazed to life in a shower of purple sparks, and the bubble of air protecting it dissipated. Lighting a fire was no great feat—even novice mages could do it—but she hadn't known that Rahj possessed magic. Was that how he'd sensed she was marked, back in Liore?

"Well, well," George said, crouching closer and warming his hands by the flame, "I see they taught you more than camel riding in those cursed dunes. If I'd known you were a mage, I wouldn't have bothered."

"I prefer not to use my power on trivial things, but it's a week to Travincal, and I'd rather not listen to you lot drown in lung butter all the way there."

Kara sat as close to the fire as she could without embers leaping on her and the fire's light burning her eyes.

She chewed on a soft wedge of cheese from her pack, unable to shake the chill from her bones. George unstoppered a hefty wineskin and began passing it around the circle. Kara quaffed from it eagerly, hoping the hearty red would warm her icy blood.

The moon lingered behind a coat of clouds, but its lambent glow could be seen through the border of trees, beckoning them forth from the shadows. It was odd to think that tomorrow would be her first time stepping forth from the borders of the Blackshear in the months since the Reaping Trials. She'd be emerging a different person.

Faedra appeared out of the woods and walked over to Aaron. She sat between his legs and leaned back into his chest, and Aaron wrapped his cloak around her shoulders. Kara's eyebrows crawled up her face. When had *that* happened? She was almost jealous. She envied their ease with one another.

"At least there will be a host of new brothels to explore in Travincal," Everett piped up. "The Chamber girls are growing stale."

"You're stale!" Thomas said, tossing a hunk of soggy bread at him. "You won't find a girl as pretty as sweet Arden this side of the Teleri River."

Jon snorted. "She won't be so sweet when you run dry of coin. And you'll be cheating yourself if you don't visit the Dovecote. Their top girl can suck a man sideways. She's got this trick she can do with her tongue... Locals say the session's free if you can last through it, but she's a very rich courtesan."

"Pssh. You're still a greenie," Athar said. "All that fancy claptrap ain't good for nothin' but bleedin' your pockets dry. True connoisseurs—like meself—know that the best girl in Travincal is Fiona. She works Cumberland's down by the docks, and she's got tits like a cow's udders." Athar groped his own generous chest for effect.

The men roared, but Jon shook his head. "Maybe so, but who wants to fight off the hordes of seamen on shore leave when you could have a much more sophisticated experience? The madam at The Dovecote books up to two weeks in advance!"

"Like flies to sap," Kara muttered to herself.

Jasper leaned over to Kara, speaking low enough so the others couldn't hear him, "They must not realize that we've got our very own whore right here. How *did* your keening go, by the way?"

Kara ignored him and kept eating—she didn't have the energy to argue with him.

"You know, my first thought was that the Commander must want you on a tight leash if he's brought you along. Didn't want you murdering any more helpless mountain folk while we're away. But maybe there's another reason, eh?"

Kara fought to quell the anger rising behind her eyes. She clenched the cheese wedge tight in her fist, her nails leaving half-moon marks deep in its surface. "Leave it, Jasper," she said.

A long shadow fell over them, then dipped as Logan dropped into a crouch beside her.

He nodded to Jasper. "We need a latrine dug. I trust you can see to it?"

Jasper's lips thinned. He nodded curtly and left.

"Thanks," Kara said. Her body buzzed with awareness of his proximity. She couldn't get the night they'd shared out of her mind. She glanced over to Faedra and Aaron, then back at her feet. She badly needed a distraction from Logan Vakarian.

"I'd kill him for you if I didn't think it would affect morale. You look cold."

Kara nodded grimly, not looking forward to the night ahead. She'd drawn the pre-dawn watch, which was sure to be a damp and drizzly affair.

Logan unhooked his black cloak and draped it over her shoulders, then fastened the silver chain about her neck. The fabric emanated warmth and wasn't damp in the slightest.

Kara jerked her head towards him. "What in the goddess's name? Did Rahj enchant your cloak?"

Logan chuckled. "No. He'd probably set it on fire if he tried. This is much more delicate work." He touched her shoulder and drew aside the folds of fabric, revealing a large rune stitched in silver thread on the inner folds of the cloak. "It's a weather resistance rune, inlaid by a clothchanter. Costs about half a year's wages, but well worth it on the road and during the winter months."

"I'm envious." She'd never seen such delicate enchanting work before. Kara burrowed into the depths of the oversized cloak and rubbed her cheeks against the dark cloth to warm her face. It smelled like him. She wanted to discuss what had happened between them during her keening, but they wouldn't have much privacy until they reached Travincal.

Jon flicked his eyes towards them across the fire then returned to his conversation, his expression strained.

"Use my cloak tonight," Logan said. "It wouldn't do for you to catch sick on the road."

She sighed and nodded. The men were doubling up in their tents for extra warmth. Kara had planned to share with Faedra, but it appeared she might have other plans. Kara glanced up into Logan's dark eyes. She didn't think he'd prove reciprocal to her suggesting they spend the night together, no matter how much she wanted to.

"Where did you go the other night? After my keening?"

Logan shifted uncomfortably on his heels. "Sometimes I just need to get out and ride, clear my head. The Blackshear is accommodating in that regard."

Kara snorted. "Accommodatingly deadly."

"You just haven't learned her secrets yet," Logan said and rose. He ran a lock of her hair through his fingers, then quickly released it. "Sleep well, Kara."

KARA AWOKE in the morning to the sounds of people shuffling outside her tent. As predicted, Faedra hadn't joined her in her tent last night, so she'd slept alone, surrounded by Logan's scent and the warmth of his cloak, wishing he'd appear.

When Kara peeked outside, dawn had come and gone, but the sky was still overcast and grey with the portent of rain. She was puzzled that she'd been allowed to sleep in. Feron had drawn the night watch; he should have woken her when his shift ended.

She stumbled from her tent, still bleary-eyed, and looked around for Feron. He was saddling his spotted mare by the bushes.

Kara came up to him and asked, "Why didn't you wake me for my watch?"

"Hmm?" He looked up over the horse's rump, expression blank and sleepy. "Oh, Logan told me not to wake you. Someone else took it."

"Bloody hell. People are going to start thinking I'm getting special treatment."

Feron shrugged. "Wouldn't complain about the extra sleep. Today looks to be another drowner."

Kara returned Logan's weather-runed cloak, pride trumping sense when he offered to let her keep it for the remainder of the journey. A mistake she regretted sorely, as the weather persisted in its dreadfulness over the next week.

They skirted the Teleri River as they headed towards Travincal to avoid passing through Sanguine territory, and the westerly winds whipping off the coast carried a bone deep chill. Several of the men came down with colds, and Kara worried that she'd be next. Occasionally Rahj would envelop their retinue in a bubble of air that guarded them from the wind and rain, but he wasn't able to hold the spell for extended periods of time. Kara was concerned that Drum and the other horses might develop rot in their hooves from the prolonged exposure to the soggy terrain.

The rain broke the day they arrived within sighting distance of the Travincal gates. A tenuous sun wavered in the sky overhead, and the air was thick with humidity. Not long after they merged onto the main market road, two sleek bays pulling a gilded carriage trotted down the path towards them. Their driver whoaed them to a halt as he approached the Stygians.

Logan rode to the front of the party with Jon and signaled for the rest of them to stop.

The driver tipped his tophat, then climbed down from his perch and opened the carriage door with a low bow. The door was emblazoned with a seal depicting two rearing stags locking antlers over a red rose. Kara didn't recognize the seal.

A richly appointed courier in scarlet livery stepped out of the carriage and down into the muck. He produced a thick scroll from his coat, pulled his feet from the mud sucking at his shoes, and cleared his throat. "The Baroness Valancourt, the august beauty and renowned patroness, requests your presence at her manor house this eve."

Logan rolled his eyes. "And we've not even passed the gates yet. Never lacking for showmanship, is she? Tell the *baroness* we'll pay her visit after we've settled in at a tavern. I need to find beds for my people."

The courier cleared his throat once more. "Upon any hesitancy to comply, the baroness requests I relay an offer of board and hospitality at her Travincal residence. Extended in good faith, so long as the Stygian Commander Logan Vakarian and his clan should remain in Travincal and surrounding areas."

"This isn't a calling party, my good man," Jon said. "We're here to work. And I doubt you've got room for us all."

"Of course, sir." The courier scanned the scroll hastily, eyes darting back and forth. "There is no mention of a contract, but she has included a stipulation. Should your retinue prove too numerous for comfortable lodging at the baroness's most palatial manor, she will provide boarding accommodations for the remainder of your people in a nearby tavern of repute."

"Mother Night," Logan said. "Jon? What do you think?"

Jon responded in a lowered voice, and they whispered fiercely back and forth for a few moments. Logan kept shaking his head, while Jon gestured wildly with his hands.

"Alright," Logan snapped, and he turned back to the courier. "It seems my subordinate enjoys reveling in luxury's lap. Let's get this over with then, shall we? Feron, ride ahead to the guild and tell them we've arrived."

"Can I bring Faedra with me? I want to show her around."

"Fine." Logan turned and gestured to the courier. "Please, lead the way."

The courier nodded and eagerly returned to the carriage cabin, poking his head through the curtained window to yell, "Follow me!"

CHAPTER SIXTEEN

Their party filtered into the parlor of the baroness's sprawling manor house after a bewildered butler ceded them entrance. Kara had done her best to knock the clumped mud off her boots outside, but they were all sorely dressed for such grand company. She was eager to get the introductions over with. The heat from the parlor hearth was stifling, and the stench of travel was thick on their clothes.

The baroness swept into the room in a cloud of fabric and lace. She was younger than Kara expected—in her early forties, overly perfumed and wearing a wig stacked impressively high and laced through with sprigs of lavender and elderberry. Her face fell when she took in their party.

"It seems the road was unkind to you," she tutted. "I trust my home will be more comfortable."

Jon grinned and swept low in a courtly bow. "Certainly, Baroness. I've longed dreamed of our return to Travincal, so that we might partake of your famous hospitality once more."

"You always have had good taste, Jonathan. Can't say the same for your Commander, unfortunately."

Logan shook his head. "How'd you know we were in town, Valancourt?"

"I ran into that leafy fellow on my weekly ride about the park. I knew then that the clans must be meeting. I don't think he'd ever leave those woods of his if he had a choice."

"Leafy fellow?" Rahj asked.

"Yes, you know. From clan Dungbeetle or whatever they're calling it now."

"Dreadnettle's arch druid?" Logan asked.

"That's the one. He was whispering to the trees, caressing them. Can you imagine?" she said, shaking her head.

"He draws his power from nature, madame," Rahj said.

"Yes? Well, that sounds like a very untidy affair. And he's very odd—all twiggy and tanned. Anyhow, I had my men look out for your party. I knew you'd come off the riverfront, avoid those red dogs. And don't you look dreadful for it? Jeffrey, come here."

The butler hurried back into the room. "Yes, madame?"

"Have the chambermaids start preparing hot baths. As many as we have rooms."

Jeffrey blanched. "Uhm. Yes, madame. Right away."

"The rest of your men should be comfortable at the Gilded Pig," she told Logan. "I'll pay for their lodgings, of course, so long as they don't bring any ill reputation to my name."

Logan looked weary and exasperated. He scrubbed a hand over his chin and nodded. "All right. The inner circle and Kara, you're in the house. The rest of you can duke it out between yourselves."

The baroness's pale blue eyes startled at the mention of Kara's name, and the mass of mousy brown hair atop her head teetered. She looked over their group more closely, eyes narrowing on Kara. "A girl? She doesn't look like much—I've seen better-kempt street urchins. Which means she's not your entertainment..."

The men shifted uncomfortably around Kara, unsure how to respond. Kara kept her lips clamped shut. The baroness's implication ruffled her temper, but she didn't want to get into a fight with their host on their first day in Travincal.

"I do recruit women, you know," Logan said, a thin layer of ice in his voice.

"Oh, really? And here I thought you obstinate. The ladies at my tea party will be positively titillated when they hear you've got a new female recruit. You must let me take her to meet them."

Kara groaned internally. The last thing she wanted was to be put on show by this woman.

Jon interceded on her behalf. "I'm afraid Kara doesn't have the societal refinements you're accustomed to. She hails from a small mountain village. We've not been able to teach her competent swordplay, let alone the social graces."

The men laughed, and Lady Valancourt bobbled her head back and forth.

"Then there's no excusing it. We must train her. Even you boors know how to don the outfit and parade among the best. She must learn to be a lady."

"Thank you, Baroness, but that's quite unnecessary," Kara said. She didn't think *ladies* usually carried decapitated heads around in a sack.

"Nonsense, child. I can see the desperate situation you're in. Don't fret, I know just the man for the job. He's been a marvel with the latest crop of debutantes. You though, my dear. You should prove quite the challenge for him."

Kara bemoaned her fate over dinner that night. The dishes were rich, and she took care not to overindulge for fear of a stomachache. She preferred the simple, hearty dinners by the hearth in Raven's Rest to this parade of tureens, white satin gloves, and waistcoats. Half of the foods were unidentifiable. Was it soup, or gravy? She might never know.

When the baroness excused herself from the table, Kara turned to Jon. "No one else is being forced to take etiquette lessons. Not even Faedra. Can't you get me out of this?" Faedra had wisely chosen to stay at the Gilded Pig with Aaron once she got wind of the baroness's plans for Kara.

"That would be impolite," he said.

"I should trade with one of the boys at the Pig, get away from all this frippery."

"Jasper and Everett are at the Pig," Thomas piped up.

"So I'm surrounded at all sides."

Jon folded his napkin in his lap. "I wouldn't be so quick to try and get out of it. She's doing you a favor, really, though it's couched in aristocratic snobbery. It's quite useful to be able to smoothly transition between social strata in this profession. We're often called into company with kings and the peerage. You may as well learn now."

"I don't know," Kara sighed. "It seems a waste of time when I could be honing my swordplay." *And sniffing out*

Sanguines in the city. "Who the hell is this lady, anyways? What are we doing in her house? Does she owe a debt?"

"Not exactly," Jon said. "I suspect this is her greasing the wheels, ensuring we keep our lips sealed about some services we provided her."

"Oh?" Kara asked, eyebrows rising in interest.

Athar looked up from his plate, a hunk of meat still impaled on his fork. "The baroness used to be married to ole' Baron Valancourt—a man of much ill notoriety, but very plush with cash. The baron was getting on in his years, and his son from a former marriage was set to inherit the title and fortune, as the current baroness never bore him any children. Baron Valancourt and his son passed away within a week of one another. Some dreadful sickness that swept through the house. The baroness inherited everything."

"So she's trying to pay for your silence with her hospitality?" Kara asked.

Jon shrugged. "It's insulting, really. Calls our professionalism into question. She's already paid a modest fortune for our services, but it seems the baroness never does anything halfway."

"Clearly," Thomas coughed.

"And killings for hire?" Kara said. "Does the Brotherhood still do them?"

Jon shifted in his seat. "I shouldn't be talking about this. Things were much less regimented before the Mercenary Guild came into power. The guild leader frowns upon assassination contracts, thinks it's a black stain upon the profession. But it's how our clan made a name for itself after the split."

"Hmmph," Athar said, "Warren has a rod up his ass. We're doing no different from the Sanguines, just manage it with less casualties."

"Yes, well, Victus can afford to bribe the guild to overlook his transgressions," Jon said.

"And the baron's son? Did he deserve his fate?" Kara asked.

Athar snorted. "I'll leave the judging for the goddess."

"Beggars can't be choosers, and broke mercenaries can't be selective," Jon said. "But I have it on good authority that he won't be missed."

After dinner, Kara went up to the room she'd been assigned. There was a door inside the room that connected it to the neighboring one, but when she tested it, it was locked. Every available surface was suffocated by pastel frills and lace. The chambermaid they'd sent to attend her bath insisted on removing the excess pillows from the bed *before* Kara could crawl into it.

"What use are the pillows then?" Kara asked, her voice sharp. The long days and short nights on the road had frazzled her nerves, and she was looking forward to falling asleep somewhere dry and warm.

"They're decorative."

"And who is coming into these bedrooms in the middle of the day to view the decorations?"

"I'm not rightly sure, ma'am. But the baroness makes all of the decorating decisions, and she's known amongst the peerage for her fashion sense." The maid stacked the pillows into a loose pyramid on a wooden bench beneath the window with practiced motions.

Kara sighed. "Look, for the rest of my stay, please leave the pillows where they are. I don't have the patience for it."

The girl's face tightened into a frown, but she nodded. "As you wish, madame."

()

IN THE MORNING Kara ignored the dress laid out for her on the settee and went down wearing her breeches and boots. The clothes hadn't been there last night, which meant someone had entered the room without waking her. She was getting sloppy. Jeffrey greeted her at the foot of the stairs, tutting to himself when he saw her attire.

"You've finally awoken, miss. The etiquette master has been waiting on you. He does loathe tardiness."

Kara grunted in response. The bed had been much softer than she was used to, but she'd been tired enough from travel to sleep till noon. She followed Jeffrey's frantic footsteps towards the ballroom. She was more concerned with breakfast than etiquette. Didn't fancy town ladies have hot chocolate and beignets brought to their bedsides in the morning? That would make this situation entirely more palatable. Or bacon. Her mouth watered at the thought.

"When's breakfast?" Kara asked.

"Three hours ago, ma'am." Jeffrey pulled one of the arching, ornate ballroom doors open and bowed low, waiting for her to enter. She peered queerly at him. "You don't have to bow. I'm a commoner."

"I am at your service, my lady." The words seemed to get stuck on his tongue.

"I'm not anyone's lady," Kara said and strode past him. The door slammed shut behind her. The ballroom was large, with a domed roof replete with sky windows and flickering chandeliers. An older man dressed in a grey dinner jacket with coattails and white breeches stood across the glistening parquet floor next to a piano. A pair of women's dancing slippers dangled from his right hand.

Kara cleared her throat.

He turned, eyes scanning over her disinterestedly. "Who are you?"

"Your newest student, apparently."

His eyebrows rose sharply on his fine-boned face, and he looked her over once more. "I thought the baroness was exaggerating when she said this was a charity case. You'll never learn to dance in those clod-hoppers, my dear. There is no blood in the ballroom, despite the many barbed tongues. Go change. I believe you'll find suitable attire in your room."

Being referred to as a charity case rubbed Kara the wrong way, but something else had caught her ear. "Dancing? I thought you were an etiquette instructor."

"And where do you think all the important business takes place? Not at ladies' tea parties, whatever Valancourt would have you think. Travincal's balls—and for that matter, those at the royal palace in Lerathil—are glorified business meetings with musical accompaniment. Now go and change into something more appropriate. I bill by the hour."

Kara sighed. "I assume those are for me?" She nodded at the slippers in his hand.

The dancing master smiled and tossed them to her.

Kara stomped back up to her room and donned the cream-colored gown draped across the settee and a pair of white stockings that ended in a band of lace around her thighs. Kara left the corset where it was. There was no way she'd be able to lace the thing by herself, and it looked dreadfully tiny. How were women supposed to breathe in such contraptions? There was a bell pull next to her bed that she could probably use to summon assistance, but she'd much rather feign ignorance.

Kara felt naked in the clothes. They were too soft, too feminine. She felt like an impostor. The dress swept the floor in delicate curves. Bits of trimmed white lace peeked out from behind the collar. It was a piece of outlandish finery by Mudbottom standards. Her family would never have been able to afford anything like it. Kara hadn't even had the traditional muslin dresses the village girls wore growing up. More often than not she'd tramped around in Wesley's hand-me-downs. Kara trailed her fingers down the lines of the dress, testing the softness of the fabric. She wiped away the tear that slid down her cheek and headed back downstairs.

The dancing master nodded in approval when Kara returned. "You'll do. And now that you're in proper attire, we can make proper introductions. I'm Philipe Galois, trainer to royals and peers for over twenty years."

"I'm Kara." She stuck out her hand.

Philipe frowned at the proffered handshake. "Just *Kara?* We'll have to work on that. People will believe what they see, what you present to them. Cultivating your public image is the first step to working among the peerage. Now, don't offer to shake my hand. Men shake hands. *Common* men shake hands. If the person you're greeting ranks above you, as most of them will, you should curtsy. If you were in a scenario where it was necessary to masquerade as nobility, or even royalty, you might proffer your hand to be kissed."

Kara curtsied dramatically low, her nose nearing the floor.

"While I appreciate the effort, that was far too deep a curtsy for the likes of me. Don't give anyone an inch more than they warrant. There is a language to bows and curtsies, one people will expect you to know if you're to fit in."

"Have you ever trained anyone like me?"

"A low-born mercenary? Of course not. They can't afford me. But the price is right, so you will learn. You're to be trained in dancing, etiquette, and court politics."

Kara wondered how much the baroness was paying for this man's attention. She was uneasy about being her newest project. People tended to expect a return from their investments.

"Now—" he pulled a pocket watch on a golden chain from his jacket pocket, "we've wasted exactly thirty-one minutes already." Philipe strode to the piano and pulled a braided golden cord that hung beneath the keys. A relaxed tune began to tinkle across the keys, as if they were being pressed by phantom fingers. "It's enchanted," Philipe said. "Not very refined, but it will do in a pinch. You don't play, do you?"

"Never."

"Harp?"

Kara shook her head.

"Flute?" Philipe asked hopefully.

Kara had squeaked along with Wesley a few times during Mudbottom's festivals. Kara waved her hand in a so-so motion.

"Well. I certainly hope you're better versed in the instruments of war."

Philipe took one of Kara's hands in his and laid the other at her waist, standing a modest distance away from her. He hummed beneath his breath, muttering an eight-count as the music reached the desired point.

"Step in time with me. We'll begin with a simple box step and work our way up to a waltz. It's one of the most useful dances to have under your belt, as there will be one at every ball."

Kara trod on his toes more than once as they swung about the room. For all of Philipe's grace, she felt stiff and awkward. Philipe paused in their dance and lifted her chin. "Look in your partner's eyes, not at your feet. If you can manage swordsmanship, then you can do this. Don't worry about misstepping—just follow my lead. Anticipate where my body is going, where it's going to be next, and follow in kind. Don't resist."

Kara's rhythm slowly improved as she learned to relax, and eventually they could make a whole circuit of the ball-room with her only making a few mistakes.

"You're a fast learner."

The ballroom doors creaked open in the middle of a song, and Logan entered. Kara skidded to a stop and bumped into Philipe.

"Please, don't stop on my account."

"Actually, if Monsieur Vakarian would not mind standing in for me, I could provide real musical accompaniment. And observing you from afar will allow me the opportunity for better critique."

"I don't think that's a good—"

"I'd love to," Logan interrupted, already striding towards her. "It's not often I get to see my recruits in dresses."

Philipe pulled the piano's cord again, and the music stopped abruptly. He sat down and stretched his fingers over the keys.

"You don't have to do this," Kara muttered into Logan's chest, reluctantly taking his hand in hers.

"Oh, but I want to."

The music began, and Kara glanced up into his glittering eyes. Logan gripped her with confidence, narrowing the space between them with the press of a hand on her lower back. He was taller than Philipe, and tilting her head back to look him in the eyes felt like surrender.

Logan spun her about the ball room with finesse and control. It was surreal. As a young girl, Kara's peers had dreamt of fancy lords sweeping them off their feet at a ball, but she'd always tried to keep her expectations realistic. And now the most intimidating man she'd ever met was twirling her around a grand ballroom and eating her up with his gaze.

"You look lovely, Kara. The aristocracy would adore you."

Kara snorted, but the comment sent a trill of satisfaction through her core.

"You dance well." She let him take control of her movements. How could her body make mistakes with his guiding her, whispering its rhythm and motions against her skin?

"I was trained well."

"By?"

"Someone from my past."

"You might be more forthcoming, Logan, after all we've shared."

The muscle in his jaw ticked. "What we shared was a necessity."

"A pleasurable one." She drew a finger over his collar, stroking the soft skin of his neck.

His breath shortened, and he shot her a warning glare. "Don't do this."

"Do what, Commander?"

His hand tightened on her waist, and he spun her faster about the room. Philipe picked up his tempo to compensate. "Don't start a game you can't possibly win."

"Did your mother teach you?" Kara asked, eager to know more about his past.

Logan gave a harsh bark of laughter. "My mother wanted nothing to do with me after my birth. A marked child—male no less. She probably would've killed me if my father didn't stop her."

Kara missed her next step. "I'm sorry, Logan. I didn't know."

"They were both Sanguines—high-ranking officers—

and the former Sanguine commander sided with Urian during the Curse Wars. Their commander led parties that hunted down and killed cursed children and any willing to protect them, town by town. After I was born, my father made his choice. He took me and anyone who would follow and formed the Stygian Brotherhood. A decision he died for." Logan's voice was hollow, his gaze distant.

Kara caressed Logan's thumb with her own, trying to soothe some of the storm that was waging across his face. She wanted to hug him. "Your father was trying to protect you. He sounds like a great man."

Logan closed his eyes and took a breath. "He would've liked you."

"Where is your mother now?"

"I don't know. I don't even remember her face."

Their dance continued in silence. As the music reached its climax, Logan dipped Kara towards the floor. She gasped as she fell backwards, but the strong arm beneath her back held her steady. Logan's other hand fluttered at her jaw, then lowered in a sensuous trail down her chest and abdomen, his tanned fingers a dark crush against the pale fabric of her dress.

Her skin flamed in the wake of his path, and she felt an insistent tug in the pit of her stomach.

The music stopped, and Logan abruptly snapped her to a standing position. She felt dizzy, flustered, left wanting. Philipe was clapping.

"Brava, brava. We will make a debutante of the little Stygian princess yet. Lessons are over for today, madame. I'll see you tomorrow."

CHAPTER SEVENTEEN

The next day over lunch, the baroness joined them. She took a seat at the head of the table, and the chatter between the mercenaries quieted.

The baroness's enormous hat wobbled unsteadily as she turned towards Kara. "Kara, my ladies and I are taking tea in the salon this afternoon. I would love for you to join us. They'd be thrilled to meet a Stygian lady, and it would give you an opportunity to practice your lessons."

Save me, Kara mouthed silently to Jon across the table. The last thing she wanted was to be paraded in front of the baroness's rich friends like some sort of curiosity.

"Ah, Baroness," Jon said, "forgive me, but I promised to take Kara on a tour of the city today. She's never visited Travincal's market or the guild before."

Lady Valancourt's lips pursed. "How disappointing. I suppose it would do her some good to be exposed to a little culture, though. Raucous as it may be. Very well. Next week, then. And do sit up, girl. I've had maids blacking my hearth with better posture than you."

. . .

"WE'LL HAVE a look at the contracts available, see who's hiring," Jon said as they approached the Mercenary Guild's headquarters later that day. A marble arch with an eagle's head sprouting from its center framed the guild's entrance, peering down on all who entered. Inside, the halls were dark and restless, teeming with members of the various clans. Jon led her into the depths of the building. The mercenaries they passed scanned them as they went by, sizing them up. Kara kept her eyes peeled for anyone in red who looked familiar.

She and Jon came to a large room where people milled about talking. A clerk was seated at a stone desk at the edge of the room, and a massive tome lay closed in front of him. A wooden board on the wall with various pieces of parchment pinned to it dominated the space.

"These are the contracts?" Kara asked. "It doesn't seem like enough to sustain all five clans."

"The public ones. Stuff any individual can take on, regardless of their clan affiliation. And it's mostly local targets. There are guild outposts with boards local to their area all over the country. This is really just supplementary stuff—side jobs. Lots of poorly-paid missions, or specific, well-paid tasks that are too dangerous for many to attempt. If you take a contract, it's yours. If the contract remains incomplete for an extended period of time or is returned unfinished, the guild taxes you for every day you held the contract without completing it. So, this board's not to be taken lightly. Don't leave the building with a sheet and your name in the clerk's logbook unless you're really prepared to make good on it."

"So where's the big stuff?"

"The guild acts as a middle man for wealthy private clients who want to work with particular clans or require more discretion. These private contracts are usually time consuming but much more profitable. The clan leaders meet the clients and try to sell their services at meetings like the one we came here for."

"Seems like it could all be better handled without the guild, honestly."

Jon nodded. "There are many who agree with you. For years the clans had their own private businesses carved out within their territories. Prospective clients would come straight to them, not the guild. But the clans grew too powerful. After the Sanguine-Stygian split and the resulting bloodshed, people wanted a neutral party to manage things during peacetime. The guild is meant to be a mediating force between the clans, though they can become a policing force if things start to get too bloody."

"They have the numbers for that?"

Jon shrugged. "Depends on who needs policing."

One of the contracts on the board stood out among its peers. It was stained with blood and tattered at the edges. Kara moved forward to read it.

Bounty contract for Saphia Kingslayer, dead or alive. Vispilian defector and disturber of the peace. Warning: highly volatile marked female. Proceed with caution. It was dated five years ago. There was a sketch of a woman's angular face beneath the words.

"Who is she?"

Jon came over to the board and chuckled. "So that's still up here, aye? Surprised they don't take it down. Plenty of mercs have tried and failed with that one. Nice thing about contracts—if your failure to complete one involves dying, at least you don't owe the guild any taxes." The award sum on the poster had been marked over and increased several times.

"Who posted it originally?"

Jon shrugged. "Public contracts are often listed anonymously, and a guild bookkeeper will arrange the reward.

People like to keep their identities secret, lest they grow a target of their own."

Jon pointed to the opposite corner of the board. "Look at this one, it was posted today." Kara noted that the contracts were in chronological order, and there were ones even older than Saphia's posted on the board. The poster Jon pointed out read: *Disturbers of the peace in Sanguine colors responsible for a domestic dispute in Travincal. Several citizens were injured. Seeking someone to give them their comeuppance. Last seen lodging at the Horn and Hound.* There was an address for the client who issued the contract, and the reward amounted to two month's wages for Kara.

Jon whistled after reading it. "Ballsy for them to include an address."

Kara's fingers smoothed over the contract's edges. She'd found her lead.

"That's not what we're here for, Kara," Jon said, laying a gentle hand on her arm.

"Something doesn't add up. The guild doesn't condone assassinations, yet they allow dead or alive bounties on their public board? Do they really expect people like—" Kara glanced back at the blood-spattered contract "—Saphia to be brought in alive?"

Jon grinned. "You're starting to catch on. The guild certainly isn't without its own hypocrisy. All public contracts go through a brief review process, and specific cases like Saphia's bounty are examined for just cause."

A voice from behind them said, "More like probable cause, given enough greased palms, connections, and brown-nosing."

Kara swirled. It was Rahj. He'd appeared soundlessly, like so many of the Stygians seemed adept at doing.

He clapped a hand on Kara's shoulder. "Enjoying your visit to our little bureaucracy? Sometimes I miss the old days. Less paperwork. I'm relieved you're here though, Jon. I need to talk to you. Guild business."

Jon looked between Rahj and Kara. "Alright. I'll meet you back at Valancourt's, Kara. Try not to tarry. This city goes to shit at night."

Kara nodded. The absence of supervision would be an opportunity to explore the city on her own terms and get acquainted with the Sanguines in town. She waited until Jon and Rahj's voices had faded down the hallway, then ripped the most recent contract from its peg and headed towards the clerk's desk.

Kara handed the contract to the clerk, an older man with thinning white hair and glasses. He raised an eyebrow at her. "Thought that wasn't what you were here for."

Cheeky bastard. "He's not my master."

"So be it." The clerk flicked his eyes over her body. "Ain't those Stygian colors? Or you just like wearing black?"

"They are."

The man shook his head. "Yer stirrin' a pot that don't want to be stirred. Why don't you pick another contract? Something you'll be breathing at the end of."

Kara smiled, but it was all teeth. "I'll play nice."

"Sure you will. Look darling, Sanguines don't take kindly to people contract-huntin' 'em. I'm not usually in the business of losing easy money for the guild, but you look new. Future profit to be made, ya know? Sure you don't wanna reconsider?"

"Give me the contract." Kara didn't want to think about the consequences, she wanted to act. She could deal with the consequences later. Or crash into them headfirst.

"Don't say I didn't warn ya. If you still have your tongue, that is."

The clerk stamped the contract with a wax seal and

opened the massive ledger in front of him. The pages crawled with names in black ink. "Name?"

Kara paused. Better to leave as little trail as possible. "Maria."

"Got a last name?"

"Not anymore."

"So be it. You got a week, Maria. Sanguines will be clearing out after that, and the guarantor is paying for expediency." He handed the contract back to her.

Kara read the address of the client. They'd be able to give her more details on the Sanguines they'd seen. "153 Oxswitch Avenue. You know where that is?"

"Other side of town. Shitty neighborhood. Fastest way's through the bazaar, if you can stand the stench."

()

TRAVINCAL WAS the southern center of trade and enterprise in Teleria. The bazaar at the heart of the city stretched as far as the eye could see. Kara didn't question where she was going because everyone on the street was headed to the same place. What was intended as a large, circular open market was turned into chaos by vendors who'd set up their stalls in haphazard rows, forcing foot traffic to loop through the bazaar in an indirect manner. There was no walking straight across to the other side.

The market teemed with people. Competing merchants shouted, hawking their wares. Street urchins ran underfoot, picking pockets and stealing produce. Other children set up in the middle of the road to beg. The wares on display were so varied and colorful—Kara had never seen the like. Swathes of vibrant fabric dyed every color of the rainbow lined many of the merchants' tables. Others held crates full of plump nuts and exotic fruits that caught her eye. She hadn't finished her lunch today, and she was beginning to feel peckish. She grabbed a handful of red fruits with tough little knobby skins from a crate and paid the merchant for them. When peeled, they revealed a soft clear pulp clinging to a dark brown pit. They were incredibly sweet, and Kara ate them until her hands grew sticky from the juice. She discarded the skins and pits in the chaos of the street.

When she passed the stall of a tall woman in chainmail with a dragonling on her shoulder, Kara did a double take. The dragon flapped its wings and puffed a ring of smoke into her face. It had iridescent ruby scales and a tiny forked tail. Its eyes tracked Kara with a knowing gleam.

The woman smiled at her. "That means he likes you. You have a lot of fire in you, eh?" Her accent was foreign and thick—Kara couldn't place it.

"Something like that. What are you selling, exactly?" The table was full of chainmail bits and thin, finely wrought leashes made of linked metal.

"The dragon, of course. And his paraphernalia." The woman stroked the dragon's neck with a heavily gauntleted hand, and Kara wondered if the armor was a precautionary measure.

"What's his name?"

The woman laughed as if Kara had said something ridiculous. "I don't know. I cannot name someone else's dragon."

"How much is he?"

"25,000 gold pieces."

Kara coughed, alarmed. It was a modest fortune. Not that she had any need of a baby dragon—how big would he grow to be, anyways? But the little fellow struck a chord in her with his inquisitive gaze.

"I'm afraid I can't afford that." It was unlikely she

would be able to splurge on such a creature in her lifetime, let alone at twenty-four.

"A pity," the woman said and averted her gaze to the next potential customer.

The dragonling was not the only living merchandise for sale at the center of the bazaar's maze. One stall hosted a menagerie full of cages holding exotic, brightly-colored birds, including a parrot the size of a young child. The birds cawed and trilled, claws scraping against the cage rails as they beat their wings.

Kara spotted the glint of red metal through the crowd and stilled, overcome by old memories. Two men in Sanguine uniforms stood on the other side of the menagerie stall, arguing with its proprietor. She became uncomfortably aware of the fact that she only had one set of daggers on her. She'd left her jeweled pair at the manor house for fear of the ruby pommels attracting thieves.

Kara moved closer to Sanguines, taking care to stay hidden behind the cluster of bodies in the bazaar. They were grilling the merchant about a blond woman with a scar, asking if he'd seen her. The merchant stuttered his responses. One of the Sanguines, a black man with a shaved head, gripped the man by his shirtfront, threatening him. His partner wore a metal helmet that obscured his face. When they were satisfied the merchant didn't know anything, they moved on to the next stall, and the next, asking after the blond woman. Kara trailed them from a distance. She didn't recognize them from the raid, but they could lead her to others.

Kara followed them until they veered off the bazaar's main loop and headed into a tavern advertising the best mincemeat pie in the city. She faltered when she saw the sign. The Horn and Hound, the same tavern named on the contract. She hesitated, fingering the edges of the contract in her pocket, then followed them inside.

The wooden door swung shut behind her, and all she saw was red. Bloody metal filled the seats. Her stomach turned. She scanned the faces of the crowd, searching for anyone familiar. The two she'd been tailing were sitting close to the door. Her blood ran cold when she saw the antlered helm cast in gilded in silver. It sat atop a table in the back by the bar.

Cervus. He was here somewhere, wearing a face she didn't know. Memories assaulted her. Da's head swinging from a gauntleted fist, the fur trim of Wesley's jacket poking out from under the blanket. Kara's mark began to burn. She felt like she was going to be sick. The Sanguines started to notice her, and cold sweat beaded on her brow. She couldn't stay. She was in her Stygian uniform; they would make her immediately. Kara spun around and left, walking as quickly as she could without breaking into a run. She wove through the bazaar in random directions, hoping to lose anyone who'd followed her out of the tavern. She wished Jon was here—not that he'd have let her get into this predicament to begin with.

After a while the bazaar traffic began to thin out. Kara had to lean against a building and wait for her nausea to subside. The richly appointed stalls targeting tourists and the wealthy had faded into food stalls with old meat left rotting in the sun, children with dirty faces running around in rags, and a much more pervasive stench. Kara drew her cloak over her abused nostrils. She was surprised they were able to keep this smell out of the rest of the city. According to the clerk, she was near the address on the contract.

Kara was a little taken aback when she found the house. 153 Oxswitch Avenue was the home of a squalid house on the outer edges of the bazaar. The windows were blacked out, and the street in front of it was full of muddy divots from wagons and horses passing through. Kara approached the house slowly, half expecting someone to dart out from the shadows and grab her. She steeled her will and knocked on the door.

"Come in," said a female voice from inside. Kara paused. She hadn't expected her client to be a woman.

Kara gingerly opened the door, taking care to keep the majority of her body mass away from the opening in case any projectiles came her way. Inside the house a woman with dark crimson lips and a loose braid sat at the kitchen table, filing her nails. Her blond hair was so pale that it almost looked white.

"You're letting in the street."

Kara stepped inside and slid the door closed behind her. The woman sized her up in a glance, barely looking up from her nails. She had an old, faded scar spanning her neck. Had someone tried to cut her throat?

Kara cleared her throat. "I'm here about the contract."

"Fresh blood, huh? I'm Saphia. And you are...?"

"Kara," she murmured in a far less confident voice than intended. Kara fought to keep her expression still. *The Saphia? Dead or alive Saphia?* The likeness was there. Kara felt as if she'd walked into something far bigger than herself.

"People don't usually take contracts against the Sanguines. Are you new?" She punctuated her words with crisp consonants, her ruby lips moving over pointed white teeth.

"Sort of."

"And your clan?"

"Stygian."

Saphia paused, then looked up from her filing. "How peculiar. I heard Vakarian had two new female recruits.

You're not the redhead, so you must be the marked one. Mind showing me? Never can be too trusting these days." There was a dangerous glint in Saphia's eye.

Kara pulled up her sleeve, revealing her mark. Who was giving Saphia intel? Someone in the clan?

"Blooded and everything. Fascinating." Saphia's lips split in a crimson grin. "Be careful who you show Namirah's brand to while you're in town. Some are eager to exploit it."

"I heard that you were marked, too."

Saphia nodded, dropping the file on the table and making her way to a bottle of wine on the counter. "Who told you that?

"There's a bounty poster for you at the guild."

"Ah. They've put that back up, have they? Shouldn't believe everything you read on the boards. Wine?"

Kara nodded. "I'm just here about the Sanguines."

Saphia passed her a glass, and Kara realized that her nails were filed into sharp, claw-like points.

"You look new. Too new to be stirring up old blood between the black and red." She made a tsking noise behind her teeth. "Your commander would not be happy about that. I take it he doesn't know?"

"Logan doesn't control me," Kara snapped.

Saphia rose one eyebrow. "Still, I'd advise you to take that contract back. You could even do it today, before you owe much on it. Honestly, I didn't expect anyone to be stupid enough to take it."

"What do you mean?" Kara took a sip of the wine after Saphia took a hearty gulp from her glass. It was a dry red that danced on her tongue then went down smooth.

"No sane person is gonna start hunting red meat when they're all in town for the meeting. Too many opportunities for something to go wrong. That contract was bait."

"You…want them to come after you?"

"Indeed. I need information, and my keening started yesterday. Two birds; one sword. You snatched up my bait a few hours after it was posted, but that doesn't mean none of their men saw it. Hell, the clerk could even be in their pocket. This location isn't secure."

"I want to help."

Saphia snorted. "You don't even know me, girl. We may be sisters of Namirah, but that's a superficial bond. Trust me, you don't want my kind of trouble."

Kara twirled a finger around the rim of the wine glass. "I don't want to help *you*. I want to help *me*."

A spark lit Saphia's eyes.

"The Sanguines were responsible for my family's death. I owe them a debt."

Saphia laughed again, then swallowed the rest of her wine. "I'm surprised Vakarian touched you with a ten foot-pole."

"You know him well?" Kara asked, bracing herself for the response. She got the impression the man had slept his way through half of Teleria.

Saphia waved her hand in a dismissive gesture. "Brief acquaintance. Quarrelsome man. You haven't fucked him, have you?"

"No," Kara whispered between tight teeth. Not technically, anyways.

"Ought to keep it that way. The curse is a bitch, but it would…complicate things. Trust me. And you should be careful with the Sanguines. Haven't you heard of Victus's latest exploit?

"I know he's been kidnapping women like us. I had a run in with one of them already, before I joined the Stygians."

"You're lucky it was just one. Victus has gone full crocked."

"Do you know where he's keeping them?" If Saphia had any new information, Kara could pass it on to Logan.

"Probably in the bleeding heart of Sanguine territory."

"Is he trying to replay the Curse Wars or something?"

"He claims it's all much nobler than that, but who the fuck knows. Could just be another of his twisted schemes."

Heavy footsteps sounded outside, and a rabid gleam came over Saphia's eyes. "You any good with those daggers?"

Kara nodded.

"Get ready."

The front door flew open, and five Sanguine mercenaries burst through the door. The two men from the market earlier were among them. They had swords drawn as they walked into the house. Kara looked to Saphia for ideas, but she had vanished. A sword slid through the belly of one of the mercs, and his screams rent the air. Saphia came into view as he fell. She'd circled the house to come at them from behind. Kara had no idea how she'd moved so quickly. A hole in the roof, maybe? The thought fled her mind as two of the mercs turned to focus on her.

Kara unsheathed her daggers and scanned the kitchen for other potential weapons. The men were approaching her from opposite angles, trying to corner her against the kitchen wall. One of them was the helmeted fellow from earlier. Kara grabbed the kitchen chair and threw it at the helmeted man, then leapt towards the other. His sword swung towards her face, and she dodged, feeling the whip of air it left in its wake. She thrust her dagger into his jugular and dug past the resistance of flesh and sinew. The man gurgled blood and flailed his hands.

Kara withdrew her dagger and felt the cold kiss of steel

meet her neck. Saphia was out of sight beyond the door, but the sounds of a struggle ensued.

"Lay down your weapons," the helmeted man said behind her. The cadence of his voice was oddly familiar. "You're not who we're here for, Stygian or not."

Kara released her daggers with a clatter. "What are you here for?" she whispered, the blade uncomfortable against the skin of her throat.

"We're collecting a known instigator." The man's green-eyed gaze darted rapidly across her face as she turned to him. He looked down at her arm, where her sleeve was still drawn up, and his breath hitched. "You... what are you doing here?"

"We gotta get outta here!" his remaining comrade yelled as he scrambled towards the door. Saphia limped after him, his sword in her grip.

The green-eyed man's sword wavered against Kara's skin. He walked backwards towards the door, keeping his weapon brandished. Once he cleared the threshold, the men fled down the alley next to the house, and Kara hurried over to Saphia. Blood leaked from a cut on her thigh, and she had a mean bruise across her right cheek-bone, but other than that she looked unharmed.

Three dead men lay on the dirty floor of the house, their dark blood slowly pooling around them. Saphia spat on the floor.

"Fucking brats—not training them like they used to. It's a pity these three aren't alive to talk. You handled your-self well, aside from getting held up at sword point and all. Surprised he didn't slit your throat."

"Me too," Kara said, still confused.

Saphia knelt beside one of the fallen Sanguines and rifled through his coin purse. She pulled out a metal coin stamped with the Sanguine sigil, a bleeding rose wrapped in thorns, and passed it to Kara before emptying the rest of the man's purse.

"Here. I'll sign your contract using an alias, and you can take this as proof for the guild clerk. He'll see you're paid."

Kara took the coin. It'd been smudged with blood from Saphia's hands. "What is it?"

"Victus gives them out at initiation, after his recruits prove their loyalty. They've gotta do some gruesome shit to get their hands on one of those."

Kara slid the coin into her pocket. She didn't want to touch it any longer. "What will you do now? You can't stay here."

Saphia shrugged. "This isn't my house. Owner's out of town, thought I'd avail myself. Still, Victus will be on high alert after losing three of his men. It's time to skip town. Maybe head into their territory, see what I can find out about the marked women he has. It'll be easier hunting with so much of the clan in Travincal." She nodded towards Kara. "You're welcome to come with me, if you'd like."

The offer surprised her. This wasn't a woman who seemed like she did friendships, or liked company much at all. "I've got over a year and a half left on my contract with the Stygians."

"Contract, shmontract. The pay's shit and the food's shittier. I'll tell you one thing, having a public bounty on your head provides plenty of fuel for keening. Though most have stopped trying on mine. It's a shame, really."

"The Stygians have been good to me. I appreciate the offer, but I can't betray them."

Saphia rolled her eyes and wiped the blood off her blade using the pantleg of a dead man. "You mean they've coddled you. They certainly haven't let you seek vengeance, not while you wear their colors. You got a taste of it today. Tasted good, didn't it?"

Yes. "I'm sorry, Saphia, but I can't."

Saphia shrugged. "So be it. Our paths will likely cross again. I'm unlucky that way. Till then, Kara of the Stygian."

"What about the bodies?"

Saphia shrugged. "Sanguines will deal with it. Moving them is too risky. Besides, they already have witnesses. You should get home before nightfall. They'll be looking for someone to punish."

Kara swallowed roughly and collected her daggers. "It was nice to meet you."

"A lie if I've ever heard one." Saphia turned to leave, then paused, her lips twisting. "How's the old battleaxe doing, by the way? Still kicking?"

"Who?"

"Aethyta."

"How do you know her?"

Saphia flashed her a bitter smile. "You mean she didn't tell you? She's my mother."

Kara's jaw dropped. "I knew she had a marked daughter, but—"

"Don't worry about it. It's no surprise she doesn't claim me. I don't have a sterling reputation, as you might have gathered."

"She's well. Still a hardass. Still making new recruits wish they'd never been born."

"Her goddess given talent. Thank you, Kara. Be well. Go with the goddess."

Kara nodded and drew up her cloak over her head. She wanted to ask more questions, but it wouldn't take long for the survivors to make it back to their inn. She left via the back entrance. The sun had sunk alarmingly low in the sky, and shadows crawled up the narrow walls of Oxswitch Avenue. Night cast a foreboding pall over the neighborhood, and the hundreds of empty market stalls in the bazaar looked eerie by moonlight. Few people walked the streets at night in this area of town. Everyone was inside, safe. Kara took a circuitous route back to Valancourt's, sticking to the shadows at the edge of the market and checking often that she wasn't being followed.

The green-eyed Sanguine nagged at the edges of her mind. And Saphia, what an intriguing woman. Was that the kind of life Kara's future held? Always running from something, killing anyone who got in the way?

She relaxed a touch when she reached the more affluent part of town. Here city guards patrolled the streets with kerosene lamps, keeping watch. Candles, lanterns, and fae lights were on inside Valancourt's manor house, and sounds came from within the parlor. Kara was loath to enter the front door like this, but she was too tired to try climbing up to her balcony. When she opened the door, Jeffrey started in his chair, frightened half out of his skin by someone who would dare to enter without knocking. Jon rushed forward from the parlor, pulled Kara's hood back, and gripped her to him in a tight hug. He was strong and warm, and Kara realized with a twinge of sadness that the last person who'd hugged her like this was Da.

Jon leaned back and gripped her shoulders. "Mother Night, I'm glad you're back. I've been sick with worry. I sent Thomas and Faedra out looking for you. I thought maybe you'd gotten lost. Where have you been?"

"I'm fine, Jon. I just wanted to explore the bazaar, look at all the stalls."

"The market's been closed since five, Kara." He released her and stepped back. "Where have you really been?"

"I went to a bar afterwards." Kara kept her bloody hands fisted in her cloak so he wouldn't see them.

The tightness of Jon's mouth told her he didn't believe her. "There's some Sanguine unrest in the city right now— I thought maybe…"

"Well, you thought wrong." Kara closed the conversation with clipped tones. Right now she wanted a hot meal and a warm bed, not an inquisition. "Jeffrey, I'm famished. Can you have something brought to my room?"

"Yes, mistress."

Kara headed for the stairs, leaving Jon in the parlor staring after her.

CHAPTER EIGHTEEN

Kara left her bedroom window open to air out her room that night. She struggled to get to sleep with the evening's adrenaline still running through her. After an hour of tossing and turning, she stretched out on top of the covers and stared at the ceiling, trying to get the image of those familiar green eyes out of her head.

When fatigue finally pulled her under, Kara was plagued by nightmares. She dreamt she was back in their house at Mudbottom, hiding from the Sanguine Rider pounding on the door. The events of that day replayed themselves in slow motion. Kara snuck out of the house and moved towards the stable, unable to stop herself. She tried to scream, to remind herself that Yuki was already dead, but no sound came from her lips.

The helmeted Sanguine from Oxswitch Avenue rounded Yuki's stall, a sinister leer on his lips. His face flashed, and his blood-red helm shifted into a mask made of bones, then back again. His eyes pierced her. Kara threw her hunting knife and watched as it sunk into his left eye. He fell to the ground and writhed. She walked over, knelt beside him, and pulled his helmet off. Dread slid down her throat.

Wesley's one clear green eye stared up at her, the other bloody and mangled. Details she'd forgotten in the months since she'd seen him came rushing back to her—his sly lips, dark hair burnished by the sun, the scar above his eyebrow he'd gotten from the pox. He looked up at her like she'd betrayed him.

Then Wesley smiled, and Kara felt metal slide into her gut. She screamed.

Kara jerked awake, gasping for air. Her shift was soaked in sweat, and her heart was trying to pound its way out of her chest. *Wesley was alive!* Elation swelled inside her. One-Eye hadn't been lying. Wesley was alive and with the Sanguines. He'd been at Oxswitch Avenue, mere feet from her. He'd recognized her, she was sure of it, and yet he hadn't said anything. What the hell was going on? Was he their captive? Were they forcing him to work for them?

There was a loud crack, and the door connecting her room to the neighboring one burst open. Kara scrambled out of bed, getting tangled in the sheets and falling to the floor in the process. Two large bare feet and chiseled calf muscles stepped into the room.

"Kara? Are you okay?" Logan asked.

Kara cursed and risked a glance up at him. Yep, completely naked. She looked back down at his legs. They were very nice legs.

"I heard you scream."

So the scream hadn't just been in the dream. "I had a nightmare. Your room is next to mine?"

"I didn't request it. I think Valancourt had her suspicions about us." Logan kneeled next to her and pushed her hair behind her ear. "Are you okay?"

Kara nodded. She was tempted to tell Logan about Wesley, but doubt crept into her mind. The clan always came first with him, and she'd already broken his rule about antagonizing the Sanguines today. Rescuing Wesley would require further conflict, and what if he thought Wesley was working for them willingly? She would wait until she could find out more to bring it to him.

"I can sense your thoughts racing. What's going on?"

Kara looked up into his eyes. They were soft and warm tonight. She trailed a hand over his chest muscles, and they flexed beneath her touch. She wanted to lose herself in him.

"Why are you *always* naked, Commander?"

"I sleep in the nude," he growled. "Stop trying to change the subject."

Kara wanted to kiss the scowl off his lips. She brought a hand to his cheek and trailed her fingers towards his mouth.

"Kara..."

She rose to her knees and pressed her lips to his. His whole body stiffened beneath her; his lips were still and unresponsive.

Kara sighed against his mouth, about to back away, when Logan crushed her body against his. He grabbed her ass and pulled her flush against his hips, then plundered her mouth with his lips and tongue. He fisted his hands in her hair and pulled her head back, then ran kisses along her jaw and licked the length of her neck.

Kara could feel the evidence of his desire growing against her core, and she ground herself against that hard heat. "Logan, please...," she said in a breathy voice.

"Please what?" he growled, nipping at her earlobe.

"I want you."

"You're not keening."

"How do you know that?"

"Trust me. I would know," he said, a sensual heat in his eyes.

"So what!" Kara ran her hand down his body and stroked his cock. He was already hard for her. He felt like steel sheathed in silk. "You want this."

Logan jumped away from her like she'd scalded him. Her body cried out in frustration. "We can't, Kara."

"Then leave! I don't want you here," she yelled. She wished she had something to throw at him.

Logan nodded and padded towards the door, revealing the taut muscles of his butt. "I'm sorry, Kara. This wasn't supposed to happen." He swung the door to behind him, but Kara doubted the lock worked anymore.

She collapsed back into bed with an irritated huff and kicked her feet at the mattress. Why did Logan have to be so in control all the damn time? Why couldn't he just let go? And then there was the dream. It had threatened to fade into her memory, but it came surging back now, replaying in her mind. Could Wesley really be alive? Was she just deluding herself? She needed to see his face again. Kara took a few deep breaths and tried to slow her racing thoughts, but sleep eluded her. She was wide awake.

She crawled back out of bed and opened the door to the balcony to let more of the cool night air in. She was about to turn around when she heard a low, sensual groan. The hair on the back of her neck stood up. She peeked her head around the door and stifled a gasp. Logan stood on his balcony a few feet away, running a hand down his stiff cock. He'd donned a black silk robe, but he was naked beneath it. Blood shot to Kara's core at the sight. She was a little miffed that he'd chosen to pleasure himself alone, but the sight of him fisting his hand up and down the length of his cock was mesmerizing. He must not have heard her open the door. His senses were usually sharp, but maybe he was caught up in the moment.

Kara contemplated returning to bed, but she didn't want to look away. The length and shape of his erection was impressive. She bit her lip at the thought of him sliding into her with it, filling her up. Her core was pulsing with need. *To hell with it*, she thought. Kara pulled her shift up and slid her hand down between her legs. She was soaking wet, and the first brush of her finger against her clit sent a jolt of pleasure through her.

Kara twisted her head to keep Logan in sight through the crack in the door and propped her back up against the doorframe. He was increasing the pace of his strokes, and the little groans of pleasure he made turned her on even more. She was tightly wound—already close to orgasm thanks to how pent up her desire had been lately.

"Yes...Kara," Logan moaned, low and long, his back arching as he reached his climax. His cum shot out of the throbbing head of his cock as he stroked it with his hand, spilling over his fingers. He was captivating. Kara began rubbing herself harder and faster, praying that he wouldn't hear the sound of her fingers against her wet lips. Her orgasm came quickly, and Kara bit back a moan as her whole body thrummed with pleasure.

Logan was still standing there, staring up at the sky like he was waiting on something, still milking his cock. If he was a horse, she imagined his ears would be curved back towards her. The corner of his lips curled up in a smile. Kara turned away and slid the door to silently, then went back to bed.

( )

KARA WENT DOWN to breakfast on uneasy legs the next morning. She hadn't slept for shit—her thoughts had kept her awake. At breakfast she was thankful Jon didn't bring up her late evening the night before. Logan was nowhere to be found, as usual.

Her lessons with Philipe passed in a blur. They went over the various members of the aristocracy at King Calim's court. The knowledge fled her mind as quickly as it entered—her thoughts were too full of Wesley and Saphia and the Sanguines and Logan. Annoyed by her preoccupation, Philipe let her go early.

Kara left the house, afraid that the baroness would try to recruit her for another tea party if she ran into her. She headed back to the Mercenary Guild to turn in her contract. The guild halls were more crowded today. Mercenaries milled about in the hallway, chatting. The big private contract meetings must be happening soon.

When Kara arrived at the contract room, the same clerk was on duty. He looked surprised to see her. His jaw dropped a little when she put the signed contract and the Sanguine coin on his desk. He quickly slid them across the table and tucked them into his desk drawer, glancing around at the room's occupants.

"That was fast. Am I to assume you'll be splitting the reward money with someone?"

"No."

He smiled, but it didn't reach his eyes. "My apologies. It's just…contracts are rarely completed so quickly." He flicked his gaze over her. "Or so painlessly. Especially those of this…variety. But we thank you for your service."

The clerk pulled the necklace he wore out of his shirt and over his head. A small key dangled from it. He used the key to unlock another drawer and began counting out coins from it and placing them in a tidy pile on his desk. He evened out the stack and slid the coins towards her. Kara scooped them up. It was the most money she'd ever held at once in her life. She slid the coins into the secure pouch the Stygian uniform had sewn into its lining.

"Is there anything else?" the clerk asked. He kept glancing behind Kara at something, worry in his expression.

"That will be all. Thank you."

When Kara turned around, Logan was leaning against the doorframe, steel in his eyes.

Kara gulped. "Commander."

"McKenna." His voice snapped like a whip.

He was pissed. She could sense the fury coming off him in waves. How long had he been there, watching? He'd definitely seen the money. She wasn't sure how she was going to be able to talk her way out of this one. Had he seen the Sanguine coin, too?

"Aren't you coming?" he asked.

Kara walked towards him reluctantly. When she got close enough, he grabbed her wrist and led her out into the corridor. She followed him through the maze of hallways until he opened a random door, pulled her into it, and slammed it shut. "This room is spelled against eaves-dropping."

It was a meeting room that held a long table and several chairs. She turned to him, and his gaze burned through her. He'd never looked at her with such hostility before.

"You took out a contract?"

Kara nodded. That much was obvious from her trans-action with the clerk.

"I heard that three Sanguine corpses turned up overnight. Victus was in an outrage at the meeting I was just at. He's threatening the clan responsible for it. Please tell me you had nothing to do with it."

"I can't do that," Kara said. There was no sense in lying; he'd see right through it.

Logan cursed and ran a hand through his hair. "Mother Night. You will be the death of me, woman. What were you thinking? Are you *trying* to get yourself killed?"

"I was trying to find information on the Sanguines from the raid. Things got out of hand."

"No shit." Logan started to pace the room. "The Sanguines are going to demand repayment in blood."

"I wasn't out to kill anyone—just investigating. They attacked us."

"*Us?*" He swiveled towards her. "Who the fuck is *us*? One of my mercenaries?"

"No. The client."

"Who was it?"

"It doesn't matter, Logan. They left the city." She didn't think Logan would take the news of Saphia's involvement well, and Kara was in enough shit with him already.

Logan stopped pacing and laid a hand on her cheek. "Were there any survivors? Do they know your face?"

"Two of them escaped." Kara hadn't fully considered the ramifications of Wesley and the other Sanguine escaping until now. She'd been too caught up in everything else. Wesley wouldn't hurt her, but the other man knew what she looked like now, and that she'd been wearing Stygian colors. Fear settled on her spine.

Logan slammed his hand against the wall. "Fuck.

They're going to be looking for you. I'll assign you a team of bodyguards. Please, don't try and go anywhere without them. Victus won't hesitate to retaliate after you killed his men. Clan on clan conflict is supposed to be kept to a minimum during big guild meetings like this, but you broke that rule. That makes you fair game."

"Bodyguards? I don't need—"

"Don't fucking argue with me about this, Kara. Until we leave the city, you need protection. They'll be discrete."

"Why not just lock me in my room?" A clutch of bodyguards tailing her was the last thing Kara needed. She had to find a way to contact Wesley before the Brotherhood left Travincal.

"I'd love to, but I know how stubborn you are. At least this way there's some chance you'll comply. I'll escort you back to Valancourt's today. You might have been followed here. Is there anything else I need to know about your little contract stunt, before it comes back to bite us in the ass?"

"No, Logan." She wasn't about to tell him about Wesley and Saphia and add more fuel to the fire.

"Then let's get out of here. Place is crawling with reds. There aren't that many women in our clan—you won't be that hard to identify."

Logan had ridden Char to the guild rather than walk, of course. A stable boy fetched him from the guild stable for them. Seeing the tall, dark stallion made Kara miss Drum. She hadn't been to visit her since they'd arrived in Travincal. Logan drew Kara's hood over her face and tucked her hair inside it, then pulled up his own. "Keep your hood up. And we need to get you some clothes that don't scream 'Stygian.' It may be a good time to put some of Philipe's lessons to use."

"How so?"

"You need to pretend to be something you aren't. No dying on my watch."

Kara mounted Char, and Logan followed, putting his hard chest and legs flush against hers. "We both know Victus is more likely to capture me than kill me."

Logan stilled.

"He's already tried once. And I overheard you and Rahj discussing the kidnappings. Put two and two together."

"You might prefer death to Victus's dungeons. But I'm not going to let that happen," he said, shaking with fury. "We'll have bracers made for you so you'll be harder to identify. Like mine."

Char's imposing presence cut a wide swathe through the market alleys, but it was still crowded and noisy. Kara kept a keen eye on the crowd—potential assailants could be lurking in any corner.

Logan pulled aside the corner of Kara's hood and leaned in next to her ear, where he could be heard more clearly over the crowd. The brush of his stubble against her skin sent shivers running through her body. "I wish you wouldn't put yourself in danger."

"Says the man who has a history of bloodshed. What does Victus want with Namirah's Chosen?"

"I wish I knew. I have my theories, but—"

"Tell me."

"Most people see keening as a weakness; Victus sees it as a strength. Killing is survival. If there's a war coming, Victus will want to have the best force that money can buy."

"Or capture."

"He has a knack for persuasion. And those he can't persuade, he'll kill or keep captive so they can't move against him." Logan wrapped his arm around her and rested his palm on her abdomen. "I won't let him take you. But you need to be careful until we get out of this city."

Kara nodded and relaxed against him for the rest of the ride back to Valancourt's.

CHAPTER NINETEEN

K ara awoke that night to a commotion outside her window. Muffled grunting and male voices came from outside. She slid out of bed, ran to the window, and looked down below. Bear was holding a man in a brown cloak as Thomas punched him. It was too far away to make out the features of the cloaked man. Kara went to the balcony door to open it, but the handle wouldn't budge, so she tried the window. It was stuck, too. *What the hell?* She double-checked that the locks were undone and tried again to no avail.

"Bloody hell." Had Logan had her door and windows spelled shut? She wouldn't put it past him. Kara tested the bedroom door and was relieved when it swung open. She grabbed her cloak and headed down the stairs. Jon was sitting in a chair posted by the door, still in his uniform.

"Jon. You're awake. There's something going on outside."

Kara made for the door, and Jon rose and stepped in front of her. "Let me check. It may not be safe."

"You're not my nanny, Jon. It's one man—Bear and Thomas have him."

"Just *wait*, Kara. It could be a trap."

Jon went out the front door, and Kara paced back and forth in the foyer. Soon the door opened again, and Jon, Bear, and Thomas dragged in a limp form by the arms. The man's cloak hung over his face, but Kara's stomach sank when she saw him. He had Wesley's build.

"Is he dead?" Kara asked, her voice cracking.

"Not yet," Thomas said.

Jon pulled back the man's hood, and Kara's fears were confirmed. It was Wesley, his face bruised and bloody. His eyes flicked up towards her through swollen lids. He was wearing dark colors that lent themselves to camouflage instead of his Sanguine uniform. She resisted the urge to run forward and check on him, though seeing him like this pained her. It'd been so long since she'd seen his face. How had she forgotten so quickly? Was her memory of Da going to fade like that, too?

"It's a good thing Logan posted us outside tonight," Bear said. "Found him skulking in the bushes outside your window, Kara."

"Do you know who he is?" Kara asked. She wasn't ready to reveal Wesley's identity to them. As much as she'd grown to trust her Stygian friends, she couldn't trust her brother's fate to them.

"What's your name, boy?" Jon asked.

Wesley gave them a bloody grin. "Dirk."

"Why do I feel like you're lying, *Dirk*?"

"Takes one to know one." Wesley tried to struggle to his feet, and Jon kicked his legs out from under him.

"Stay on your knees. I take it he's a Sanguine who's lost his way. Probably followed someone back here," Jon said.

"Thomas, have the stablemaster prepare us an unmarked carriage. I'll hold him."

Thomas left, and Kara paced the foyer and pulled her cloak tight around her.

Wesley's eyes tracked her. Jon yanked his head back by his hair. "Keep your eyes to yourself, or I'll pluck them out."

Wesley grunted and looked at the floor.

The sound of hoofbeats outside signaled the carriage's arrival. Kara wouldn't be able to follow them on foot and keep up—not at this time of night, when the moon was full and there was no one to blend in with on the street. The stable boys would know if she went and got Drum, let alone anyone Logan had guarding her.

Thomas returned with a burlap sack that he pulled over Wesley's head. Kara winced and looked away. Too late she realized that Jon had seen her expression. Bear and Thomas pulled Wesley up by the arms and escorted him to the carriage, but Jon stayed behind.

"Do you recognize him, Kara?" Jon asked.

"No. I don't think so."

"I didn't think you'd be soft on the Sanguines, given your history."

"I'm not. I was just wondering if you're planning on killing him." *Please say no.*

"No," Jon said, and Kara let go of the breath she'd been holding. "That would just piss Victus off more. But we are going to get some answers out of him. We'll let him go when we leave the city."

When they left the city? She'd never get to talk to Wesley at this rate. "What are you going to do with him?"

"We'll set him up somewhere secure. Can't do it here— too many prying eyes. We need to be discrete."

"I'll come with you. I can help."

"It's better if you stay here. He could have backup, and the manor is easier to secure. Though you ought to be wary of any servants you don't recognize."

Fuck. Where would they take him? Would they torture him for information? Who would do it—Logan himself? She blanched at the thought. How the hell was she going to get Wesley out of this mess? She had a few important questions of her own. She contemplated telling Jon who he was, but it could backfire. If the Stygians knew of their connection, they may keep her away from him.

"Where's Logan at? Shouldn't he be here for this?" Kara asked.

"He had business to attend to tonight."

Kara thought she knew what *business* he was attending to, and it made her grind her teeth. The thought of Logan keening with someone else drove her crazy.

"Go back to bed, Kara. You're safe here," Jon said, then he left.

( )

THE NEXT MORNING, Jon brought a stack of folded clothes to Kara's bedroom. It contained two modest dresses, some shawls, white stockings, and brown flats. The dresses were in muted green and brown tones. The color of the fabric and the style of the clothes were non-assuming and would blend in well with a crowd.

"Did you buy all this?"

Jon nodded and pulled a small velvet bag out of his pocket and handed it to Kara.

Kara sat the clothes on the bed and opened the bag. It held a pair of silver cuffs that were wide enough to cover her mark and a pair of leather bracers with brown laces.

"The leather bracers are from Logan, but they don't

blend in everywhere, so I bought an alternative at the market."

"They're beautiful, Jon. It was very thoughtful of you." Kara set the bag down on her desk and began digging through her coin purse for money, but Jon waved her off.

"It's a gift. All of it. You don't need to pay me."

Kara paused. Silver wasn't cheap. "I feel like I owe you something."

"Just stay alive. I've lost too many friends already. I don't think you should be leaving the house at all with the target you've painted on your back, but if you do, wear a pair."

"You're not gonna give me a lecture on how much I fucked up?"

Jon's lips tightened. "I wouldn't be telling you anything you don't already know. And I feel like I'm partially to blame. I brought you to the guild, showed you the contracts—left you there alone. Should have known you wouldn't be able to resist temptation."

Kara smiled. "It's not your fault, Jon. I went looking for trouble."

"Well, you certainly found it. I don't like this, Kara. I'm not on your guard rotation, but if you need me—"

"I'll be fine. You worry too much."

Jon took the leather bracers out the bag and motioned for her hands. "Let me help you lace them up."

Kara held out her wrists for him, and Jon nimbly wove the laces through the eyelets. His thumb brushed against her mark when he came to it, and Kara suppressed a shudder. When he finished, he pulled the laces taut.

"That man being discovered outside your window wasn't a coincidence. He may have just been a scout. More will follow."

Kara hugged Jon and was surprised by how tightly he returned the embrace. "I promise I'll be careful."

Jon planted a kiss on her brow. "I'll hold you to that, Ace."

KARA SPENT the rest of the morning formulating a plan for gaining access to Wesley. After lunch, she pulled Thomas aside in the dining room and waited until the waitstaff had cleared out.

"Where's the Sanguine prisoner being kept?" Kara asked.

"Cutting right to the chase, are we? No 'How are you, Thomas? How are you finding Travincal?'"

"You want smalltalk, we can smalltalk, but I need this to remain private."

Thomas sighed. "I'm not supposed to tell anyone the location. Jon made me swear."

"But I'm a Stygian. What's the harm?"

"The less people who know, the better. Why do you need to know?"

"I want to ask him some questions, see if he can name the men responsible for what happened to my family."

Thomas frowned. "You can't kill him, Kara. They were very clear about that. And he may not have even been there."

"I know, but I have to try. I'm never going to get a better chance than this. I'll owe you."

"Fine. But this better not come back on my head." Thomas looked around at the dining room's many doors, then leaned forward and whispered the directions in Kara's ear. "There will be guards there. That one's on you."

Kara raised on her tiptoes and kissed Thomas on the cheek. "Thanks, Thomas. You're the best."

Thomas blushed. "Just be careful. The Sanguines are dangerous. Don't let him fuck with your head."

( )

EVERY MORNING, Kara dressed in the green dress Jon had brought her and took a stroll around the baroness's gardens, using its high, twisted hedges to spy on the Stygians following her. A retinue of two or three guards—it varied day to day—followed her everywhere she went once she stepped foot out of Valancourt's. They were discrete and never stopped her from going anywhere, but she could feel their eyes on her. After identifying who made up her retinue for the day, she would go into the city and scout out the path from Valancourt's to the house where they were holding Wesley. She used circuitous routes and never approached the house directly. Someone in her guard might know the location, and she didn't want to raise any suspicions. She grew more anxious as the week went on, her mind conjuring horrors of what might be happening to him. But she had to get this right, or they were both fucked.

It was a week before Kara felt comfortable enacting her plan. Her guards this morning weren't men who knew her very well, which was key. Kara led them on her normal route through Valancourt's garden and into the city until she reached the Foxhole, a brothel for the less discerning customer. From her scouting, Kara had learned that the place had two entrances, one on both sides of the building. She approached the Foxhole, then turned and waved at the crowded street with a beckoning motion. One of her guards, a tall, balding man she believed was named Nathan approached. He was wearing street garb too, and could easily blend in as a merchant or tourist.

"What is it?" Nathan asked. "Spot something?"

"No, not exactly." Kara sidled up to Nathan and put a hand on his shoulder. "This is trouble of another sort. I'm keening. I need to satiate the curse. I may be a while; I like to get my money's worth, you know?" Kara winked at him, and Nathan's cheeks colored. "Can you and the others wait for me out here and watch the building? I don't think the madam would take kindly to you looming in her drawing room."

"Alright, I guess. But if you're not back in an hour, I'm coming to check on you."

Kara pouted her lips. "I do hate to be rushed."

Nathan eyed her up and down. "I think that'll be plenty of time."

He turned and disappeared back into the crowd, and Kara went inside the brothel. An hour was the best she could hope for, really, but she'd have to make wise use of her time. The safehouse where they were keeping Wesley was a ten minute walk from here, and handling his guards would require some improvisation.

The Foxhole was located in a rundown building. A tired looking woman with her hair in a bun approached Kara. The madam, she presumed. The woman looked puzzled. Kara imagined she didn't look like her average customer.

"Can I help you?" she asked. "This isn't the flower place, you know. That's Foxglove's, up the street."

"I'm well aware, madame. It's just—" Kara made her voice shake and twisted her fingers together. "A strange man has been following me through the marketplace. I'm afraid he means some ill will towards me, and I don't want to lead him to my house. I was wondering if I could pay for a room and wait here until he goes away?"

The woman's look turned sympathetic. "You don't have to pay, dear. I shelter women in need. Is he outside now? Want me to go say something to him?"

"No, no. I don't want to draw any more attention. I believe he'll get bored and go away. But I insist on paying —for your troubles." Rather than ask her how much a room was, Kara drew out two gold coins and passed them to the woman. She needed to secure her silence and cooperation.

The woman's eyebrows shot up her face, her mouth gaping a little. She led Kara to a room close to the building's other entrance. Perfect.

"Please let me know if you need *anything*, ma'am. You can stay as long as you wish."

"Just privacy, please," Kara said. "I may take a nap to pass the time."

The room held a bed barely big enough to fit two people, a wooden chair with peeling paint, and a bowl with cloudy water and a rag in it. Kara ignored the squalor, focusing instead on her mission. She quickly stripped the green dress off, fetched the brown one from her bag, and put it on. Then she draped the white shawl over her shoulders and tied it around her neck. Kara pressed her ear to the door, listening for movement. She could hear thin strains of conversation, but it was distant. She opened the door, left via the Foxhole's back entrance, and headed for the safehouse.

When Kara arrived at the address, she almost walked past the house in question. It looked inconspicuous from the outside, blending in with all the other houses on the street. She was making good time so far, and she hadn't seen any sign of her guards.

Kara strode up to the safehouse and entered like she belonged there. Two Stygian men she recognized from Raven's Rest but didn't know by name were on guard. They started when the door opened, then relaxed when they saw her.

"Kara. What are you doing here?"

"I'm here to question the prisoner. The Commander thought a female face may make him more talkative."

The men glanced at one other, then back to her.

"Vakarian said no visitors…" the guard on the left said. The one on the right was already reaching for the key ring on his belt.

"He changed his mind. You think I'd be here other-wise? I've got better things to do than fuck with Sanguine scum."

That seemed to satisfy the left guard. "Fine," he said. "But make it quick. Shift change is soon."

There was a midafternoon shift change? Curious. It might be worth staking out the house to see how frequently they changed shifts. She'd spotted a small cafe across the street that she'd be able to see the door from, provided they were careless enough to use the front entrance.

The guard with the keys unlocked the door behind him and slid aside a bolt. "You'll be needing some light," he said, passing her a torch from a nearby sconce.

"He's kept in the dark?"

"Of course."

Kara moved through the door and down the staircase leading to the basement. It was a storage cellar that'd been cleared out and converted into an interrogation room. The room was pitch black. Kara fanned the torch across the room. There was a solitary bucket in the corner, but no bloodied tools or other signs that Wesley was being tortured.

Wesley sat in a chair in the center, his arms and legs tied with thick rope knots. A burlap bag covered his face. As Kara approached, he stirred, head swiveling towards her. "Wesley," she whispered, "It's me." Kara eased the sack off his face, expecting the worst.

One of his eyes widened when he saw her. The other was swollen shut and purple with bruising. He was gagged, his nose crusted with blood. The blood had leaked down his face and stained his shirt, but other than that he looked hale. Kara had been afraid that they were starving or torturing him to get the answers they wanted.

This was the first opportunity she'd had to get a good look at her brother. He was no longer the thin, pale boy she'd known at Mudbottom. He'd filled out with muscle, a side-effect of having plenty to eat and exercise, and his eyes had a sunken, haunted look about them.

Kara untied Wesley's gag and pocketed it, then enveloped him in a tight hug.

Wesley coughed, clearing his throat. "Kara? Goddess, am I glad to see you. Quick, untie me. Do you have a weapon?" His voice was raspy, his lips cracked from dehydration.

Kara stepped back and shook her head. He didn't need to know about the daggers strapped to her thighs beneath her dress. "There are guards outside. They think I'm questioning you. How are you alive? I thought you were dead."

"We can talk about this later, Kara. You need to get me out of here. How armed are the guards? We may be able to take them together—we can break the chair into pieces."

"I'm not attacking the members of my own clan, Wesley. I came to make sure you were okay. To find out what the hell happened to you."

Wesley's eyes went wild, sliding from side to side. "You

can't let them keep me here, Kara. You don't know what they're capable of."

"Have they done anything so far? Are there wounds under your clothes?"

"No, but it's only a matter of time. Vakarian has questions—questions I don't have the answers to."

Kara frowned. She couldn't deny that Wesley may have useful intelligence, but he should be willing to give it up freely. "I'm working on a plan, okay? But I can't get you out today. You should tell him what he wants to know. Or me."

"Did he send you, then? How tight are you wrapped around his thumb, that you'd interrogate your own brother?"

Kara fought the urge to shake him. He was under a lot of duress—that was why he was acting like this. "Logan didn't send me. They don't know who you are."

"You can't let them find out. They'll think you're a traitor."

Kara chewed on her lip. "I don't intend for them to find out. But I need answers. What the hell are you doing with the Sanguine Riders? After what they did to Da?" Kara's voice broke at the mention of their father.

Wesley averted his eyes. "I didn't have a choice. It was join or be killed. They wanted me because I was young, strong. They...they killed Da as an example. To make the villagers pay up."

"And you're still with them?" Kara's voice shook, her hands itching for a fight.

"I can't just leave, Kara. You ought to know that. I have a contract. Deserters are killed, or worse, and I'm of no use to anyone dead."

"You could run. Hide from them."

"They're too powerful. Their reach extends all over

Teleria. They know my face. I'd be hunted down. Executed, if I was lucky."

A heavy footstep on the first floor startled Kara. She was losing track of time. How long had she been down here, talking to Wesley? She needed to get back to the Foxhole before the guards got suspicious.

"And what about you, little sister? In bed with the Stygians? *Saphia*?"

"I did what I had to do to survive," Kara growled. "Were you at the Reaping Trials in Liore?" Had he been right under her nose that whole time?

Wesley shook his head, and greasy strands of hair fell in his eyes.

Something about Wesley's story was odd to Kara. Was Victus so desperate for bodies that he was recruiting men with reason to want him dead? Was it another part of his plan to gather an army? "Why would Victus recruit someone who hates him?"

"It's all mind games, Kara. He loves to fuck with people's heads. To keep you under his thumb. He relishes in that hate. Why'd you take the black?"

"You were always interested in joining them. I wanted to avenge you and Da, so I decided to train with them until I could bring you both the justice you deserved. They brought Da's head to town. Swung it around like…like a toy. And then I saw your coat on a dead man. I thought I'd lost you both." Kara was breathing hard, tears running down her face. Her mark itched beneath the leather bracer.

"Kara," Wesley said, trying to move his arms against the restraints. "It's okay. Everything's going to be okay. You just have to get me out of here. We'll figure something out."

"What were you doing at Valancourt's?" Kara

snapped, trying to pull herself out of her grief. "How did you know which room was mine?" Kara wanted to be sure none of the Stygians had sold him information.

"When I saw you at Saphia's, I panicked. I wasn't sure I could believe my eyes. You looked so different. What if I was losing it? Then I realized you were working for Vakarian. We've had eyes on you since that day at Oxswitch Avenue. They know where you sleep. I didn't know if I could trust you. Then I realized it didn't matter—you're my little sister. I came to the manor to try and talk to you, find out what I could before Victus sent us after you. I came alone that night."

Kara sighed. "And ended up here. You can't go back to Victus, Wesley. The things he's doing are terrible."

"If I don't go back, I have to run. Forever."

"Maybe the Sanguines will think you're dead, murdered by the Stygians. If I let you go and the Brotherhood finds out, I don't know if they'll forgive me."

"*Forgive you?* Are you mad? You can't risk staying, Kara. You'd be a traitor. What do you think the Stygian Brotherhood does to traitors? I'm not leaving you with Vakarian to die. I already lost you once."

Kara had a hard time believing that Logan or Jon would hurt her. Then again, she'd never been on their bad side before. And they'd never trust her again if she absconded with a Sanguine prisoner.

"Look, Kara. We'll leave together—escape the clans. We can carve out a life for ourselves somewhere far away from them."

"We could be running forever."

"At least we'll be together. Think about it—we're all each other has left. It's what Da would have wanted."

The prospect of leaving the clan made Kara realize just how much she'd come to think of them as family. The thought of never seeing them again made her feel empty inside. Could she do it? Could she leave the life she'd built with them? And could she let go of avenging Da since Wesley was alive?

More noises came from upstairs, and adrenaline shot through Kara as she tried to calculate how much time had passed. "I have to go. The next time I come, that'll be it. Goddess protect you, brother."

Kara gagged and covered Wesley again and squeezed him on the shoulder, then forced herself to walk away. Her heart unclenched a little when she saw that no one new had arrived upstairs. The guards were just stretching their legs.

"That was fast," the amenable guard said. "Usually they spend hours down there with him."

"Who does?" Kara snapped.

"Vak—erm, the interrogators."

Why was Logan spending hours questioning Wesley? What did he think Wesley knew? A trickle of unease crept up her spine.

"You get anything useful out of him?" the other guard asked.

"Maybe. We'll see if the information checks out. Thank you for your time, gentlemen. You can lock back up now."

Kara half jogged, half ran back to the Foxhole. She didn't care if it drew attention to her—if Logan got wind that she'd dodged her guards and restricted her movements further, she may not be able to free Wesley. Kara darted in the back entrance of the brothel and stripped down in the hallway, pulling her green dress over her head and stuffing the brown one into her bag. There was no need to pinch her cheeks or muss her hair to complete the ruse—her breakneck pace had accomplished that already.

The madam and a male patron stood at the other end of the hall, staring at her. She nodded to the madam. "Has that man been in here looking for me?"

The madam shook her head slowly. "I think you're in the clear."

"Thank you."

Kara exited the building and headed straight for the crowd of foot traffic headed towards the market. Nathan appeared out of the crowd and began walking beside her.

"In a hurry? You start a brawl or something?" he asked.

Kara forced a grin. "No, no particular hurry. Just a pep in my step. A jingle in my jangle, if you know what I mean."

"I'm not sure I do."

"You got me, Nathan. I am in a hurry. I worked up a fierce appetite, and the street food here is to die for. I can't get enough of those fried rats on sticks being advertised as chicken. I don't know how I'm gonna go back to Olly's cooking."

Nathan's lip curled in distaste. "I take it you have more business to attend to in town?"

"It won't take long. I need to visit the market."

Nathan nodded and disappeared back into the crowd.

Kara sought out one of the herbalist's stalls she'd seen on her first visit to the market. The merchant's table looked a lot like Bart's supply cabinet, crowded with pickled-looking things in jars and dried herbs hanging everywhere. The merchant manning the stall wore bright silks and multiple pieces of jewelry.

He beamed at Kara as she approached, revealing two rotten teeth and one gold one. "Welcome to The Herbarium, supplier of quality ingredients to the most discerning—"

Kara cut him off. "I need something to help me sleep a dreamless sleep at night. I have intense nightmares."

He nodded twice. "I have exactly what you need." He reached under the table and produced a blue vial full of liquid. "One drop—heavy eyelids. Two drops—a dreamless sleep. Three drops—you will surely sleep past sunrise. Four drops—only use if you are perhaps recovering from an injury, or need a patient to be still. Five drops and more? Your dreamless sleep may never end."

"What's in it?" Kara asked. It was beginning to sound more like an opiate than a sleep aid.

"My own personal, proprietary blend of coconut oil, valerian root, and milk of poppy. Only found here, at The Herbarium."

"Right. How much?"

"Fifteen gold pieces."

Kara narrowed her eyes. The guy was trying to rip her off. "There's a lot of drops in that vial. I don't think I need that many. Do you offer it in a smaller size?"

The merchant wagged his finger at her and said, "One size only. Many drops for many nightmares, miss. Can you put a price on a good night's sleep?"

"Yes, actually. I'll pay seven."

The merchant looked aghast. "You insult me. Thirteen, no lower. A special discount—for buying in bulk."

"Ten," Kara said. "Take it, or I'll find someone else that will."

"A shrewd mistress you are. Very well. Remember my warning about the dosage. The Herbarium isn't liable for any accidental comas. For one more gold piece, I will write down the dosage instructions."

"No thanks." Less than five. She could remember that.

As Kara made her way from the market back to the manor house, her mind raced. She had to get Wesley out—

he was the only family she had left in the world, and she couldn't let Logan hand him back to the Sanguines. But the Stygians wouldn't take kindly to her releasing a Sanguine prisoner, and sooner or later they would find out it was her. How would Logan react? She couldn't risk telling him. She and Wesley were going to have to run, and she could return and explain everything once he was safe.

CHAPTER TWENTY

Kara spent the next week in and out of the cafe near the safehouse, taking meticulous notes about the pattern and times of the shift changes and who was on guard duty when. She would attempt to free Wesley when the same guards were on duty, since they'd let her in to see him before. She pilfered two flasks from the kitchen at Valancourt's and filled them with the baroness's liquor, then added four of the sleeping drops to each container. She'd tested the elixir on herself in smaller amounts to ensure that it was effective. The only side effect she'd had was waking with a fuzzy feeling in her head after a deep, restful sleep.

Once Kara had everything prepared, she still hesitated, insisting to herself that she needed more time. Every time she saw Logan or Jon or one of her friends, a hollow ache filled her stomach. She missed them already, but she needed to act soon. Deep in her heart, she didn't want to leave. She'd finally found acceptance. She'd help Wesley to safety, then come back and deal with the fallout. He'd been imprisoned for two weeks; his condition might be much worse now than the first time she'd visited him. And the Brotherhood could be leaving Travincal any day now. A new private contract for the clan hadn't been announced yet, but she suspected business with the guild was winding down, as the members of the inner circle had been spending more and more time around the manor. It was more keen eyes around than Kara was comfortable with.

Logan was her biggest obstacle. He left the manor at random times of the day and night, and she knew he'd been interrogating Wesley. If he showed up at the safe-house or found them before they escaped the city, they'd be screwed.

Kara's resolve wavered as her plan solidified. She wasn't sure if she could actually go through with it. Anxiety dulled her appetite, and she slept poorly, waking up throughout the night from nightmares, soaked in sweat.

And then her keening began. She should have seen it coming—enough time had passed. According to Logan, there was roughly a month between episodes. She recognized the signs this time. Her dreams were hot and restless, and she woke from sleep with a needy ache between her legs. As usual, Logan featured prominently in these dreams. Maybe it was all in her head, but she felt like she could sense him on the other side of her bedroom wall as she lay in bed at night. Feeling him just out of reach was slowly driving her crazy. She needed to take care of her keening before freeing Wesley. There would be few opportunities while they were on the run. She could always try a brothel again, perhaps with a man instead of a woman this time, but her mind rebelled at the idea.

Kara was keeping up her lessons with Philipe for appearance's sake. After lessons one day, Logan and Jon entered the house as she was leaving the ballroom. Kara froze in her steps. They were both shirtless and dripping with sweat, their waists belted with swords. They must have been sparring—intensely, from the looks of it. Tight breeches hugged their legs, and the sculpted muscles of their chests rippled with each labored breath. Jon looked delicious, but she couldn't keep her eyes off Logan. A trail of dark hair peeked out of his waistband, drawing her eyes downward. His breeches did not conceal much.

Logan's eyes caught Kara's as she trailed them over his body, and she jerked them back up to his face. Her body called out to his. A bead of sweat trailed down between her breasts from her sudden flush.

Logan's eyes flashed with fire. It was like he could tell everything she was thinking, feeling. She felt exposed, vulnerable. Jon looked between the two of them, his expression tight.

"Hello, boys," Kara said with a shaky breath.

Jon stepped towards her, and Logan growled, his expression turning feral as he palmed the hilt of his sword.

Jon stopped dead in his tracks and slowly turned towards Logan, lifting his hands in surrender. The wide line of his scar looked red and angry in the morning light.

Kara couldn't take the tension. It coiled between her thighs and between the two men, threatening to explode in passion or violence. The last time she'd keened, she'd nearly killed Jasper. This was a different kind of sensation altogether. Kara turned towards the stairs and fled.

She half-expected Logan to chase her. The heat of his gaze was on her. She *wanted* him to chase her. Hunt her. Take her. She was disappointed when she didn't hear booted footfalls on the stairs behind her. Instead, Jon was yelling.

"One time, you said! What are you thinking? Fucking snap out of it. Get out of here if you can't control yourself."

She couldn't hear Logan's response. The front door slammed shut, and Kara sighed. He'd left.

She went inside her room, and her attention immediately went to the door connecting her room to Logan's. She tested the knob, surprised when it swung open. The broken door jamb had been repaired, yet he hadn't locked it. Kara entered his room and shut the door behind her. The decorations were sophisticated, regal, and dark. There was none of the frippery that dominated her quarters. The bed was covered in an embroidered gold duvet and black silk sheets. She fought the urge to strip naked, wrap herself in his sheets, and inhale his scent like a drug. She could touch herself between his sheets and leave the scent of her desire there to torment him.

Kara shook her head, trying to clear it. Two wine glasses and a few books littered the desk. She flipped open a book on Telerian geography to the bookmarked page. A map of the Black Hills, Sanguine territory, spread across both pages. She put the book back, then searched the drawers of the desk for any correspondence she might find related to Wesley or otherwise, but there was nothing. She wasn't that surprised. Logan wouldn't leave the door unlocked if he was going to leave any valuable information lying around, and the baroness's maids likely had a set of keys. On a whim, Kara tested the backs of the drawers and the bottom of the desk for false bottoms or a hidden drawer, but found nothing.

When she looked up from her search, she spotted a decanter of wine sitting on the mantle above the fireplace, half-full. Kara had the vial of sleeping elixir on her. She'd taken to carrying it everywhere in case she needed to enact her plan spontaneously. If Logan drank the wine tonight, she could try and get Wesley out. The two guards from before were scheduled to be on duty. Kara drew the vial out from between her breasts—curse dresses for their lack of pockets—and unstoppered the decanter. She transferred four drops of the elixir into the decanter using the vial's glass dropper, then paused and reconsidered. More drops would be safer, considering the volume of liquid, but what if he drank it all in one sitting? It wouldn't be out of character for him. Would five drops kill him? Kara couldn't risk it.

The door's latch turned, and Kara nearly jumped out of her skin. She twisted the vial closed and slipped it back into her dress, then turned around, still holding the decanter as Logan entered the room.

"Logan!" she started. He was still shirtless. She loved the sight of his bare chest, with its dusting of dark hair over golden skin. She hoped there was nothing out of place still from her pilfering.

"What are you doing here, Kara?"

"Waiting on you." She shook the decanter for emphasis. It had the bonus effect of stirring up the drops of the elixir. The flavor of it wasn't too obvious when mixed with alcohol, but Logan had eerily good senses. "I was about to start without you."

"Start what, exactly?" His voice was intense, low. He began to close in on her like a predator circling his prey, and a shiver ran up Kara's spine.

"Drinking," she squeaked. He was emanating menace and desire at the same time. Kara slid his two glasses towards her and began to pour, having to focus to keep her hands from shaking. She passed him one of the glasses, letting her fingers brush against his.

"What are you really doing here, Kara? I know you didn't invite yourself into my room for a drink."

Logan had yet to taste the wine. He caught her glance and said, "I'm keening. I shouldn't partake."

Kara stilled, the tension between her shoulders building into a twisted knot. So much for that plan. Was she about to be forced to drink the elixir? She set the carafe down on the desk.

"I'm keening, too," she said, heat pooling between her legs.

Logan's gaze raked over her, and he stepped closer. "It was bound to happen sometime," he said, his voice strained.

Kara held his gaze with hers. "Maybe we can help each other."

Logan gave a short laugh. "No, Kara."

"You helped me before."

"That was different. You were suffering."

"I thought you enjoyed it."

Logan's eyes went amber and didn't shift back like they normally did. "You know I did. But I wasn't keening then. I could lose control and hurt you."

"Like with Jon?"

Anguish contorted Logan's face for a moment before he regained control of his features. "So he told you."

"I asked him. You were just a kid, Logan. And so far gone with the curse—I can't imagine the pain you must have been in. You can't keep blaming yourself for that."

"You're not going to ask me how the story ended? About what happened after I nearly killed my best friend?"

Kara stilled, waiting.

"I woke up in the morning next to the body of what I assume to be an innocent merchant. I have to assume, because there was nothing recognizable of him left. Just his horse and his wagon and his blood. So much blood. And *pieces* of him. I remembered none of it."

Kara snaked her fingers between his and pulled him

towards her. "You weren't yourself, Logan. That wasn't you."

"But that monster's inside of me, just waiting to come out. It always will be."

Kara unlaced their hands and wrapped herself tight around him in a hug. Logan stiffened, then gradually relaxed. He tentatively wrapped his arms around her, wineglass still clenched in one hand, then rested his chin on top of her head and breathed in the scent of her hair

"Let me help you sate the curse. Your keening was starting that night you came into my room, wasn't it? How much longer can you resist?"

"Not long," he admitted, his nose trailing down to the curve of her ear. "I tried to sate the curse yesterday and changed my mind like a fool. My demon is particularly fond of *you* for some reason. Before your first keening, I thought a taste would be enough, but that only made it worse. You're all I can fucking think about, Kara. It's driving me mad."

Before her first keening? He'd been *fond* of her for that long? "I have a confession to make. I watched you, that night on the balcony."

"I know."

"What?" Kara squawked, pulling away from him. "You knew I was there? Why didn't you stop?"

Logan arched an eyebrow at her. "Why didn't you?"

Kara's cheeks heated with blood.

"You sounded delicious, Kara. I could hear you pleasuring yourself and smell your arousal on the wind. It took all the control I possess to resist coming back to your room."

"I liked watching you, too."

Logan's free hand clenched into a fist so tight his

knuckles turned white. "You need to leave before it's too late. Please."

Kara stepped towards him and ran her hands down the broad planes of his chest. "You can be rough with me if you want," she said as she trailed her hand down and stroked the hard heat of his arousal through his breeches.

Logan groaned. The wineglass shattered in his grip. He dropped the shards, and Kara lifted his palm to her mouth and licked the trail of blood there. His cock pulsed beneath her touch. Then the ring around his iris went red, and he broke.

Logan jerked her against his hips and kissed her, dragging his teeth across her lips and roving his hands over the soft planes of her body. Kara wove her fingers through his dark hair and responded in kind.

"I've tried so hard to resist you," he growled in her ear. "I'm done trying."

Logan spun her around and ground his hips into her ass. Kara ground back. Their bodies fit together like a glove. He pushed her against the wall and cut through the lacing of her dress with his dagger, then ripped the dress open and pushed it down her hips. The vial fell from between her breasts into the soft cushion of fabric, and Kara's heart stuttered.

Logan pressed his lips against her shoulders and kissed and licked his way down her back until he got to her butt.

"Spread your legs."

His commanding tone made Kara even wetter than she already was. She obeyed, pressing her hands against the wall and spreading her legs, pushing her ass out. Logan bit her lightly on the butt, making her yelp. He kissed his way towards the center of her need slowly, torturously. The soft graze of his lips against her skin made her shudder. Then he ripped her underwear off with his teeth, and his mouth was on her, his tongue lapping at her sensitive folds. He wrapped an arm around her hips and rubbed her clit with two fingers. Pressure built inside her, and Kara moaned in pleasure. His hands gripped her thighs, holding her legs open as she began to squirm against his mouth. Kara's nails bit into the wall, and Logan kept going, pushing her to the brink. And then she was peaking. Pleasure curled up her spine as she came. She cried out Logan's name and rolled her hips, exulting in the satisfied growl he made between her legs. Her legs shook uncontrollably in the aftermath, and Kara fought to stay standing.

"Bed. Now," Logan said. His voice was hoarse and deep.

Kara stepped out of the pool of fabric her dress had made on the ground. "You might have to carry me," she said, half-joking. "I can't stop shaking."

Logan picked her up without hesitation, scooping her legs out from under her, and strode over to the bed and tossed her on it. The silk sheets felt sinful against her bare skin. He watched her with molten eyes as he crawled onto the bed. The mattress sunk with his weight, and Kara shivered in anticipation. He hovered over her, the desire in his eyes calling to her own. He bent and scraped his teeth against the smooth, sensitive skin between her neck and her clavicle, and Kara shuddered as heat flooded her core. Then he began to caress her breasts, lifting their heft and tweaking her nipples. His mouth was all over her, claiming her.

"Do you have protection?" he growled between kisses.

"From what?" she murmured, lost in a haze of pleasure.

"Childbirth. I can't trust myself to pull out when the keening has this strong a hold on me."

Kara's hand went to the contraceptive charm at her

neck that she'd taken to wearing daily. "Yes. Bart gave it to me."

"Remind me to give that man a raise."

Kara laughed and slid down his body, running her tongue over the ridges of his abdomen like she'd imagined doing a thousand times. She unlaced his breeches with shaky hands. He helped her shrug off his pants, and his unrestrained cock sprung up, rigid and huge. Kara swallowed her spit. The full length of his erection up close was intimidating. She wanted to take him in her mouth and find out how he tasted. The head of his cock beaded with precum as she stared at it. Kara licked up the bead of moisture, and Logan sucked in his breath and pulled away from her.

"I'm too close, Kara. I need to be inside of you."

Kara leaned back on her elbows and spread her legs open for him. Logan moved over her and stroked the length of his cock between her lips, stimulating her clit and coating himself in her wetness. Kara arched her back, biting her lip.

Their eyes blazed at one another as he slid into her, stretching her out. Logan groaned. He took it slow, gradually filling her up with inch after inch of him. She moaned as he stretched her out, feeding her his cock until he was sunk in to the hilt and they were both panting. She was uncomfortably full, but she wrapped her legs around his waist and pulled him in even deeper. Logan snarled, baring his teeth, and slowly slid in and out of her once. The slow glide of his cock against the knot of sensitivity inside her sent pleasure coursing through her.

"Gods, yes. You feel amazing." She arched her hips, meeting his stroke and scraping her nails down his muscled back. "More."

He thrust again, torturously slow, a wicked smirk on his

face as he watched her come undone on his cock. Her second orgasm was already close. She ground herself into him, watching as his abs contracted with each thrust.

"Harder, Logan. Unleash yourself," she moaned as a delicious pressure built inside her. Logan slid out and buried himself inside her with a sharp thrust. He reached between her legs and stroked her sensitive clit. She was so close.

"Come for me, Kara. I want to see your face when you come." He stroked her with one hand as he moved inside her, filling her over and over again, and it sent her over the edge.

"Logan," Kara moaned. She clenched around him as her neck tensed and her back arched in pleasure.

Logan clenched his teeth and hissed. "Mother night. You feel so good when you squeeze me like that. You feel perfect." His thrusts became faster and harder, and the expression on his face intensified. He was close. His eyes were a molten red, the ropey muscles of his body rigid and tight. He was completely gone, turned over to the demon. The expression on his face was feral. Their love-making grew rougher, his hips pumping into her relentlessly as he fondled her clit, driving her insane. Kara screamed in pleasure and dug her fingers into Logan's back. She squeezed her inner muscles around him as her pleasure ramped again, and Logan groaned and shuddered. He bit her on the shoulder, hard, as he came inside of her, filling her up. When he was done, he collapsed against her and buried his face in her neck. Kara stroked her hands through his hair and down the sweaty planes of his back.

"Are you okay?" he mumbled against her skin. "I lost control—"

"I'm fine, Logan. I feel wonderful." Kara had never felt

so much pleasure in her life. She might be a little bruised, but she was euphoric. She didn't want this moment to end.

Logan rolled to the side, sliding out of her, and she missed the fullness of him inside her. He lay back on the pillows and pulled her against him. Kara burrowed her head into the crook of his arm.

They lay together, blissfully content for a few minutes. Then Logan rolled out of bed and padded naked to the door. He slid the bolt on his door and the one connecting their rooms closed, locking them both.

"What are you doing?" Kara asked, sitting up.

"Making sure we aren't interrupted. Stay with me tonight."

Kara laughed. "It's mid-day."

"We've a lot of time to make up for." His eyes promised fire.

"But we aren't keening anymore."

"I don't care," Logan growled. "I still want you." He stopped by the desk, and his gaze fell to her glass of wine that sat untouched. "You didn't drink any of this."

Kara stilled. She'd forgotten all about the drugged wine. "You were very distracting," she said, forcing a smile.

Logan picked up the glass and sipped from it, then carried it back to bed with him.

Kara's mouth fell open. The urge to yell at him not to drink it surged within her. *And then what?* She'd have to tell Logan Vakarian that she'd intended to drug him. He'd be so angry with her. He'd force her to explain why, and her opportunity to free Wesley would vanish. Kara stuffed the urge down her throat. Guilt roiled in her belly.

"What's wrong? You've gone pale."

She scrambled for an answer. "It's just...what of your list of concerns, regarding us sleeping together?"

"They're still there. But you drive me to distraction

regardless, so we might as well enjoy what's between us, no?"

"And what is that?"

Logan stood by the bed and caressed her cheek, sipping the wine in his other hand. The glass was already half empty.

"Undeniable lust. The desire to drag you into my bed or take you against a wall every time I see you. The urge to murder any man who looks at you the wrong way."

Heat coiled low in Kara's belly. She forced herself to picture Wesley tied to a chair in a dank basement. *You have to rescue your brother. He's the only family you have left.*

Logan finished off the glass of wine and crawled into bed. "Now, where were we?"

Guilt tore at Kara, wedging its way into her chest. Was she about to ruin everything between her and Logan? Would he be able to forgive her? "Just hold me."

"I've a mind to do a lot more than hold you." Logan pulled her on top of him. Her naked flesh pressed against the hard planes of his body, and lust stirred within her. His cock was hard again between her legs.

"Soon," Kara whispered. She buried her face in the skin of his neck to hide her pained expression. Her tears leaked onto his chest, and Logan ran his hands through her hair and down her back, calming her. "What's wrong?"

"Just hold me." They laid like that for several minutes, the sweep of his hand between her shoulder-blades growing slower. The sleeping elixir acted fast. Soon Logan's breathing slowed, his hands coming to a rest.

Kara pulled away from him. His eyes were closed, his chest rising and falling in a steady pattern. Kara poked him hard in the chest to test his responsiveness, and his eyelids didn't even flicker. Her guilt was a heavy stone in the pit of her stomach. She wanted to stay with him while he slept, to be there when he woke up, but this could be her only opportunity to help Wesley.

Kara kissed Logan on the lips and slid out of bed. She cleaned off the evidence of their lovemaking using a pitcher of water on the sidetable, then gathered her ripped dress and the vial. She opened the door between their rooms and took a moment to look back at him. He looked so young and peaceful in his sleep. Her chest tightened at the thought of leaving him. What if something went wrong, and she never saw him again?

Kara stepped into her room and closed the door. She took a deep breath and tried to put her mind into a cold, analytical space. Logan would be asleep for hours. This was the best chance she had. She summoned the image of Wesley's bruised and bloody face to try and steel her resolve. She owed this to her brother. She just hoped that Logan Vakarian would understand.

Kara put on a fresh dress and took the pack she'd prepared for this occasion out from under the bed. It held the doctored flasks, rations, supplies for the road, and her jeweled pair of daggers. Then she rifled through her desk drawer for the envelopes and stationery stored there. They were bone-white, the envelopes embossed with a border of thorns and roses. Kara pulled out her quill and ink, wet the nib, and began writing.

CHAPTER TWENTY-ONE

Kara left Valancourt's at dusk and retraced her steps to the Foxhole. She counted three guards tailing her, including Nathan. When she walked up to the building, Nathan approached her through the crowd.

"Back again?" he asked.

Kara nodded. "A vice, I know. But I prefer it to others."

Nathan's eye narrowed on her pack, and her heart tried to beat its way out of her chest. "What's in the bag?"

Kara stilled, then painted a confident smile on her face. "My daggers, a negligee. I like to set the mood, you know? It can be intimidating for them to find weapons strapped to my thighs."

Nathan coughed. "Alright, alright. But I don't think it's wise to be visiting the same place multiple times. Someone might recognize you. There are plenty of other brothels."

"I'll pick somewhere else next time, okay?"

Nathan grunted. "Fine. Make it quick, it'll be dark soon."

That's what she was counting on. When Kara

entered the brothel, the madam was nowhere in sight, and the front room was empty. Kara pulled a brown cloak out of her pack and donned it, hood and all. Sounds of pleasure emanated from the rooms around her as she walked to the building's other entrance, an uncomfortable reminder that she'd abandoned Logan right after they'd made love.

Kara exited to the street. The packs of people out were dwindling as night approached, and Kara moved at a fast clip. There was no activity outside the safehouse when she got there. She entered as she had before, without announcing herself. And then she froze.

Thomas was sitting in a chair next to the obstinate guard from her last trip. The easy-going one was missing. Their hands went to their weapons and began unsheathing them. Kara pulled her hood back, and they paused.

"Relax. It's me." The hardass slid his sword back into his scabbard, but Thomas didn't. "Where's whatshisface?" she asked the guard. "From last time."

"Mel's sick. Probably the damn crotch-pox, if you ask me. Vakarian send you to interrogate the prisoner again?" the guard said.

Kara nodded.

"He did, did he?" Thomas asked.

"Yes."

Thomas searched her face with scrutiny but didn't say anything further.

Kara pulled the two flasks out of her pack and tossed them to the men, then pulled out her personal flask filled with water. "I brought you boys a present. Courtesy of the baroness." She nodded towards the guard from before. "I didn't get your name last time."

"Otto."

"Cheers, Otto. Thomas." She unscrewed her flask and

took a swig. Otto followed suit, but Thomas didn't drink. He pocketed the flask instead.

"You ruined my cheers, Thomas. That's unlucky—we'll have to do it again."

"I'm not drinking on duty, Kara. What if the Commander shows up? He'd hang us by our balls. I need to stay alert."

"Suit yourself," Otto grumbled.

Kara tried to keep the panic rising in her chest suppressed. She couldn't force Thomas to drink. He hadn't been part of the plan. "Spoilsport. I have some more questions for the prisoner. The Commander thought he may be more willing to talk after a few weeks of captivity."

"I'm not letting you down there, Kara."

"Why not?" Kara tried to keep the bite from her voice.

Thomas looked from her to Otto. "We need this prisoner *alive*. I know you have no love lost for the Sanguines."

"You say that like that's a bad thing, sonny," Otto said.

Kara snorted. "Fine. Otto can come down there with me, if you prefer. He'll make sure I behave myself."

Thomas hesitated. Indecision warred in his eyes.

"Please, Thomas."

"Fine. Otto, go with her. Yell if you need anything."

Kara didn't feel the relief she expected when Thomas acquiesced. Instead she felt guilty for lying and manipulating her friend. She'd have to make it up to him later.

Thomas unlocked the door. Kara grabbed a torch, and she and Otto moved down the stairs. Otto dragged his chair behind him. "Ain't sittin' on that floor," he grumbled. "Mother only knows what's on it by now."

Wesley was still tied to the chair with the burlap sack over his head. Kara took the sack off and made sure he saw Otto behind her before undoing his gag. He looked better than she'd expected. His cheeks were sunk in, there were dark circles under his eyes, and he was starting to smell from not washing, but there were no signs of harm. The skin that was visible was free of any fresh bruises and cuts. The Stygians may have been depriving him of sleep or feeding him meager portions, but it wasn't on par with the torture she imaged they were capable of.

"Prisoner. I see you're still breathing. How unfortunate," Kara said.

Wesley kept his eyes trained on Otto. Kara could hear him unscrewing the lid to the flask again.

"Now that you've had some time to come to terms with your situation, I'll ask you again. Why were you sent to Valancourt's?" Kara asked.

"Maybe if you lot actually knew how to torture people, I'd have told you that by now," Wesley said, smirking.

Kara asked Wesley questions for the next thirty minutes, and Wesley prevaricated or outright ignored her. Something crashed to the floor, and Kara spun around. Otto had nodded off and lost his balance, tipping his chair sideways. He was sprawled out on the floor. Kara checked his head for any blood, but he was unmarred, just out cold.

Kara pulled her dagger out and began sawing at Wesley's bonds.

"What's wrong with him?"

"I drugged him, but there's another one upstairs. I don't know—"

Thomas's voice came from the stairway. "Kara? What's going on? I heard something."

His voice was getting closer rapidly. *Mother Fucking Night.* Wesley barely had one hand free. Kara sprinted to the wall beside the door, put her back flush against it, and didn't move. The door swung open. Thomas took a step inside, and Kara jumped on his back. She wrapped her right arm around his throat and secured it with her left, applying pressure to his artery. He was so fucking tall. She wrapped her legs around his torso in an effort to not slide down his back.

Thomas thrashed beneath her. His hands clawed at her arms, struggling to pry them off, leaving deep gouges in her skin. He tried to shake her off, but she clung on. Then he slammed her back against the stone wall, and it knocked the breath out of her. Her back felt like it'd been lit on fire. Thomas made to do it again, and Kara kicked him in the gut with her heels. He was beginning to fade. The fingers clutching her arms went slack, and Thomas fell to his knees. Saliva leaked out of the side of his mouth as he went still. Kara let go of him and caught him before he fell flat on his face, then guided his body to the floor. His face was ruddy and unnaturally still. Regret rose in her throat, and tears threatened to slide down her face. Kara bit her lip, trying to distract herself with pain. She held her fingers to Thomas's throat to feel for his pulse. It was slow, but there.

Wesley stared at her with something akin to pride. "Well done, sister."

"Shut up. He's my friend."

"You'll have to hurt more of them before this is over."

Kara ignored that comment. She didn't want to think about the future anymore. She could only think about the next ten minutes, the next hour, lest she be overwhelmed. She sawed off the rest of Wesley's bonds and gave him a drab brown cloak from her pack. His wrists and ankles were red and raw where the rope had chafed against them.

"Get Otto's weapons," she told him. "But don't kill anyone unless your life's in danger, please. These are my friends."

"If you insist."

Wesley stripped Otto's still form in methodical, practiced motions. "Do you have clothes for me?" he asked. "The ones I'm wearing are disgusting."

"No, I didn't have the chance to buy any."

Wesley unlaced Otto's boots and took them, his pants, and his coat. Kara tried not to think about how cold this basement would get come nightfall.

Kara stripped Thomas of his weapons, money, and keys with the cold remove she was becoming practiced at adopting, then considered his face. She plucked his glasses off, folded them up, and slipped them into a pocket in her pack. He'd be pissed, but it would slow him down once he woke up. She locked the door behind her after she and Wesley ascended the stairs. The next shift would need to bust down the door or remove it by the hinges.

When she and Wesley left the safehouse and took to the streets, it was dark out. The moon was new, so there would be little light to track them by once they got out of the city. They headed towards the eastern gate that led out of town, down near the wharf district. Kara's heart was still racing from the fight with Thomas, from the realities of her actions coming to bear. She and Wesley shared few words. Their intent was singular—get far away as quickly as possible.

As they neared the stable she'd planned to purchase horses from, Kara began to feel short of breath.

"Wesley, wait." She leaned against the wall on the side of the street, letting it support her weight. Her vision was blurring at the edges.

"Kara? What is it? Are you hurt?"

"I can't breathe." The breaths she drew were short and weak, and the motion constricted her chest in pain.

Wesley felt her forehead and her pulse, then pressed along her back with his hands. "How does that feel?"

"Sore, but not excruciating."

"Are you panicking?"

"Yes." Her hands were cold and clammy, and each breath she took was tight.

"Okay. You need to calm down. We have to move."

"Has telling a panicking person to calm down ever worked in the history of mankind?"

Wesley cracked a grin. She hadn't seen humor light his eyes like that in so long. Images from that day at Mudbottom threatened to spill into her mind. The memory of Da's face, frozen in agony, was etched on her brain.

Wesley slapped her in the face, and anger pulled Kara back.

"What the fuck?"

"We don't have time for this, Kara. You can freak out later." That was when she saw he'd drawn his dagger. He grabbed her left arm, unclasped the silver cuff, and slid the blade against her mark.

"Don't!" Kara tried to pull away, but he held on with surprising strength. The blade pressed into her skin, and blood welled up. He traced the same circle pattern over her mark that Logan had before the Reaping Trials. It stung fiercely, but she didn't fall unconscious this time. Instead, a rush of strength suffused her. Heat surged through her veins like lightning. Her breathing went back to normal, and some of the pain from her fight with Thomas faded.

Doubt began to creep into Kara's mind as she looked up at Wesley. "Where did you learn to do that?"

"There's no time right now. We'll talk about it later."

What exactly had her brother been doing for the Sanguines?

Two night watchmen rounded the corner of the street they were on. She and Wesley stopped talking and began walking, lest they draw attention to themselves. Kara wrapped her wrist up in her cloak so that she wouldn't drip blood. Hopefully the cut healed like it had last time.

"You do the talking at the stable," Kara said, passing Wesley her coin pouch. "I don't want him to see my face if we can help it."

When they arrived it was quiet, but the horses heard them and began to shuffle and nicker, waking the stable boy.

"We're closed for the evening," the boy mumbled as he sat up from his pallet and rubbed the sleep out of his eyes.

"We need two horses. Now. I'll pay extra for your inconvenience," Wesley said.

"What kinda horses?"

Wesley dropped a pile of coins into the boy's hand. "Fast ones."

The boy perked up when he saw the sum. He led them to the stalls of a tall dappled grey gelding and a bay mare. "They're the best of the lot."

"We'll take them," Wesley said.

They made short work of saddling. Kara mounted the grey as Wesley slipped another two gold pieces into the boy's coat-pocket.

"You didn't see us," he said.

The boy nodded fervently. Hopefully his secrets weren't bought as easily as his loyalty.

She and Wesley would ride these horses hard, then trade them out at the next town they came to. It was one of the reasons she hadn't risked bringing Drum. She'd rather leave her in Logan and Rohan's care than that of a stranger.

They kept to a brisk trot on their way out of the city. The guards at the east gate gave them a quick once-over but didn't ask them any questions. Once they cleared the view of the gates, they kicked the horses into a gallop and rode like the hounds of the goddess were on them. Kara had left the Stygians quite the mess at the safehouse, but they would move swiftly once the next shift's guards discovered Wesley was missing.

The cold night air whipped in Kara's face as they rode. They put as much space between them and the city as possible. She hadn't planned much past their escape; her main concern had been getting Wesley to safety. She'd spent little time considering where he would go after she freed him or how long it would be before she could return to the Stygians—if they would even have her. What would Thomas tell Logan? Would they think she was a traitor? And what would Logan think, when he woke up in his bed expecting her to be beside him, only to find her gone?

( )

THEY DIDN'T SLOW their pace until they were several miles out of town and the horses were well-lathered. They rode for a few more hours, but they'd need to make camp soon. Kara wouldn't be able to ride all night without tying herself to her saddle, and Wesley was in worse shape than her. She was already sore from a combination of her and Logan's lovemaking, her fight with Thomas, and their mad dash on the horses.

"Let's stop for the night," Kara said.

Wesley nodded, and they picked their way off the road and into the woods. The forests in this region were sparser than the Blackshear. There was less cover for them to hide in, and they had to search a bit before they found a thicket of trees beside a large rock outcropping that was suitable for making camp.

Wesley was strangely silent while they unsaddled the

horses and rubbed them down. Maybe he was just over-whelmed.

"Are you familiar with this region?" Kara asked.

"Next major town's Portswell, about four days' ride from here. We can resupply there. It's mostly wilderness and trade roads in between."

"Alright. We'll steer clear of the roads during daylight. I don't want merchants or other travelers spotting us."

"Where are we heading to, Kara?"

"I figured we'd take the ferry in Portswell across the Teleri River, then go from there. We can head east, away from Sanguine and Stygian territory."

"And then?"

"I don't know. I didn't think that far ahead." Wesley unrolled the blanket she'd packed him and began to lie down. "Wait, Wes. We need to talk."

"I'm exhausted, Kara."

"I just betrayed my clan for you. You owe me some answers."

He sighed and rolled his neck out. "What do you wanna know?"

"What happened to Da?"

His face shuttered, and he scrubbed his hands over his eyes. "I don't like to think about that day. You deserve to know, though. We were on our way back from hunting when we saw the Sanguine riding party on the edge of town. We tried to get back to the woods before they spotted us, but they were moving fast. You know Da wasn't too swift on his feet anymore."

Kara fought the nausea rising in her throat. She sat down beside Wesley.

"You alright?"

"Yes. Go on."

"The Sanguines wanted their tithe. I tried to tell them to wait, that it was back at the house, but that set Da off. I think he was afraid they'd ride ahead and ransack the place with you inside, before we could get back. He mocked them, called them heartless dogs. That pissed them off. One of them said, 'We don't need the whole family,' and the leader agreed."

"Cervus?"

Wesley's eyes were wary, but he finally nodded. "He told Da to choose. Him, or me. One of us had to die. An example, he said. It happened so fast." Wesley's voice cracked, and Kara scooted closer to him and squeezed his hand.

"One of them drew their sword. I didn't think they'd do it. I thought they were bluffing. I could see the fear in his eyes, Kara. They made me watch everything. Even after."

"Which one of them killed him?"

"I don't know. I was panicking. They were wearing helmets. It's like a blur in my memory—I don't want to think about it."

"And afterwards?"

"They restrained me and left me with a guard outside the village. Along—along with Da's corpse. When they came back, I could see the houses burning in the distance. I had no idea you were still alive until I saw you at Saphia's. Cervus told me I could join them or end up like Da, so I did what I had to do. I learned to adapt."

"You're free now, Wesley. You don't have to go back to them. Maybe Logan would take you."

Wesley cut her off. "Not all the Sanguines are bad men, Kara. Cervus's group is particularly nasty. I doubt Victus approved what they did."

"You can't be serious. Da's dead because of him."

"I'm just saying that they're not all evil monsters. You donned the black—you know what I mean."

"It's not the same at all."

"No? Have they not killed indiscriminately? Don't be a hypocrite, sister."

Kara busied herself with unpacking her blanket and clearing a spot to sleep on the ground, trying to keep her frustration off her face.

"So what's your plan? Are the two of us to live a quiet life by the seashore, eking out our living on oysters and clams?"

"I don't know, Wes. My first concern was your well-being. I'll have to return and explain what happened to the Stygians once we get you to safety."

Wesley jerked his head up. "What? You want to go back?"

"Yes."

"You can't, Kara. They'll kill you."

"Once I explain—"

"There will be no time for explanations. You're a traitor. A deserter. You can't go back there."

Kara didn't see the point in arguing with him. The clan would be pissed, sure, but death? Wesley was overreacting. "Will the Sanguines come for you when they learn that you deserted? They'll be leaving Travincal soon, if they haven't already."

"I've been thinking about that, actually."

"Oh?"

"We need to be realistic, Kara. How do we plan to live? Guild contracts? If we go that route, our risk of running into one of the clans is high. They might even put bounties on us."

Kara shrugged. "We could do anything we wanted. We

both know the farrier trade, thanks to Da. It may not be particularly lucrative, but—"

"Kara, I didn't want to leave Mudbottom so I could go to some other country shithole and do the exact same thing."

"You have a better idea?"

"Hear me out. I think the Sanguines would take you on. The Stygians aren't going to want you back, and Victus is enamored of the power of the mark."

Kara shook her head. She couldn't believe what she was hearing. He must be in shock still. "Victus locks up women like me and holds them against their will, Wesley!"

"If you came willingly, you wouldn't be locked up. You could be around other women like you. Ones who want to fight the coming war."

"What war! I betrayed my clan and rescued you to get you away from the Sanguines, not send you back into their arms. They killed Da. I would never betray his memory like that, and if you had any respect for him, you wouldn't, either."

"I've told you they aren't all like that. And it was just a thought," Wesley mumbled.

"Do you really want to go back?"

Wesley was silent for a few moments, then he shook his head. "I liked being a part of something bigger than myself, but you're right. I'm sorry, Kara. I'm just anxious about the future. I worry that they'll come for us."

Kara sighed. "Let's get some sleep. We should ride at dawn."

()

THREE NIGHTS LATER, Kara sat huddled in her blanket, chewing on a piece of jerky and wishing she could start a fire.

They should reach Portswell tomorrow. There'd been no sign of the Stygians tracking them, even when they intentionally doubled back to check if they were being followed, but they couldn't risk someone seeing the smoke. Kara was beginning to miss regular meals, access to fresh water, and even the baroness's bed. She bundled up in her cloak at night to sleep, but she often woke up in the morning with numb fingers and lips. Wesley hadn't been doing a very good job of rationing the food, either. Her pack was nearly empty. Kara tried to rationalize his behavior by reminding herself that he'd been held prisoner for two weeks and probably hadn't been fed much during that time. Right now he was in the woods, trying to disguise the tracks they'd made when they'd left the road to make camp. They'd need to stop in Portswell tomorrow to get supplies before making the ferry crossing.

Kara stilled as a gust of wind brought a familiar scent to her nose. The bushes rustled faintly. She glanced behind her to where the horses were picketed. They were both there. An uneasy feeling curled up her spine. She was being watched.

"Wesley?"

No response came. She drew her daggers and stood, backing away from the noise.

Logan stepped into the clearing, and a fist clenched Kara's heart. He was wearing his Stygian uniform, with weapons strapped all over his body. His hair was pulled back into a tight knot, and his sword was drawn. The planes of his cheeks were hollow, his eyes bloodshot. He looked like he hadn't been sleeping.

Kara lowered her daggers from their raised position.

"Logan." She failed to keep the longing out of her voice.

He didn't say anything. His eyes were roving the camp site, settling for a second on the two horses. Kara's mind was racing. If Logan was here, where were the other Stygian men? Surrounding the campsite at this very moment? Had they already captured Wesley?

"Are you hurt?" he asked, his voice cold. She couldn't read his face. There was a layer of ice there, keeping her out.

Kara shook her head. She had no idea what to say to him.

"Are you here of your own volition?"

Her throat clenched. "Yes."

His face shuttered, his gaze going dark. "Are you with the prisoner?"

Kara nodded slowly.

"When I woke up and you weren't in bed beside me, I knew something was wrong. I thought the Sanguines had you, Kara. I thought a courier was going to bring you to me in pieces. Why did you leave me?"

Kara's heart broke a little at the pain in his voice. "You didn't see my letter?"

"What fucking letter?" he growled.

"In my room—"

"No, I didn't sack your room looking for a letter. I panicked. I was ready to go kick Victus's door down, damn the fallout. And then the safehouse shift change came and went, and there was no report. When Thomas told me it was you, I didn't believe him. I told him I'd slit his throat for slandering your name. I made a thousand excuses for you, Kara. I told them you wouldn't betray us, especially for one of them."

"How'd you find me?"

"It wasn't that hard, darling. I know your scent intimately. You had my blood on you. Filled with my seed. I could have tracked you anywhere."

How hard had he ridden to catch up to them? He

should have been asleep for hours after she left, and she and Wesley had been keeping up a relentless pace.

Logan stepped towards her, and Kara resisted the urge to move closer to him.

"I didn't want to hurt anyone. I tried to avoid it."

Logan blinked, and realization dawned on his face. "Otto was still out cold when we found him. Thomas said you brought them flasks and prodded them to drink. Did you drug my wine, Kara?" He smiled, but it was full of malice. "You didn't drink any of it, did you?"

"I'm sorry. I didn't mean for it to happen like that."

"*Why?*"

"He's my brother, Logan. I rescued the prisoner because he's my brother."

Logan tilted his head to the side and peered at her. "Your supposedly dead brother. Pray tell, why would your brother join the Sanguines if they killed his father?"

"He didn't have any other choice."

Doubt warred across his face. "If that's true, why wouldn't you ask me for help? Why didn't you tell me?"

"I didn't think you'd be willing to help a Sanguine—to jeopardize your clan by starting a conflict with them. Even for me. I couldn't let you give him back to Victus."

Logan frowned. "I would have helped you if you came to me, but you didn't, which makes me think you're lying. Are you Victus's spy? You've proven your talent for manipulation. You were able to evade your guards, dispatch the ones at the safehouse, and seduce and drug me. With nary a scratch on you. Well done, Kara. If that's even your name. Victus knows me well, even after all these years. Sent me someone masquerading as an unawakened girl from a squalid mountain village who was looking for vengeance and begging to join my clan. The perfect bait."

Was he serious? It felt like he'd slapped her. "You've got

it wrong, Logan. I would never work for Victus."

"You're quite the accomplished actress. The way you fumbled through training, your sweet, ignorant questions about the curse. The way you fucked me," he growled. "You had me fooled. I should've had you spy for *me*."

"Logan, please stop." But he was gone. She could see his mind spinning as he tried to convince himself he was right. Hope crumbled inside her chest.

Logan's free hand clenched into a fist. "What was your mission? Infiltrate, earn our trust, then report back on what you learned as you got closer to me? What have you told them? That contract against the bloody Sanguines—it was all a ruse, wasn't it? Travincal was your first opportunity to meet your contact and report in person. No wonder you were reluctant to tell me who'd posted it."

Logan stepped forward, raising his sword. "What I don't get is why you blew your cover. You were in a golden spot. You're not heading for Sanguine territory, which tells me it wasn't orders. He must be someone important to you. Maybe he is your brother, but the story about your father was a lie. Or is he your lover, Kara? How does he feel about me fucking you? Have you told him yet?"

Kara shook in silent fury. Her mark was blazing against her skin. Did Logan really believe these ludicrous accusations, or was it just his anger talking? "Don't do this. You're being ridiculous. I'm not a Sanguine spy. I didn't deceive you about my identity. I was reluctant to tell you who posted the contract on the Sanguines because it was Saphia."

"*The* Saphia? Saphia Kingslayer?"

"Yes."

Logan arched an eyebrow. "Interesting."

"Do you believe me now?" Kara asked limply.

His expression remained hard and unrelenting. "Let's

pretend for a second I do. Something doesn't line up, Kara. Why isn't your brother dead or in a cell? Victus has no shortage of men. He demands a brutal proof of loyalty from his new members, and he's not the type to keep around a liability. What if your brother killed your father? Have you thought of that possibility?"

Some of the blood drained from Kara's face. "No— Wesley would never—"

"You told me he was interested in joining a clan. Maybe he contacted them before the Reaping to get a foot in the door. *Maybe* he heard Victus was collecting marked women. You shouldn't trust him, Kara. I know you grew up with him, but people change. Especially when they feel like they're out of options."

"I know my brother. He wouldn't do that." *Right?*

"The Sanguines came to your village early to collect you, yet your father's death didn't trigger your curse. Consider that."

Kara paled.

They both went still at the sound of footsteps. Wesley appeared out of the treeline, sword drawn. Kara's chest constricted. She didn't want anyone to get hurt.

Logan stepped between her and Wesley. Kara glanced between the two men. "Don't hurt him, please."

"If you insist," Wesley said.

"I wasn't talking to you." She heard the dark sound of Logan's chuckle.

"I'd heard the rumors, but I thought you had better taste than this, sister. The leader of the Stygians? Really?"

"Shut up before I rip your tongue out of your throat," Logan said.

Wesley had the sense to stay silent, but he kept his sword trained on Logan.

"Stop it. Both of you. Listen, Logan, if you let him go,

I'll come back with you. I was planning to return and explain myself once Wesley was safe. You can put me in a cell if you want until we figure this thing out."

Logan looked through her instead of at her. "You think I *want* you back? Sanguine spy or not, you're a traitor. You betrayed me and the clan. Your value now is in the information you carry, which you've likely already passed along if you're working for Victus. I should kill you both."

Wesley's face tightened into a snarl. He looked like he was about to lunge at Logan.

Kara tried to blink back the tears welling in her eyes, but they overflowed and started to stream down her face. She tightened her hands into fists and dug her nails into the palms of her hands. "I can't come back?"

"No, Kara."

Kara searched Logan's face for any sign that he didn't really mean it, that it was just his anger talking, but there was nothing there. Just cold indifference.

"She wasn't meant for this life, Vakarian," Wesley said. "She's better than your lot."

"If you're leaving, do it now. Before I change my mind. The others will be here soon." His gaze pierced her to her marrow.

Kara devoured his face with her eyes, trying to memorize every detail of it. She fought the urge to run into his arms. He didn't want her back. He didn't want *her*. And he was letting them go rather than taking them prisoner. She felt crushed. Would she ever see him again?

"Goodbye," Kara whispered.

Logan held her gaze for a long second, the muscle in his jaw flexing. Then he turned around and walked into the woods.

Kara silently begged him to turn around and look back, to give her some sign of hope. She wanted to run after him, but her feet wouldn't move. Wesley pulled her towards the horses, and Kara heaved back a sob. She mounted her horse and tried not to break into a thousand tiny pieces.

CHAPTER TWENTY-TWO

Kara spent the next week in a haze. The day after Logan found them, they'd reached Portswell and made the river crossing after resupplying and trading the horses for fresh ones. Kara went through the motions of survival—ride, eat, sleep, repeat, but she was hollow inside. She was haunted by the things Logan had said, by his suggestion that Wesley had more to do with Da's death than he'd let on. His question about why Da's death hadn't triggered her curse kept her awake long into the night while Wesley slept peacefully.

Wesley tried to cheer her up by reminiscing about their childhood, but it wasn't working. The fact that Logan might believe she was a spy—that she'd been pretending since the beginning—hurt like hell. She couldn't fault him entirely. Her actions had been duplicitous, and he was the leader of the Stygian Brotherhood. He had to remain vigilant for threats such as spies and traitors. On the other hand, she wanted to rage at him for not believing her. For not taking her back with him regardless of what she wanted. She was having trouble coming to terms with the fact that she may never be able to return to the clan. When she'd set out to rescue Wesley, she'd always imagined some future where she'd be able to go back to them and pick up where things had left off, but now she was branded as a traitor.

Her somber mood was beginning to affect Wesley. Like her, he was increasingly lost in his own thoughts and distracted, and they grew less vigilant about covering their tracks and checking their perimeter when they camped at night.

They continued their journey east, to a mid-sized town called Midburn that sat on the border of the Royal Fields surrounding Lerathil, the home of the royal palace.

"There's a contract board here. We'll see if we can pick up some easy jobs," Wesley said when they rode into town.

They rented a room at the local inn so they could get hot meals and a bed for the duration of their stay. Once they were settled in, Kara dug through her pack to collect their soiled clothes for washing. She checked Wesley's pockets for valuables and paused when she felt something hard and round in one of them. Kara reached into the pocket and pulled a coin out. The blood drained from her face. It was a Sanguine coin. Just like the one Saphia had pulled from the dead man's pockets at Oxswitch Avenue. A token of loyalty...a token of initiation... Why would Wesley have one of these? Her hands shook. She dropped the coin, and it rolled across the floor.

The door to the room opened, and Wesley walked in. He'd gone to get food for them so they could avoid eating in the common room.

"I got you some soup and bread. It's watered down, but I paid for extra meat."

Kara ignored him. The coin had rolled to a stop and fallen flat beside the bedpost.

"Come on, it's gonna get cold."

"I'm not hungry," she said through clenched teeth.

Wesley's spoon clattered against his bowl as he set it down. "You've got to snap out of this funk, Kara. You're acting like you were in love with the guy. You fucked him, I get it. But you're Namirahn. You're gonna do a lot more fucking before you're done."

Rage boiled up in her, swift and ready. She was ready to fight, ready to feel *anything* again. "Fuck you, Wesley. How do you know so much about the curse now, anyways? Da always kept us in the dark."

"I learned it during my time with the Sanguines."

"Please tell me you didn't have anything to do with Victus kidnapping marked women."

Wesley's eyes slid away from hers. "Look, Kara, I was assigned there—I didn't have a choice in the matter."

"Assigned *where?*"

"It's at a base in the Black Hills. I couldn't tell you how to get there—even Sanguines are brought in under the cover of night, blindfolded to keep the location secret. Only the highest ranking officers know the location."

Kara was beginning to feel sick to her stomach. A ball of dread twisted in her gut. "What did you do there, Wesley?"

"I don't want to talk about it."

"I don't give a shit what you want! I have a right to know."

"I was just an errand boy, okay? I brought them meals, delivered messages, sat watch."

"That's all? How'd you know to use my blood to draw that pattern on my mark? Back in Travincal."

"Sometimes I had to do things I didn't want to do to

survive. To not be killed. You have to understand that, Kara."

"What did you have to do, Wesley?" Kara's ears rung in her head. She was afraid of his answer.

"Sometimes there were…difficulties, and I had to sit in on the torture sessions."

Kara had to make a conscious effort to quell the shaking in her hands. *Difficulties?* "Victus is torturing them?"

Wesley kept his eyes averted, but he nodded. "If they were noncompliant. Sometimes he wanted information— names of other marked women. Most of them are fine. Some of them even want to be there, but the trouble-makers were dealt with harshly."

Just how far had her brother gone to blend in with the Sanguines? "Did you tell them about me, Wesley? Did you tell them I was marked?"

"Kara—"

"Answer the question."

"Everyone knows about the marked female Vakarian let join his clan, Kara. It wasn't a secret—"

Kara inhaled deeply through her nose. "You didn't know it was me until that day at Oxswitch Avenue, though. Did you tell them who I was afterward?"

Wesley stirred his soup and avoided her gaze. "No. That's why I came alone to Valancourt's."

Kara didn't know if she believed him. The knot of doubt tightening in her gut told her not to. She felt like she barely knew her brother anymore.

"Was there any truth to what Logan said?"

"What do you mean?"

"Did you have anything to do with what happened to Da?"

"Seriously? How can you suggest that?"

"I found your coin."

"What?"

"The Sanguine coin. I know what it means."

Wesley bit his lip. "They give that to everyone, Kara. It's a means of identifying a legitimate Sanguine, that's all. What did you do with it?"

A *legitimate* Sanguine. The words burned her ears. "You know, I always wondered why the Sanguine Riders came early for the tithe. They never came early before."

"You're being paranoid, sister. That asshole Vakarian wanted you to doubt me, and it's working. Are you really going to believe him over me?"

"*Did you have anything to do with his death?*" Her mark felt like a brand being laid against her skin, and she fought the temptation to go for her daggers.

Wesley stood up from the table abruptly. "Don't forget that he was *my* father, Kara. My blood. He uprooted our entire life for *you*, some stranger's cursed brat, and then mom got sick in those fucking mountains. Both of my parents are dead because of *you*."

His words burned in her ears. A sinking sensation flooded her chest. Wesley resented her, and she couldn't blame him. How long had he felt this way?

"Get out, Wesley," Kara whispered.

"What?"

"Get. Out. I need to be alone."

Wesley took his soup and left, slamming the door behind him.

( )

KARA SLEPT LATE the next morning. It'd been too long since she'd had the comfort of a pillow and mattress, and she intended to get her money's worth. The room was cold when she woke, the fire in the hearth having died down overnight. Kara rolled over and looked at the other bed. Wesley was missing, but he might have risen early. He hadn't come back to the room last night until she was already asleep.

Kara stilled when she saw the curled scrap of paper on his pillow. She slid out of bed and walked towards it slowly, afraid of its contents.

The paper shook in her grasp when she picked it up. Scrawled in black ink with Wesley's messy handwriting, it read:

Goodbye, sister. I know where your loyalties lie, and I don't want to be your burden. Go to him. He would be a fool not to take you back. Stay safe. Don't look for me. You may not like what you find.

Remember me as I was in the woods.

Kara dropped the note and backed away from the bed, then collapsed to her knees. She'd left the Sanguine coin on the floor last night; she hadn't wanted to touch it. She looked by the bedpost where it had fallen, then scoured the rest of the small room for it. It was gone.

Kara grabbed her pack and dug through it. Her clothes were there, but all of Wesley's were gone, along with half the money they'd had. She wanted to scream and beat her fists against the wall. Was him fleeing an admission of guilt, or weakness? She hadn't sacrificed everything for it to end like this.

Kara quickly dressed and tore downstairs. "How long ago did he leave?!" she demanded to the bar keeper.

"Who?"

"My brother! The man I arrived here with."

The man paused for a second, thinking. "Last I seen him was hours ago, ma'am."

Fuck fuck fuck fuck. She'd just found Wesley, and he was gone again? This couldn't be happening. Damn his letter, his abandonment. She needed answers. Kara fetched her horse from the stable—Wesley's was missing—and saddled up. As soon as she slid her feet into the stirrups, she paused. Where would he go? East, towards freedom? Or west, back to the Sanguines? Kara lowered her eyes and heeled the horse westward, into the woods.

She was only a few miles in when she discovered she was being followed. Her pursuers weren't trying very hard to be discrete. Shadows moved behind the trees, flanking her. At least two people—maybe three. Unease curled up Kara's spine. She didn't know what to do. The deeper into the woods she led them, the further she'd be from anyone who might hear her scream. Kara turned her horse as far as she could without it looking like she was heading back for town, and the shadows adjusted around her.

She doubted it was the Stygians. They could track her sight unseen until they wanted to reveal themselves. Had the Sanguines caught up to her and Wesley? Worse, had he already rejoined them and led them straight to her?

The shadows moved in closer. They were herding her. She didn't want to fight them three against one if she could avoid it. Kara wrapped her hand in the horse's mane and kicked him into a gallop. They whipped through the forest at a dangerous speed. She had to duck low along the horse's neck so she didn't take a limb to the face, and the low branches they sped under scraped against her back.

The shadows drew even with her on the other sides of the trees, and there was still a ways back to town. Their horses crashed through the underbrush. Two on the left, one on the right. Her rented horse wasn't fast enough.

They were going to catch her. Kara veered to the right, chasing the lone horseman.

He came into view through a gap in the trees. Slick red metal covered his back and arms. She was going to have to get close. Kara heeled her horse until she drew even with him. He glanced up, surprise clear on his face.

Kara cut her horse in front of him, forcing him to slow. He pulled a mace out of a sheathe on his saddle and swung it at her. Kara's mark flared. She ducked his swing and hooked her dagger into his wrist, digging it in until hilt met bone. He screamed and dropped his weapon. He tried to yank his arm back, but Kara pulled him into her saddle and sunk her other dagger into his chest, driving it beneath his breastplate. He gasped and clutched his chest. She yanked her daggers out of him and pushed him to the forest floor.

Kara scanned the trees, looking for the other two Sanguines. A heavy weight crashed into her from over-head, pushing her out of the saddle. She caught her fall with her wrist, and a shooting pain ran up her arm. Her wrist bent at an awkward angle when she tried to move it.

Her assailant rolled on top of her, pinning her to the ground. He must have climbed a tree and waited in ambush. Kara tried to scramble forward in the dirt, but he yanked her back by the hair and sat on her spine.

"Where do you think you're going?"

Tears bit at her eyes as he pulled at her scalp. One of her daggers lay in the dirt, just out of reach. Her fingers inched towards it. The merc leaned forward and snatched the dagger just before she could. When Kara felt the shift in his weight, she dug her feet into the ground and heaved, tossing him off of her.

She tried to scramble to her feet, and he lunged for her. The ruby pommel of her dagger flashed through the air, then hot fire slid into her gut. She gasped, air escaping her lungs. Her hands clutched at the hilt of the knife. It'd gone all the way in. She bent around the pain pulsing through her abdomen.

She heard the *thwip* of an arrow, and fletching sprouted from her assailant's skull. He sunk towards the earth, blood leaking between his eyes. Kara looked in the direction the arrow had come from.

Her savior appeared from the trees on horseback, wearing an antlered helm gilded in silver. Cervus had found her.

She pulled her dagger out of her abdomen, clenching her teeth to keep from screaming, and covered the wound with her hand. Hot blood pulsed out between her fingers. There was too much of it.

Cervus dismounted in one smooth movement, his massive bow strapped to his back.

"I enjoyed the entertainment, dear, but he's not allowed to hurt the merchandise. Knew I shouldn't have brought him. Too feral."

Cervus began walking towards her. Kara tried to crawl away. The horses were nowhere in sight—they'd probably bolted during the commotion. She wasn't confident she'd be able to make it far on foot.

"You've proved exceedingly difficult to kidnap, Kara McKenna. But it seems your brother knows you well. He said you would come."

"Where is he?"

"Gone. You'll see him later. Said he didn't want to watch. I was tempted to make him, but he's done well.

Maybe he was bluffing. Maybe they'd captured Wesley and forged the note and...she was grasping at straws. Her vision blurred at the edges, and a seductive voice curled in her ear. *Stop making excuses for him. He isn't your blood. He is meat.* Kara shook herself.

"Your brother told me everything. I loved the part where Vakarian convinced himself you were working for us. That man is too paranoid for his own good."

Hope withered inside of her. "You might as well kill me. I won't be Victus's puppet."

"Be happy to, but Victus wants you alive. There's a bloodline to preserve."

Cervus neared her. Kara rose on unsteady legs, trying to block the pain that blossomed in her abdomen. She clutched her dagger in her good hand. She had to fight. If she could make it to his horse, maybe she'd have a chance.

She swiped a hand through the blood leaking out of her abdomen and smeared it in a circle around her mark, praying it would work like it had with Logan and Wesley. Kara shuddered as fire suffused her, invigorating her. There was weakness beneath the flames, like a shadow flickering at the edges, but it numbed the pain in her gut. For now.

"You could be happy with us," Cervus tsked. "You would be treated like the queen you are. Not relegated to a crumbling tower."

How did he know that?

Cervus drew his sword. "Victus wants you alive. He said nothing about whole." When he reached the edge of his range, he whipped the sword at her so fast that she felt the sting across her chest before she even saw his blade. This was bad. He was wicked fast and had a deadly reach. Blood blossomed where he'd cut her and dripped down her abdomen.

Cervus sliced into her over and over again, quick exterior cuts that drained her will and energy more than they actually hurt her. Every time she tried to dart in and strike at him, he blocked her with that long blade. There was no end in sight to his stamina; he wasn't even winded, and Kara was moving sluggishly. She could feel the power of her blood infusion waning bit by bit. She had to try something different, and soon.

Kara fingered her dagger, adjusting her hold on it. They'd circled each other, so he no longer stood between her and his horse. She threw her dagger at his face and dashed for the horse. Cervus dodged it and grabbed her by the back of her shirt. He yanked her to the ground and punched her in the face.

Kara's head bounced off the ground, and stars blossomed in her vision. Pain radiated across her cheek and into her jaw. She whimpered.

"I'd play with you all day if I could, little dove, but you're losing too much blood. Victus would skewer me if I let anything happen to you."

"Help!" Kara screamed at the top of her lungs in a last bid for freedom. Thunder rumbled in the distance.

Cervus stuffed a dirty rag into her mouth. "No one's coming to help you, Kara. You're mine. When you're chained up all day, wondering how you ever got there, think of your dear brother Wesley. He's been ever so helpful."

Cervus turned away from her and scanned the trees. A shadow of worry crossed over his face. Kara's ears were still ringing from his punch—was someone there?

"Come out, or I'll give your whore something worth screaming about," Cervus yelled.

A black blur burst out of the trees wielding a sword, and Cervus's mount bolted. He cursed.

Logan galloped towards them atop Char. Kara's heart clenched. How was he here?

Cervus wrapped his huge hands around Kara's neck as

they charged forward. "I will snap her like a twig if you come any closer, Vakarian," he shouted.

Logan stopped Char hard, and the stallion's hooves made deep indentations in the earth as he slid to a standstill. Logan's eyes glowed a deep, violent red, and the muscles in his neck and shoulders were pumped with blood.

"Get off your horse and drop the weapon."

Logan dismounted slowly and laid his sword in the grass, never taking his eyes off Kara. He scoured her face and body, taking an inventory of her wounds. The worry in his eyes concerned her.

"All of them."

Logan unbuckled the harness holding his daggers and throwing knives and let it slide to the ground. Even unarmed, he emanated menace. He was breathing heavily, the pent-up rage in his body barely contained. Logan took a step forward, and Cervus's hands squeezed her neck, blocking her air.

Kara struggled to hang onto consciousness. A heavy weight tugged her under, beckoning her into its warmth. When she glanced down at her hands, they were stained with blood.

"Don't move if you want her to live." Cervus dragged her to her feet, picking up his sword and keeping it trained on her back. His eyes flicked around the clearing, weighing his options. He was starting to panic.

"Give me your horse, Vakarian."

Logan patted Char on the rump and sent him forward. Hope blazed inside Kara. She'd never seen anyone ride Char other than Logan. Maybe this could work.

Cervus grabbed Char's bridle and yanked him around. Char snorted and stamped a hoof, perturbed by the unfamiliar scent. Cervus shoved the tip of his sword between Kara's shoulderblades. "You first."

The motion of stepping into the stirrup and pulling herself into the saddle with a stab wound nearly undid her. Kara groaned behind gritted teeth and slumped forward over the pommel. She was having trouble keeping her balance with everything spinning. Her body was cold and weak. Cervus kept the blade trained on her as he mounted, sinking his weight into the stirrup and swinging over. Just before Cervus found his seat, Logan whistled, and Char exploded into a rear.

Kara leaned forward and wrapped her arms around Char's neck as he jerked into the air. Cervus grabbed for her, yanking at her shirt as he pinwheeled towards the earth. Logan crossed the distance in seconds. Cervus had dropped his sword in the fall, and his helmet rolled off behind him. Logan slammed into him, shaking the ground with the impact. He pounded his fists into Cervus's face over and over, each punch echoed by a brutal thud.

Char fell back to the earth, and Kara's grip went limp. She started to slide off his side, unable to support her weight any longer. It was safe now. She could finally succumb to that hazy black warmth. Kara hit the ground with a thud, and Logan cursed. He gripped Cervus's head between his hands and twisted his neck in a fast, brutal motion. The pop was sickening.

Then he was next to her, lifting her off the ground. He propped her up in his arms and drew up her shirt. He sucked in a breath when he saw her wound.

"You're not allowed to die on me, McKenna."

"How are you even here right now?" Kara mumbled. Couldn't he tell that she just wanted to sleep?

Logan pulled a knife from his saddlebag, ripped through the laces of his bracer, then sliced open his mark.

He held his bloody wrist to Kara's mouth. "Drink!" Kara sputtered and coughed as hot liquid flooded her tongue. His blood was rich and tangy, and she choked on it going down. "You have to swallow it, love. I'm sorry." Logan yanked her collar down and drew a rune on her chest with his blood. He pressed his hand to it and whispered fiercely, cradling her against his chest, his lips pressed into her brow so hard that she could feel his teeth. It sounded like he was saying *please*.

Warmth slid through Kara, snaking down her throat and arms and legs. It felt like he was inside her, bolstering her strength. She was drunk on him. He ran a hand through her hair and felt her forehead with the back of his other hand. "That's it, that's it baby. You're going to make it." He lifted her in his arms and carried her to Char. Logan whistled in a lower tone this time, and Char folded his legs and lowered himself to the ground. Logan situated them in the saddle and signaled Char to rise.

Kara sighed against his chest and snuggled into his warmth as they began to move. She closed her eyes and let oblivion slide over her.

CHAPTER TWENTY-THREE

K ara awoke to the sounds of arguing.

"Heal her!" Logan yelled.

"You fed her your blood then used blood magic on her—that's forbidden, Logan," said a woman with a familiar voice.

"Heal her, or I will do much worse."

Kara tried to open her eyes and see who was speaking, but they were weighed down.

"I'll do it. But I want to be clear that I'm doing this because of the contract, Vakarian. Not for you. You can't just show up in Lerathil every time you have an emergency, demanding my services."

Lerathil?

"You were the closest mage I trusted. Please, Serena. I'll owe you."

"I'll hold you to that."

Kara managed to crack one eyelid open and peer around the room. She frowned as the woman speaking slowly came into focus. Serena? What was Serena doing here?

"She's coming to," Serena said.

Logan turned to look at Kara. She'd never seen him look so haggard. Dark circles ringed his eyes and his hair was sticking up at odd angles. He knelt beside the bed and folded her fingers in his. "Serena's going to help you heal. You lost a lot of blood. You remember her, right?"

Kara nodded. Her face was swollen and tender, and pain shot through when she turned her head "Where am I?"

"At the royal palace in Lerathil," Serena said.

( )

KARA SPENT the next two weeks in bed, much of it in and out of consciousness. Serena came every few days and laid her hands on Kara's wound and chanted until a web of vibrating yellow energy spanned her abdomen and slowly sunk into her skin. Logan was there every time she woke, sometimes reading in a chair by the window, sometimes plastered against her skin in her sleep, his strong arms pulling her tight against him. Sometimes staring at her face like it held the answer to every question he'd ever had.

Eventually Kara felt well enough to get up and move around, and he escorted her as she walked the empty stone halls to rebuild her strength. She wasn't sure where Serena was keeping her, but she never saw anyone other than her and Logan.

Kara didn't know what to say to him. She was torn between gratitude that he'd saved her and anger that he'd believed she could be a Sanguine spy. Wesley's betrayal hung heavy in her head, preoccupying much of her thoughts, and she had a tiny ball of resentment inside her that she hadn't been the one to kill Cervus. They often sat in silence, Logan waiting for her to say something and her never knowing what to say. It was excruciating.

On one of their daily walks about the halls, Kara caught the toe of her shoe on a flagstone and nearly tripped. Logan caught her so quickly that it felt like he'd been anticipating it. Kara shrugged him off and stepped away.

"You think I'm fragile now."

"No I don't."

"You do. You touch me like you're afraid I might break."

"I want you to recover well."

They both knew that was an excuse. Her appetite had returned. Her wound had closed days ago. Serena now only visited to chat, not to heal her. The blank stone walls were beginning to get to her. "We need to talk about what happened, Logan."

They made their way back to her cell, as Kara had begun to think of it. When Logan closed the door behind him, Kara spun on him and pinned him against the wall.

"What are you doing?"

"Trying to find your fire." Kara pulled his head down to hers and kissed him. She channeled all of her lust, rage, and confusion into the kiss. She tangled her tongue in his mouth and scraped her nails down his chest, breathing hard. She dove beneath the hem of his shirt and slid her hands up his sculpted chest.

His lips responded to her, but he kissed her back sweetly, patiently. Like a suitor. It drove her insane.

Kara pulled away from him. "Why'd you come after me if you thought I was a traitor, Logan? After I drugged you."

"Because I'm a fool."

"A fool to come find me?"

"A fool to let you go. I should have believed you, Kara. I let rage cloud my judgment. The accusations I made against you were unfair, and I'm sorry for them. I hate that I hurt you, that I doubted you like that."

Kara took one of Logan's hands and squeezed it in hers. "You're not entirely to blame in this. I'm sorry, too. I should have trusted you enough to tell you about Wesley. And the sleeping elixir—I didn't mean for it to happen like that, Logan."

"If I'd dragged you back to Travincal with me that night in the forest, none of this would have happened. You wouldn't have been hurt. I hate that I let it happen."

"It needed to happen. I needed to know the truth about Wesley. But I don't understand why you're still holding yourself back from me. Is it this place? When are we returning to the clan?"

A shadow passed over Logan's face, and Kara knew something was wrong. "What aren't you telling me?"

"It's the clan, Kara"

"Is Thomas okay?" She held her breath while she waited for his answer.

"He's fine. Maybe embarrassed that you got the better of him, but fine."

Relief swept through her. She'd have to do some serious groveling the next time she saw him. "Then what is it?"

"I understand your motivations now, but the clan doesn't. They'll need time. They think you betrayed them. *I* want you back, but I have to do what's best for the clan. If I can't do that, then I shouldn't be leading them."

"What about my contract?"

"Do you really think that will make a difference?"

A stone dropped into the pit of Kara's stomach. He

was right, as much as she hated it. "How long do you think they're going to need?" *How long do I have to be alone?*

"I don't know, Kara. Before we left Travincal, I secured several royal contracts. I had you in mind for one of them. If you're interested in it, it'd be a good way to begin earning back their trust."

"*Royal* contracts? As in from King Calim?"

Logan nodded, and Kara sucked in her breath. This was the real deal.

"What's the job?"

"Calim suspects Victus is making a power play at court, maybe with the aims to end the monarchy altogether. At the very least he wants to put his men in positions of power. We suspect there are several royals already in his pocket."

"What about the cursed women Victus has been abducting and torturing? Wesley confirmed it. We need to do something, Logan."

Logan nodded, his eyes looking haunted. "Did he or Cervus give you any information on where they're located?"

Kara shook her head. "Somewhere in the Black Hills."

"Cervus was an officer, he would have known. I wanted to interrogate him for information, but there was no time. You were dying, and it was too dangerous to leave him alive. I have people working on finding it, but it's a well-kept secret, and the Sanguines have a tight hold on their territory. If Victus has anyone important at court, we might be able to learn more from them. You'll be spying for me *and* the king."

"Spying on who, exactly?"

Logan grinned. "Everyone. You'll need to identify whose loyalties lie where. As a woman, you'll have access to conversations and locations that men won't. But you must be careful to maintain the identity you're given, Kara. They can't find out who you are. The Baroness's lessons should come in handy."

"I'll do it."

"Are you positive? It will be dangerous."

Kara shot him a look. "Perfect."

"That's what I was counting on."

"Now, will you kiss me like you mean it?"

Logan's eyes flashed fire, and he dragged her to the bed.

FREE BONUS CONTENT

()

Want to read the scene of Kara's first keening from Logan's point of view?

Sign up for my newsletter at **sarasellers.com** and receive a link to this free exclusive.

I'd love it if you could leave me a review. Reviews are the lifeblood of authors like me, and they allow me to keep writing. Thank you!

ADVANCED READER TEAM

()

Want to be part of my advanced reader team that receives
early access to new releases?

Sign up at **sarasellers.com/links**

THE STYGIAN CROWN
PREVIEW

( )

Continue Kara and Logan's story in the sequel, *The Stygian Crown*, out now. Keep reading for a look at the first two chapters.

PROLOGUE

L ogan palmed the letter between his fingers. It was worn down and wrinkled from how many times he'd read it, crumpled it up, then straightened it back out again over the past month. The paper was streaked orange from desert dust. He should have burned it a long time ago, but it kept pulling him back. He couldn't get her out of his head. Part of him wished he'd never read it.

DEAR LOGAN,

   I shudder to write this, but you deserve an explanation for my disappearance. Leaving you is the last thing I want to do right now. The Sanguine prisoner you've been holding is my brother, Wesley. The one I was searching for when I joined your clan and the closest thing to family I have left in this world. I hope you'll understand my deception. I can't let you hand him back to Victus. We've been through enough pain already.

   I know you won't let us go easily. I beg of you, don't search for us. I need to help him start a new life away from the clans, however *long that may take. I hope to one day return to the Brotherhood, once my brother is safe. I hope to return to you. I will miss you to my very marrow, Logan Vakarian.*

Yours,

Kara

P.S. Sorry for drugging you.

LOGAN CRUSHED the paper in his fist.

CHAPTER ONE

O *ne month earlier*

"Do you really have to go?" Kara asked, tracing the whorls of dark hair on Logan's chest. She sprawled naked on top of him, one leg hooked around his as he cradled her in the crook of his arm.

"I have to leave and rejoin the rest of the clan. They expected me a week ago."

"And you still can't tell me what the mission is?" Logan had negotiated another contract for the Stygians, one that took him away from Lerathil, but he refused to share the details of it with her.

His eyebrows knit together. "Classified, I'm afraid. It's safer if you don't know."

Kara closed her eyes and sighed against his skin. "Are you going to be gone longer than a month?" She hated the question, hated what it meant. Afraid to hear his answer.

"I'll make it back in time. For both of us."

"But what if you don't?" The keening would come for them both regardless.

"I'll be back, Kara."

"There you go again, making promises you can't keep." She hoped she was wrong.

"I don't make that promise lightly," he said, a low growl in his throat.

"And while you're away I'm to fake being a noble and spy on members of the Lerathilian court. Without your help. No pressure."

"You'll do fine. Serena will help you. Just don't do anything I wouldn't do," he said, a wry grin spreading across his face. "Now, enough of goodbyes. We still have tonight." Logan flipped her beneath him in one smooth motion and pinned her down, his great muscular body stretching out over hers. He dipped his head to her neck and nibbled at her collarbone until she shrieked, then caught her scream between his lips.

"I'm going to miss this," Kara whispered between hard, frantic kisses. She wrapped her legs around him and pulled his hips towards hers until the hard heat of him rubbed against the crux of her thighs.

Logan hissed between his teeth. "Goddess, me too."

( )

THEY GOT little sleep that night, and the following morning Kara escorted Logan to the stable yard, the dark circles beneath her eyes hidden deep within the hood of her cloak. She squinted and winced at the sudden sunlight as they exited the castle's side door. They'd spent all their time since she'd healed from her encounter with Cervus and the Sanguines in the same removed set of halls and rooms beneath the servant's quarters, so far from the center of the castle that even the servants rarely trod them. At least her new identity would mean freedom, of a sort.

Kara's eyes adjusted to the light slowly. The palace

stables were constructed of ornate stone and curving arch-
ways, and large enough to hold a small army of horses.
Dim-eyed stablehands led finely-bred steeds with shining
coats to their hitching posts to be saddled. Kara's hands
fisted in the fabric of her cloak, a trickle of unease running
through her. She felt out of place, and the game hadn't
even begun. A stablehand appeared from beneath one of
the stable's curved arches leading Char, who began to jerk
his head and prance on the lead when he saw Logan.

"You better bring my horse back with you, Vakarian."
Her mare, Drum, was still with the rest of the Stygian clan,
wherever they were.

Logan laughed. "Of course, my lady."

Kara winced at the honorific.

Logan pulled her towards him and found her face
within the cloak's hood, grasping her cheeks in his hands.
"No goodbyes. I'll see you soon." He tilted her head up to
kiss her, and his lips were desperate and hungry when they
met hers. They said farewell, even if he wouldn't. She
wrapped her hands around his neck and clashed her lips
with his, tasting him. The spicy flavor of his blood danced
on her tongue, and Kara realized she'd nicked his lip with
her teeth.

Logan groaned and pulled her to him, crushing her in
a tight embrace.

She buried her face in his neck and breathed deep,
trying to capture the smell of him for safekeeping.

"Stay safe, little spitfire," he whispered.

"You too, Logan."

And then he was gone, striding towards Char and
mounting in one smooth motion. He nodded to her once,
and Kara tried to sear how he looked now, hair out of
place and lips red from her brutal kisses, into her mind.
And then he was galloping away.

The hole in Kara's chest spread, threatening to collapse.

Someone coughed, and Kara followed the noise. Serena leaned against am imposing stone column to the right, her dark hair framing her olive face and expressive brown eyes. Her hair was loose, and she was dressed in a simple cream blouse and leather breeches.

"Don't worry, he'll be back. He's got that look in his eye."

Kara quickly snuffed the flame of jealousy that threatened to rear its head. There was nothing between Serena and Logan now besides tense friendship, and the woman had saved her life on multiple occasions.

"Are you ready to begin?"

"Yes." Staying busy would distract her from missing Logan.

"Then follow me, my lady."

Kara stilled. The title was going to take some getting used to. Serena led her back through a different entrance into an unfamiliar wing of the castle. She struggled to keep from gawking at her surroundings. White marble floors covered in royal blue carpet runners led to an imposing split staircase at the head of the room. An enormous crystal chandelier dangled overhead, catching sunlight from the windows and refracting it. The entrance hall was flanked by statues carved into creatures of legend—a siren, her face contorted in ecstasy as she was swallowed by a wave. A horse with wings that spanned ten feet across, each feather wrought in glorious detail. Kara traced her hand over a wingtip, running the pads of her fingers across the individual barbs.

"It takes some getting used to," Serena said.

Kara drug her eyes from one extravagance to another as she followed Serena up the marble steps. She hated that she thought it was beautiful. The second story featured endless hallways and doors leading to an untold number of rooms. Portraits of royalty hung on the walls, their austere gazes staring down at her.

Serena stopped in front of a room at the end of the hall and opened the door, ushering her in. "Your new quarters."

The room wasn't as garish as the one she'd stayed in at Baroness Valancourt's in Travincal, thank the goddess, but it was still uncomfortably lavish. A fire blazed in the hearth, which was carved out of the same white stone as the statues. Gold and grey veins streaked through the marble and splintered out across the mantelpiece. A bed large enough for three people sat in front of the fire. It was dressed in stark white linens, and a diaphanous blue curtain hung from the four-poster canopy, flowing down to the floor. Kara wanted to climb into the bed and shut herself inside the curtain for a while.

Serena strode past the bed to a walnut-colored armoire and snapped open the doors, revealing a dark green gown beaded with white pearls. "Put this on. I'm taking you to meet the king."

"Excuse me?" Kara's jaw hung slack.

"We need to hammer out the details of your employment, and he wants to meet you before you begin."

Serena passed her the gown, and Kara stood there, clenching the heavy fabric. "This is all happening very quickly."

"If you can navigate Vakarian, you can navigate anyone. You'll do fine." Serena opened a drawer in the armoire and began chucking pieces of white fabric onto the bed, including stockings, a slip, and a corset.

"Who am I pretending to be?" Kara laid the gown on the bed and began to undress.

"Lady Celine Grey, newly come to court in search of a husband."

Kara paused, her shirt halfway over her head. "*What?*"

"It's the best cover. You can bond with the other debutantes or attend soirees with their mothers, and it will allow you to get close to any single men you're investigating without raising suspicion."

"Mother Night. Did Logan know about this plan?"

"What do you think?" Serena asked, arching an eyebrow.

Kara sighed. "And is Lady Celine real?"

"No, but Robert Grey, the Lord of Briarcliff, is, and he's in hot water with King Calim. He doesn't come to court often, and his estate is remote enough that people shouldn't be too suspicious at your sudden appearance. I'll leave it to you if you want to be public about being marked or not. This is Lerathil, so everyone's got a Namirahn somewhere in the family tree. You'll find judgmental assholes all over Teleria, but by and large you wouldn't be scorned for it."

What would it be like to not be judged for her curse? She'd had a taste of that with Logan and the Brotherhood, but now she was wearing a mask again. Kara donned the undergarments and stepped into the dress, unused to the feel of such soft fabric against her skin. She pulled it up and pushed her arms through the sleeves, then turned so Serena could help her lace up the corset and gown.

Serena tackled the laces with deft fingers. "You'll have a lady's maid to help you with this most of the time. You can reach her with the bell-pull by the bed."

"I don't need a maid in my business all the time."

"Well I have duties other than lacing up your dresses," Serena said, yanking the laces taut. "And unless you learned to do your hair like a Countess's daughter from Philipe Galois, you're going to need her."

Serena finished lacing her up, and Kara pinned her hair up in a simple twist. Countess's daughter or not, it would have to do for now.

Serena took a step back and looked her over. "You clean up nice, McKenna. Calim is going to eat his teeth."

Kara slid on a pair of ivory slippers and followed Serena back to the first floor, then down several sidehalls. Serena navigated the labyrinthine palace with confidence, but Kara was beginning to doubt her ability to find her way back to her room without getting turned around.

They entered a room behind a tall set of double doors, and Kara sucked in a breath. Bookshelves lined the room, stretching two stories high. Rolling ladders rested against the bookshelves, and several spiral staircases led to a floating walkway that bordered the second level of books. Fae lanterns bobbed along the second-floor banister, teasing passerby to peek over the edge.

Against the far walls, three enormous hearths blazed with glowing green fire, like the cavernous maws of some many-mouthed eldritch beast.

"Spellfires. So the smoke won't damage the books and there's no chance of a real fire spreading." Serena locked the library doors behind them. "There are reading rooms here, if you ever need a break. Though they're mainly used for illicit rendezvous. Come, the king awaits."

Kara followed Serena's gaze to the library's sole occupant. A man reclined in a plush leather chair, a book in his hands and reading glasses halfway down his nose. He wore an unassuming doublet in royal blue and black breeches tucked into tall boots. A plate of half-eaten lemon cookies sat on the end table beside him. He wore no circlet or crown, though Kara supposed she would not want to wear a crown all the time either, were she queen.

Kara approached him and executed one of the slow, graceful curtsies Philipe had trained her to do by making her balance a book on her head. "Your highness."

The king glanced up at her and recoiled, dropping his book in his lap. Then he shook his head and met her eyes again. "Apologies. You look a lot like someone I know."

The king's close cropped brown hair was greying at the temples, his eyes a warm chocolate color. Kara was surprised by the lack of royal seals or jewelry on his person, not even a ring. Was he as humble as his wardrobe?

Calim motioned for her to rise. "You must be Vakari-an's girl." He had the crisp consonants and polished accent of an aristocrat.

"I'm my own person." Kara tried not to let her annoyance show on her face.

Had his lips twitched at that?

"Of course, forgive me. Where are you from, again? I won't ask your name—best to forget it ever existed while you're here."

"The Balmoran Mountains."

Calim took off his reading glasses and cleaned them with his sleeve, a thoughtful expression on his face. "Interesting. You don't look like mountain stock."

"I was adopted."

Calim's eyes flickered to Serena, then settled on Kara's face, analyzing. "Impressive, seeker. I could almost believe we were related."

Serena smirked, settling onto the couch across from Calim and crossing her legs. Kara was unsure if it'd be rude to sit in his presence, but Calim gestured for her to take the chair next to him.

"What's your education like? Vakarian didn't give me much to go on."

Best not to tell him she'd been homeschooled by a soldier turned farrier. Kara shrugged. "Just a village school in the north. I can read and write and do sums, but they rarely got philosophical. Philipe Galois of Travincal taught me etiquette and dancing, though. I can blend in in the ballroom."

"Well, you came highly recommended. Vakarian doesn't give praise lightly, and I trust him and Serena. Shall we talk business?"

Kara nodded. "I'd like to discuss my pay." She needed the money to come to her, not the Stygians, since she wasn't sure how quickly the dustup over her breaking Wesley out of their safehouse would settle once they returned.

Calim broke into a grin. "Of course. A mercenary's favorite topic. You'll be generously compensated for every week you remain in my employ. There will be bonuses for any information you bring me that proves useful in identifying the Sanguine sympathizers. Find out which nobles are in their pockets. Since it's a Stygian contract, will you be giving Vakarian his cut? Or do I need to set it aside for him?"

Kara smiled, and it was all teeth. "I'll give it to him." *Once I'm accepted back into the clan.*

"All your expenses will be taken care of," Serena said. "I've made you an appointment with the best modiste in the city already. Is your room to your satisfaction?"

Kara nodded. "Do you have any leads on the Sanguine threat? Where do I start?"

"To begin with, familiarize yourself with the palace and the courtiers in residence," Calim said. "Try to find your way into their good graces. There's new information that's come to light since I negotiated this contract, though."

"What is it, your highness?"

"Please. I'm just a man with a crown. Call me Calim."

Kara gulped. How in Teleria had she ended up here, with the king of the realm, being told to call him by his first name? It struck her anew that she was talking to the grandson of Urian, the man partially responsible for the creation of Namirah's curse.

"Calim." His name stuck in her throat.

"We believe there's a threat to my sister, Princess Ariana's, life."

"From the Sanguines?"

Calim nodded. "That's our suspicion. Ariana's betrothal to the Prince of Gavroche will be announced soon. Their marriage stands to strengthen the crown in both trade and military might, make us a real contender in Teleria again. There are some who'd prefer we remain weak."

"The Vespertines will protect her," Serena said, "but people know who we are. They see us coming, know our habits and schedules. You, however...You don't have to be by her side day and night, but we'd like to you look out for danger. And find the person plotting to kill her before it's too late."

"My sister and I are the last in line to the throne. We have no heirs. We must dig out the roots of dissidence, or the problem will fester and grow. The palace is large, but our army is small. If the Sanguines took Lerathil, or, goddess forbid, instilled their own puppet monarch on the throne, I don't think even the guild could stop them. Or the Stygians," he said pointedly.

Kara's mind whirled. Hunting a princess's assassin sounded like a good way to end up dead. It'd be lucrative, though…and Logan or no Logan, she needed to secure her own money with her status with the Stygians still in limbo.

"Where is Princess Ariana right now?"

"She went to find herself in the desert," Serena said, "but she'll be returning soon. Her ladies-in-waiting would be a good place to start. They have powerful spouses, men who always tend to want more. You'll need to be in their good graces if you want to get any information out of them."

"And will the princess know my true identity?"

Calim faltered, and his eyes darted to Serena's again. "For now, no. We'll inform her if it becomes important. Are you up to the job?"

Kara nodded. "I'll take it."

Calim's face broke into a beaming smile. "Splendid. My sister's due to return to court soon, and I've been planning a masque to celebrate her return. Many foreign officials and dignitaries, as well as some of our own diplomats, will be there. Hopefully you'll feel at home in the palace by then and will be able to gather some information."

CHAPTER TWO

K ara got lost twice on her way back to her room, and when she finally found it, she was exhausted and overwhelmed. A headache pulsed at her temples, threatening to grow. She fell face-down into the soft bed and groaned when she realized she'd need help unlacing this blasted gown.

There was a gentle knock on the door. "Come in," she moaned, assuming it was Serena.

A young woman with mousy brown hair pulled into a sleek bun entered and immediately curtsied, her nose nearly scraping the floor. Kara rolled to her feet, waiting for the girl to rise and introduce herself, but she continued to hold the position. *Bugger.*

"Ah, please rise."

"Pleased to make your acquaintance, my lady. I'm Merry," the girl said. Her eyes were a clear, pale blue, her collarbones sharp beneath her plain dress.

Kara was tempted to say *good for you*, but decided not to rile the girl. "I'm—"

"Oh, I know who you are, of course, Lady Grey. They

told me you were coming weeks ago. I've been eagerly awaiting your arrival."

Weeks? Logan must have been planning for her to take this contract since before she'd fled with Wesley. *Yet he never mentioned it to me.* That man needed to learn to be less withholding.

Merry frowned at Kara's pinched expression. "Shall I draw you a bath, my lady?"

"That sounds divine. Where are the baths located?"

Merry smiled and made her way across the room, where she pressed a wooden panel on the wall that swung open. A hidden door. "There's a tub in the antechamber."

Kara raised her eyebrows. An attached bathroom? Her very own tub? What had she done to deserve this? She crossed the bedroom and resisted the urge to whistle when she followed Merry into the bathing chamber. A tub made of clear glass sat in the center of the room, flanked by a sink fixture and a tall oval mirror ringed with silver filigree.

Several braided silk ropes hung beside the head of the tub, and three runes were etched into the bottom of the clear glass.

"Are you familiar with water runes?"

"No," Kara said, trying to keep the awe out of her voice.

"Red silk for hot water, blue for cold. Black for an evaporation spell."

"I think I'm in love."

Merry giggled. Kara was relieved to see a crack in her shell.

Kara spotted a matching set of runes and silk ropes by the sink. She tugged the red rope experimentally, and warm water filled the bowl, as if it seeped in from the glass itself. She suppressed a squeal of delight. "Can you please help me with my dress?"

"Of course, Lady Grey." Merry swiftly undid the laces of the dress and corset, and Kara let them drop in a puddle at her feet. She stepped out of the circle of clothes and pulled her slip overhead, then started on the stockings.

Merry gasped. Kara's eyes flew to her left wrist, but her silver cuff was still in place, hiding Namirah's curse mark. Had her scars surprised her?

Merry averted her eyes as she bent to pick up the dress, her cheeks a bright pink.

"Apologies, Merry. Modesty isn't an affliction I suffer from." She must be new if she was unaccustomed to people undressing in front of her.

"No worries, my lady. You just surprised me. Will you require anything else of me this evening?"

"You're free to go. Thank you for your help."

Merry curtsied and scurried away, and Kara heard her hanging the dress up in the armoire before the bedroom door snicked shut.

Kara experimented with the ropes and filled the tub until she had water that was almost too hot to stand, then sunk into the tub with a sigh. She leaned her head back against the rim, wishing Logan was here to massage her neck and head until her headache vanished and she melted in his arms.

She imagined he was here, sneaking into the bathroom and diving his hands beneath the water to touch her. Imagined he was in the bedroom beyond, standing naked in front of the fire, waiting on her to finish her bath to take her into his arms. Imagined he was anywhere but gone.

()

Kara accompanied Serena to the palace training yards in the morning. Apparently the Vespertines, the palace guard, and what little of the royal army remained stationed here trained together often. She hadn't been able to practice regularly since the clan had left for Travincal, and she sorely missed it. Exercise was one of the ways she kept the volatility of the curse under control. Serena loaned her clothes to wear after Kara accepted her invitation. To Kara's surprise, she'd said it wasn't uncommon for the women of the court to join the sessions, either for exercise or to learn self-defense. Kara was relieved to be in a pair of pants again, even if they were embroidered with a filigree.

A tall man with straight blond hair and piercing blue eyes approached Kara as she stretched her legs on the training yard green. He bowed low to her. She tilted her head up to get a better look at him. He was handsome, with a chiseled jaw, aquiline nose, and bronze skin. His tan breeches hugged muscular thighs, and the vee of his green shirt revealed a dusting of blond hair. *A target appears.*

"Welcome to Lerathil, Lady Grey. We've been eagerly awaiting your arrival. I'm Viscount Kendrick. But you can call me Aidan." Serena must have planted the seeds of her arrival far in her advance, as no one seemed surprised by her sudden appearance.

"Kendrick?" Kara paused, scouring her brain. Why did that sound so familiar? Then it clicked into place. *Jasper!* That was his last name.

"Do you have a brother, Aidan?"

"Several. Have you had the misfortune of meeting one of them?"

Kara smiled. She'd have to judge Aidan on his own merits. "I've heard talk, is all."

"Count yourself lucky, then."

Aidan dropped into a stretch beside her, and the court ladies that'd been chatting on a bench nearby quickly rose and came closer, beginning their own stretches as they watched him.

Kara chuckled under her breath. "It appears you have an audience."

Aidan glanced up. "Ah. I've grown inured to it. Do you spar regularly, Lady Grey?"

"Please, call me Celine." It was odd enough being addressed as 'Lady' all the time. "And I do from time to time. I enjoyed many outdoor activities in the country."

"I've been to Briarcliff. The land there is wild and beautiful."

Shit. She needed to be careful about bringing up the earl or Briarcliff in general before she had the opportunity to learn more about them. "But not so beautiful as the palace, of course."

"If you say so. I find I prefer the ruggedness of country living as I age. Pray tell, what tempted you out of it?"

"The threat of spinsterhood."

Aidan cracked a smile, transforming his face. Kara blinked at him. No one should look that good while touching their toes. She was beginning to understand what the ladies of the court had lined up for.

"And you? What brings you to the palace?"

"I command a portion of the royal army that's stationed here."

Kara forgot herself for a moment when she said, "For a man so fond of nature, you seem to have chosen the wrong profession."

Surprise flickered across his face. "Indeed. Army outposts grow fewer as mercenary control spreads. But you're familiar with that, with your borders so close to Dreadnettle's."

Kara nodded. "They certainly contribute to the wildness. Perhaps you can retire to a hermitage." She finished stretching and dusted her hands off on her pants. As a captain in the army, Aidan seemed unlikely to be a Sanguine sympathizer. But honor often knelt to coin. And he *was* related to Jasper.

"You must be an accomplished swordsman. Would you care to spar?"

"I wouldn't want to hurt you—"

"Nonsense. You insult me, my lord."

"Very well, Celine." The way her new name rolled off his lips sounded seductive.

Kara caught Serena's eye as she and the viscount took up practice swords. The mage was in the middle of a cluster of Vespertines, giving them instructions for their workout.

She and Aidan began slowly, going through a set pattern of attacks and deflections. His gaze was bored, unfocused. His eyes flitted between the other groups of people around the yard. Kara gave him a quick rap on the collarbone to wake him up.

"I said I wanted to spar, not trade blows like children." Kara deviated from the pattern again, darting in to give him a cheeky poke in his inner thigh. She was going to have to threaten him to get him to take her seriously. Aidan deflected the swift blows she followed up with, his eyes widening.

"You're fast. Who did you train with?"

Keep it vague, Kara. "The man who taught me to ride was an excellent swordsman."

"And you an excellent student." Aidan began to duel her in earnest, increasing his speed and varying his blows, though she sensed he was still holding back. If he'd trained with the same tutor Jasper had, he'd be quite the swordsman.

The thudding of the wooden practice swords meeting

soothed her with their brutal lullaby. She almost missed the feeling of Aethyta's gaze on her back, the clap of her hands ringing in the air. A pang went through her as she wished Jon or Logan were here to spar with. They always challenged her.

A few of the Vespertines gathered around, watching them fight. Kara wanted to show off her full skills to impress them, but she controlled herself, pulling her swings and letting Aidan score hits she'd have normally blocked or dodged.

They continued for several more minutes, then Kara pulled off, acting winded. She could slowly escalate Celine's abilities and stamina, just as she had her own. She might already be pushing it.

"It's refreshing to have a new sparring partner."

"Likewise, my lady. You're quite accomplished."

Kara paused. Aidan may be able to give her more information on the situation at the palace, but she'd need to be alone with him if she wanted him to be candid with her.

"Could I interest you in giving me a tour around the city sometime, Lord Kendrick? I haven't had much chance for tourism, and you must know the city well." Kara had no memory of her trip into the city, when Logan had rushed her to the castle as she bled out. The heads of the court ladies twisted around like owls, listening in. This wouldn't win her any fans amongst them—Kendrick was obviously a hotly contested bachelor.

Aidan blushed. "Of course, Celine. It'd be my pleasure."

()

THAT EVENING, Kara and Serena went on a ride around the castle grounds, which extended beyond the palace proper and encapsulated a section of Lerathil's rolling green countryside. Kara was given a fine mare from the stables to use, which made her miss Drum all the more.

It was the first chance she'd had to get a good look at the palace from a distance. Its seven white spires pierced the sky, each peaked with blue slate tiles. High white walls surrounded the palace proper, separating it from the city below. The scenery was beautiful, the air crisp without being cold, and Kara had every material thing she could ever want at her beck and call, yet she still felt ill at ease.

"Thank you for inviting me to the training yard today. I needed it."

"I figured you were probably getting antsy, being cooped up in the castle the last few weeks."

Logan had kept her plenty entertained, but Kara didn't think Serena would appreciate that knowledge.

"My offer still stands, you know. To join the Vespertines."

Kara swung her head towards Serena. "Really?"

"Why not? You're smart. And a brilliant fighter."

Sometimes Kara wondered what the past year would've been like had she taken Serena up on her offer, back during the Reaping Trials. But the Brotherhood was part of her now, even if she wasn't part of it.

"Things are still…in limbo, regarding my contract with the Stygians. I need to see that through before making any decisions."

"Well, keep us in mind. The mercenary life is hard, and the women in the Vespertines are a good sort. I'll introduce you at the next training session."

As Celine. Which meant their relationship would begin on a lie.

"Speaking of training, I don't know that Kendrick will be of much help with the Sanguines, unless you're just looking to get your mind off Vakarian."

Kara snorted. "As if that's possible."

Serena snapped her head back and laughed. "Oh, I don't miss *that* feeling. What's bothering you?"

Kara smiled at her. The mage was fast becoming a good friend and her sole confidante at the palace.

"The man's impossible. I don't know what we are, what I mean to him—if he just sees this as temporary or something more."

"And you never will, unless he's changed."

"I wish he would tell me the things he says with his body. That he'd trust me more. I don't know what he's so afraid of." *That you'll betray him again,* her mind whispered.

"Probably the same things you are."

"How did you deal with it, when things ended between you?"

"Ours was no great love story, Kara. I broke things off between us."

"What? Really?" Someone had dumped Logan Vakarian? Kara's esteem for Serena grew.

"He was never there, even when we were together. Not really. I'd look in his eyes, and he'd be a thousand miles away. Plus I've got some commitment issues of my own."

"If you'd rather not talk about this, please tell me."

"You're fine. I'd like to help. My advice? Don't wait for him. I worry that you'll get hurt it if you do. The clan has always been first in his heart. You're young, beautiful, deadly with an assortment of weapons. What's not to like? There are plenty of other men out there."

Men who don't know the real me. Men who, if they did, would look at me in fear and disgust, or as a curiosity to be sampled. Logan saw the beast inside her and didn't flinch, because that beast lived in him, too.

"However…" Serena started, and Kara looked up at her. "When he brought you to me, on the brink of death—I've never seen him so rattled. And Vakarian doesn't rattle easily. Nor does he promise favors, *ever*, and he promised one for you. I'm no romantic, but that must mean something, Kara." Serena reached down and patted her horse's neck. "So, you'll probably destroy each other or live happily ever after."

Kara barked out a laugh. *Why not both?*

"I don't think I've thanked you properly for saving my life, by the way."

"You wouldn't have made it to me if Logan hadn't cast a blood spell on you. A very dangerous and forbidden spell, by the way."

"Forbidden? Why?" She could recall the sweet copper taste of his blood in her mouth, the surge of warmth after he'd drawn the rune on her chest, but everything after was darkness.

"The sanguinata. Blood binding. He gave you his blood then bound it with yours, letting the power in his blood invigorate you."

Kara swallowed. "Is it…permanent?"

"I have no idea."

"What makes it so dangerous? I've noticed no ill effects."

"Your blood could've been incompatible, causing your body to reject it. Or if you had died while his blood was still in your system, it could have weakened and killed him."

"*Oh.*" Logan had risked that for her? Had he known it was a possibility?

Serena paused, gazing out at the sunset blanketing the

distant hills. Her horse lowered his head to grab a chomp of grass. "Do you want to see him?"

"Of course, but I've no idea where he is. He didn't deign to share that information."

"There might be a way. Come to my workshop tonight."

KARA FOLLOWED Serena to her workshop after they put the horses away. The grooms offered to take care of them, but Kara enjoyed the routine of unsaddling and brushing down a horse. It helped her center and calm herself.

Serena's workshop was in one of the palace's seven spires, atop an endless spiral staircase that reminded Kara of her old room at Raven's Rest. The final step opened into the workshop, opposite an arched window that gazed out over the city. The spires, lit by the moon and stars, were breathtaking to behold from this height. Why couldn't she have been born in a place as beautiful as this? Where the curse was so omnipresent that it seemed less a burden. Kara leaned out the window and looked down at the drop below—at the sheer height she was at—and imagined what it'd feel like to ride a rope pulley all the way to the ground. She could almost feel the wind rushing through her hair.

Kara turned back to Serena, who was reaching on her tip-toes to retrieve a plain-looking black bowl from a high shelf. The room was lined with potions and crystals and weapons etched with runes, but despite all the things in it, it didn't feel cluttered. Everything had its place.

Serena brought the bowl over to the sink beside Kara. The inside of the bowl was carved with complicated, inter-locking runes. Most runes Kara had seen were simple, like the ones etched to the bottom of her bathtub or stitched into Logan's cloak, but this looked like someone had knotted twenty runes together and arranged them in a symmetrical pattern.

Serena filled the bowl with warm water and placed it on the table in the center of the room. "A word to the wise regarding this bowl. Don't jump to conclusions. Now, look into it and think of the person you want to see. Focus on a strong, positive memory of them."

Serena stepped away to her work desk, and Kara stared into the water. She pictured Logan on the last night they'd been together, when he'd been content to lay beside her and trace the lines of her body with his fingertips, eyes dark with emotion.

The water grew cloudy, then an image wavered on its surface.

It was Logan, his skin sun-kissed and jaw thick with stubble. Kara resisted the urge to caress his image in the water. Wherever he was, the sun hadn't set yet. It wavered low on the horizon. The steady bob of his frame was consistent with someone riding a horse. The image in the water shifted, drawing back, and Kara frowned. A beautiful woman in blue silks rode beside him, laughing at something he said. She curled a possessive hand around Logan's bicep and pointed to something in the distance.

Kara tasted blood. She'd bitten her tongue, hard. There was something about the image that was nagging at her. The black horse the woman was riding looked familiar. Logan and the woman turned, and the horse's profile came into view. It was Drum. The bitch was riding her horse.

Kara raked her fingers through the pool of water, distorting the image. It faded with a tingle.

"Shouldn't stick your hand in things you don't understand," Serena tsked.

"Does this bowl show the present?"

Serena nodded.

"I've seen enough."

"Are you sure?"

"Yes."

Kara regretted coming here, regretted asking the question she'd feared to have answered. She was risking her neck at the palace to get back in the clan's good graces, entirely out of her element, and he was gallivanting around goddess knows where with some woman. A woman riding *her* horse. Kara had never felt jealousy like this—this ragged clawing at the edges of her stomach. She should have made Logan clarify exactly what they were to each other before he left, but when he'd asked her to wait for him, she'd assumed that meant he'd wait for her, too.

Kara took a few deep breaths, trying to calm herself. It was only a hand, only a horse. She was overreacting. It could be entirely innocent, and he deserved an opportunity to explain himself.

"Uh oh. Amber eyes. What did you see?"

"Nothing good."

"You wanna talk about it?"

"Suffice it to say that you might have been right."

"Hmm. Sometimes I think that bowl's cursed."

"Do you spy on people with this all the time?"

"It's a lover's bowl. Only good for seeing people you have a deep bond with."

"Does the bond have to go both ways?"

Serena nodded. "Though I don't recommend it as a replacement for daisy-pulling. The bowl is much more fickle than that."

"Can I take it with me?" Kara already wanted to look into the bowl again, regretted disrupting the image. What if she missed something important?

"Will you use it responsibly?"

"Probably not."

"Don't torture yourself, Kara."

"Is that a yes?"

Serena sighed. "Fine. Just *don't* try to contact the dead. Trust me."

Kara poured the water out into the sink, and the runed stone quickly absorbed it. An odd idea wormed its way into her mind. "What happens if you fill the bowl with blood instead of water?"

Serena looked sharply at her. "Mother Night, what would even possess you to ask that? I don't know, and I wouldn't like to find out. I don't practice blood magic."

"Do you know someone who does? Logan told me I'd be able to use it eventually."

Serena frowned and chewed her lip. "There is another mage at the palace…a man named Salizar. I wouldn't choose him as your teacher, though."

"Why not?"

"Some people crave power so much that they have no respect for how they acquire it. There have been rumors among Namirah's Chosen at court lately. He's peddling a supposed antidote to the monthly keening."

Kara stalled, heart fluttering in her chest. "That exists?" Logan would have mentioned such an alternative to her, right?

Serena glanced at Kara and twisted her hands together. "Perhaps I shouldn't have told you of this. I doubt it works, Kara. He's still refining it, and some of the women have gotten sick from it. Besides, Salizar does nothing without an ulterior motive. Some things are better borne."

"You don't know what it's like, Serena. To lose control, lose yourself. If it works, that would be…"

Serena lowered her eyes. "You're right. It's your decision. Just be careful."

Kara caught Serena in a hug. The mage's body was stiff, arms at her side. She slowly relaxed and returned the embrace, gingerly patting Kara on the back.

"Thank you," Kara said.

ACKNOWLEDGMENTS

()

I hope you enjoyed this glimpse inside my mind. *Sanguine and Stygian* has been an important part of my life for the better part of the last decade, through many ups and downs, starts and stops, and changes of scenery. I'm thrilled to finally share it with the world.

To all my early beta readers: Lindsey Sellers, Amanda Iles, Marisa F., Tara Sharp, Gabrielle Vizcaino, Sevannah Storm, Linn Lahlberg, Nelson Valenzuela, Katherynn Rune, Ambria Flanders, Spencer Barns, Josh Booker, Tori Avery, Grandma, Mom, Dad, and Rex, thank you for your time and effort! This book wouldn't be where it is without your feedback, encouragement, and support.

I'd also like to thank all my fellow PitchWars 2019 mentees for their endless enthusiasm and friendship, and my mentor, Paris Wynters, for seeing something in *Sanguine and Stygian* and helping me shape it into what it is today. To Sami Ellis, CJ Connor, Megan Scott, Megan Van Dyke, and many others—may the party parrot live forever. Another big thank you to Maxym M. Martineau and Mary Ann Marlowe for seeing potential in my book, and Pintip Dunn for being the mother duck to all us wayward ducklings.

ABOUT THE AUTHOR

( )

Sara Sellers lives in Georgia with her three cats. She likes the sound of rain, the smell of gasoline, and the taste of boiled peanuts. She has a soft spot in her heart for K-dramas and training montages.

Find out more at www.sarasellers.com

Join my reader group at facebook.com/groups/sarasellers

tiktok.com/@sellerssara

facebook.com/authorsarasellers

x.com/sellerssara

instagram.com/sellerssara

threads.net/@sellerssara

pinterest.com/sellerssara

goodreads.com/sarasellers

amazon.com/author/sarasellers

bookbub.com/authors/sara-sellers